After a blissful minute of silence, Gwen faced Pearl. "So you really ⸻ ⸻ of volunteering?"

Pearl stared ov⸻ ⸻ "I am. Want to come? It's ⸻ t, two pairs of boots, a trip ⸻ ⸻ ⸻u can get until the war ⸻ entire world are dead. Oh, ⸻ ⸻ ncer, a raincoat. The one you never afforded for yourself because you gave half your pay to that ungrateful aunt of yours."

"A raincoat. Golly," Gwen mused half-seriously. "A worthy reason to join. Plus, if I go with you, I could listen to you complain all the time."

Markham threw a pillow at her.

"I might look into this, just to learn what it's got to offer," Gwen teased her, but inside a seed of interest grew roots.

"Ask Dalton. She knows more."

"Why?"

"She's going. O'Bryan persuaded her."

"Doc is going to France?" Gwen couldn't believe it. O'Bryan didn't seem like the adventurous type, nor the noble type, either. She misjudged him. Why would he volunteer?

"For a million soldiers," Anna chimed in. "You need thousands of doctors and nurses. Dentists, too."

"Of course," Gwen murmured. *How many people do you need to care for millions of men? How many scalpels and needles? How much ether and debridement solution? How many sterilizers and...just how do you get all that where it's needed to save lives of men in pain and bleeding?* "I want to learn more."

To Carl,

Heroic Measures

by

Jo-Ann Power

I hope this will lead you to the next book! Enjoy!

Jo-Ann Power

This is a work of fiction. Names, characters, places, and incidents are either the product of the author's imagination or are used fictitiously, and any resemblance to actual persons living or dead, business establishments, events, or locales, is entirely coincidental.

Heroic Measures

COPYRIGHT © 2013 by Jo-Ann Power

All rights reserved. No part of this book may be used or reproduced in any manner whatsoever without written permission of the author or The Wild Rose Press, Inc. except in the case of brief quotations embodied in critical articles or reviews.
Contact Information: info@thewildrosepress.com

Cover Art by http://graphicfantastic.com

The Wild Rose Press, Inc.
PO Box 708
Adams Basin, NY 14410-0708
Visit us at www.thewildrosepress.com

Publishing History
First Mainstream Historical Edition, 2013
Print ISBN 978-1-62830-087-1
Digital ISBN 978-1-62830-088-8

Published in the United States of America

Dedication

To my dear husband, Steve, who declared this book
must be published in time for the Centennial, and who,
in his abiding generosity of spirit and love, eagerly
traveled in the United States to museums and libraries,
then went to France as my research assistant,
my interpreter, my photographer, my chauffeur,
and my charming dinner companion!
My loving gratitude.
This book would not be a reality without
your encouragement and your belief in me.

~*~

Also to my cousin, Kathleen, who years ago read
the novel in its much cruder form and remembered
how it brought tears to her eyes then.
Thank you for your encouragement
and your enthusiasm for the story.

~*~

To my best friend and colleague, Desiree Holt,
I owe my heartfelt appreciation for her enthusiasm and
joy in the creation of this novel, her kind
and ever-flowing advice and most of all, for her reading
of the manuscript and her comments and insights
on its plot and characterization.

~*~

To my charming daughter, Ann,
who diligently corrected my French,
my love and appreciation.
Merci beaucoup, ma chérie!

Acknowledgments

Every historical novelist owes a huge debt to the innumerable authors of non-fiction whose works form the bedrock of his or her fiction. My indebtedness to those historians who have helped me form a picture of those women who joined the Army Nurse Corps during the Great War is incalculable. Although I list all of these professionals and resources, please know that all interpretations of fact are mine, as are any errors of it.

For research that began more than twenty-eight years ago when many of the primary documents were as yet unorganized nor catalogued, I am grateful that these archivists handed me boxes brimming with photographs and letters and often pointed me toward microfiche files marked only with handwritten notes and dates. These dedicated professionals included those of the United States Archives, Washington, D.C., the Library of Congress, Washington, D.C., the staff of George Washington University and Medical School, and the U.S. Army Heritage and Education Center, Carlisle Barracks, Carlisle, Pennsylvania.

As I resumed research for the novel in the past few years, I saw that many of the original documents not only had been catalogued and notated but also that the wealth of information had expanded. For that, we owe thanks to the historians and museum curators throughout the United States who preserve the remnants of our past with loving care.

In the continental United States, I am very grateful to Eric Gillespie, Director, and Andrew E. Woods, Research Historian, at the Colonel Robert R. McCormick Research Center, First Division Museum at

Cantigny, Wheaton, Illinois. I am grateful to Mr. Gillespie for his kindness to open the research facility to me. Mr. Woods's expert knowledge and insights of the museum's holdings added invaluable detail which in many instances I found nowhere else. Thank you.

To the staff of the U.S. Army Medical Department Museum at Fort Sam Houston, in San Antonio, Texas, I give my thanks for their marvelous exhibit and interpretation of artifacts. To the historians of the U.S. Army Medical Department, Office of Medical History, I am grateful for their expert recording of medical care during the Great War. Their detail of conditions, supply lines, hospital establishment and operations, plus the formation and use of mobile surgical units, was crucial to my rendering. I also thank Doran Cart, Senior Curator at the National World War I Museum in Kansas City, Kansas, for supplying me with a picture of the dress uniform of a captain in the British Expeditionary Force.

Abroad, I encourage you to visit the Great War halls of Musée de l'Armée, Hotel national des Invalides, in Paris, France. Here you will see a complete description of the four years of war with countless objects, photographs, uniforms, replicas of cannons like Big Bertha and tanks like the French Renault F17, plus one of my favorite pieces—one of the famous "Taxis of the Marne." I also highly recommend you take a short train ride out of Paris to the new and stirring Musée de la Grande Guerre in Meaux, France. Here in the small town where the French halted a German advance on Paris in September 1914 you will view a superb recreation of trenches, medical care treatment, and artifacts of soldiers' grueling life in the trenches. I recommend especially that you take time to sit and view the unique collection of raw film footage of scenes on the front lines and back of them.

In France, 30,921 World War One American war dead lie buried in the shade of beautifully tended linden trees in our cemeteries. The staff of the American Battlefield Commission manages the facilities. These dedicated people are a font of knowledge about the area and the establishment of the commission. I encourage you to walk inside each visitors center and introduce yourself. These men and women work there to assist Americans who wish to visit family members' graves and to educate all about the heroism of those whose remains rest in their care.

In particular, for their generosity to share their knowledge of their cemetery, the commission and the surrounding battlefields and monuments, I am indebted to the following:

•Geoffrey Fournier, Superintendent, Oise-Aisne American Cemetery, Fère-en-Tardenois, Aisne, France;

•Flora Nicolas, Cemetery Associate, Aisne-Marne American Cemetery, Belleau, France;

•Nadia Ezz-Eddine, Cemetery Associate, St. Mihiel American Cemetery, Thiaucourt, France;

•David Bedford, Superintendent, Meuse-Argonne American Cemetery, and Dominique Didiot, Cemetery Associate, Meuse-Argonne American Cemetery, Romagne-sous-Montfaucon, Meuse, France.

To all readers, I encourage you heartily to visit the World War One American cemeteries in France and pay your respects to the nurses, soldiers, marines, YMCA workers, volunteer female doctors, Salvation Army workers, and thousands more who lie in repose in these serene parcels of land where they fought and died. They deserve your regard, your time and effort to journey there to grant them your thanks for their loving service.

To those of you who may not travel abroad just yet, I encourage you to visit the museums and monuments throughout the United States which display the artifacts and tell the tales of those who went to fight "the war to end all wars." With that hope, more than a million men and women joined the armed forces and journeyed thousands of miles to foreign lands in an age when few had ever ventured beyond their farms or towns. For that courage, we owe them not only our respect but our deepest gratitude for their dedication to a cause they deemed just and worthy of their sacrifice.

Chapter One

June, 1917
Scranton, Pennsylvania

Gwen paced before the window next to her bed, then stopped to match the time on the wall clock to the hands of her new wristwatch. Anna better show up soon before Gwen had to leave for observation in surgery— because none of the four others here would deign to unlock the door for flighty, flirty Anna Carlucci. Except for Gwen and the four trying to sleep, most student nurses had already departed for the lesson, promptness a virtue near sainthood in training. The four in the dormitory had worked the wards last night and were just settling down into their covers. None was likely to interrupt her precious rest to aid anyone, least of all Anna.

Muttering about the petty competitions and resentments among her colleagues, Gwen gathered up her stockings and plunked herself on her bed to finish dressing.

Why did Harry keep Anna out until dawn? He should know better. Anna should!

Gwen checked her watch against the clock. *Why do I take care of her and defy the rules?*

By admiring her free spirit, do I encourage her carelessness?

Pebbles sprayed against the window. Jumping at the clatter, Gwen threw down her stockings on the mattress and hobbled over to peer through the glass at her friend. Her very late friend. In the dim light of dawn, Gwen saw Anna standing at the bottom of the stairs leading up to the student nurses' dormitory. She glared at Gwen, tapping her toe, hands on her hips, impatient as ever.

"Finally," Gwen murmured, hating to wake up the four who had stood night shift. One long white stocking on one foot and none on the other, she padded across the cold wooden floor toward the far entrance, unlocked the door and swung it open.

Anna sailed inside, a smile wreathing her round face, black eyes dancing with mischief from another of her recent all night adventures.

"About time you got here," Gwen whispered. "Surgery starts in half an hour—and you're attending. Plus, we have to show up in the dining hall or—"

Anna waved a hand at her, crossing the wooden floorboards on tippy toes. "Don't be a fuddy-duddy."

"Well, if Gwen won't," the contralto voice of Pearl Markham pierced the silence of the nurses' quarters, "I will. Pipe down, Carlucci. We know you've been out with Harold—"

"Harry," Anna corrected her, sniffing because she often told them how proud she was to have a regular beau and none of the other nursing students did. "Go back to sleep, Markham."

Gwen frowned at her irrepressible friend, catching a whiff of men's cologne mixed with...beer. "You've been drinking?"

"Only a bit, Miss Fussbudget. Let me get my uniform on, will you?" She flounced around her bed, discarding her skirt and blouse, working at her camisole and her lace-up boots.

"You'd better brush your teeth," Gwen warned her. "If Dalton gets close to you and smells alcohol, she'll haul you before the Superintendent. We're to get our caps the first of August and this won't go well with the Super."

"Not to worry." Anna grinned at Gwen, then swayed on her feet. "I'll swish my mouth with some stuff Harry gave me. He uses it with his patients."

"Mouth wash," came the growl from across the room. Pearl Markham could be a real bear, especially when deprived of her proper rest. "Best of luck with that, kiddo. Now can you kindly shut up and get out of here? Flo and I worked like dogs last night and you two have no pity." With a huff, she rolled over to face the wall.

"Amen," muttered Florence Aldridge across the aisle.

Sinking down on her bed, Gwen picked up her stocking and resumed dressing. She loved energetic, sunny Anna who always found the bright side of anything, even chemistry class. But as she became more and more enchanted with Harry Winchester, she grew more and more irresponsible. For a lot of reasons, that courtship was not wise, and Gwen feared it could only end in heartache for Anna. Harry's mother, one of the leading lights of tiny Peckville's society, disapproved of all "newcomers" to town. Anna's parents, Guido and Carla Carlucci not only were considered new, though they arrived at Ellis Island before Anna was born, but also they were olive-skinned Italian. The Winchesters gave themselves airs that as English descendants, their Anglo-Saxon blood and their Protestant ethics blessed them. Furthermore, their goal was to ensure that others like them remained pure. Anna would not be welcome in that family.

Gwen understood this kind of thinking. It was the same as her Aunt Mary's.

Picking her pinafore apron off the hanger on the wall hook, Gwen laid it carefully on the mattress so that she could attack it without wrinkling the cotton. To obey their head nurse, Bernice Dalton, each student not only washed and ironed her own uniforms but also starched them to a fare-thee-well. "Darn things can stand up on their own," Gwen grumbled, attempting to tie the stiff sashes behind her.

"Let me." Anna tugged at the long swathes of material that Gwen crushed each time she dressed. "You know she likes the bows to be big and flat."

Gwen nodded, pouffing up her own huge sleeves and smoothing the front of the apron. Perfection was another quality Dalton admired. She was only the latest, but kindest woman who had demanded that of Gwen. Her aunt had required it of her since the day she went to live with her. At least here in nursing school, Gwen understood the need for such exactness. It saved lives.

"Done. Come on." Anna hooked her arm through Gwen's and the two of them marched toward the door and the day's duties. "I'm ready to beat dear old Bernie at her own game."

Gwen waited until they had closed the door on their sleeping colleagues before she answered. "Hope you are up to this. Did you study the procedure?"

"Sure. What's so hard about it?" she asked, winding fistfuls of her dark hair into a knot and jabbing pins into it to secure her floppy white student cap over it. "Doc O'Bryan will sew up little flaps of soft and hard palates."

"Yes, but he'll ask you questions." *And this operation has to be perfect. This child is dear to me.*

Anna patted Gwen's arm as they sailed toward the main hospital building and the entrance to the nurses' dining hall. "I'm ready. Stop worrying, *si*?"

"*Si,*" Gwen lied. But she was concerned. The patient was the darling of her mother's eye and her mother had been Gwen's best friend since they met that dreadful day nine years ago when their fathers died in the mine cave-in. "But a hare lip procedure can be delicate. You have to get the nostrils evenly aligned and no scarring—"

"I know! I read the instructions!" They scurried through the cafeteria line, taking a tray, a cup and saucer, utensils. The aromas of oatmeal and cinnamon, coffee and bacon swirled in the air and Gwen's stomach growled.

"Spencer, Carlucci," the head dietitian called to them from her office doorway. "Better step on it. Dalton is looking for you, Carlucci."

"Thank you, Miss Rawlins." Anna bobbed a curtsy, catching her hat as it fell over her brow. "I'm going in now."

Gwen put a bowl of oatmeal on her tray.

But Anna took none.

"Aren't you eating breakfast?"

Anna's dark eyes narrowed on Gwen's bowl.

"Mmm. No, thanks. Not for me. I can't right now."

Gwen glanced at Anna who appeared not just tired but pale. "If you don't feel well, then—"

"I'm fine! Stop worrying. See you in surgery." She fluttered her lashes in pretended horror. "All the ghouls and goblins will be in one room. Some days I cannot believe I signed up for this training." Then she turned and disappeared through the door.

Gwen stared at her cereal. *I have to stop being responsible for her. She has to do it for herself. And I must think more of me.*

She took a bite of her oatmeal and sipped at her cup of tea, her stomach calming now that she was alone.

"Psst! Gwen," Jane Benson poked her head through the dining room door. "Can you talk?"

"Jane?" Gwen glanced from her friend toward the dietitian's office. "What are you doing here? Patsy is over in the operating room and you should—"

"I know, I know. But I had to see you." Jane was so overwrought about her daughter's corrective surgery that Gwen had spent her Sunday off last week at Jane's and her husband's home describing the procedure of closing the child's palate. Ever since Jane had given birth and their little girl had been malformed, Jane had blamed herself. So had her husband. This punishment, Jane declared, for some sin she had committed in her past. No amount of telling her otherwise had changed her opinion or her husband's. Gwen had rebelled at their explanation, reminding them over and over again that sometimes things like this happened. Besides, she asked them, would God be so mean to do this to a charming little moppet with red curls and a doe's pleading brown eyes?

Gwen hurried toward the hall and took in her friend's anguished face. Her hair was not its usual upswept perfection. Her pert straw hat tipped over her brow, askew. "You should be over in the waiting room, Jane. Is Edward with you?"

"No. He had to go in to the bank this morning."

Or he wanted to stay away and let you carry this burden alone. Gwen patted her arm. "Please don't worry. Doctor O'Bryan is very good in surgery. I've observed him three times now. He's calm and oh, so careful."

"What if his hand slips and...and he makes her look worse than she is?"

"Oh, Jane." Gwen drew back, astonished at how negative her friend had become since Patsy was born with an open palate. Some of that attitude was a reflection of her husband's embarrassment over his child's looks. But some came too from a fatalism that could afflict people who lived with unusual circumstances and physical challenges. "He won't. You have to trust that he won't. This is his job, Jane. He does this all the time."

"But slicing into people is not easy."

Gwen winced at Jane's callous terms. "Not easy, but he was trained for this." Gwen squeezed her friend's hands. "Please don't make this worse on yourself. Go to the waiting room. I know Doctor O'Bryan will be out to talk to you afterward. And I must go myself. I'm late." She smiled at Jane, the woman's long face pale with terror for her baby. *And for herself, too.* "Hurry. Patsy will be repaired."

"But not perfect. Edward hates that she will not be

pretty."

"He can't predict that she won't be." Gwen's tone was harsher than she intended. "Besides, loving her will make her beautiful in her heart."

"Of course." Jane nodded, looking like a lamb to the slaughter.

Gwen could not tear her eyes from Jane as she hurried off. Edward Benson exerted the greatest influence on his wife's attitudes. If only Patsy would learn that her father did not have the most useful outlook on life, the little girl stood a good chance of becoming a raving beauty.

"Spencer!"

Gwen startled, glancing over at the head nurse who stood with one meaty hand to the operating theater's door.

"Yes, ma'am," she replied, rushing to finish her scrub and turn off the hot water spigot. Shaking the droplets from her fingertips, she reached for a clean towel from the rack. "I'm done. Headed upstairs."

"No. Get in here," Nurse Dalton growled.

"But—" Gwen pointed up to the observation room. "I'm to go up—"

"Not anymore. You are late. Did you think I would not notice?"

"No, ma'am."

"You are needed in here. Quickly, quickly!" The woman motioned her forward with one sweep of her arm. "Your friend there, Carlucci, just threw up."

Gwen's eyes grew wider by the second as Anna, limp as a noodle, was frog-marched by two orderlies from the OR where Dalton, in all her battle-axe glory, held court.

What a disaster. Anna would pay for this, maybe even with dismissal.

"You get to redeem your class's reputation, Spencer, if you can hold your breakfast down better than Carlucci." The portly woman sniffed as Anna passed and looked at Gwen with the grim sadness of a scolded puppy. "Get a mask. Gloves. Hurry up."

Throwing the towel into the hamper, Gwen scurried toward Dalton.

"Stop. Mask! Gloves! Now!"

Gwen grabbed one of each. She hadn't done a stint in surgery yet and she wasn't eager to do it this morning either. Hot on the matron's heels, Gwen needed the woman to know that she shouldn't be in this operation. Not for this surgery. Not this morning. She should be observing with many of her other classmates up in the amphitheater above the floor, looking down at Doctor O'Bryan. Her turn to stand in surgery was next week.

"I know this child," she blurted out to Dalton by way of excusing herself.

"Good," the woman said with a half glance over her shoulder, marching on. "Then you have an interest in her care."

"Yes, but—" Gwen bumped into Dalton who had halted in her tracks.

"But *what*, Spencer?" The matron's glassy gaze darted over Gwen's face.

Terror of Dalton's disapproval didn't matter as much to Gwen as dread of the nurse's dismissal from training. The woman was known to liberally and loudly list all the sins of a student nurse in front of anyone at any time she felt so inspired. Gwen could take her bullying and scolding, but she'd cringe at any public shaming. Dalton would up-braid any trainee, if she thought a student possessed no backbone. Gwen had one all right, but now was the time to mind her Ps and Qs. "You said we should separate our personal feelings from our professional demands."

"Marvelous. Then today you get to practice that rule. Come along and do stop clenching your fists. Save your fingers. Doctor may ask you to hand him instruments, not throw them at him."

Me? Gwen shivered at the chill traveling her spine. She could not assist at this surgery, surely. Another. Next week…

"Come, come." Dalton pivoted and pointed toward the surgical table where the small bundle of one-year-old Patricia Benson lay anesthetized.

Gwen followed like a sleepwalker. Sweat beaded on her chest and ran down her cleavage. Her throat began to close like it always did when she had to fight to save herself. *Breathe. One. Two.*

"You have studied this deformity. Have you not?" Dalton prodded her.

"Yes, ma'am." Gwen swallowed, the diagrams of harelip malformations dancing in her mind. *Patsy has a left cleft lip, not as severe a condition as a cleft palate. We want to close that up so that she can eat and breathe more easily.*

She followed Dalton into the circle of light trained on the cadre of three others in the center of the room. Doc O'Bryan waited, still and mute, too stoic for Gwen to read. The nurse anesthetist, Therese Reynard, rolled her eyes at Gwen, impatient with the goings-on. A younger doctor stood behind O'Bryan, eager and nervous. Up in the gallery, Gwen heard one of her classmates gasp. Others whispered. Gwen heard her own name mentioned in quiet tones laced with fear.

I swear I will never be late again for observation.

"Doctor," Dalton said, squaring herself before the physician whom Gwen had known since the day he pronounced her father dead at the mouth of Number Two Carbondale mineshaft. "We are ready."

O'Bryan skewered his gray gaze on Gwen. Behind his half-mask, he scanned each member of his team, then took one step toward the table and the tiny daughter of Gwen's best friend. "Pulse?" O'Bryan began the litany of pre-surgical checks that would lead him to the first cut into the deformed face of a darling child who nonetheless was the apple of her mother's eye.

"Very well," he concluded, his baritone a rich resonance that earned him praise from those who heard him declare good tidings or bad. O'Bryan, according to her Aunt Mary, knew how to console a widow or a mother with eloquent phrases of solace. Too bad, she loved to add, he knew little how to curb his desire to sing in the local tavern after delivering such news.

"He is weak," her aunt always had concluded. "The drink will kill him."

"Scalpel."

Doc's demand snapped Gwen back to the moment and she clamped the instrument in his outstretched hand.

He had been drinking the day her father and her uncle died in the cave-in of Number Two. Gwen had smelled it on him. At twelve years old, she was wise to the ways of those who sought comfort in spirits. The whiskey, a favorite of her uncle Len, was a grossly familiar aroma to her. She had smelled it on her uncle every time he came to their house and argued with her dad. Doc O'Bryan, she had noted that day and many days thereafter when he came to console her Aunt Mary for her losses, might have a snoot-full, but he never argued. Never raised his voice.

Since Gwen had entered the student nursing program here at Moore Hospital nearly two years ago, she had been in Doc O'Bryan's presence at least four times each week. To her surprise, she never saw him tipsy. Never detected on his person any whiffs of alcohol. He seemed clean, sober, unlike that morning when, like the rest of Peckville, he had rushed to the mine entrance at first alarm.

The thundering explosion beneath the earth had shaken the entire town. Gwen had just taken her spot along the long benches of grade six between Jane and her cousin Helen when the floorboards of the schoolhouse shook beneath her feet. Townsfolk rushed outside, murmuring, crying. A woman screamed. Gwen grabbed Jane's hand. Jane took Helen's. The three of them checked each others' eyes. They were children, yes, but this terror had happened before. Every year or two, a mine exploded or a fire ravaged a new shaft. Each time the sirens blew, everyone expected men would die. Men would suffocate. Or burn. Or lose an arm or leg. Few would escape to tell tales of the disaster.

The colliery's whistle screeched across the valley confirming the news.

Whoop. Whoop-whoop. Whoo-oop.

At the memory, the sound ringing in her ears,

Gwen winced.

"Protractor."

She slapped it in O'Bryan's hand.

She, Jane, and Helen had rushed to the schoolhouse windows. Their teacher yelled at them to return, but with their friends, they ran out to the street. No one stopped them. The men in those mines were their fathers.

People gathered along the road, yelling. Cave-in. Fire. Gas. Men and women ran everywhere. Where were the miners? Were they coming up?

Did my father escape?

"Needle."

She gave O'Bryan the tool.

"Gauze. Gauze!"

"Yes, sir!" Gwen responded and held it out.

"Not like that!" Dalton barked.

Gwen reversed her offering to O'Bryan. "Sorry, doctor. Excuse—"

"Quiet, girl!" Dalton hissed.

Gwen bit her lower lip, her gaze locking on the doctor's and offering the apology she could not give in words. The firm rule was no talking in the operating room. Only the doctor did that. He ruled supreme here, needing his wits about him.

"See here." O'Bryan directed them to examine his handiwork. "Now you can see here that we have closed her up. How does it look, Spencer?"

"Doctor?" She was shocked he asked her opinion.

"Tell us."

Was he trying to put her on the spot? He wouldn't. Couldn't. She saw the human body as an intricate puzzle, piecing fitting and locking, working beautifully together as if it were a machine. "The patient's top lip will heal very symmetrically over time. Her nasal passage will be clear. Her palate will harden as most children's do."

"Precisely. Now, Spencer, tell them up there what I would have had to do if Patsy had had a cleft palate as well as lip."

Gwen blinked at him. Was he testing her knowledge further? He hadn't done that before with any of her classmates who had taken their turn observing his surgical talents here on the floor. In fact, he hadn't asked anything of them, but to be perfectly mute and invisible. "You would have had to first determine if both hard and soft palate were cleft. Then, depending on the severity, surgically join one, then the other."

"Very good. So," he said as he swung to squint up into the lights toward the twenty-odd women in the amphitheater, "we have a case here that should bode well for this little girl. She may go to school without fearing nasty tricks and damaging ridicule from feckless little boys. Then twenty years from now, she will most likely marry one of them and call herself complete. Isn't that right, Spencer?"

"Yes, doctor."

"Very well. Hubbard," he addressed the young doctor to his right, "you will close for me. Mind you, small stitches on the inside as far as you can. She will scar less so that way." Untying the strings of his voluminous white operating attire, O'Bryan whirled away for the far door and the physicians' entrance to the operating theater. "Spencer?"

Surprised by the summons, Gwen stiffened. "Doctor?"

"After you have scrubbed up, meet me in the hall."

Oh, what had she not done well? If anyone had to chew her out, it would most likely be Dalton, not the doctor. *Unless he is going to give me my notice himself.*

She watched him leave, heard her classmates above her murmur their dismay at his words. Iron in her spine, she refused the impulse to clap a hand to her mouth. She would not be sick. She couldn't lose this. *Could not.* This was her way out of the hopelessness of life on Prospect Street. She had fought so hard, so long to escape that cage.

Pushing away her fear with her need to work, she collected and assembled the used surgical instruments and took them to the sterilizer. Fascinated by Reynard's quiet competence, she watched the anesthetist monitor Patsy's pulse and withdrawal from ether. As the child slowly stirred, Therese administered a small dose of morphine. She pushed the little girl's bed toward the recovery room and paused at the door.

"You did well today," Therese told her with a small smile. "It started badly, but you saved the day."

"I certainly don't feel that way. And O'Bryan wants to see me. That's doom."

"I'd bet not. But go see."

Nodding, Gwen went for the hall. In her rush this morning, she had not gathered up her hair into a secure chignon—and tendrils fell over her eyes and cheeks. Before O'Bryan and Dalton came to give her what-for, she should repair her untidy appearance. Grabbing her cap off her head, she groaned as the weight of her waist-length waves spilled like heavy draperies down her back. Her pins pinged on the floor like chimes.

In counterpoint, Dalton's footsteps clanged on the

hard wood of the scrub room. "Spencer!"

Gwen stood at attention, resigned to hearing the worst about her performance this morning.

"Yes, ma'am." Gwen braced herself for the browbeating she was about to receive. At least, no one else was in the room to witness it.

"You let Carlucci into the dormitory this morning?"

No use to deny it. Someone probably saw Anna waiting at the bottom of the stairs. Or spotted Gwen opening the door for her. Dalton had learned somehow, some way that Anna had breached the student nurse's curfew. "I did."

"Is your friend's happiness more important than your own?"

Gwen's ready answer would reflect only her loyalty to her friend, none to herself. She bit her lip.

"I see. Think on that, girl. You have a future, but only if you control your present. Anna Carlucci has one goal in mind for hers. Your vision is another. Help her seize hers or seize your own. You may not have both."

With that warning, the woman paused and frowned at Gwen. "Doctor O'Bryan had an appointment he must keep and could not meet you as he asked. He wanted me to tell you that he was proud of you this morning. He has great hopes for your future."

As Gwen stared at her, her mouth dropping open in astonishment for praise she coveted, Dalton marched away. Gwen stood for a long minute, her mouth curving in a grin as the O.R. door flapped to and fro on its hinges.

Scrubbed up, she caught her hair to her nape and secured her floppy student's hat tightly over her ungainly bun. Then she raced toward chemistry class. She would not miss it. She would also take Dalton's advice. She had escaped disaster this morning. She would ensure she avoided it in the future.

Chapter Two

The trolley chugged to the end of its line and all passengers except Gwen lined up to leave the car. Noting the black swirling clouds to the east, she hoped the storm would hold off until she walked the twelve blocks home. She had never bought herself a raincoat with her meager salary. Worse, because of the fiasco this morning about Anna, she had been flustered and left the dorm forgetting her umbrella.

"Mid-Valley Sanitarium," cried the streetcar conductor. "End of the line. End of the line."

The car slowed and Gwen gathered up her reticule and her packages.

A brisk wind blew her hair as she alighted and she caught at her hat, jamming it on her head. Lot of good that did. The blue felt slid off again. She gave up, inhaled the electricity in the fresh air and shook out her curls. The red gold mass dropped like a heavy curtain over her shoulders. No Dalton here to scold her for her loose hair, she allowed herself the joy of her free afternoon.

A large black touring automobile pulled next to her and paused, the engine clacking away in a mighty racket. The driver honked the car's ridiculously loud horn.

"Gwendolyn Spencer! *Kommen sie* here in this car right now!"

"Mrs. Learner?" Gwen bent to get a better view of the lady beneath her wide brimmed straw hat. "How nice to see you."

"*Ja.* You, too, *liebchen.* Get in. It will rain soon, and you will be a *vet* duck." The roly-poly woman laughed at her own joke, motioning all the while for Gwen to hop inside.

"Oh, thank you for this." She tucked her gifts inside the Model T, slid into the comfortable leather seat, and shut the door. At once, the lady shifted the gears of her car and off they puttered down Main Street.

"You were walking," the woman said with her faint German accent that made her sound exotic. *You ver walking-a.* "Keeps you fit, but if you are soaked through, then what will your Aunt Mary say of you?"

That I am careless and daft. Gwen gave her aunt's employer a polite smile. "I have my free afternoon today."

"Her half day, too."

When she is at home is the only time she permits me to visit. She shifted in her seat, pulling at her spotless white gloves and smoothing her long navy skirt.

"*Wie gehts...ach,* no. I am to speak English out of the house. My husband insists. This war. This war." She stared at the road, her mouth thin with anxiety. Since Congress had declared war in April, many in town ridiculed Germans, even those whose families had been here for decades. The radio was full of talk about the evil Germans. Cartoons in the newspapers and magazines portrayed the Kaiser and his soldiers and allies as monsters. Many people feared anyone who had a German sounding name and because they were incited, some acted like vigilantes. The Learners had suffered, putting out one fire at their home and two at their beer plant. All, the police said, were works of arsonists, but they had yet to arrest any suspects. "I hate this war and that my son is gone to fight it."

Gwen's stomach clenched. She panicked that Mrs. Learner's oldest son Felix might be injured. Last summer, he had sailed to France with two of his college friends to join an aero squadron comprised of American pilots. Gwen had not had a letter from him in over three weeks. From newspaper articles, she read about the risks flyers took and how Lex courted death daily flying in the Lafayette Escadrille.

She put a hand to the lady's sleeve. "Is he well? Do you have news?"

"Yes, he is happy, my boy Lex," she said, beaming and using the Anglicized nickname he himself had chosen as a boy. "I have a letter from him Monday from France. He says he is taking good care. Eating well and enjoying the wine. *Ach*, but you know young men."

"I know Lex," Gwen added with a chuckle, relieved to hear of him in fine health. Lex, the oldest of the Learners' two sons, had volunteered, no novice to the sport of flying. As the heir of the wealthy German brewing family, Felix Gerhardt Learner had money and time to spare. He had taken up flying when he attended Yale University. Last year after a vacation with one fellow enthusiast in New York City, he had come home to Scranton at Christmas only to announce to his family that come June, he was off to France and *La Grande Guerre*. As a third-generation German American, Lex was careful not to say he was off to fight the *Hun*. Nor would he destroy the *Heinies*.

"I am one," he had said to Gwen that day he led her to his mother's garden and told her of his departure. "But I am more of an American."

"It's not our fight, Lex." She grabbed his hands and held on tightly. She didn't want him in someone else's war, fighting someone else's battles.

"It will be soon."

"Maybe not. In any case, why go now?"

"Because I have a skill they need. Please understand," he pleaded with her, his hands to her shoulders, his hazel eyes reflecting exuberance for life that she understood in herself and rarely saw in others. She could not argue with him further.

"He goes from town to town near Alsace," Mrs. Learner rambled on. "Near Germany. Did you know my grandfather and mother came from Alsace to America? Yes, it is true. Funny, how we all go around and around, *ja*?"

"He says he does not fight in the air." *What had he called those encounters?* She should remember from his last letter.

"*Ach, nein.* He takes pictures of the ground. Can you believe it? Pictures."

"That should be safe." Gwen prayed it was.

"Is it? Who knows, eh? Enough of my rascal Lex," his mother said with perhaps too much cheer. "How goes your training? Do you still like it, this hospital work?"

"I do love it. I will get my cap soon and then I will be…what do you call it, *auf Deutsch*?" Gwen had acquired a smattering of German in the past twelve

21

years that first her mother and then her aunt had worked as Mrs. Gerhardt Learner's housekeeper.

"*Eine Krankenschwester.*"

"Yes," Gwen said with pleasure. "That. A cranky sister."

They both laughed.

"Hello! Hello!" Mrs. Learner gestured to the butcher who waved to her as he stood by the side of the road emptying his trash into an old tin can. He called back, his voice lilting with the brogue he brought with him from Scotland.

"Herr Arnold cut me a big pork roast last week. He is too generous. Go on like that and he will make no money."

Gwen noted that Mister Arnold did not wave at her. Did he think she was a chip off the old block of Mary Spencer? *Probably. Who in town had not felt the lash of Aunt Mary's tongue?* Gwen shivered, the breeze blowing sharper and her mind pointing ever toward the woman she was soon to encounter.

"Your own sister is to have a birthday soon. Are those her gifts in your lap?"

"Yes, it's true. I have a few items for Susannah and…other things for the rest of my family."

"You are a kind woman, Gwendolyn Spencer."

She smiled faintly at the woman's praise, but kept the real reason for her gifts to herself. Explanations of who she was and what she and Susannah had endured at the hands of their maternal aunt took too long. Besides, who would understand?

"How old will be your *schwester*?" Mrs. Learner asked, her attention on the road filled now with four other automobiles whose drivers had no idea of what a straight path really was.

"Eleven. On Wednesday."

"Your aunt tells me she wants to place her at the mine office."

Gwen's heart raced. *How dare she tell you that. How dare she try after all I have said.* "I hope not," she told her, being far more polite than she would be with Aunt Mary. "Susannah is very bright."

Mrs. Learner nodded. "*Jawohl.* A peach *mit* golden blonde hair *und* cream skin. And the eyes. Oh, my!"

Gwen grinned at the praise. "She looks just like our mother. A real beauty."

"Like her lovely sister, I will add. And too *schönig*—too pretty to put to the mines, Gwendolyn."

"I agree. No child should have to work near those pits. Susannah is talented, too. Loves to play the piano."

"*Ja.* She plays here at the house and learns much from my Wilhelm. He is good but not good enough for her. She is better. We must see that she saves her hands for the piano."

"I would like her to have proper lessons and after I graduate I will make certain she has them."

"You give so much, *liebchen.*"

"She is my sister and I am happy to do it." *I must take care of her, see that she survives her childhood with some measure of hope.*

"Your aunt is very determined."

I know this. First hand.

"But it is the way in your family, *nicht wahr*? To work in the mines? Your cousin is a breaker boy, is this not true?"

"He is." Winslow, with eyes like blue flame and hair the color of wheat, had gone off to sit on the coarse boards outside the main colliery when he'd been only eight years old. Now a skinny lad of fourteen, he had sallow skin and sunken eyes and the film of boredom in his once lively gaze. He caught colds easily and often in the winter, when he coughed, he hacked like an old man. His condition terrified her. But Gwen could not save him from the black coal dust that floated like a ghostly shroud around the mines and burned in the mountainous culms. She had not been old enough to object to Aunt Mary's orders for Win to work there. She'd not been strong enough or maybe even wise enough then to object to her aunt's avarice.

But Mrs. Learner knew none of this.

"We Spencers came from coal country in Yorkshire. My dad knew how to mine. My uncle, too."

"There should be more to life than going down into the pits and staying there, Gwen."

"I agree, Mrs. Learner." She considered the woman who had always been so kind to her. When she would go to the Learners' to help her aunt after school, the woman had given her bowls of stew Aunt Mary said she could not afford to make for the family at home. She'd also given her sweets. Clothes, cut down, from her own closet, that Gwen had shared with her cousin, Helen, nearest her own age. Or she'd cut them down further herself to fit Susannah. "I do indeed."

"I know you do, Gwen. You fought not to go there. You fight now for Susannah."

Whether her statement was an injunction, an encouragement, or a simple statement of fact, Gwen did not debate. She simply valued her support and nodded. "I will."

"Fine thing, this is for you and her. Well, here, I

will drive straight, *liebchen*. You, I will let out. Only another block and no rain yet. Is that good?"

"Wonderful, Mrs. Learner. Thank you for the ride."

"All the time is a good thing to help another, *ja*?" The woman winked at her.

Gwen chuckled. This woman had certainly helped the Spencers in countless ways. She had employed her mother as her housekeeper, allowing her to bring Gwen with her when she was very young and having her come after school. She had kept her mother on even during her pregnancies, allowing for her recuperations after her numerous miscarriages. Then, after her mother died, Mrs. Learner had hired her mother's sister, Mary, as her new housekeeper. She had even endured Mary's tart personality and her officiousness. Over the past twelve years, Mrs. Learner had learned more about her aunt and her mother and all her family, than perhaps even Gwen herself. Wisely, the woman also kept that knowledge to herself.

With a wave, Gwen let herself out of the car and said her thanks. She took the turn off Main Street up to Prospect and hastened to beat the storm. By the time she climbed the front porch steps and circled around to the hallway door, her joy in the conversation with Mrs. Learner was a cold and distant memory.

She knocked on the rickety screen door frame. The inside door sat ajar, but in the past two years, Gwen had never entered the house uninvited. Aunt Mary would raise a fit about having to answer her knock, but Gwen had a point to prove. She no longer lived here—and she refused to fall into the trap of acting like she did, thereby allowing her aunt the opportunity to reprimand her for it. No, she had learned that lesson early in the weeks immediately after she had left this house to enter nursing school. She had chosen to quit this place and she would never return. Not even in the small deeds that might make her beholden to her aunt for any service. Once, she had been an intruder. Now she was a visitor here. She would remain so all her life.

She knocked again and cocked her ear to listen to the sounds coming from the back yard. Someone whooped and hollered as they chased the chickens and the rooster. The ruckus was so familiar. Susannah, who had never liked "smelly old chickens," was most likely trying to catch one to kill for supper.

Where was Aunt Mary? In the kitchen?

She knows I come usually about two o'clock. She's just being stubborn, making Susannah or Helen come to let me in.

"Hey, there, Gwennie!" Walking along the sidewalk toward her was her cousin Winslow, home from his early morning shift.

She walked to the railing and grinned at him.

Covered in soot, his gray shirt grimy with it, his black overalls thick with it, he trod up the steps, carrying his lunch pail and his soft hat. He greeted her with a hand up and a genuine grin of perfect teeth gleaming in comparison to the rest of him in gray dust. "No, don't hug me. Let me wash up first. How are you?" Inches in front of her, he looked her over, his pale blue eyes sparkling in welcome. "You look good. But tired, yeah? What did you bring us? Steak? Lemon drops? Chocolate?"

She rolled her eyes.

He imitated her. "No stalling!"

"Salami from Carlucci's delicatessen." She dug in

one of her bags, brandishing the gift that Anna had insisted her parents give her for saving her from the worst type of punishment this morning. "A nice hard cheese."

Win bent over her knit grocery bag to peer in. "That from Carlucci's, too?"

"Yes. Please do not tell me you object to their goods because they are Italian?"

"Hey, cuz." He chuckled, derision in his tone, then opened the screen door for her. "Not me. Let's go in. The wind is stirring up and I'm catchin' a chill out here."

She hoped he wasn't. Prone to chest colds, Win could become congested even on a mild June day like today. The mines did that. A pity the work could do that, especially to a young man.

"Hey, Mama!" He called from the hall toward the kitchen. "Gwennie is here!"

Nothing for it now but to face her aunt. Gwen walked toward the back of the house, past the parlor where her father and Uncle Len had been laid out in their caskets, one along each wall. She avoided that parlor at all costs. But her eye caught on the sideboard…on a porcelain vase. New. Expensive looking. Resentment flamed in her chest, the old burning that could add fuel to an argument…if she allowed it.

"Hello, Aunt." She strode toward the oval oak table and put her bags down on a wooden kitchen chair. The days when she would offer the woman obligatory kisses had ended two years ago. Why pretend affection when all love had died long ago?

Mary turned, a tall woman with an oval face and

strong jaw. Substantial, many might have once said for her height and weight. Even her hair—watery blonde but aging in streaks of bland gray—gave her an aura of faded glory, once attractive, now merely sallow. Her eyes, the same almost colorless bright hue as her son's, dissected Gwen. Behind her rimless round glasses, she took her time assessing her niece and the packages she had lain down. "You are early today."

"Mrs. Learner gave me a ride up Main Street."

"That is why you look windblown. Do you wish to wash?"

"Thank you, yes." Gwen made for the washroom at the back of the house, walking around her aunt, careful not to swish against her voluminous skirts. "I have a few things for the family."

"Useful, I hope?" her aunt asked.

"Very." *Would I ever come without an offering?*

"Oh, what did you bring, Gwennie?" Her sister Susannah rushed to her through the back door as Gwen turned on the spigot. Her arms out wide for an embrace, chicken feathers stuck to her fingertips, she flung herself against Gwen. "I am so happy you are here!"

Gwen pecked her little sister on the lips and hugged her close. Susannah smelled as she had as a small girl, baby powder and soap. But her golden hair that hung in ringlets from a large band at her nape smelled of the lavender Gwen had bought for her. "I am tickled to come for your birthday dinner."

The girl, fresh from the sunshine, blushes on her English porcelain complexion, squeezed her tight. "And what did you bring? Anything interesting?"

Aunt Mary tsked. "Stop that at once. Ungrateful and ill mannered, too. Let your sister wash. You do it, too. Then offer Gwen refreshment and a seat. She has come a long way to see us."

Gwen trained her eyes on her sister, knowing full well that their aunt was more devoted to chastising Susannah than she was to teaching the girl fine etiquette. "I have brought many items this Friday. You shall see them as I show them to Aunt."

"You do tease me," Susannah chided her as she rushed toward the chair where Gwen had laid her gifts.

"Not at all. I simply wish for Aunt to put the goods in the ice box."

"Hurry and dry your hands then so we can begin," Susannah urged, rising on her toes this way and that to try to peek into the crocheted bags in the chair.

"I have a treat for Win, too, and I don't want to start without him. Wash up." The girl sped away.

"Helen sends her regrets," her aunt said. "She must work until the store closes at seven o'clock. Mr. McIntosh lost his clerk this week to the army. Helen volunteered to take the man's shifts, which will be a good thing for all of us."

A wonderful development for Helen, who will now earn more money and pray that induces you to smile. "I have heard of many who wish to go. Two of my friends have brothers who didn't wait for the draft. They volunteered. They said they want to see the world, but I doubt they'll see anything beautiful."

"But imagine, they're going to Paris, Gwen," Susannah said when she returned, her sky blue eyes dreamy. "I've read about Paris. How big the streets are, everyone is rich and the ladies are all so stylish."

"You read too much," Aunt Mary scolded her, picking up a peeler to work on a pile of potatoes.

29

Gwen dug into the first of her two large bags. "I brought you salami and cheese."

Her aunt wrinkled her nose. "Oh, those things from the Italians are so strong."

"I like them," said Win as he entered the room, his face and hands washed, his shirt and overalls changed, his feet bare. "I'll eat them if you won't, Ma."

"I like them, too," Susannah said, her face alight in expectation. "We have boring things."

"Pasties," Win groaned. "I eat them for lunch and dinner. Can we cut into the salami, now, Ma?"

"And the cheese, too?" Susannah beseeched their aunt.

"Yes, I suppose. But not too much. It'll spoil your dinner."

A silence fell over the kitchen. No one dared to ask what the dinner fare was. That way led to huffs and puffs by their aunt. And if she were in a particularly vindictive mood, she could pretend such insult that she deprived the inquiring person of it.

"In any case," Gwen said, sliding her hand down inside her bag and widening her eyes at Win, "I have— ta-dah!—steak. Two big sirloins."

Both younger children ooed and ahhed over that. Win took the brown-wrapped package of meat from Gwen's hands as gently as if it were a glass. Susannah clapped in anticipation of Gwen's other items.

"I brought a few oranges and lemons." Placing the fruit one by one on the table, Gwen did not have to check her aunt's expression. Her aunt would count them and gauge them for freshness from where she stood, immobile and placid. Citrus was considered a delicacy in a house that had received them only as weekly donations from the members of the local Methodist church. "And for you, Win, I have a small pair of scissors."

"What?" He looked puzzled. "What will I do with them?"

"They are for your nails, my dear." *So you can trim them after handling those huge lumps of coal and shale each day.* "If you keep your nails trimmed, you'll have less to scrub out from under the edges and you won't break and chip them as often on the coal."

"Oh, okay. Thank you, Gwennie." He bussed her on the cheek, then walked away opening and closing the blades.

Susannah said not a word as she stood before Gwen, her lips pursed in expectation.

"And for the charming girl with the birthday, I have four presents."

"Four?" Susannah lifted her shoulders in rapture. "Oh, Gwennie, how will I thank you? What will they be?"

"The first one is a pair of nail scissors just like Win's." Gwen extracted it from her bag and this one had a red bow around the center.

"But I don't break coal."

God willing and I have a say, you never will. "I know. But these are for you to play the piano with your beautiful long fingers. Nails trimmed and—" She produced another object from the depths of her bag. "Buffed. This slides along your nails like this." Gwen demonstrated to the girl. "When you play, you will do so with elegant hands. Like a lady."

"Like a lady who lives in Paris." Susannah took the object from Gwen and marveled at the object, then used it on her nails just as Gwen had taught her. She caught the edge of the buffer on one ridge. "I suppose that ladies in Paris don't try to catch chickens for dinner, do they?"

Gwen smiled. "Maybe not. But you will play more easily and that is what is important."

"Yes, I will. I promise. But…but you said you had *four* presents?"

"Ah. I do." Gwen stuck her hand inside the bag and fished at the bottom to catch between her fingers the pages of the two items she wished. "These"—She placed the sheet music in her sister's outstretched hands—"are for you to play at Mrs. Learner's."

Susannah squealed at the gift of music in her hands. "Oh, Gwen, you are the very best sister! The very best. Oh, my. These are so good. 'It's a Long Long Way to Tipperary' and 'The Band Played On.' Everyone will be jealous I know these." She clutched the pages to her chest, then crushed Gwen to her heart and broke away aghast. "But I don't know if I can read the notes."

"You will learn," Gwen assured her.

"I must ask Will," she said, referring to William Learner who had nourished her love of music and the piano. "He will know the words."

"I bet you could figure out the tune now. Try humming it."

"I can't, Gwen. I can't sing."

Gwen tipped her head. "Sweetheart, you never know until you try."

"Thank you. Oh, I must try now!" She spun on her heel, caught Win's hand. "You sing so well. I bet you even know these words."

"Yeah, matter of fact, Suze, I do," he admitted sheepishly catching a look at his mother.

"Come on and help me."

"Okay! All right! Can I go, Ma?"

"Yes, the two of you may leave for a few minutes. But I need that chicken cleaned for dinner. Do that now. I must talk to Gwen."

The two children bustled off, happy but dismayed that they still were required to gut a fowl.

Gwen folded her hands, girding herself for the coming fight. She had known what it would cost her to bring these gifts to Susannah long before she paid her hard-earned money for them. She met the steely gaze of her aunt and held. "Susannah will have these. She needs them."

"She will work at the mine. I have already told the principal she will not return to school in September. She must contribute her fair share to this family."

"I contribute for her."

"In what? Scissors and buffers and sheet music?"

"You know I give more than that." *I always have.*

"It is what is necessary to keep us alive. You with your airs and your fine nurses' training don't see that."

"But I do." Gwen lifted her head higher. Mary's insults always stung. *When will I learn to ignore them?* "I have for years. Just how much do you need from us?"

"To pay for our home—"

"The house is rented. I know how much you pay to Mister Dunwitty each month. I know what you pay for food at Arnold's Grocery."

"How dare you ask—"

"I don't have to ask. I see what food costs. I know

the price of an orange." She lifted one from the table and placed it down again. "I know the cost of living in this house."

"I do not make enough from Mrs. Learner to pay for two children of my own and the two of you."

"One," Gwen corrected her and stood. "Only one now." *Since I left almost two years ago, you have one less mouth to feed.*

Her aunt inhaled, filling herself up with her righteousness. "The years you lived here were very hard on me."

"I know they were. I am the oldest. I remember. Susannah was two years old. A baby. Win was four. Helen and I, twelve, old enough to help clean and cook, but not worth much else unless we picked coal at the entrance to the mine."

"You were good then, the two of you," her aunt conceded. As if that statement were enough now to compensate for the desperation that the woman had poured into them like poison, she sniffed as if she were to cry real tears. She tried to play for sympathy—and used it as a wedge to justify any behavior she felt useful.

But Gwen had long seen precisely how menacing, how calculating Mary was—and for no other reason than to dominate them without question. "Helen and I were good girls. We went to work each morning at five with the first shift of miners. And we filled buckets with the nuggets that had fallen from the rail trams. We earned money that we brought home to you."

"That is enough, Gwendolyn. I know these things. I had to take you in and your sister. Where else would you have gone? Len's and John's brother Charles did not want you, could not take you."

"He had three children of his own and a sickly wife."

"He did." Aunt Mary threw down her peeler and strode to the washroom.

As ever when they argued over Susannah's future, Mary maneuvered to draw Gwen to her. Like a spider luring her prey into her web, Mary understood how to position herself to manipulate another.

Gwen huffed. *No.* She would not follow her. She would not bow.

When Mary reappeared in the kitchen, Gwen switched tactics and gave her what due she owed her. "I recall the look on your face each Monday when the ladies' society from the church would bring their weekly fruit and vegetables. I know how you felt when the warder came from the Miner's Relief Fund with the stipend."

"You remember? Good for you. That money was ours by rights. The coal company never inspected the gas leaks in that shaft. My Len and your father died for no reason."

Her heart broke for the woman her aunt had been that day her husband and her brother-in-law were crushed and gassed in the collapse of Carbondale Number Two.

She remembered the pain. The black void of that day. Her daddy had died there. Her uncle, too. And since she had lost her mother in childbirth only a year before, her father's passing made Gwen and her sister orphans. Yes, she shuddered to think of what would have become of the two of them if Aunt Mary had not volunteered to take them home with her. She and

Susannah would have gone to a crude abode filled with other homeless, parentless children.

They might have been torn even from each other. Made to work in the local silk factories, equally as hazardous as picking coal lumps from the entrance to the mineshafts. They would have lost each other, not only in the indifferent atmosphere of an institution but also in the impersonal attitude toward poor children that excused rash and abusive behavior.

Aunt Mary had saved them from those horrors. But in her need to acquire the means to pay her rent, buy food and clothing and pay the occasional doctor bills for four children, the woman—who had never been mild-mannered—had become a shrew.

She harped about money to them, calling each child a burden, a stone around her neck. She criticized them unmercifully. Gwen, the oldest of the four, was less intimidated than Win or Helen. Susannah, a baby, had been too young to intimidate.

Gwen's father and mother had praised her, laughed with her, taken her for Sunday strolls in the park and read to her each night from books, wonderful books, Father had bought for Mother. They told her, too, that she must be wise and mind her elders, learn from them too.

They encouraged her to read and write. Delighting in her child's flights of fancy, they applauded her made-up tales of faeries and knights. They enjoyed her descriptions of imaginary friends. Promising that if she did well in school, she would have a better job and a finer life than they had, they were a joy to live with. After that wealth of happiness, Gwen was puzzled by Aunt Mary's behavior—and from the first, she rebelled at the woman's callous treatment.

Two months after Father's death, when Gwen turned thirteen, her aunt insisted that she leave school. She refused. Mary used the back of her hand to make her point. Gwen had never been struck by an adult. She recoiled but days later, she appealed to the principal to let her stay in school. When Mary stood in the woman's office and heard her recommendation to permit Gwen to remain in school, she told the official that she had the right to take the girl and do with her as she would. Silent, Mary took her by the arm, marched her home and used her belt to punish her. Gwen relented and went to pick up coal. For two years, she obeyed until one afternoon, she begged Mrs. Learner to allow her to take a hipbath in the back parlor. She cleaned herself of every inch of black dust and applied at the tuberculosis sanitarium to be a charwoman. She was very young to do such savage work, the director declared, but she liked Gwen's spunk. She got the job.

Mary, incensed by her niece's insubordination, nonetheless took her wages and spent them as she wished. Worse, she went after the other children with a vengeance. If they did not show promise in their studies, she withdrew them from school and forced them to work. Win, she had sent to the colliery at age eight because he could not read well and occasionally stuttered. Helen, at thirteen, went to work at the mine entrance. She stayed there until five years ago when Gwen persuaded her to apply at the local dry goods store to become a clerk. Helen was a whiz with arithmetic and when she told the owner so, Mr. McIntosh tested her skill, asking her to keep his books. He paid her well for that and now that Helen had more hours of work because McIntosh's man would enlist in the Army, Gwen was certain Aunt Mary rejoiced. This meant more money in her pocket.

The woman took from each child all their wages and only as each one had grown older and demanded a bit of their earnings, had she dispensed pin money to them. A fraction of their total wages, the ten percent pleased Win and Helen. Never Gwen.

To her, the pittance only fueled a desire to find a way out of the house, out of that life, out of that misery that was a series of days without a kiss or a hug, a thank you or even a small smile. The allowance was the proof of her bondage.

"I realize you feel put-upon, Aunt. And you resent the tragedy that combined our families. But you have taken it out on us for more than nine years. It is time to stop. Helen brings you her salary. Win brings you his. You still receive some money for Susannah from the Relief Fund."

"That ends next year when she turns twelve."

"Is it so large a sum that in its lack, you will send her to that hideous place and deprive her of what she loves?"

"We do not have a piano. I hate asking the Learners to let her play theirs."

Your pride was ever your albatross. Buying china and cut glass, lace tablecloths and skimping on meat and cheese. But inviting the reverend and his wife for Sunday dinners and tithing at the church. "The Learners enjoy having her there. They always have from the time she was a baby in my mother's arms, they welcomed her. They don't consider their love for her charity."

"And to accept all that? I owe them. I owe them. I will not!"

"Yet you make us four owe you."

"To pay your way."

"For us to contribute to the running of the house is certainly just. For us to show you our gratitude for keeping us together as a family is only right. But you cannot control so much of our lives that you squeeze the very breath from our lungs."

"I do no such thing."

"You seek money to pay the bills. But the truth is, you seek more and more of it. No amount ever satisfies you. No amount ever will. You demand we give up our days and sacrifice our dreams. We cannot do that. There is a limit to how much of one's life you must lay down for another."

"Oh? Why did you not ask that of me nine years ago?"

"I couldn't. I was a child. I was grateful to you for loving me enough to bring me here amid our grief. But you killed my love with your demands and your resentments."

Mary seethed. "You will use any excuse to salve your conscience that you left here and went to nursing school without my permission."

"That is not true. I feel no guilt that I left to better myself. You did not want me to go because my salary scrubbing floors at the sanitarium lined your pocketbook so well. Fifty dollars a month sounded more attractive to you than the twenty-five I earned as a student nurse. But I had to go. I was dying here. I'm sorry that you disapproved of my decision. But I have made compensation for my leaving to you each Friday when I visit."

"Meanwhile, you treat yourself well." The woman clutched her two hands together, focusing on Gwen's wristwatch.

Swallowing a retort, Gwen refused to justify her purchase. Mary would never acknowledge anyone's need but her own.

Her aunt took one step closer, a threatening lift of her nose. "And you bring trinkets for the others."

You buy them for yourself. Gwen ground her teeth and held her ground. "Items they need and cannot buy for themselves. Things you will not let them buy. And I bring more you never acknowledge. Say it."

Mary glared at Gwen, her nostrils flaring, her backbone steel.

Gwen reached inside her reticule and pulled out the fat envelope stuffed and sealed as each week's gift always was. She raised it in the air, a sword, an offering, a recompense for love never given, succor always sought, understanding ever needed. "The same amount as always. From me. For you. And Helen, Win and Susannah. Let them have a bit of joy in life, Aunt. A little goes so far. You can afford it."

Tears welling in her eyes for all their confrontations that never pierced her aunt's armor, Gwen looped her reticule handle over her arm, then picked up her empty crocheted bag. "Do not stop Susannah from going to the Learners to play the piano. Do not."

"You cannot threaten me."

Gwen spun, not bothering to conceal her disdain. "If I wanted to threaten you, I would say do not stop Susannah from going to the Learners or playing piano or I will cut you off from my weekly contribution to the family."

"Your Quiet Ones—" the woman blustered, pointing a shaking hand to the envelope and the money that Gwen would no longer give as a silent contribution to her aunt's tyranny. "—do not buy my compliance."

"I never gave them to you expecting that they would, Aunt. Perhaps I should have demanded it. We might have had a different life."

"I will put her to work at the mine."

Gwen bristled at her aunt's intransigence, no longer appealing but now demanding one last time for mercy. "Do not break her heart."

"You break mine."

"Do I?" What gall Mary possessed. "I doubt that. In fact, I wonder who did break it and do I pay—do we all four pay—for your heartbreak?"

"Get out."

Gwen nodded. "I wish I could take all of my loved ones with me."

Chapter Three

Monday morning, Gwen was early for hygiene class. All the other students still dressed or ate their breakfast. With no intention of giving Dalton any additional reason to look sideways at her performance, Gwen had vowed to herself yesterday to keep a spotless record until she earned her cap. Once she was certified as a trained nurse, she would earn more than her training allotment of twenty-five dollars a month. She'd get three times that on the wards here at Moore. Perhaps more than that if she moved to Harrisburg or Philadelphia. If she were very fortunate, she could earn that much in a week as a private duty nurse. Surely then she could afford to take Susannah from Prospect Street. And while she wanted to take Helen and Win as well, she had no right to do that.

"You are dreaming again, Spencer." Bernice Dalton appeared suddenly at her elbow as they strode the long corridor to the classroom.

"No, ma'am." *Dreaming is something I doubt I have ever done.*

"Have your read your textbook for this morning's lesson?"

"I have, yes."

"Tell me how the British in the battlefield use

Carrel-Dakin's solution for debridement."

The head nurse could not stump her on this. "They use it as a flush running it from hosing over the affected areas. Insert the tubes into the wounds, sterilizing even after major operations."

"Why?"

"The faster you clean a wound, the greater the chance of releasing all contamination from the body."

"And why is this is important?"

"Gas gangrene can affect any part of the body, and any foreign object carrying dirt or debris can cause infection."

"Superb." The woman stopped, waiting for Gwen to open the classroom door for her. As Gwen did, she examined her. "Crying is not good for your eyes."

"No, ma'am."

"A few tears are useful. Wash the membranes and allow for release of anguish."

Gwen nodded, horrified that this woman somehow had learned about her sadness of the past few days.

"Then there comes a time when you must stop. Bad for your health to wallow in despair." She faced Gwen and in the glare from the strong overhead lights, she set her jaw. "Then you must make a decision to go forward or back."

Gwen searched the head matron's expression. Dalton came from Peckville. She knew the town, the people, the mining company—and the rumors about Mary Spencer and her relationship with her children and her nieces. Dalton might also have heard about her recent row with Aunt Mary. Neither of them had spoken since Friday afternoon. Many of their arguments over the years had aroused neighbors' irate comments and much gossip. Gwen herself had overheard some whispers of that talk whenever she'd been out and about on Main Street or even at the TB sanitarium where she was friends with many of the residents. One of the most outspoken critics of her aunt was the TB San's director who also happened to be Bernice Dalton's cousin. In fact, Gwen often suspected that the one person who was most responsible for accepting her application into nursing training two years ago was Bernice herself.

"I won't go back," she heard herself whisper. "I won't. I want to make something of myself. My sister, too. I want to take her away from there."

"That may be difficult to do. You are not yet of age."

"In February, I turn twenty-one. I can save money and after I have my cap, I can rent rooms in a boarding house."

"What life will that be for a child?"

"What life will she have if she stays there?" Fear chilled her spine at the thought of her beautiful Susannah dulled by drudgery, warped by spite and vindictiveness. Gwen caught her breath. "I'm sorry. I do not mean to argue with you."

"You don't. We simply talk."

Gwen focused on her folded hands. She disliked others knowing how erratically her aunt behaved. The woman's callousness tarnished all she touched. Her actions shamed Gwen. "Yes, of course."

"You are intelligent, Spencer. You have ambition. I like that in my girls."

She resisted the insulting notion that Dalton considered her merely a child. The last time she had felt young was most likely the day before her mother died. "I have had to acquire it. Need demanded it."

"It did indeed. But I said to you Friday morning, you must learn to live for yourself."

Inhaling, Gwen met her gaze. "I will. I am."

"You may have to, Spencer. Sooner than you planned."

"What do you mean?"

"Your aunt came to see me yesterday."

"On Sunday? My God. Is Susannah ill?" Had Mary taken a belt to her in punishment for Gwen's words?

"No, nothing like that."

"Why then would she come here?" Mary was capable of so much harm. She scarcely understood her malicious effect on others.

"She told me she would have the town constable arrest you if you came anywhere near her house. Told me she would accuse you of robbing her."

Gwen glanced around, stunned. "But that's ridiculous! Why would I do that?"

"Spencer, you have taken from her the one thing she cannot afford to lose."

Gwen worked at words. "I'm…I'm sorry. Explain that to me."

"You continually deny her the ability to order her life—and all around her—as she chooses."

"Yes, by God." Gwen straightened her spine. "She chooses poorly."

Dalton's plain round face softened into the first compassionate smile Gwen had ever seen. "She does indeed. But do not tempt her. Stay away from her. At least, until you graduate."

"She'll take my sister from school. Put her to work.

I cannot—"

"You or your sister, Gwen. Which will it be? Take your choice for the next few months. Who will you save?"

Outrage clogged Gwen's throat. Tears pooled and burned as hotly as her hatred of her aunt. "I will choose to graduate."

Dalton reached out to pat her arm. "That's the Gwendolyn Spencer I see. Find the place in this world for her to shine and laugh and love. Your sister will be best served by that woman."

****

The months turned hotter, July rainy and August sweltering. Gwen worked the wards, eager for the breeze from opened windows, encouraging the orderlies to keep the patients' water pitchers filled with water. Lonely for her sister and cousins, Gwen divorced herself of her fears about Susannah, her cousins, and Mary. Instead, she pored over her texts, learned her lessons and took pride in how competent she felt.

Even Anna Carlucci was up to snuff. She had studied each lesson, arriving on time at classes and observations. True, much of that devotion was prompted by the fact that Harry Winchester had left town at the end of June. He was a dentist, only one year in practice in Scranton, but still he volunteered to join the Army Medical Corps as a captain for a base hospital forming in Philadelphia.

While their colleagues bent to their studies, too, spurred on by their approaching graduation, they talked constantly of the hundreds of thousands of war casualties in Europe. In the dormitory at night, many students discussed joining the American troops shipping out every month. Gwen marveled at her friends' desire to sail off to another country. What would it be like to live among people whose language she did not speak? To work on hideously wounded men missing arms or legs? Could she cope with the terror of cannons and bullets? She tried to imagine the enormity of that challenge. How did one accept such destruction of one's body? She bought newspapers and gobbled up reports of the war, mesmerized by the tales of devastation and misery. As each day passed, she grew perplexed by her own intrigue to know more…and her compulsion to join up and do her own bit.

But how could she leave her sister?

"Hey, everyone! I have another letter from Harry." Anna waved the paper around the dormitory, then dropped on her bed to read his latest missive. Five nurses, all of whom talked of going abroad, gathered round her.

Gwen had no letters, not even from Lex in the past few weeks. The lack stung. A stamp cost three cents, but no letter came from Susannah, who had no money of her own. Aunt Mary had probably prohibited her from writing to her. What could she do but hope her aunt shook off her latest fit? In the meantime, she would make the most of today and now. Plumping her pillows behind her back, she smiled at Anna and picked up a novel from her nightstand. "How is Harry then? Enjoying the sights of South Carolina?"

"Hmm? Oh, yes. He says the training is frightful. Eight hours a day they are in classes. Some of their instructors are French. Imagine."

"I wonder how hot it is there," Pearl Markham groused as she turned the page of a newspaper, feigning disinterest in Harry's words. She, like the others in the room, was dressed only in her camisole and slip. "If it's cooler, I might just join the Army to escape this heat."

"It's cooler, all right." Gwen glanced up at Pearl, half serious, half incredulous. "And it rains so often in France, you'd be swimming instead."

"That works for me."

"I'm joining," Anna piped up.

Pearl and Gwen gasped together. "What?"

"It's true. I am going. The Army Nurse Corps for me."

"Since when?" Gwen asked, shocked at this new development.

"Since Harry talked about it."

Pearl snorted and snapped the newspaper in her hands. "Of course."

"Do not make fun of me, Markham."

"Fun? Let me tell you about fun, Carlucci." She adjusted her glasses and read from the front page. "'Although the French troops took the ridge from the Germans within five days, they fell back from the line quickly. The offensive was abandoned in disarray in early May, and the town returned to German control. The French High Command now lists its casualties at one hundred and eighty thousand men.'"

A hush fell over the dormitory.

"My God," whispered Anna.

"Too many," said Flo. "And we worry about one or two patients a day."

Gwen's insides melted. One hundred and eighty thousand wounded, lying on a battlefield. What did that look like? Sound like? Who could aid those men? Who would try?

She had seen men carried into the hospital, their arms or legs crushed in machinery or in automobile accidents. She had seen men and women suffer with cancers of throat or groin or breast. She had witnessed little Patricia Benson cry after her surgery, moaning for relief. None of them had asked for that pain. All wanted only some saving grace. But how did a man rise up out of a trench and march across a field knowing it might be his last step, his last breath, his last moment on this earth? What did he tell himself, what phrases could he summon in his soul to justify obeying an order that would cost him his all?

"Thousands of men to splint and sew up. A few to save, then send them back to kill someone else. That's what we're in for." Pearl took a glimpse at Anna, who had gone white as the sheets on her bed. "And that, my dear Carlucci, will not be fun."

"No, of course it isn't, Markham. You make me out to be an idiot. I'm not. I got into this class because I have a few brains in this noggin."

Gwen shook her head, contemplating the bigger conflict and its costs. "Can we please not argue? Pearl, stop needling Anna. And you." She zeroed in on her friend."Stop acting like a love-sick ninny. If you want to go to France, for God's sake, go because you want to help the wounded, not because Harry Winchester might be available for a few kisses after the bombs stop falling."

"Well!" Anna got her dander up. "Whose side are you on?"

"Yours, dammit."

Anna gasped.

Pearl chuckled. "If you want a man, terrific. If you

want Harry, good for you. He's a nice guy. But if you want to get our respect, stop rubbing our noses in the fact that we either don't have a man or don't want one."

"Some of us don't see a man as our meal ticket to better living," Flo Aldridge offered from across the room.

Anna opened her mouth, ready to hurl some kind of insult at Flo.

"Don't, Anna." Gwen shot her a look. "Just don't argue, please."

The dark haired woman settled back into her pillows. "I do want to go for good reasons."

"Yeah?" Pearl challenged.

"Markham." Gwen struggled from her bed. "Button your lip."

"She shouldn't go if she thinks it'll be a picnic and she can sneak out at night to cuddle with Harry."

"I don't. You saw how I'm learning anesthesia. I put old man Dodsworth to sleep properly the other day. You know I am good. You ask Therese Reynard if I'm not good as her. Ask Bernie Dalton." Anna stuck out her tongue at Pearl.

Gwen raised her brows at Markham, hoping she would acknowledge Anna's skill and end this conflict between them.

"You are good, Anna." Pearl conceded. She rattled her newspaper, training her mind on the page again. "Go over. You'll do a lot of men a service to give them peace while we sew them back together again."

After a blissful minute of silence, Gwen faced Pearl. "So you really are thinking of volunteering?"

Pearl stared over the rims of her glasses. "I am. Want to come? It's a set of uniforms, an overcoat, two pairs of boots, a trip to France, and all the work you can get until the war ends and all the men in the entire world are dead. Oh, and especially for you, Spencer, a raincoat. The one you never afforded for yourself because you gave half your pay to that ungrateful aunt of yours."

"A raincoat. Golly," Gwen mused half-seriously. "A worthy reason to join. Plus, if I go with you, I could listen to you complain all the time."

Markham threw a pillow at her.

"I might look into this, just to learn what it's got to offer," Gwen teased her, but inside a seed of interest grew roots.

"Ask Dalton. She knows more."

"Why?"

"She's going. O'Bryan persuaded her."

"Doc is going to France?" Gwen couldn't believe it. O'Bryan didn't seem like the adventurous type, nor the noble type, either. She misjudged him. Why would he volunteer?

"For a million soldiers," Anna chimed in. "You need thousands of doctors and nurses. Dentists, too."

"Of course," Gwen murmured. *How many people do you need to care for millions of men? How many scalpels and needles? How much ether and debridement solution? How many sterilizers and...just how do you get all that where it's needed to save lives of men in pain and bleeding?* "I want to learn more."

"Forget it, Spencer." Flo gathered her laundry in her arms, headed for the stairs. "They won't take you. You're too ornery. Plus you're too damn pretty. They want ugly women. Like me. No temptation for the men."

Pearl sniffed. "Don't discourage her, Flo. Thousands of American boys might come home just because golden-haired, pansy-eyed Gwendolyn Spencer smiled at them."

"Be serious, Markham," Gwen replied. How she looked had never bought her any advantages over the challenges of daily life. When boys had looked at her when she was a kid, they taunted the skinny girl with wild pigtails and big red freckles on her nose. When she'd grown taller and gangly, Lex had called her a gazelle. His friend from Harvard—what had been his name?—had tried to kiss her a few summers ago as they strolled in the Learners' garden. But in the last two years, when men looked at her, they saw a woman in a uniform. Dedicated. Smart. Or she hoped they did. At the least, they respected her and that satisfied her mightily. "I'd hope they'd return home because I laid hands on them and helped them heal."

That appealed to her. To do work she loved and be appreciated for it. That made her heart feel rich.

****

The next afternoon, after her round of the children's ward, Gwen tucked her scissors in her apron pocket and looked forward to a nap. She'd been on duty at seven after tossing and turning all night long.

Debating going to France had filled her head with visions of travel, a concept she had never contemplated before now. Wouldn't it be thrilling to go to another country where everything was new? The people, the sights, the language? She'd had that same sense of adventure she'd experienced when she left the sanitarium to go into training. She'd learn every day how to section a colon or patch up a broken arm. She'd be so much more qualified when she returned home that she'd command top salary. Oh, there'd be problems. She knew no French. Only the smattering of German phrases she had heard the Learners speak over the years she'd been in their home. But she wouldn't have to speak German and she supposed not French, either. She would travel with Americans and work with Americans.

But how could she leave the only place she had ever known? The only people she had ever known? How could she leave Susannah?

The merry-go-round of her thoughts had tormented her.

Now the only way to end the ceaseless argument was to ask Dalton for more information.

She paused in front of the matron's office door. If she asked, if she learned more, if she was tempted, would she go abroad and regret it? Would she miss her home?

She snorted.

Home no longer existed. In reality, she had had no home for nine years. She had had a roof over her head and food put in front of her. But she had worked hard in return mostly at jobs she hated and gotten no thanks for her labors or her contributions. Thanks she did not need so much as she had wanted—*no, craved*—some respect for her compliance with her aunt's demands. Some little consideration for what she had given freely…until now, when she would give no more. Especially when her aunt would be so bold, so heartless as to cut her off from her own sister.

She raised her hand and knocked twice.

"Come in," Dalton called, and Gwen opened the door. "Hello, Spencer. Finished your rounds?"

"Yes, ma'am. May I talk with you for a few minutes?"

Dalton nodded, pushing aside papers on her desk. "Do sit down. You look haggard. Not sleep well?"

"No, ma'am."

"Not feeling well?"

"I am healthy, thank you."

"What's your problem, then? Not that aunt of yours, I do hope."

"I have not seen her. Have not gone near her since you told me of her...her threat." The last word stuck in Gwen's throat like a stone.

Dalton folded her hands over her ample middle and sat back in her chair. "Out with it. I must do my weekly check of items in the supply room."

Gwen met the woman's gaze. "I wish to learn more about volunteering to go abroad with the Army Nurse Corps."

Dalton's round face registered a small pleasure. Her mouth curled up briefly. Her hard blue eyes actually twinkled. Then her brows arched. "Carlucci has talked to you?"

"Pearl and Flo, too."

"Carlucci will go. She tells me she wants to be with that dentist of hers." Dalton cleared her throat, frowning and showing her disdain of Anna's rationale. "Love of one man is not the reason one volunteers to go to war. But her grades are good. Her health, too. And the War Department says we need all the trained nurses we can muster."

Dalton shifted in her chair, eyeing Gwen for interest. "Shall I continue?"

"Please." Going abroad, sailing on the ocean

seemed such exotic acts, demanding little of a traveler except enjoyment. Going to war would require no joy, only guts, nerves of steel, and tremendous heart. Did she have those qualities? Enough of them to do a proper job?

"Some estimates say we will not have enough graduate nurses and we must find a way to educate more and do it quickly. The British are so short-handed that they have had to allow women from other professions into their wards. They have sent them to school in a camp for a few weeks before they post them to their hospitals. God knows what these women are good for except to feed patients or undress wounded, but that is not for me to justify. This is war. And need is need. The work is backbreaking. The demands are often round the clock. We need trained help who are strong and determined. So then you must tell me, why would you go, Spencer?"

Gwen contemplated her choice of words. Dalton was so critical. So discerning. And yet, why should Gwen worry if the reason she gave was not honorable enough for the matron? Dalton had accepted Anna's application, even though she completely disapproved of the young woman's motivation. "The work—" She lifted her shoulders and surrendered to her need to go. "The work calls to me. If I can aid one man, I can help two or twenty or a hundred. I have come here—" She waved a hand to denote the hospital. "Come here to do some good. I am appalled that there could be so many people wounded and in pain when I work here dallying, wasting time pampering one or two. It seems a pity to keep my knowledge to spend on a few when so many are in need."

This time, Dalton did smile. And the radiance of it warmed Gwen's heart as little else had in years. "You are right. You are needed. And you would be among the best to go and serve, Gwen."

Gwen. Dalton never addressed her charges by their first names. That was more affirmation of her worth than she had ever hoped for from the head nurse.

"You need to know that once a nurse volunteers, she is assigned to a base hospital. We will not form one in Scranton. But in Philadelphia and Pittsburgh, Baltimore, too, there are groups organizing and they require fifty nurses each. Maybe more in the coming months. Who knows? After signing up, you would go with other women volunteers to a training camp for approximately two to three months. The British and French have sent over medical teams to teach us what they have learned after three years of fighting."

Gwen tilted her head in question.

Dalton's face turned gray. "How to treat men quickly. How to distinguish among types of wounds. Those that will heal quickly. Those that won't."

"Triage?" Gwen had heard of this system of separating the wounded into three groups, based on who would benefit from immediate surgery, who could wait for treatment without detriment, and who would not survive no matter the treatment.

"Yes. But in camp, a nurse would also learn how to take cover in a shelling and how to use a gas mask."

Gwen straightened. "The Germans attack hospitals?"

"Bombs and shrapnel fall willy-nilly. Gas drifts on the wind," Dalton said, her voice trailing off with the horror of what she relayed, "and when the winds change course so does the gas. Armies can attack their own men. Not good. Not wise. But then, this is war and nothing about it is good or wise."

"I want to go," she blurted. "I want to serve, but I—I hate to leave my sister."

"If she is like you, she is strong and will survive whatever has been placed in her path."

Gwen gave Dalton a half-hearted smile. "Good of you to say, ma'am. But she is only twelve."

"I believe you were that same age when your father died."

How did she know that? "That is true."

"Doctor O'Bryan has told me about the death of your father, so soon after your mother, too. A pity. But you have done well for yourself, Spencer. Despite it all, you have studied and worked hard. I would welcome you on my team."

"I am grateful to you for this discussion." Gwen rose. "I'll think it over."

"Wait." Dalton gazed at her with surprise. "Don't you want to know how much it pays?"

Money had always been a determining factor in her life. Money was the reason her aunt had put her to the mines. More money, the reason she left to work in the TB San. To enroll here in the student nursing program, she had rejoiced that at the end of it, she would earn more than she had ever expected, but she would also do it in an occupation that stimulated her curiosity. She smiled at the older woman. "I never even thought about it until now."

"That's good because the amount is a really a sin."

"But it's war. I didn't expect a fortune." Brought up short by her complete lack of forethought about pay,

Gwen marveled at the novel freedom. *I didn't expect more than food and a bed.* "What is it?"

"Sixty dollars a month. Plus you buy your own uniforms."

Gwen inhaled. In a hospital, she could earn seventy or more a month. But in private duty, she could command thirty to fifty dollars a week. That *was* a fortune. "Well, at least I can say I didn't get rich during the war."

"Noble."

"Is it?" Gwen pondered that.

"To risk life and limb and heart and mind, yes. You must see this is the gallant thing to do."

Gallant? Noble? "I see it as the decent thing to do."

"Splendid. But you should know you have one problem, Spencer."

"Oh? What is that?"

"When you applied here, you told me you were eighteen years old."

"Yes, I was."

"That you had no record of that. That the only note of your birth was with the Peckville Methodist Church and since they had a fire there at the turn of the century, there was no official record of your birth."

"That is true."

"It would be well for you to remember that. If you choose to join the Corps, that is."

Gwen bit her lower lip. "I'm afraid I still do not understand."

"The Corps calls for graduate nurses ages twenty-five to thirty-five."

"Oh." A cold wave of disappointment rolled over her. "That's...terrible."

"I agree. If they need nurses who know what they are about, they must not care for age. Such an arbitrary measure, don't you think?" Dalton's brows rose, the look of innocence on her face a unique expression for the usually dour lady.

Gwen nodded, realizing the woman was implying much more than she said. "Would you sign a recommendation for me? If I decided to go, that is?"

"I would indeed. And I would have a lapse of memory regarding your date of birth."

Dalton would lie for her? Gwen sat taller in her chair. "That is very kind of you."

Dalton rose. "I know what you are capable of, Spencer. We need nurses like you. I need you. Let me know what you decide, young lady. And soon. I go with a base hospital from Philadelphia in October. Think on it and tell me your decision in a few weeks."

So soon?

Could she change her entire life in so short a period?

Gwen thanked Dalton again and left to walk the grounds of the hospital. The sun was hot and bright, warming her body and heating her enthusiasm for volunteering as she sat on a bench and watched a few autos meander along the street in front of the hospital entrance.

Could she volunteer and allow Bernice Dalton to lie for her? What price would Dalton pay for that? What price would Gwen pay? Or did her age really matter compared to the need for skilled medical personnel?

Age was a marker of time, not maturity.

But what would happen to Susannah? Would she, as Dalton said, survive without her for a while? A year?

Two?

Perhaps Gwen could find a way to ensure Susannah had a little joy in her life. The piano lessons at least.

And if she provided for her sister, could she leave Scranton and America, and go to the front lines with the expectation that she would work now, not for her aunt, not for her sister, nor even for her own personal gain?

Could she give up her days and nights to risk fatigue, disease, and yes, perhaps, even death, to fulfill a longing she could not even describe except to say she owed it to those unseen, unmet thousands who needed what skill she could render?

Was it courageous to volunteer and leave everyone, including Susannah, behind? She was no heroic figure. No woman seeking honors or glory.

She yearned to go because, for once in her life, she wanted to work for a cause greater than she had ever done.

Dare she do it?

****

Five weeks later on a Friday afternoon, Gwen took the streetcar once again. Today, she did not go to Prospect Street, but to Graham Mount and the large white and yellow Victorian home of the Gerhardt Learners. Climbing the steep hill to the top, Gwen trudged the slate sidewalk and smiled to herself. Memories of playing on these flat stones danced in her mind. They were among her most pleasant recollections of her childhood. She and Lex used to compete to jump the farthest and skip the most slates as they raced to the back door to plead for her mother's cool tea and iced cakes.

Today, she was not getting treats, but giving them. And the anticipation of the gifts she was about to bestow hurried her onward. Climbing the steps to the elaborate house with the wooden gingerbread filigree hanging on the eaves, Gwen lifted her skirts and hurried. This was the last time she would come here for years. The thought sent a streak of melancholy through her and she paused to glance up at the home where she had known so much laughter here with Mrs. Learner, Lex, his brother Will—and her mother.

Shoving away her gloom, Gwen took the rest of the steps to the front door and knocked. Will appeared, his round face alight with joy to see her.

"Come in. It is about time you visit us. I told you when we came to your graduation that we wanted you to dinner last week for mother's birthday."

"I know. I wanted to," Gwen said as Will reached over and took her into a bear hug. "But I had many things to do. I came today so that I would not see my aunt here."

"Keeping secrets, are we?" he teased her lightly, but put up a hand. "Ah. Ah. No need to explain. I know her. We all know her. I was in the music room practicing a bit of fluff. Mother is upstairs and I know she will be thrilled to see you."

"Wonderful." Gwen walked alongside him to the room where a piano, a harp, and a cello stood as witnesses to the delightful times that originated within its pale pink walls. Afternoons when Lex had played Chopin for her. When Will had tickled the piano keys with Tin Pan Alley songs and sung "Casey would waltz with a strawberry blonde and the band played on." When her own sister had first performed an ear-thumping version of one of John Phillip Sousa's band marches. "I always liked the window seat."

"To view Mother's roses, I know. I'm afraid they're past their season now, but the chrysanthemums bloom."

"I see that," Gwen said as she took her favorite place on a chintz-covered cushion and craned her neck to view the garden. "I will admire it all until you return."

"Have you had any letter from Lex lately?" Will asked, his voice lowered. "We haven't gotten a thing in weeks. Mother is worried sick. My father, too. Lex has lost so many of his friends in those airplane crashes so I wondered—?"

"No. I'm sorry to say I have no word. I worried about him, too."

"She'll ask you if you've heard. He's a bugger not to write."

Gwen had read more newspaper stories about the war in the past weeks. Every day or so articles popped up about the members of Lex's Lafayette Escadrille flying French planes and fighting the Germans in the air. "He's busy, Will. Working hard."

"You're right, of course. As long as he's not in Paris on leave going to the Moulin Rouge."

"What's that?"

"Can-can dancers? No? Never heard of them? Good you haven't. They're ladies—or maybe not—who lift their skirts to show their legs when they dance."

Gwen frowned. "Thank you for that description. I doubt he's there."

"What a good answer!" Will shot her a smart salute, and went away, returning in minutes, trailing his mother behind him.

"Gwen, I am so happy to see you!" Mrs. Learner took both her hands and bent to kiss her on both cheeks. "Do not rise. Ve vill have Wilhelm get us some tea, *ja*?"

"No, that is not necessary, Mrs. Learner."

"You come to visit. You take the streetcar and so you are thirsty. And I am sure you need a cake or two. Am I right?"

Gwen chuckled, as she removed her gloves. "Yes, you are right."

"Good. Wilhelm, do go. That's a good boy." The lady took a Chippendale chair with the grace and aplomb of a woman who knew how to command a room and a conversation. "I am pleased you are here. We were so happy to see you at the hospital for your graduation. I am very happy," she said, leaning close, "you invited us to attend."

"I was delighted to. You are dear to me."

"And you to us, my child. But you are no longer a child, but a lovely accomplished woman."

Compliments from others made her uneasy. The praise she earned for leaving the mines and the sanitarium was what she valued—and it was her own. "Well, I try to be, thank you."

"You succeed. So. You come today when your aunt is not here. I am glad you did. She would not approve. And it is very sad for her that she cannot open her heart to even attend the ceremony for your cap—"

Gwen thrust up both her hands. "Please, do not talk of her and us. I am here for another reason. Well, really two reasons."

"Oh?" The lady sat back in her chair once more.

"You sound quite serious. What is this?"

Gwen fiddled with her gloves. "I come to ask you a favor."

"I see. What is it? For you, we will do all."

Gwen bit her lower lip. "This is a bigger favor than most. I am most hesitant to ask it, not having asked too many in my life."

"You have worked hard instead, dear Gwen."

She tried to smile. "I want you to know that I will continue to work hard. That I would not ask this of you if I could find any other way to accomplish my goal."

The woman tilted her head. "What is this you ask of us, Gwen?"

Gwen opened her reticule and took from it a large envelope, fat and sealed. She hated that it resembled all those other envelopes she had given to Aunt Mary for so many years. But the appearance was of no importance. The intention was.

She placed it squarely in her lap and looked Mrs. Learner in the eye. "I want Susannah to have piano lessons. I am not certain if my aunt will force her to quit school this fall. I told you at my graduation that my aunt and I do not talk these days. Also, I do believe that she prohibits Susannah from writing to me. But if my aunt has her way, Susannah will be working each day. She will not be able to come here as often as she has in the past, but if she does, if she can, I want you to offer her Herr Schuler's instruction of the piano. And this," she said as she placed the envelope in the lady's lap, "is payment for some of those lessons."

The woman looked at the envelope as if it were some exotic creature. "I cannot accept this, Gwen."

"Oh, you must!" Gwen captured the lady's hands.

"I want to leave Susannah knowing she has some light in her life. That she can have her precious music and that she can enjoy some portion of her days."

"What's this?" Will reappeared with a tray of cups and saucers and a tier of small cakes. Younger than Lex by four years, Will lately had grown as tall and handsome as his striking older brother. The resemblance made Gwen smile and yet made her yearn for the man who had been her best friend of many years. "Are you ill, Gwen?"

"No, Will. No."

"She wants us to have Herr Schuler give Susannah piano lessons."

Will chuckled. "Well, hell—"

"Wilhelm!"

"Sorry, Mom. But Gwen, Schuler already does teach her!"

Gwen surveyed Will's face. His hazel eyes, so like Lex's, danced in merriment. "He does?"

"Of course. When he comes and she is here, he spends as much time with her as me. I—" He glanced at his mother and smiled, sheepishly. "I asked him because she is so talented."

Gwen was struck by his generosity and grateful, too. "She never said."

"She never wanted your aunt to know of it. Discretion is her best game." He winked, then placed the tray on a nearby deal table and began to sort out plates and utensils. "Suzie is good. Very, very good, Gwen."

His declaration warmed her to the tips of her toes. "This," she said, casting her gaze on the envelope still in his mother's lap, "is to pay for his services."

"Nope!" He crossed his arms and glanced at his mother, then shook his head. "Nope. Won't take it."

"He is right. Ve vill not. You can give it to your aunt."

"No. I won't. We—we argued. I will never go back there. Never give her any more money."

"Oh, dear Gwen." Mrs. Learner wrung her hands. "She is a lonely woman."

"Bitter."

"I know, but a hard worker. Even if she cannot—"

Cannot love. Gwen got to her feet. She hated talking about her aunt. Worse, she could not abide being shamed and she loathed pity. "Please, Mrs. Learner, Will, let me pay for this. This is as much as I can give now. But I will have more. Just not for a long time."

"Are you not taking a post at the hospital?"

"No, no, Mrs. Learner, I decided not to do that. I will work there only until—" She resumed her seat and tried for some calm demeanor. "I am going away. For a long time. And I won't have any means to send you any more money for Susannah. Not until the war is over." She rushed on, hating the questions that would come and the need to answer them quickly so that these two would not argue with her.

"I have joined the Army Nurse Corps, and I am in the war until it is won. I leave next week for Camp May in New Jersey."

The two before her gaped at her.

Smiling valiantly, she told them both, "I will be paid, but in France I will have no way to wire you money. That's why I'm giving you this now. For her. I am told I can buy a life insurance policy. Ten thousand dollars, they say it is. A large amount, I am glad to tell you. I will make it payable to her. And you will please make certain she gets the money and not my aunt. Promise me this."

They each nodded and agreed.

"I am going to the front where I can ease the suffering of those men who fight for something bigger than themselves. Like Lex and his friends. I'm proud to do my bit. Contribute what I know. And this eases my worries about Susannah. Please do this for me. I need to hope that she will endure whatever she must while I'm gone and find a way to live the life she wants."

Chapter Four

"Faster! Faster!" The drill sergeant blew his whistle and clicked off his stopwatch. Standing atop the side of the makeshift trench, he scowled at the nurses eight feet below him. "You're all *dead*! Do you hear me?"

Gwen winced at his bark, in no mood for his surly behavior. After an hour of marching in step around the parade ground in the bitter November winds in nothing but her white uniform and a sweater, she was ready to bite his head off. "The devil himself can hear you."

Pearl Markham stood next to Gwen and scoffed. "He's also pissed."

"What's that, Markham?" he growled like an old dog at Pearl, squatting to look her in the eyes. "You want to die?"

She cleared her throat. "No, Sergeant."

"Good. You want to live, you put that mask on within ten seconds." He stood, barrel-chested martinet that he was in his Army browns. "Do. You. Hear. Me?"

"Can't help it."

"Markham, I'll ignore that. If you were a man in my platoon, I'd send you to the stockade. I'm told we need you nurses or I'd have you for breakfast. Now, let's do this again. Ten seconds, ladies. Ten! Or your lungs are burned. You can't breathe and you can't see. You know why? Yes! You are blind! Ready?"

He lifted his whistle to his mouth and blew. The forty-two women scrambled to lift the unwieldy contraption over their hair and yank it down over their noses.

Glancing around, Gwen thought they each looked like monsters with huge glassy black eyes and long gray snouts. The material, heavy Army canvas, draped down over their shoulders. And in their white cotton uniforms, the women looked like angels with hideous heads. Shivering cold angels.

"Dismissed!" The sergeant sent them on their way.

Climbing up the crude wooden ladders to the top of the trench, the women fell into groups as they left the drill field. They had free time between bouts with the cranky sergeant. This morning, they had more than usual because their British doctor who taught a course in shell shock had kept to his cot with a chest cold.

"Thank God we're done with the masks," Gwen groused as she ripped off the contraption and scratched her head, ruffling her disheveled hair even more than the mask had. "If the gas doesn't kill you, the lack of air will."

Pearl made a sound of disgust. "I was going to strangle him with his own whistle."

"He needs to go to charm school," Flo murmured.

"That cure won't take," Pearl said. "He's constipated. He needs an enema."

"And where are our uniforms?" Gwen complained, rubbing her arms as they hurried to their barracks. "They're wool, aren't they? And it is almost December. Don't they know this in the War Department?"

"I told you to take my afghan last night," Anna said. "I've got that other blanket my mother sent me."

"Thanks, tonight I will take it. That is, if you're certain you're warm enough without it."

"Your aunt should send you things," Anna said with compassion.

"No." Gwen shook her head. "I told you, Anna. I don't ask."

"Carlucci," Pearl barked. "Don't pester her for what she hasn't got. Bad enough she has that woman to contend with. Don't worry, Spencer. We'll make sure you survive the winter."

"Yes," said Flo. "If any of us survives that sergeant."

"I don't know why we're still stuck here in New Jersey," Gwen said. "The doctors got their orders last week."

"Some did," Anna added. "Harry's to go off to a special school. But he wrote me that they got their typhoid shots and they whined like kids." She leaned over to confide so that others wouldn't hear her. "They also got a lecture on syphilis."

Gwen rolled her eyes. "Want to bet we don't get that particular lecture?"

"Instead they'll instruct us on how to tie our knees together," Pearl said and the four of them got a good chuckle out of that.

In imitation, Gwen hobbled along. "Tough to work like that. Whatever happens, they can't leave us here. What good are doctors without nurses?"

"Useless!" Pearl added. "They'll forget where their asses are pinned."

Gwen opened the door to the barracks and shooed

her friends inside. "Hurry. I need to sit by that fire before I crack like ice."

The group of them huddled in front of the pot-bellied stove and rubbed their hands together.

"Wish we had coffee," Flo mourned.

"Kerosene would taste better than the swill we get in the chow line," Pearl said.

Gwen smiled. "I'm ready for lunch. Potatoes and just what is that meat they put in there?"

"Horse," Anna announced to the horrified grins of her companions.

"Getting in the swing of this, are you, Carlucci?" Pearl gazed at her with full approval for the very first time.

"I do believe I am, dear," she cooed with as much sass as Pearl had always thrown at her.

"Good. You might live," Pearl said.

Gwen elbowed her. "Stop that."

"Yes, yes, I know." Pearl nodded and tried to re-pin her dark hair into a bun. "I'll be nice to Anna. We could all die."

"And that," Gwen said, "is no way to march forward. We're going to need each other. Bury the hatchet now, will you?"

Flo agreed. "See, Pearl? Someone who can speak the truth without being snide."

Pearl bristled. "I am not snide."

Every other woman turned to skewer Pearl with their hard gaze.

Then Anna giggled. "Besides, how will you catch a man if you're never nice?"

"Oh, well now!" Pearl dusted her hands off and rose to her feet. "That did worry me!"

"Wonderful." Gwen hated the constant bickering between these two—and she hated being the mediator. If there was anything she learned from dealing with her aunt, it was that some people never changed. "I am finished with you two. Why not just get into a boxing match and be done with it?"

She strode to her bunk, reached under her cot, pushed aside her trunk and fished in her suitcase for her old sweater. Yanking it on over her other one, she ignored Pearl and Anna and the others who sat silently in their little circle before the stove.

Then she walked out of the drafty barracks, letting the flimsy wooden door slap against the frame. As the head of her class, Gwen had taken on the responsibility of taking any of their questions or problems to Bernice Dalton. She and the head nurse had become friends in the last few months, even if Gwen made certain to show the older woman the deference her position demanded.

Inside headquarters building, Gwen found Dalton at her desk outside the sergeant's office, poring over a pile of papers.

"Hello, ma'am," she greeted the matron. "I hope those are our orders."

Dalton sat back, her fingers drumming on the wood. "As a matter of fact, Spencer, I do have news."

"Good. I'm ready now. When does Uncle Sam say we're leaving?"

"Next Friday."

Gwen felt her heart pound. "That's wonderful."

"For New York."

"What?"

"We're to report to a hotel in New York City where we will receive our uniforms and live in a hotel until we embark for France. But before we leave, we will march down Broadway with American soldiers. A parade, Spencer, a big one." Dalton lifted a sheet of paper and read from it. "Five thousand volunteers. Two hundred and fifty-six nurses. Eighty ambulance drivers."

"A parade." She really disliked pomp and circumstance. Especially when men were wounded, dying, and she had work to do. "We want to go to France."

"Hmm. Yes. But first we march down Broadway."

"How far? Do they want to wear us out before we get there?"

"They want to applaud you."

"Better to spend their time rolling a few bandages."

"It's all for patriotism. Makes the home folks happy. Makes them feel proud."

Gwen sighed, resigning herself. "Some people have to see what they're supporting."

"What they're donating money for."

Gwen tried to smile, but crossed her arms to capture the warmth of the room to her body. "Have they given enough money yet so that we can get the wool coats we were promised?"

"Yes. When the weather turned yesterday, the quartermaster appealed to the warder and you and your friends will be fitted today. He will be here after chow."

"Lunch?" Gwen grew warm already, just thinking about it.

Dalton nodded, her gaze drifting over Gwen's body. "Yes. He'll have with him a supply of shoes and boots. Right away, you'll get two pairs of shoes, one pair of leather boots and one of rubber, too."

"And a coat?" *Please, god, let him have coats.*

"Yes. A long blue wool coat and, you will be pleased to note, a raincoat." Her broad face split in a kindly grin.

Gwen sighed in pleasure. "I may dance back to my barracks."

"Do restrain yourself. Sergeant Borden may not like the lack of discipline."

Gwen huffed at the thought of the irritable sergeant. "Borden tends not to like anything about us."

"He's paid to be a bear to get all of you in line. Responding without thought in a crisis is critical. You know the value of that. Besides, after you receive your uniforms, I am certain he will see you as his sweet little chickadees."

"That man has not met a chick in the past forty years."

Dalton gave her a tolerant look. "I hear he has a wife and children. Perhaps he likes to see his charges looking exactly like every other one. That way, when one is wounded or lost, he need not grieve too deeply."

That sent a chill straight up Gwen's spine—and Dalton's point was not lost on her. "A way to cope? I see, I see. I will remember that."

"Do."

"Thank you, ma'am. I am grateful for your time."

Dalton picked up her pen, glancing over the rims of her glasses. "You are welcome. Take off that hideous sweater as soon as you get your new uniforms, will you, please? You look like an orphan."

"Yes, ma'am. I agree. In fact, I might burn it."

"Do that. Quickly."

****

74

"What will we do Christmas Day if we're still here?" Anna asked as the four of them walked from the theater down Broadway to their hotel in Washington Square. "I'd like to go to another play, but the theaters aren't open Tuesday night. All the restaurants will be closed, too, I'd guess."

"Bet we can't go to the picture show, either," Pearl complained.

"We should buy ourselves something special to eat," said Gwen. "Make our own feast at the hotel. What do you think?"

"They wouldn't ship us out on Christmas, would they?" Flo asked.

"I wouldn't be surprised," Anna said. "Meanwhile, I'm growing older as we wait."

"I'm growing mold," Gwen muttered.

Flo stared at Gwen. "Listen to you, growing a funny bone."

Gwen nodded, pleased with herself. Being away from Scranton, out from under the shroud her aunt cast over her, had worked a new freedom into her attitude. She liked being head of the twenty-four nurse contingent from her hometown and Dalton's right hand. She liked the authority and could tell by the way the other women accepted hers that they thought her wise and fair. That, more than any other approbation, made her humble and yet proud of herself.

"Spencer is growing perspective, Aldridge," Pearl proclaimed. "That's what comes of being Dalton's fair-haired girl."

"Hey," Gwen challenged. "Don't complain. I got us our uniforms, didn't I? And I made them find your mother's package with all the sweaters in it, didn't I,

Pearl?"

"She got the sergeant to get the paymaster to give you your back pay, too, Aldridge," Pearl said.

"Why can't that man get it right?" Flo asked her.

Pearl huffed. "Because you lost your pay booklet, that's why. It says right there on the front, keep with you always. *Always* means night and day."

"Along with my scissors and my identification tags, two of them, mind you. And my gray ward uniform buttoned at the cuffs and up to my neck, *precisely* the way the sergeant demands. God! I am a mad woman with all the rules."

"Chocolate," Pearl mused dreamily as she hunched down into the collar of her long navy blue coat. "That's what I'd like for Christmas dinner. Lots of it, too. Hot chocolate and some of those Italian pastries with the cream that you bought last week, Carlucci. What were they?"

"Cannolis. I'll walk over to Ferrara's after class tomorrow."

"I'll go with you and stop in the liquor store for beer and wine," Gwen said, loving the idea of fun at Christmas. The Learners had always had their cook do a huge feast and Gwen enjoyed sipping her glass of wine. Back on Prospect Street, the holiday had always been a dour event. The food was the same fare as any other day, soup or stew with bread. Her aunt detested the idea of gift giving, claiming she had no money for frivolities. Here in New York on their way to war and demanding work, Gwen figured they all needed good food and fun. And wine. "Red or white?"

"Hell." Pearl brightened. "Make that two red and two white."

"We can go to that other store next to Ferrara's, too, and buy hard salami." Gwen inhaled, almost smelling the aromas. "Good crusty bread."

"Beats whatever Cook is serving in the chow line," Anna said. "God, that man has no imagination."

Gwen grimaced at the recollection of the chow that tasted like plywood. "That man has no say in what he cooks. I hear he has to take what the quartermaster buys off the local farmers."

"Wonder what we'll get in France." Anna opened the door to their hotel lobby and all piled inside.

"Snails," Gwen told them.

"*No.*" Flo was aghast, halting in her tracks. "Who told you that?"

"A book I borrowed from the hotel lobby is a travel guide by an Englishman. It said the French eat frogs, too."

Flo covered her mouth, making a face. "I'll starve."

Gwen led the file up the stairs, snickering. "The author said the French cook them really nicely."

"Yeah?" Pearl asked, as they trudged up the second story to their third floor rooms. "Do I want to know how?"

"In duck fat." Gwen delivered the news and the others groaned.

"I can't do it." Flo raved on about why people didn't just eat meat and potatoes or chicken, at the very best. She was still complaining when they reached the top floor and each of them put the key in the locks of their respective rooms. "I won't eat. I will tell them I am sensitive and must have simple things. Toast. Jam!"

"Nurses!"

The four of them spun to see Dalton at the end of

the hall and they straightened, all humor gone immediately.

"Where have you been?" She strode forward, face grim as she buttoned her navy wool coat up to her chin.

"To dinner and a show," Gwen told her, recognizing Dalton wished for brevity, not guff.

"A musical," added Anna. "Great fun—"

"We've been searching for you all evening. Pack your trunks and suitcases."

Gwen's heart pounded. "We're leaving?"

Dalton nodded. "We are. We've had clearance from the Navy that our ship can sail. All the other nurses left hours ago. You are the only four left. Hurry."

"We're shipping out at night?" Gwen frowned. Wasn't that dangerous? "Don't we need to see our way out of the harbor?"

Dalton shook her head. "I am not a sailor, Spencer. Neither are you. Best to let them do their jobs and we'll do ours. Pack."

At the dock, the five of them climbed out of the taxi. Waiting as the driver removed their regulation luggage from his boot, each woman stared at the giant hulk beside the dock. Gwen had never seen anything larger, except for buildings in New York. This ship of glistening black steel made a sinister silhouette against the dark gray sky. The enormous hulk impressed Gwen for its size…and the lack of any lights. Sailors in uniform hastened up and down the ramps, escorting groups of soldiers boarding by the light of small hand-held lanterns.

A sailor met Dalton and the four younger nurses at the foot of the gangway with a sheaf of papers. "You are the matron?" he asked Dalton and she told him she was. "Show me your orders for these four. Where's your manifest?"

She pulled a list from her reticule.

Gwen peered over her shoulder to see that most of the names on Dalton's paper were crossed off.

"Good. Identification tags, please?" he demanded of the five.

Each woman had to unbutton her overcoat, then her dress shirt to pull out a silver chain on which hung two identical silver tags. These he stared at, one by one, reading by the light of the lamp he held aloft. "Good. Come with me, ladies."

Up the steep ramp Gwen trudged behind Dalton, her three friends behind her. All of them were silent. The monstrous size of the black ship cast an eerie spell over her. The joy of the Broadway musical had dissolved in their haste to throw their uniforms and shoes into their trunks, gather their suitcases and purses, then take the taxi with Dalton to the port.

"We are on level four," Dalton told them when they arrived on the main deck. "Follow me."

The matron led them to a small opening off the deck and to a staircase down. For three levels, they curled round and round, following her into the bowels of the ship.

Gwen had never been on a ship, and everything about this one seemed novel, frightening, and a contradiction of large against small. The staircase was only wide enough for one person to pass. The passageway was only slightly wider. But when Dalton opened the door that led off the corridor and the light inside illuminated the interior, Gwen thought she had never seen anything so awful. In a huge room with walls of steel and rafters from which hung enormous pipes, stood hundreds of women. Some talked to their friends. Others bent over their trunks or suitcases unpacking their uniforms. A few sat on the few wooden chairs available. But from the thick pipes, every few feet hung nets. Big nets.

Dalton turned to survey the four of them, her lips tight. "These are our quarters. The matrons have cots. Every nurse has her own hammock."

Gwen's mouth dropped open, then snapped it shut. *Surely, we're not to sleep in those?*

"You will keep your own trunk and suitcase directly beneath your hammock. Chow lines are through that far door. Breakfast, I am told, is at five promptly. The bathroom is through that door there. And the showers are just...there. You will select a hammock now, quickly, then come with me so that you can be issued a rubber suit and a life jacket."

Gwen was too stunned to do anything but accept her directions. Her friends obviously felt the same way. Here they would have no privacy, but disrobe with the hundreds of other women on this deck. "A good thing modesty is not an item we packed."

Pearl snorted. "I have nothing anyone wants to see."

"Include me in that," Flo said. "What if we get a backache?"

Dalton didn't so much as blink. "You will ignore it."

"Of course, we will," Flo agreed with a resigned flap of her arms.

Pearl frowned. "Will we have drill? Classes?"

"Only life boat drills," Dalton said. "In case of attack."

Anna gasped. "Attack? Who would attack us?"

Dalton surveyed Carlucci with an icy sweep. "German U-boats. They patrol our shores."

"Here?" Pearl grumbled. "But they aren't supposed to hit medical personnel."

"And how would they know what we do, Markham? Hmm? Besides, there are soldiers on this ship. And a few of our doctors."

"Really?" Anna brightened. "Do you know if—"

"Yes, Carlucci. Your dentist Winchester is aboard. I saw him here earlier. He says to meet him after the drills are over. Up on the gun deck. Next level up from the main one."

Anna clapped her hands. "Oh, I am just so grateful for that, ma'am. Thank you!"

The matron fixed her with a gimlet eye. "Be certain you keep your wits about you, Carlucci. Do nothing on this ship you will be ashamed of. Casts shadows on us all. Do you understand me?"

"Yes, ma'am."

Dalton caught Gwen's attention for a moment, her expression harsh with warning. "I expect each of you to maintain decorum. This won't be the last time we are in the presence of vast numbers of soldiers."

A passing nurse agreed. "No time to sample their saliva."

Cries of "Euuw" and "Nooo" went up, followed by a cacophony of chuckles.

Waving a hand, Dalton left them to their unpacking.

****

Hours later, Gwen walked the main deck with Flo and Pearl. "I'll never be cold again in this rubber suit. Took us half an hour to get in it, hope I don't have an urge to go to the bathroom before I am allowed to get out of it."

"Just cross your legs, sweetie," Pearl said, pulling at the neck. "Who makes these things?"

"Tire companies," Gwen offered.

Flo laughed.

Pearl snorted. "I'll say. They're bulky as hell. But I suppose if it means I survive this boat sinking, I'm all for it."

"Do not be so gloomy," Flo reprimanded her.

"I wonder why we don't get going," Gwen said, peering over the rail like hundreds of other nurses did. Someone above called out her name and she looked up to the next deck. "There's Anna and Harry. Hi, there, Harry!" Gwen waved. "Wonder what that class was the dentists had to take."

"Facial surgery," Pearl said, watching the tugboats line up to take the ship out of port. "Special detail because there are a lot of men with jaw injuries. Anna told me."

"I'd like to take that one myself." Gwen smiled at Pearl, happy her two friends were becoming less antagonistic toward each other. For months, Pearl had loudly disapproved of Anna's devotion to getting Harry to marry her.

Gwen had at first assumed Pearl thought Anna less devoted to nursing than she ought to be. But lately, Gwen heard a note of wistfulness in Pearl's voice and Gwen questioned the cause. Seeing Pearl with the soldiers in camp, Gwen noticed how she tended to be more gruff than usual around them. She acted as if she were one of them, a woman able to walk and talk and crack jokes as well as they.

Certainly, Pearl was no fragile flower. She was tall and big boned, crusty, funny, even risqué. She was not pretty, but she had nice even features. An oval face, sapphire eyes and glossy wavy black hair. Gwen smiled at her now and wondered to what extent Pearl's looks and physique shaped her own thinking about herself and her attractiveness to men. Did Pearl want a beau for herself and thought she might not get one? Didn't everyone want someone to love and love them back?

Do I?

Gwen rubbed her arms and watched one tugboat latch on to the side of the ship with a huge rope. She couldn't push the question away.

When she had been fourteen, playing chess with Lex in the garden room one summer day, she had looked up at him and in the brilliant sunlight striking his blond hair, she thought what it would be like to kiss him. On the lips. He had caught her admiring him and asked if she was stalling or dreaming. She'd moved her queen—and never told him where her mind had wandered. He was her friend, after all. Not her beau. And he was four years older than she. Too old. Besides, he was soon to go to college. She never would. Daughters of coal miners did not rise so high to interest well educated men, especially not one who was the heir to the biggest business in the city.

"I can't believe we're finally leaving the country." Pearl's pensive voice intruded on Gwen's reverie.

"I know. None of it is like we imagined. Not as fast or as terrible," Gwen said. "It's so different, it feels like a dream."

Flo shivered and huddled down into her suit. "Do you ever ask yourself if you did the right thing to volunteer?"

Pearl shook her head. "Absolutely not. I was bored with Scranton, P.A. I want to see the world...even if it is blowing up."

Gwen could have said that too. But just as she was certain Pearl covered her deeper motivations with bravado, her own were as broad and, dare she admit it, grand. But at core, her answer was simple, maybe too simple. But it was hers. "It's right for me. What good is my training if I can't use it for the most people? For the best cause?" She realized too that part of what she'd said echoed Lex's statement to her last winter.

"Bah!" Pearl piped up. "If they don't get this boat chugging out of this port, we won't be using our training for anyone but ourselves. We'll go mad. Or get a rash. By the way, I want you to know that I used that latrine." She stuck out her tongue.

"Bad as an outhouse?" Gwen laughed.

"We used to have one at our house before my dad put in a toilet. It was so cold in winter, hot in summer. The roof leaked when it rained. And lord did it smell." Flo shuddered.

Gwen remembered the one they had on Prospect Street. Last year, with money she had given her aunt, Mary had hired a plumber to install a toilet and a sink. "Ours was as bad. I used to hold my breath when I went."

A loud boom shook the deck. The railing vibrated. The ship rocked, banging against the dock with clanging thumps. A few of the wooden boards broke away from the pier, sending chunks of wood into the air. The splintering sound raked the night air.

"Oh, God. What is that?" Gwen's teeth clenched. She grabbed for Flo with one hand and Pearl with the other. They fell together on their fannies on the wet deck.

The ship swayed.

Nurses on deck with them screamed. Some tumbled into others, piles of arms and legs flailing.

Gwen stared at each friend. They froze, all three, in shock.

"What in hell just happened?" Gwen asked her friends.

Pearl shook her head, her mouth opening and closing convulsively.

Flo went white.

Others cried out. Nurses nearby sat up, cupping their knees, their elbows or their heads. Some were bloodied.

Above them on the next deck, men yelled and ran. The din rose to a roar, a mix of hoarse cries and thundering feet. Some screamed for fire hoses. One begged for a doctor. "Christ! Get us a doctor!"

"Have we been hit by a U-boat?" Gwen crawled to the side to survey the dock.

"In port?" Flo looked like she'd seen a ghost. "We could be going down."

Gwen blinked. What had happened up there? The boom had come from the deck above. She cleared her head while others ran below or sat and wailed. "No, they'd tell us. Make us go to the lifeboats. Like we did in the drill."

"So what was that boom?" Pearl looked around

her.

Gwen struggled to her feet and offered a hand to Flo and Pearl. "It came from the next deck up. Anna's up there. She might know. Let's go ask."

"Right you are," Pearl agreed.

Gwen motioned for them to go up through the stairwell. But the portal was clogged with people trying to do that very thing. Meanwhile, everyone asked others if they had any idea what occurred.

A sailor appeared at the top of the stairs. "Go down. Back down! You can't come up here!"

"Why not? What happened?" People shouted all sorts of questions. Hundreds milled about, muttering and full of fear.

"Not sure yet. But we think a gun misfired."

Gwen checked the expressions on Pearl's and Flo's faces. The three clutched each other's hand. "Let's go to our quarters. Anna will come down soon and tell us what happened."

Both women agreed with her, but their brows wrinkled in trepidation and their chins quivered.

"No use staying here. They won't tell us anything more," Gwen urged as they turned to thread their way through the throng, down the stairs and into the massive deck room where only a few of the nurses had returned. There the three of them sat on Dalton's trunk, side by side and fretted. "Dalton will find out. She'll come. She'll tell us."

"And why doesn't Anna come?" Pearl asked, but neither Gwen nor Flo offered an answer.

Minutes ticked by. In small groups of four or five, more nurses drifted in. All looked disheveled and unnerved. Some told tidbits of rumors. A few cried or sniffled.

One woman, her hair standing wild as Medusa's, grew especially loud and erratic. Yelling that it was the Heinies who had "hit us with a torpedo, they were going to make certain our boys had no doctors or nurses. If they don't get us now, they'll hit us in the ocean."

A few criticized her, some none too kindly, and she retired to her hammock in a snit.

But as more women straggled into the quarters, they told stories that began to sound alike.

"A cannon misfired."

"A sailor told me."

"No one knows why or how."

"This is a German freighter. Did you know that? We took it when the war started."

"Oh, so that's why the side is draped in that canvas."

"To hide the German name? Why do they care?"

"So the Bosch won't kill us for spite."

"Hey, pipe down. I'm going to try out this bed. Never slept in a hair net before."

"I didn't see a canvas," Flo said. "Did either of you?"

Gwen and Pearl shook their heads. Gwen's throat grew thick. Fear loomed like a giant spectre inside her. Anna wasn't here yet. *Where is she?*

A few nurses nearby asked for help to get out of their rubber suits. Gwen and Flo and Pearl assisted each other.

Most women climbed into their hammocks and tried to sleep. But Gwen, anxious for her friend, walked the floor. Flo and Pearl did, too.

Weary, she sat on Dalton's trunk. This was not right—Anna should have returned. Dalton had given her strict orders to behave modestly although Gwen didn't believe that Anna had ever acted improperly with the man. Anna wasn't stupid, just in love. She knew to be late was a minor infraction of rules, but if she became pregnant, she be drummed out of the Army. Sent home and in disgrace, too. Not a good thing for any nice Italian girl. For any nice unmarried woman. And if she were to bear a child outside of—

Bernice Dalton appeared at the door, her face ashen, her gaze searching the room and landing on Gwen.

Gwen sprang to attention.

Pearl grabbed Gwen's arm.

"Oh, no," Flo murmured.

The matron stood before them, tears beading on her lashes. Only when Dalton swiped at her cheeks did Gwen notice that her fingers were bloody.

"Tell us," Gwen whispered.

"Anna is dead. Harry, too."

No. Gwen's head reeled. "How?"

"A cannon. German. Misfired. The captain talks now with the gun crew who were manning her. They didn't know…really…how to operate it correctly."

"Why fire it tonight?" Gwen asked, focusing on the ridiculous, pushing away the absurd. *Anna isn't gone. Cannot be. Why would she be? And Harry, too?*

"I don't know. I don't know. It's an accident. A terrible accident." Dalton clamped a hand over her mouth, fighting for control. "The captain says he will tell me more when he learns."

"Where is she?" Gwen gazed at the portal to the

passageway. "Where? I want to see her."

"No, you don't."

"I do! I was her friend. Her best friend. And I have the right to see her!"

"She is not…presentable."

Gwen sprang to her feet. "I don't care. I want to see her. You will let me."

"I can't."

"Why? *Why?*" She wandered, lost in a maze of impossible words that told of death and sorrow and improbable endings. Strewn in her path were bodies of those who had died before. Her father. Her uncle. Her mother. Now Anna. "She'll want me. Everyone wants someone they love when they die. Please. Let me."

Dalton took her by the elbows. "Collect yourself. I cannot persuade them. I am not as powerful as you think, Spencer." Pushing away, Dalton dug a handkerchief from her pocket and blew her nose. "They took her below. Harry's body, too."

"Below," Gwen repeated as if someone had doped her with morphine.

"To clean her up before they transport the bodies."

Gwen sank down like a stone to the truck. She knew Anna's parents. Kindly, generous Guido and Carla would be crushed. They were so proud of their only daughter, so delighted that she was to be a respected nurse. Now, she would be forever lost to them. Lost to Harry and to love and marriage and children. Lost like Gwen's mother had been to her father. Lost like her father was to her and Susannah.

Tears dribbled down her cheeks. "How will they bury her?"

Dalton gulped. "Send her to her parents. We are

still in port so they can do that. She will go with a military train back to Pennsylvania."

"She'll go with Harry?"

"She will. They will travel together."

"They'll like that," Gwen whispered. Then she looked up and saw how Dalton had barely managed the words. She put a hand to the matron's arm. "Would you like a cup of tea?"

"No. I...yes, I would." She covered her face with her handkerchief and behind that shield, she let her body silently bury her grief.

Gwen stared at Flo and Pearl, both of whom were weeping, undone. "Help me take Dalton to the mess, will you? Let's all get some tea."

"They won't do that for us," Pearl said, her dark brows knit in anger.

"They will tonight," Gwen told her and she meant to plead or argue, whatever it took, until the cook gave them something, anything to pass the shock of the untimely death of their friend.

****

Hours later, their ship had still not left dock. Gwen huddled in her hammock as she watched the December sun fill the round portholes with dawn's sad brilliance. The bodies of Anna Carlucci and Harry Winchester had been taken down the ramp and placed in an ambulance half an hour before. Gwen had watched the orderlies load them to the back of the military truck and she had bid her friend farewell with a kiss on the wind.

Now she could not close her eyes without recalling Anna and Harry on the deck above calling down to her, happily reunited after months apart. What if Anna had gone to meet him later? Would she be here alive, sleeping in her hammock?

Gwen twisted and turned in the netting. No position was comfortable. No memory soothed her. No explanation for tragedy consoled her. Angry at fate, yearning to escape her grief, she tipped herself out of the ungainly ropes and flipped open her trunk. She swung her wool cape over her shoulders and headed toward the far door to walk the deck and mourn.

The brisk air whipped her long hair around her face and the chill froze her unshed tears as if they were crystals on her heart. She was leaving her own country and perhaps, like Anna and Harry, never to return. She had accepted that possibility, but never gave credence to the odds. Death was for the old, the infirm, the unfortunate. Her job was to help others cheat it.

Though she had seen patients in her wards die, she believed she herself would not. Could not. Naïve to think herself invincible, she persisted these past two years during training assuming she was too young, too healthy to succumb to anything so feeble as disease or injury. She prided herself on her stamina, her will to change her circumstances. She'd enjoyed success at her own hand. She could not die when she was so willing to live. But here was Anna gone. Young, healthy, cheerful Anna had expected more from life and had volunteered to help save others so that they might have years to prosper and grow, love and learn. But that frail shield had failed Anna.

Gwen needed a stronger one herself. Good intentions alone did not survive disease or accident. Determination alone did not guarantee longevity. Not in a battlefield. Not in chaos.

A hand to her throat, Gwen gazed out on the black

void of sea before her. She herself might not return home. How silly she had been not to realize this. How young and foolish to flick the possibility away as if it were a flea. Her alienation from her aunt and her success at rebuffing her had hidden her own vulnerability from herself.

She would change that, if she could. Now, before this ship left port.

Gwen twisted from the rail, needing to take care of one neglected responsibility before the last packet went down the gangplank. She needed to write a letter. Two, actually.

One went to her sister, whom she loved with all her heart and who, she had been told by Mrs. Learner, was forbidden to visit her before she left America. Going to France was now a journey that took her into a vast, unimagined land where neither time nor circumstance nor even noble intent could guarantee she would return in any way she might predict. She would write to Susannah to record those events. It was the least, now the only part of herself she could share with her young sister.

The other letter would cover the one to Susannah. That one would not ask for forgiveness nor understanding, but for the courtesy to allow one sister to write another while she served thousands of miles away.

She prayed her aunt would have the heart to permit the girl to read her words.

Chapter Five

Gwen braved the January wind to lean on the rail and watch the uniformed men on shore heave together to secure the ship's hemp moorings to the dock at St. Nazaire. They called to each other in their own language, keeping a tempo by which they hauled the ship to its rest. Gwen doubted that the language they spoke was French, having learned a few useful phrases of it at Fort May. But she marveled at their appearance. They were tall, sinewy, bald, bearded and dressed in pale khaki shirts and bloomers that reminded her of the outfit Mrs. Learner wore to ride her bicycle. What was more fascinating about the men was that they—like those in the distance who wore darker khaki American Army uniforms—were Negroes.

If she never had to board a boat again, it would be too soon. The ten-day trip across the north Atlantic in dead of winter had been a bitter journey. Her feet, even as a child, had always been cold. But sailing on this tin can, she had often sworn that her toes had fallen off. She was not alone in her misery. Two of the nurses near her had come down with pneumonia last week and had gone into sickbay, not to return. Dozens of others roamed the ship, sneezing, coughing, and complaining. Flo had taken to her hammock for the past three days.

She recovered slowly. Gwen and Pearl rejoiced that their friend had developed nothing more than a severe head cold.

Shivering, Gwen flipped up the collar of her wool coat and squinted into the distance where trucks stood. Each flew one American flag on the hood. The muddy, treeless landscape was a hive of activity as the Americans unloaded lorries, checked manifests, and sorted boxes of supplies.

"Interesting sight, isn't it?" Dalton appeared at Gwen's side, huddled in her navy wool coat and hat, her gaze chilly as the temperature.

"Everything we need to fight a war," Gwen surmised.

"Let's hope. I doubt any of it will equal the splendor of the Holley Hotel in New York."

"Give me anything but another hammock." Gwen pressed a hand to the small of her back, then lifted her chin toward the sight on shore. "I don't see any white men. I wonder why that is."

"A sailor told me just now that the ones in the pantalets are French Africans. Men from France's colonies who fight for them."

"And our men out there?" Gwen asked. "Did he explain anything about them?"

"I guess they volunteer like anyone else. But he said we put them in units together and have them work the supply lines."

"They don't go to the front?"

"No."

"Don't you think that's odd?"

Dalton rolled a shoulder. "He said it's the law."

"A law that prohibits a man from fighting?

Especially when we're at war?"

Dalton agreed, her tone disparaging. "I don't make the rules. I just live by them."

"We're definitely in the Army." Gwen sighed. "Do you know when can we disembark?"

"As soon as those French officers in the tower up there finish our paperwork." Dalton pointed to a turreted lighthouse near the shore. "The harbormaster has to approve our entry."

"We've been here for nearly an hour. Shouldn't he let us get off as soon as these sailors lash the ship to the pylons?"

Dalton crossed her arms. "There is a long distance between can and should. We'll see how quickly the French know the difference."

"Then what do we do?"

Dalton tipped her head in the direction of the American trucks. "Those take us to the local train depot. Then we climb aboard for a trip to Paris."

Gwen's only other train ride had been the one from Philadelphia to New York and the memory of lush velvet seats and steam heat in the car had her reveling in the comfort soon to be hers. "Any idea how long it'll take?"

Dalton's brows rose high as the woman peered at her. "Eager to get to work?"

"You know I am. Wherever we land, first thing, I want a hot bath."

"Oh, that wishes come true."

****

They didn't.

Lunch was served on board before the captain appeared in the mess and announced they would depart within the hour. Gwen jumped up from the table, eager as a jack rabbit and said to Pearl, "God, am I glad to leave this mess. Another round of tinned lobster and boiled potatoes and I'd jump overboard."

"I'd swim with you, but the water would be too damn cold."

Minutes later, Gwen sat her rubber suit in her hammock and patted the darn thing a fond farewell. Dragging her suitcase and her trunk, she got in line for the gangplank. She and Pearl tried to share carrying Flo's suitcase, but it proved too clumsy to get through the tiny corridor to the gangway.

"I'll carry yours and Flo's," Gwen told her. "You help her off. We need only walk to trucks beyond the dock. She can make that easily. Then we get on our train."

But on shore, the women stood in marching formation, ankle-deep mud with not one vehicle in view.

"Nurses!" An American officer with lots of brass on his uniform hollered from a bullhorn. "We'll march to the trains."

"And what if I prefer not to?" Pearl grumbled.

Flo sighed, too weary to fight. "Let's just go."

In the end, the three of them joined the hundreds of other nurses trudging their way through muck to climb aboard a rickety French train. Unlike the sumptuous accommodations of the New Jersey to Manhattan railroad line, this car was dirty, old, and cold. Disappointment swept through Gwen, but she said nothing. How much were they supposed to endure? And if conditions were poor for them, what would they be like for the wounded? This was not at all what Gwen had expected. She plunked onto the straight wooden bench and prayed their journey would be quick.

"Thank heavens." Flo sank onto the seat like a sack of potatoes. "I don't think I could have gone any farther. I'd die. You two are in my will."

"Do not say such things," Gwen barked. Visions of Anna flashed across her mind and her lingering anger over her friend's passing electrified her. She had a hard fast rule since her father's death to never criticize, never complain. She had devoted herself to enduring any hardship, always focused on how and when to make the best of her situation. That resolve had eroded badly in the last ten days. What's more, so had her friends'. On the trip across the Atlantic, both of them had turned inward. Flo was morose. Pearl taciturn. Meanwhile, Gwen picked apart her own motivation to volunteer, until she thought herself a fool. She couldn't tolerate her own despair, let alone her friends'. "Do not even joke. It won't help you face what's to come."

"You're right, I know." Flo bit her lower lip, but lolled her head against the wooden backboard. "But I get this weird feeling now and then…ever since Anna died. Like ghosts walking on my grave. I might go, too, you know?"

Pearl cursed. "Don't dwell on it."

Gwen locked her gaze on Pearl and arched an inquisitive brow.

"Do not look at me with that eagle eye of yours, Spencer."

Gwen set her jaw and challenged Pearl. "Will you take your own advice?"

"If you do."

Swinging away, Gwen trained her eyes on the long

line of American soldiers marching below her window. Pearl was right. She had burrowed into herself since Anna's death, picking at the scab of her grief. Ripping open her motivation to come to war. Had she been wise to volunteer? What if she were wounded and lost an arm or leg? How would she earn a living? How could she provide for Susannah? Could she bargain with God to learn the answer? Or like Flo, should she wager only the darker forces of the universe knew such secrets?

She pulled off her gloves, finger by finger, resolved to give her friends at least the face of courage. "I admit I'm not my usual self since Anna's accident. I promise to be better. Not be a grump. I will laugh. And do you one better, now and again, Pearl."

"Good. I'm getting tired of being the circus clown."

"You were never that," Gwen said. "I thought your humor was your own."

"Maybe I'm entitled to be skeptical of what we've gotten ourselves into."

Gwen nodded. "Makes two of us. But we're not going back."

"Not unless you care to swim."

"Right," Gwen said. "And I am not getting back on the *Siren*."

"God help the next group that gets on board. I wouldn't wish it on my enemy."

The three exchanged looks then, the enemy taking on new meaning.

"Forget I said that." Pearl tried to settle into her seat, but fidgeted like a floundering fish. "Could they make this buggy any more uncomfortable? I'm not feeling very jovial at the moment. My lord. How many can this train hold?" Pearl leaned against the glass, her breath forming a frozen circle on the window as an endless parade of soldiers passed them by. "That's a hell of a lot of men."

Segregated as the nurses had been on the ship, they hadn't really seen too many men except the hundred or more officers who ate in the mess at the same times they did.

Folding her arms, Gwen wondered how many of them would become her patients. *Please, God, let them be few.* "I want them to hurry on board."

"Eager to work your elegant little fingers to the bone, eh?" Pearl razzed her.

"Yes." She sat back in the straight-backed bench. "Just like you do."

"*Bonjour! Bonjour! Mademoiselle! Un peu de pain? Oui?*" A short fat little man with a handlebar moustache appeared outside their compartment in the corridor. Carrying a crocheted bag of skinny loaves of bread, he was dressed in a black cape, a comical flat black hat and a large red and white polka dot bow tie at his shirt collar. He grinned like a fool at the three of them and gestured to his bread. "*Voulez-vous?*"

"What now?" Pearl slid open the compartment door and stared at the Frenchman. "Do you want money? We have only American dollars."

"He doesn't understand," Gwen told her.

"Makes two of us," Pearl said as he thrust a loaf of bread into her hand.

"*Je* love *Américains!*" he rattled off exclamations of what Gwen thought was French joy and ambled along to the next compartment. "*Un peu de pain, mademoiselle. Oui, oui. Oh, non, non. No dollars.*"

Gwen chuckled that the last word sounded like *dollarrrrrs.* "I appreciate men who bring food. Hand a piece of that over here, Pearl."

She held out the long loaf.

Gwen broke off a piece and popped it in her mouth. As she chewed, she rolled her eyes in ecstasy. "That is…fabulous. Wish we had some butter."

Flo munched on hers. "Or jam."

Pearl broke off a piece for herself. "The cook on board our ship could take lessons from this little man."

"He," Gwen said with a roll of her eyes, "is a distant memory."

The three of them polished off their treat, then brushed crumbs from their uniforms.

Gwen perched herself into the corner of the seat, trying to find a more comfortable position. "I plan on eating well here in France."

"And I plan on peeing here in France." Pearl added as she got up. "I'm off to find the ladies' convenience. Want to come with me?"

"No, you go." Flo shooed her out the door to the corridor.

Within minutes, Pearl appeared and shoved back the compartment door. "You will not believe this. We have no ladies' convenience."

"Well, that cannot be." Flo was aghast.

"I am not kidding. I asked Dalton. She sits up in the next car with another matron. We have no toilet. None. Not for us. Not for the men, either."

Gwen, who felt the urge to go herself, sobered. "This is not funny."

"I know!" Flo agreed.

"We are to hike our skirts alongside the tracks!"

Pearl announced, gesturing like a madwoman to the trees. "So if you don't wish to tie your legs in knots before Paris, you'd better get off with me now."

"How long until we arrive?" Flo asked, her voice rising to a screech.

"Who knows? Necessity calls." Gwen stood and brushed down her skirt. "Come on, we'll take turns manning the bushes while we each do our duty."

Flo rose to her feet. "Damn if I thought I'd be watering the bushes of France when I volunteered."

Opening the outer door, Gwen took a whiff of fresh air. She stepped down to the muddy ground, her hand up to help her friends alight. "And here I had big hopes for a hot bath."

"Best not to hope," Flo grumbled as they trudged behind a cluster of tall evergreens.

Gwen told them she'd take the first watch and folded her arms like a general in charge. "We'll expect nothing. Accept anything and make the best of it, right?"

****

By dawn, the train chugged into a tiny French town. As it slowly approached the tracks, Gwen slid open her eyes and prayed this was their final stop. The car shuddered from side to side and one, two, three loud blasts made her sit up and cock an ear. Outside, two lorries traveled the main road parallel to the tracks. A few men and women trudged along the side path, their faces grave, their attention drawn to the forest beyond. She followed their gazes, seeing nothing but the horizon in the faint light. But the ground shook with every new thump. She realized these were the pounding of cannons.

Alarmed that they arrived in a war zone without some advance warning, Gwen checked on her friends. Flo was asleep slumped over her suitcase, her hat askew, snoring. Pearl had sagged into a corner of the wooden seat facing Gwen. Her mouth lay open, lax, her head wedged at an odd angle. She'd have a stiff neck today. They were too exhausted to be alarmed, too needy of rest to be awakened. These cannons would not be the last she heard.

Gwen stretched, wincing at the numbness in her own muscles. She scrubbed a hand over her face, licked her lips and wished for a toothbrush and a washcloth. Her hair hung around her shoulders in tangles. Where was her hat? Ugh! Crushed beneath her fanny! She crouched over to check the floor for her pins and spied them on the filthy floor. Well, they'd stay there. She was a mess and until they arrived wherever they were going, she'd remain a fright. How many times had they stopped last night? Three times? Four? How many more stops before they got to their camp?

All French trains, they had learned from another nurse who had it from a French conductor, could not run on the same tracks. A few ran on different sized rails than the others, and it just so happened that the second train they boarded was one of those that could travel no farther than the next town.

After a ride of no more than an hour, all the Americans—soldiers, nurses, and doctors alike—had been ordered to disembark. There they were split, all doctors and most of the nurses waiting for one train, while Gwen and approximately forty other nurses were directed to board another. They soon learned that this one, too, lacked ladies and men's toilets, decent seats and heat. Thousands of men and forty or more women, sleepy, exhausted, jammed into another ancient conveyance, just as wretchedly uncomfortable and ridiculously slow as the previous one.

She marveled at the lack of efficiency. This was no way to win a war.

And if I ever travel on another train in my life, I will first demand a soft, warm seat.

Along the platforms, a few American officers ran to catch the train and swung themselves up into the cars where the nurses were seated. Gwen hastily gathered the length of her unbound hair and tucked it up under her hat. It wouldn't do to look untidy if they were getting off at this stop. She rose to open their compartment door and saw Dalton passing along the corridor, poking her head into the stalls, waking the nurses and giving instructions.

"We're getting off here. Grab your belongings. Wake up. Come on. That's right."

"Is this Paris?" Gwen asked. "The outskirts of the city?"

"I'm not sure, Spencer. We've been ordered to disembark here. Not sure why. We'll learn. Maybe they've had a push of some kind and need nurses."

"They'd better have heat," Flo grumbled.

"I'll vote for coffee," said another nurse as all of them pressed into a corridor and made for the exit.

"Tea," said another.

"Do they have bathtubs?" asked one more.

Snide remarks were her only answers.

"Oh, why did I think we wouldn't have to walk too far?" bemoaned another as they drifted through the tiny one room station to the snow-covered road. There, half a mile or more away stood four vehicles. All sported red crosses on the sides.

Are they ambulances? Gwen craned her neck, marching in formation with her friends, grateful for her heavy wool coat and hat and her sturdy leather boots. In the crisp morning air, the forty-odd women strode quickly toward the trucks.

"What do you know?" Pearl grinned. "This time, we get a ride."

"And a hand up," Gwen said as she allowed one soldier to help her up the rungs into the back of the conveyance. "Any idea where we're headed?"

"I hear the general has a cold," he told her, the twinkle in his eye making the morning seem warmer.

"You're kidding, aren't you? A general—"

"*The* General, Nurse." He winked. "Pershing himself has a cold."

"The American commander is sick and he gets all of us to tend him?" Gwen laughed, incredulous. "That can't be."

"Sure 'nuf, he can, ma'am," the private told her as he motioned for her to sit on the rough-hewn plank and hooked up the back flap of the truck. "Y'all be good now, hear?"

He slapped the metal side of the truck twice and the thing jerked forward, then sped down a bumpy road. A three-legged horse would have given them a smoother ride.

"Cancel the coffee," said the woman who had wanted it back at the station.

"Give me a toilet," joked another.

"You are having a pipe dream, girls," Pearl added.

"We're going to cure General Pershing's cold,"

Gwen told them, crossing her arms.

"Aw, come on!" someone shouted.

"That's crazy," another one said.

"He can't do that."

Gwen who had an unobstructed back seat view could see through the snow-laden forest that they neared a village that crawled with activity. "I think we're about to find out that he has. Look here!"

She pointed to the American flag flying on a pole in the center of a clearing. Beyond that lay a broad road jammed with American soldiers, trucks, ambulances, wagons and every kind of horse and mule she'd ever seen. At one end of the lane stood a huge tent with a red cross on the roof flaps.

"If that's where we're working," Flo muttered as she hugged her reticule to her chest, "I'm surrendering to the Germans now."

"Toodle-loo, Aldridge." Pearl slapped her knees. "As for me, I'm going in. I'm finding Old Man Pershing and asking him for a cup of his own coffee and the use of his latrine." She stopped to think. Then stared at Gwen. "You would expect he'd have one of his own, wouldn't you?"

"If I were Pershing," she said, nodding with conviction, "I'd have it gold-plated."

Flo wrinkled up her nose.

Within minutes, the trucks drew up to the hospital tent and all the nurses hopped out. Scrambling into formation, they strode two by two into the hospital where along each side stood a single row of beds. Empty beds. Except for one at the far end. There lay one man in a uniform of muddy gray.

"Good morning, nurses." A short officer with a

huge paunch strode into the tent to stand before them. Hands behind his back, he glared at them as if he'd never seen so many women before. "I am Colonel Scott and you are in Temporary Hospital Number Sixty. We only just finished erecting this tent yesterday and, as you can see, we have one patient. One. We will soon have more. Many more. The general in charge of this sector has diverted your train here. It's temporary. Then you'll resume your original route farther west to Compiègne. We have an emergency. Is there any one among you who speaks German?"

German. Gwen frowned, waiting for one of her colleagues to respond to the colonel.

"Anyone?"

Gwen raised her right hand. "I speak a little. I understand a bit more."

"Fine."

"Sir, you should know that my knowl—"

"Remain here," he ordered her. "The rest of you may go with Captain Holder." Another officer appeared as if by magic at his side and ordered the nurses to follow him.

The colonel stared at Gwen as if he dissected her under a microscope. "I imagine you would like coffee and the use of the facilities?" Before she could answer, he nodded and rattled on. "Good. I will have your breakfast brought to you. The latrine is through that exit there. I assure you privacy. Wait a minute until the others have left."

Dalton stepped to her and patted her on the back. "You and I will talk after you have done this for the colonel."

"But, ma'am," she whispered, worried, "I don't

speak German well."

"He clearly wants you to talk to that man there." Dalton tipped her head toward the ill soldier in the gray uniform.

"No, I can't. He looks feverish. Delirious. Perhaps unconscious."

"You will do what you can. It is what you are here for, Spencer."

Gwen's gaze landed squarely on the dark-haired man in the bed. "Very well. I'll try."

"Your name, Nurse?" the colonel asked of her when his captain and the nurses had departed. When she gave it, he continued, "Spencer, good. Go to the latrine. I understand you have traveled from St. Nazaire all night. The trains, I know, are less than one would hope."

To say the least. "Where can I wash my hands?"

"I'll have a large bowl brought to you."

"A bowl?" She needed more water than that.

"It's what I can offer you, Nurse."

"We were told we would have sterilization trucks."

"None here. Not yet." His lips thinned, miffed at her.

As upset as he, she set her shoulders. "Okay. Boiled water then. Two bowls," she told him, her attention fused to the handsome fellow in muddy gray, so flushed, against the bleached white sheets. "One for me. One for him."

"Your matron is correct. This man is your patient."

Was he safe to approach? Would he try to hurt her, kill her? That was the job of a soldier, no matter his nationality. Yet, he would not be the last man she'd encounter who was out of his mind with pain or disease. "How did he get here? To this hospital?"

"Our ambulance drivers brought him in last night. One of our officers on the front line had pinned a note to his uniform requesting urgent care. The stretcher-bearers told our field corpsman that he stumbled across No Man's Land and fell into our trenches yesterday. Extraordinary he's still alive. But he's quite bleary with fever and keeps babbling about a new German advance. In German, of course. Our general staff will want him well so they can interrogate him."

In classes at Fort May, officers had instructed the nurses not to speak to enemy patients in their wards. They were to be healed as quickly as possible so that they could be sent to prisoner of war camps and "persuaded" to tell the Americans about their troop movements and supplies. Gwen's hackles rose. She would heal a man's body only to have it destroyed again. This time, willfully. She swallowed her objection. That irony she could not cure.

She walked closer to him. Reclining so quietly, the man looked whole, but she could not make assumptions. "Is he wounded?"

"No shrapnel or bullets. He has deep barbed wire wounds."

"You're sure? He looks awful."

"Unbuttoned his uniform as he raved on, yes, we did. No wounds, no, ma'am."

She stood at his bedside and her heart went out to him, he was in such a sweat. Perspiration beaded on his forehead and ran down his cheeks, creating rivulets of dirt. His thick, coal black hair was matted with mud and plastered to his skull in clumps. He was a tall man, broad-shouldered. His neck was tautly muscled. His body, even in the filthy ill-fitting uniform, looked remarkably healthy for one who must have been fighting for more than three years. Did the Germans eat so well in their dugouts that this man had no hollows in his cheeks? "Where are his wounds?"

"His arms, worst are on his palms."

Gwen lifted his hands, his nails jagged, encrusted with filth. His skin, beneath the grime, was smooth and bore no calluses. His fingers were tapered and elegant, dwarfing her own. Jagged barbed wire had sliced through the center of his flesh, carving deep, angry slices. "Anywhere else?"

"His stomach. A few scratches."

Clenching her teeth, she drew down the sheet and undid the remaining buttons of his tunic. "Why has he not been cleaned? His wounds dressed?"

She stared at the lines across his ribcage. Here, he was not as severely cut as on his hands. Thank god. Yet whatever he had touched had created a raging infection.

She pivoted toward the officer. "Colonel, if he is important, you need a proper German translator which I hasten to emphasize, I am not."

"I have sent for one to headquarters. But in the meantime, I have no doctor. Only you. This man came across the German lines, Spencer. He's infantry, from what we see of his insignia. A captain. Whatever he knows, we must know it, too. And to our advantage, he thinks he's still in German-held territory. So clean him up, make him comfortable, tell me what he says until my intelligence man arrives from Chaumont."

"Chaumont?"

"Pershing's headquarters."

"I see. All right. Please get me blankets. Lots of

them. Iodine packs, rubbing alcohol, scissors, and bandages. Let's see, what else? Hypodermic with tetanus. A supply of Carrel-Dakin solution and lots of water to bathe him."

The colonel shook his head at her. "I don't have all that, Spencer."

Frustrated, her anxiety blossomed like an evil flower. "Why not?"

"The trains, the supply lines, as you have witnessed first hand, are not up to snuff. We haven't received our supplies."

That doesn't help me much. Or this man. "What *do* you have?"

"Blankets, water, iodine."

"Morphine?"

"None."

She shook her head, fuming at the inefficiency, livid that she was charged with aiding a patient without any proper means to do so. She unbuttoned her coat and draped it on a stool. Then tore off her hat. Her hair tumbled over her shoulders to her waist.

The man noticed, sucking in air.

Probably told not to remark on the nurses' appearances. Fortunate for me this morning that he has other priorities.

Plus she needed his respect and compliance. "Please bring me what you have, sir. And find someone with a needle and thread. A wooden spoon or something similar for him to bite on while I sew up his hands. That is, if I can ever get his wounds sterilized."

The colonel beamed at her. "I have a daughter who's about your age. Feisty for one so young, aren't you?"

One rule of her student nurses' training was never to smile at a patient. At Camp May, they'd been instructed not to show any emotion to any man in uniform, officer or drafted. It gave away a nurse's authority. This colonel might not seem like a threat to her power, but she would take no chances. Not since this soldier's life depended on it—and her reputation as well.

She would do well to use her training here and now to her own advantage. "I'd like to get to work, sir. And I request that you treat my colleagues to lots of hot coffee. Hot oatmeal, too, if you can have your kitchen duty prepare that. My friends have had a rough crossing, sleeping in hammocks, followed by hideously long rides in ridiculous trains. And while not all of my friends are as young as I am, all of them have volunteered to help every man who needs them."

The officer nodded, showing no sign he took umbrage at her starched attitude. "Your point is well taken, Spencer. I'll do my damndest to give you want you want."

"Thank you, Colonel." She spun back to the man on the bed, a hand to his grimy forehead and another to his wrist where his pulse beat too quickly. "So will I."

Chapter Six

Alone with her patient, Gwen examined him more fully. At the moment, he lay peaceful. His fever, still violent, was her most pressing concern. She had to get his temperature down before he broke into convulsions.

She bent over him, looking for other indicators of his condition. She lifted one eyelid. Clear. Not bloodshot. She took his pulse again. Rapid. Fighting infection. His skin was pale and when she pinched the back of his hand, his skin puckered. He was dehydrated. She gently pried open his palm. Sliced so deeply one white bone glistened at the base, his flesh oozed. But she bet that once she cleansed him, it would be pink. Not black. Not gangrenous.

Not yet.

Where are my supplies?

She sat on the side of his bed, careful not to jostle him. He was tanned. Hardy. His face oval. His cheekbones perfectly high and wide. Striking, he might even be handsome save for a nose that was a tad too long and a thin white scar from the corner of his left eye to his temple. He had suffered a deep cut to his lid at one time, but the surgeon who had patched him up had botched the repair. His left eye drooped and she wondered if his vision had been impaired by the shoddy suturing.

Her gaze dropped to his hands. No wedding ring. No wife, then.

No business of mine.

She fidgeted, pulling her concentration back to her duty…and failing. He was such a puzzle, her German captain. Fit but wounded. Smooth hands cut to ribbons by barbed wire.

How did you survive No Man's Land? Did you purposely come across? How? On your hands and knees? Or on your belly? Thousands and thousands of men never made it on their feet, let alone on their stomachs. Certainly, none with intent. Bullets, grenades, shrapnel, exploding mines, gas attacks—all lessened the odds of survival in that hell. Why would you chance destruction from them? How did any soldier risk his life and limb, day in and out?

She recoiled at the thought. Soon she would encounter more men than this one who toyed with fate. She would be responsible for repairing their bodies so that they might tempt it once again.

Men were a mystery to her. Her father had been a big, boisterous, laughing man and except for the death of her mother, he appeared to embrace each day with a stalwart heart. Her uncle, Aunt Mary's husband, had been his brother's brooding shadow. In Gwen's two years of training, she had cared for a handful of male patients. One man, a carpenter, had fallen two stories from scaffolding and broken both legs. Two days after Doc O'Bryan set his bones in casts, his wife had taken him home to tend him. The other man, his ribs crushed in an automobile accident, had suffered internal bleeding, unconscious in her ward for five days. And though Gwen had taken a thorough course in anatomy—and had excelled in it—she had never touched any man so thoroughly as she must touch this one.

Stop stalling.

She peeled his tunic back as best she could. Dried mud fell from the fabric in clumps and she brushed them to the floor. She'd use scissors to cut away the rest. His trousers, she decided, at least for now, she could leave on him. Her focus should be his hands and his torso.

Ignore the rest.

Killing the urge to snort at her predicament, she watched his lips move in whispers that soon became shouts.

She put a hand to his cheek and murmured soothing words.

He raged at her, yelling that she was his friend.

"*Nein*, you must be calm, *mein Herr*."

"*Komraden!*" He barked, his arms flailing. Then he rattled on in such a rush, she could distinguish no words she knew from her years with the Learners.

"Stop that. You make yourself worse." If he didn't understand English, perhaps he'd heed her tone.

"*Ja, gut, gut, mein Freund!*" Her patient shouted as in warning, then whipped out his arm—and bashed her in the ear.

"Enough of that," she said, staggering, a hand to her head. "Where is my water and iodine? Damn."

Shocked she had cursed, she sank to the stool. She sat on her coat but didn't care. She allowed herself a minute to clear the stars from her eyes. "You have a powerful fist, *mein Freund*."

"*Ich weiss…*" And off he went into another tirade full of words she did not know.

"*Ja, ich weiss nicht,*" she muttered, aflutter now as she spied a soldier wheeling in a cart filled with her supplies. She thanked him profusely, blessing him for the steaming bowls of water, the field packets of iodine, a heaping supply of bandages, a pot of coffee, and a cup.

"The colonel regrets we have no cream for your coffee, Nurse. Private Summersby, at your service, ma'am. Colonel says I'm to get you whatever you want." A grin split his plump pink face. "You tell me and I'm to rob heaven to bring it to you."

"Thank you, Private. I appreciate that. I'd like… Oh, I'm not sure. A sandwich?"

He snapped his fingers. "Done. What else?"

"Hmm." She rolled up her sleeves, ready to wash in the delicious looking warm water. "Bring me that translator as soon as he arrives."

He pivoted for the exit and she set to work.

Her patient was not cooperating. She put cool compresses to his forehead. He thrashed and they fell off. She tried to wash the muck from his face. He grimaced and muttered at her. She splashed water onto a cloth to let it cool so that she could rub him down. Over his forehead, down his cheeks, his shoulders and torso, she cooled him, time and time again. Her arms grew weary. Her back grew stiff. The water grew cold.

She stayed at it, a check of her watch telling her she'd wiped him down for more than an hour. He was too delirious to accept any water from her, making her grumble to herself about his condition. Then he went from bad to worse. He developed chills, rolled to one side, his teeth clattering so loudly she thought he'd break them. She had the orderly lift him, sliding blankets under him and then piling them over him, until he calmed and slept.

Succumbing to the lull, she dozed in her chair.

Awaking with a start, she blinked to refresh her memory of where she was, what she was about. Automatically, she reached for her cloth and wrung it out to begin again. But when she moved to soothe his brow, he lay silent and serene as he stared at her. His forest green eyes glowered at her. If he'd been well, she would have fled the room.

Instead, she began to wipe his brow. "You, sir, are delaying my noble intentions with your antics."

He grabbed her wrist.

She jerked away, but he held fast.

"I cannot help you if you insist on restraining me."

His eyes grew wide. His lashes fluttered as he surveyed the room—and her again.

"Let me go," she demanded and yanked away. This time, he did release her. Quick as a rabbit, she reached for a roll of bandages, unwound it, grasped his hand and tied his wrist to the wooden bed frame. "That should hold you."

He wrenched at it, shaking his bed and murmuring to be free. *Frei. Frei.*

"Okay. Okay." She stood fast and thought hard. What could she say to calm him? She couldn't sterilize his wounds or sew them shut if he was going to carry on like a mad man. "We need sturdier beds, that's for sure. I'll tell the colonel. As if that will do any good."

Her patient scowled at her, as if he actually considered her problem. She considered his silent state.

Looking at him, she recalled when Winslow had been a boy, bed-ridden with chicken pox. She had repeated his favorite nursery rhyme to him until he joined her and talked himself to sleep.

She knew no nursery rhymes in German. Had no vocabulary in that language to make word games.

"What can I do with you?" she asked him as much as herself. Then she smiled.

He tipped his head, wary, on alert to her actions.

She threw her cloth into the bowl. From her years in the Learner household, she recalled one song she often sang with them. *Auf Deutsch.*

"*Bitte*," she pleaded with her German captain who was now examining her eyes, her hair, her mouth and chin as if he had never before seen a woman. "Do you know this song?"

And there, in the hollow tent, she offered up her battered version of the one ditty whose words she only partially understood. Lex had once told her it was a German drinking song meant for bars, but she hoped this might be just the ticket to inspire her patient to cooperate.

In her tone deaf contralto, she began. "*Du, du liebst mir in herzen. Du, du liebst mir in Zinn. Weiss—*"

"*Weiss?*" he asked her, his dark brows arched.

She paused. At least he was polite about it. "*Ja. Weiss mir viel Schmerzen,*" she sang.

He tossed his head on his pillow, grimacing, grinning. "*Nein. Dass ist nicht richtig.*"

"Well, *mein Herr*, it is right because that's all I know." She charged onward. "*Weiss nicht wie gut ich dir bin.*"

"*Ja, ja. Ja, jaaaa,*" he sang with her and into the

last stanza. *"Weiss nicht wie gut ich dir bin."*

At the end, he seemed tranquil but puzzled.

"Nurse?" Private Summersby flipped up the flap of the tent and stuck his head in. "Are you singing in German?"

"Yes, Private. Don't worry. I'm only trying to calm our guest." She stared at the officer and nodded at his placid expression. "It seems to work."

"Whatever you say, ma'am." Summersby disappeared. Gwen and her patient were once more alone.

"Bring me more sterile water, will you, please, Private?"

She turned to her patient again.

"Bitte," she repeated, this time, more softly. *"Ich* must—" Oh, hell. What was she doing trying to speak a language she did not know. What if she said something entirely wrong and this man thought her a lunatic?

Hopefully, he'd understand her intentions from a serene tone of voice. "I'm sorry but you are going to have to stop jumping around. I have a job to do and your hands need to be cleaned, stitched and bound. So please, *bitte,* lie back and let me try to get your fever down."

As if she waved a magic wand, the man sank back and focused on her with curious eyes. Better still, he was cooperative, offering up his hands to her service. Within the next few minutes after Summersby supplied her with fresh water, she had flushed the worst wound on her patient's right palm. Though he groaned and bit his lower lip, he gave no objection. Nor did he take his eyes off her.

She spoke to him throughout her ministrations, as

if she addressed a child. And she did so in English. She had seen Doc O'Bryan work with a few mental patients and she took a cue from that. Doc had been serene, measured in his movements, talking sweet and low. He had even managed to get one hysterical patient to talk rationally to him. She couldn't converse with this man in any useful way, but she could tell him by her actions and her tone that she was no threat.

"I've got to open your wound wider, Captain. I know this will hurt like the devil." *Actually, more like hell.* Yet thankfully, in his pain-filled eyes, she saw trust as well as resignation. She pointed to his palms. "I have to probe to see if debris is lodged inside. And I have no morphine."

He nodded.

She gulped, never having sutured before. She needed a doctor, for God's sake. Pressing the spoon into his other hand, she said, "Use this."

Refusing the spoon, he shook his head once.

"You must. Like this." She stuck her finger between her teeth and pretended to bite it. "Hopefully you won't faint. I promise to be quick."

"Just do it."

She blinked.

"You heard me." His voice was rusty, hollow.

"You speak English?" *With a British accent, too. Just like one of her instructors at Camp May.* She sat taller.

"I do." He ran a hand through his hair, yelped as his open wound touched his head. "God, in heaven. I feel like a wrung cat. Where in hell am I?"

If he could curse, he could think. "Darned if I know. France, somewhere between Compiègne and

119

Chaumont."

He gawked at her a second, then snapped shut his mouth. "That's a big bit of territory for an American girl to know."

"Well, I do not know, at all. It's what I've been told. Are you British?"

He rolled his eyes. "Last time I looked I was."

She waved a finger at his tunic that she had dropped in pieces to the floor. "Not the last time the rest of us looked."

Inhaling, he sank further into his sheets and squeezed shut his eyes as if he blocked horrid memories. "Yes, well. Weeds of war and all that. Who's in charge here? Not you. You're too young—and too pretty. Where's your matron?"

Pursing her lips, Gwen shifted, irritated by his comments of her age and appearance. The implication that youth and passing good looks meant one was dumb and incapable of great deeds made her itch with indignation. She'd show this man, English or German or whatever he was, when she sewed him up that her skills were as sharp as any older nurse. And a damn sight better than the hack who'd fixed his eye. "She's gone off with my unit of nurses somewhere. Much as I can tell this is an American camp and the colonel in charge is—" Caution swept through her. What if he had lied to her? *What if he is a German? A spy?* She stood up. "Wait. Rest. I'll be back."

"What?" he asked, looking too weary to breathe. "I thought you were—"

"Drink this," she told him, passing him a glass of water. "All of it."

"Where are you going?"

"To get the colonel."

"Patch me up first. I'd prefer not to get gangrene and lose my hands, you see. Then you can—"

Another challenge. This man was a thorn in her side. "You won't lose your hands. I guarantee it."

"Really?" He fixed her with a stony look. "How can you assure me of that? I scrambled across ten, maybe twenty yards of No Man's Land and from the feel of it, I've brought all the muck of it with me."

"I looked at your wounds. You have no necrotic tissue. And I have cleaned you thoroughly."

"Wonderful." He wiggled his fingers. "Sew me up."

"I was ordered to get the colonel when I had gotten you to talk."

"You mean with your limited German?"

She inhaled, pressed her lips together. "Yes. My very limited German. Sorry it didn't meet your standards."

His face went lax with remorse. "I apologize. I wager they got the only person they knew who spo—"

"I'm getting the colonel."

He sighed heavily. "Go then. Hope he has half a brain."

She looked back at him. He sat, palms up on his sheets, sagging with fatigue. "Unless you can prove somehow you are English, they're going to arrest you. Take you as a prisoner of war."

He snorted. "They jolly well better take me to Chaumont."

"Chaumont? You want to go to Chaumont?"

"Yes, I need to depart as quickly as you can debride my hands and stitch me up." He brandished the spoon, lifting and lowering his eyebrows like a clown in a circus. "They need me in Chaumont."

"Why should I believe you? Why should anyone?"

He cursed, citing her delay. "An excellent question. I do have an answer. I doubt it would make much sense to you."

Those kinds of insults she had dealt with on Prospect Street. She hadn't succumbed to them there and she'd not accept them here, either. Even if her lowly status as a nurse did not merit any revelations of import. "You should try."

His lips thinned in anger. "And if I pass your muster, will you be able to get me a pass to Chaumont?"

Enough of his insolence. Picking up her skirts, she swung toward the exit.

"Wait!"

A hand to the flap, she glared at him through the haze of her irritation.

Summersby jumped up from his stool. "Ma'am? Is there a problem?"

She thrust up a hand to ease the private's alarm and directed her attention to her patient. "Make this worth my time."

"I went across German lines to get information about a new advance we think they plan."

His words rang true and they rocked her.

He is a spy. For us.

Why she believed him, she couldn't say. Shouldn't. She had no means to judge. Stepping outside, she told Summersby to get the man more water to drink. "More for me to bathe him, too. Which way do I go to find Colonel Scott?"

"Down this lane. The tent with all the flags in front."

"Thank you, Private."

"But…Nurse? I can't leave him. He's our prisoner. What if he runs?"

Gwen shouldn't give too much away. What if she was wrong to accept his explanation? What if he was, in fact, a German spy and she… Oh, hells bells. What if she was simply too young and inexperienced to detect his lies? Her doubt rankled. One thing she did understand was his condition. "He's too weak to run anywhere, Private. He'll be there when you return."

****

When she did return, she had Scott in tow. She'd told him nothing except their German was now awake, aware and spoke English. She thought it the best discretion to let the colonel discern the veracity of the man.

"Nurse Spencer tells me you speak our language. Might I ask you where you learned it?"

"At my mother's knee, Colonel. Captain Adam Fairleigh, His Majesty's Forces. Forgive me, sir, I would greet you appropriately but our erstwhile nurse has strapped me to the bed." He glanced at Gwen, his dark green gaze alive with gleeful reproach.

"Then you must need restraining," Scott replied. "What the hell is this that you say you're with the Brits?"

"I am, sir. I am attached to General Pershing's staff, Chaumont."

"As what?" Scott was not buying his explanation easily. "How do you speak Hun so well and why in God's name are you in one of their uniforms?"

Fairleigh arched both brows, looking at the short American down his very elegant straight nose. "Liaison to the American Commander, sir. Since December. I speak excellent German," he told him in a measured, haughty tone, "because my maternal grandmother came from Saxe-Coburg, the same principality as our late Prince Albert. And I, like many in my family before me, attended university in Heidelberg on the Rhine. I speak German, sir, as well as I do English. Before the war, that was no crime, but an asset. I use that to our allies' advantage."

"I see. And how do you come by this uniform?"

Their patient was no longer so quick or cocky. Instead, he glanced from the colonel to Gwen and back again. "I took it off a dead man."

Gwen swallowed hard at the savage image of this man removing clothing from a corpse.

"I had managed to crawl across a zone where they were not shelling. I thought if I could reach one of their forward trench lines, then I—"

"Preposterous. How did you get that far in your own uniform?"

"I went in peasants' rags. Christ knows, there are a lot of them, impoverished, broken by this miserable war. Our lines abut an old village where only a few huts still stand. I thought if I—"

"Why discard your rags for a German captain's uniform?"

"Well, sir, he was not only dead but conveniently my size."

That shut the man up.

Gwen could only marvel at this creature in the bed.

"When I came upon their trench, I could hear their

conversation below. Luck was with me. That bunker was a communications center. If I could get in there, I might learn quite enough to make my mission worthwhile. Of course, I couldn't do that, couldn't speak German to them and have them believe I was one of them if I wore French farmer's culottes, could I? So I crept around…among their dead whose bodies they had not retrieved." He stared at the American with blank eyes. "I happened upon the captain who seemed my height. Then I waited until night fell and—"

He halted, regarding Gwen once more. Sucking in a huge breath, he went on. "I buried my rags and crawled into their trench. They accepted my story. I was privy to their orders that were to move their gun emplacements. Then, as you can expect, I was stuck with them, considered one of them. I had to run with them. I had no opportunity to escape until two nights later when the French opened a barrage in our sector."

He lifted a hand, let it drop to the sheets. "I managed to hang back when they retreated with their line. I set out to No Man's Land and prayed to Christ I'd find my way across to French lines. This took me…I'm not clear. A day. A night. Two?" He shrugged. "Here I am."

"Who is your American liaison in Pershing's staff?"

"Colonel Samuel Rustings."

Scott nodded, a hint of a smile curling his lips. "I see."

"I gather you know him."

"Same class at West Point."

"Well, then. If you telegraph him, he will verify who I am and my mission. He knew I went out, you see."

"A man from headquarters is already on his way here."

"Splendid."

"We thought we had ourselves a Heinie."

The man's mouth quirked in bitterness. "Sorry to disappoint you."

"Oh, you'll do, sir. What did you say your name was?"

Gwen noticed that Scott had not addressed him by his rank.

"Fairleigh."

"We'll see what our man from Chaumont has to say about you. In the meantime, my private is outside the tent."

Fairleigh inclined his head in acknowledgement of his warden.

"Nurse." The colonel didn't bother to look at her, but stared at the man whom he still clearly did not trust. "Finish up here. Untie him. "

"Thank you, sir."

"Good day, then."

When Scott had departed, Fairleigh regarded her with appraising eyes. "What is your name?"

"Spencer."

"Nice name. Spencer."

"Thank you." She pulled her cart closer to his bed. No matter who he was, he was to be made whole as efficiently as she could.

"I am sorry, Spencer, for being an ass."

She saw on his face honest contrition. Unaccustomed to apologies from those who insulted her, she had no reason to trust the value of his. Yet she gave him credit for the courtesy of it. He had done such a brave act. What kind of man would do as he had done? A fool. An opportunist. A man who saw this was work which he and he alone was best suited for? Was that hubris? Cunning? Or duty? If indeed, he *had* done it. If he hadn't lied.

"Spencer, I am grateful for your help. Please do patch me up. I'd hate to lose my hands because I lacked good manners."

He was making conversation to heal their rift. That, too, she applauded. She picked through her gauze looking for the needle she had misplaced when she had left him. Brusqueness served her where experience did not. "Lie back then and be good."

"You give no quarter, do you?"

She whipped around to look at him. "I am not here to give quarter, sir."

"Chilly. Do you they teach you to be frosty like that in America?"

"Yes."

He feigned a shiver.

She fought a smile. "Put that spoon between your teeth. This needle will hurt."

"I wager it will hurt less than your German. You should have warned me that it was so bad."

"Careful." Fingering her needle, she began to thread the eye. "You need me to be gentle as I sew. Besides"—she could taunt him now that he was rational and at her mercy—"I doubt I'll ever sing with you again."

"I will endeavor to ensure you do."

His attempt to charm her flattered her as no other man had ever done. She would do well to ignore it. She might be inexperienced with men who would be beaus, but she would never lure them being coy. That was best left to other women who nurtured ambitions to be wives. She had never allowed herself that luxury probably because she had not yet met a man whom she would allow herself to love. "This is war, sir. Neither of us has the time."

"Then sing to me instead."

"When I put my needle in your skin, I will hear *you* sing and off key, too." She threatened him, hiding all the humor his compliment inspired. "The spoon, sir. Now!"

Chapter Seven

"Wake up, Spencer." Pearl nudged her shoulder the next morning. "Brought you coffee. Chow's on in the mess, and we're leaving as soon as trucks arrive to take us north."

"Thanks, Pearl. You are a gem to bring me this." Gwen sat up, swinging her legs over the edge of the cot and reaching for the tin cup. "Where are we going?"

"Colonel didn't say." Pearl stood next to her own cot, where all the nurses ordered off the train yesterday had slept together in a tent. She jammed her flannel nightgown into her suitcase. "But I'd guess it's where we should have gone yesterday before they pulled us off for that German."

"Englishman." Gwen shoved her wayward hair over her ears and scrubbed the sleep from her eyes. She had spent yesterday afternoon tending to the man, subduing his fever, encouraging him to drink and eat. Then, before supper last night, his American counterpart from Chaumont had appeared in the hospital tent. With much glee at finding his friend and comrade alive and well, Colonel Rustings confirmed for Colonel Scott that this man was indeed Captain Adam Fairleigh, His Majesty's British Expeditionary Forces, adviser to General Pershing.

Eager to return to headquarters, Rustings slapped his buddy Fairleigh on the back and declared they would depart then and there. "That is, if Colonel Scott could donate a Doughboy uniform to your cause."

Gwen stepped forward. "Pardon me, sirs, but I do not recommend that. Captain Fairleigh is dehydrated, malnourished from his nights on the battlefield. He is very weak from exposure and surgery."

Fairleigh grinned like a fool, looking pleased at her warnings. "Nurse Spencer may set her hounds on you, Rustings, if you take me away before she permits it."

The implication that she was a dedicated nurse gratified her, but she would destroy any inference she might wish Fairleigh to remain here with her for other than medical reasons. "If you take Captain Fairleigh out into this frigid night air, Colonel, you may have a case of pneumonia on your hands. Go if you must, but you pay your own consequences."

Rustings, a tall burly man with a booming bass voice, arched his bushy brows at her then at Fairleigh. "Feisty little lady, you have here."

That riled Gwen, too. These men might be in charge of battles, but she had her own to wage keeping men fit to fight them. "Colonel, I assure you I know my business as well as you know yours—or I wouldn't be here. Take Captain Fairleigh if you must and if you kill him, well, then that is your regret—and one less man to fight this war. However you should know that Colonel Scott went to considerable trouble to stop a train, order me and forty-odd nurses off, divert us from our route, all to find someone who might repair the captain's health. I have tried. If you disobey my orders, you pay the prices."

Fairleigh grinned at her, raising one arm to cheer her on, his heavily bandaged hands resembling huge white hams. "You tell him, Spencer."

Rustings just chuckled. "Who's arguing? I'm not fond of driving back over that one lane ditch they call a road in the dead of night. We'll leave tomorrow. Ah. I'll amend that. We'll go *if* he looks fine to you, ma'am."

"Wonderful. I'll see you in the morning, Captain."

Peeved that she'd had to fight to be respected but tickled she had thwarted the American colonel, Gwen had reported the events to Colonel Scott, and afterward, Dalton. She'd eaten a supper of bread and cold chicken soup, then found her way to the nurses' tent and her own cot. And there she had slept like the dead until Pearl awakened her.

She stood, hoping for a shower before she dressed and ate. Pearl told her the best they had this morning was a sponge bath. "Oh, well. Nothing new, right? I'll be quick then I should go check on my patient. Make sure his fever is still down. Check his stitches."

"Hurry. Dalton is on the warpath with Colonel Scott that they took all of us off the train for the sake of one man. She won't be happy if you hold us up any longer."

"I'll be fast. Where do we make formation?"

"Outside the colonel's tent."

"Okay. I'll be along. What's for breakfast?"

Pearl looked at her deadpan, her eyes beady behind her rimless spectacles. "Nothing worth writing home about."

"That good, huh?"

"So tasteless, it has no name. Get going or Dalton

131

will leave you behind."

****

When she entered the tent, Fairleigh slept peacefully. His complexion was now a more healthy color. His head to one side, his mouth was parted, and he snored softly.

She smiled, safe because he didn't see her. Hating to wake him, she had to put her mind to rest before she left. She strode closer to him, placed her tray down on the cart, then put a hand to his shoulder. "Captain, I apologize for waking you, but I am to leave soon with my corps."

His dark lashes fluttered as he came round and cast her a mellow smile. "You have your hair up this morning."

Caught off-guard by his personal remark, she shrank back. "I borrowed a few pins."

His eyelids closed. He licked his chapped lips. "Liked it better down."

"How do you feel?" She put her palm to his brow. Normal. Her fingers to his wrist. Slower today.

"Better. Hungry. Thirsty."

"Good. I have remedies for that. Coffee. Tea. Boiled egg to build you up. And something the kitchen patrol calls oatmeal."

"I'll take it all." His green eyes, so much more alert today, scanned her features. "Where are you going?"

"I have no idea." She poured water from a pitcher into a cup and held it to his mouth to sip. "I'll find out when I get there."

His hand covering hers, he drank eagerly from the water. "What is the name of your group?"

"Base Hospital Philadelphia."

"The city of the Declaration of Independence."

"Yes, it is. Drink more. I want to take a look at your hands before I go. Do you have medical staff attached to Pershing's Headquarters?"

"We do."

She took one of his hands, snipped away at his bandages and gently uncurled his fingers. "I hope to heaven they have debridement solution. Tell them they must set up a drip for both hands immediately. You should sit and allow the solution to cleanse your wounds for at least forty-eight hours."

"That's a long time, Spencer." His voice this morning sounded less rusty, more resonant, and vastly appealing with all that British crispness.

She met his gaze and though his eyes showed humor, they held another softer emotion as alluring as it was dangerous to her decorum. "It will be a longer time, Captain, if you lose your hands to amputation."

He winced as much at her words as at her probe of one section of his wound. "You are not kind, Spencer."

"No. Truthful. Let me feed you, then I will apply new dressings before I go."

She cleaned him up and fed him, did everything necessary except accompany him behind the screen to the latrine. When he was once more under the sheet and blanket, curled against his pillow in clean Army pajamas, she admired his angular good looks. She could do it with impunity because she'd never see him again. But regret that she was leaving him surprised her. Gave her butterflies.

She fiddled with a button on her coat. "I—I must go. The trucks will be here by now."

He reached out to her, trapping her hand under his

bulky bandages. "I am very grateful that you are such a hard-headed nurse."

That had her beaming. "Thank you, Captain. I shall continue to be one."

"You'll save a lot of lives."

"I hope so. Best of luck to you, sir."

"And to you."

She turned and hurried from the tent.

Outside, the cold air blew away the warmth of his regard. He had forgotten, as she feared he might, yesterday's promise to seek her out again. He upset her balance, and she did not want him near her again. He could fascinate her, and her goal in life was not to be intrigued by a man. Maybe in the future, beyond this war and her duty, but not now certainly. She was here to help others like him, not moon over one man like a ninny.

She swung herself up into the back of the truck to the applause of her companions.

"How's the Heinie, Spencer?"

"Saved his ass, we hear."

"Heard he was pretty," said another nurse.

Pearl who sat across from her merely snickered. "You are blushing, kiddo."

She cupped her cheeks. "It's only the wind." It would never do for her think about him. They had nothing in common, save the war. "Any idea where we're headed?"

"My guess is yours."

Flipping up the collar of her coat, she tugged on her gloves. The sky was laden with clouds that portended snow. And just like yesterday before she was called in to stand attendance on Captain Fairleigh, she heard the regular booms of cannon. As their driver took them out of the American compound, they drove through a French village. A few small stone houses stood intact. One hut with a thatched roof had only three walls. The fourth side was no more, only mere rubble scattered on the ground. In the weeds, a toddler of two or three cried into the skirts of his mother as they stood among the ruins. Not all who suffered in war were soldiers.

The truck skirted a river. Flowing swiftly, the dark green waters carried debris of all kinds downstream. Broken planks, a chair, a tea kettle, a small porcelain figure that was a child's doll minus an arm. Gwen looked up at the trees. Bare of leaves, lined with snow, the skeletal limbs waved in the winds. No birds perched here. At least not this morning.

The thunder of cannons grew louder, closer. How far upstream was it? How far away were the front lines?

By dusk, the trucks drew along another river. This one sped along, carrying broken wooden boxes, old tires and the black corpse of a bloated cow.

"They need to get that carcass out of there," Gwen said to Pearl. "We'll have typhoid on top of everything else."

"The driver's slowing down. If this is our destination, let's pray they have wells."

He pulled up, the other vehicles making a semi-circle in the dirt road. Unlocking the back flap, a private helped each nurse climb out of the back.

Flo joined Pearl and Gwen as they surveyed the sight before them.

"A wooden city," Gwen said of the half-built dozen or more structures. Only two wooden buildings looked completed with red crosses painted on the tarpaper roofs. Beyond that lay rows and rows of tents.

"And what are the odds those tents are ours?" Pearl asked, crossing her arms and stretching her back. "Hammocks are one thing. Cots another. But if I'm living in a tent, I'm praying they have decent food to keep us happy."

"Don't count on it," Flo grumbled, citing how they hadn't had lunch and she didn't care what she ate as long as it was hot and fast.

"And what's that?" Gwen pointed to a set of rounded gables that pierced the sky behind a line of trees. An aged stone castle shimmered, a giant silver phantom against the gray sky.

An American Army colonel emerged from one of the completed buildings and strode down the steps to offer a perfunctory smile.

"Good evening, nurses," he said. "No need to make formation. I think you are probably tired, having traveled most of the day. I am Colonel Hightower, head of this facility. We are pleased to have you with us. About time, eh?"

He nodded, weariness in his moves. "Welcome to what will be your base hospital. This behind me is Chateau du Jardin. We are on the estate of Count Chatillon at his invitation. As such, we are in his home as his guests.

A number of nurses grumbled. Gwen and Pearl exchanged wide-eyed glances.

"Yes," the colonel continued in a tolerant tone, "I see your dismay at our current state of disarray here. I assure you our engineers will build this out. Not sure how quickly. But it will become a compound, a fully functioning base hospital with our own wards, pharmacy, x-ray labs and sleeping quarters. At capacity, we will process approximately one thousand casualties at any one time. At present in rooms of the chateau, we have twelve doctors and four dentists. Our only two nurses are Frenchwomen who are volunteers and yes, they are woefully overworked. You are our first American nurses and more well trained than the two Frenchwomen who try so hard to fulfill our needs in the wards and the OR. As you can see we have not finished constructing your quarters, but those two buildings behind me will become your operating theaters. We expect them to be finished by Thursday. In the meantime, we work in the chateau itself."

A general murmur from the nurses made him frown but he continued, "We do have supper ready for you. But before you go to chow, you should take your bags and claim a tent and a cot."

Now the murmur swelled to a collective groan.

He pursed his lips, looking strained. "We will receive beds. Not quite what you are used to at home, perhaps, but slightly more comfortable than cots."

"Sheets?" someone asked.

"Yes and a blanket."

"One?" Gwen could hope for more than that. Even now, she shivered in the chill.

"Two. Wool."

"Heat?" asked another.

The colonel's forehead wrinkled. "When we're finished building we will have gas heaters. From what I have seen of them, they are not always reliable. But for now, nothing. I suggest you sleep in your coats."

"Oh, brother. And do you predict it will snow

137

tonight?" Pearl asked him.

"I think so, yes. Your name, Nurse?"

Whether he intended to punish Pearl for her and others' outbursts, he nonetheless looked pleasant about it.

Pearl stared him down, stalwart and ready for any attack. "Markham, sir."

"Good. Markham, I will see to it that you get one of the first blankets from the supply train."

"Thank you, sir."

"You may disperse to the tents. Meet in the mess hall in half an hour. Your latrines are yours alone. No men permitted."

"That's a swell rule," Gwen said to Pearl and Flo.

"I hate to ask him about bath water," Flo put in. "I'd prefer to be surprised."

Hightower cleared his throat to gain everyone's attention. "After supper, we will march up to the chateau. I will show you the current operating theater and introduce you to your doctors. You should know most of them, but we have a few additions to the roster."

"Do the doctors sleep in the castle?" Flo looked bitter.

Gwen bet they got preferential treatment. Beds, blankets, hot meals. "And what have they been doing while they waited for us?"

"They've been operating." Hightower flicked his gaze over her in derision. Then he scanned the crowd before him. "I need half of you as volunteers for the night shift. The rest of you go to bed. You'll take the day shift."

Gwen focused on the castle. "They're working up

there?" *How could they be without many nurses or supplies? And where were their patients?*

"Must be," Pearl said.

"I'll do it." Gwen raised her hand.

****

With the moon high and brilliant in the black sky, Gwen hastened with Flo and Pearl and seventeen other nurses along the dirt road from the base. As they approached the stone entrance gates of the huge old chateau,

Gwen smelled the air. This odor was not manure from animals. Not rotting hay from the fields. But sweet ammonia. She walked on, casting an inquisitive glance at Pearl. They locked gazes. Pearl flared her nostrils to indicate she smelled it, too.

"Hurry." Colonel Hightower stood to one side of the stone gate. Holes of all diameters marred the beauty of the six-foot tall walls. Jagged pieces of metal, as big as she, stabbed into the earth at obtuse angles, piercing the ground where they had fallen from the skies.

Gwen girded herself for what she was about to see. But as she passed the gate, it was what she heard that made her skin crawl. A new sound to complement the continuing thump of distant cannon spoke of animals in pain.

Gwen halted. The ground on either side of her for yards and yards up to the house crawled with life. Vibrated with desperate murmurs, some for morphine, others for God, many for their mother.

Among the writhing, moaning bodies, a few soldiers—medical caduceus on their sleeves—hunched to talk to this man or that. Another soldier put his hands to one man's neck to take his pulse, then threw a blanket over his face.

"Who are they?" Pearl whispered, horror in her voice.

"British, I think." Gwen noticed a few blue uniforms among the dark brown. "French, too."

"Nurse? Nurse?" A man caught Gwen's hem. "How long?"

She stooped down to him. His eyes wandered, focus impossible. The left half of his uniform was gone, cut away for a bandage, bloody and crusty, on his shoulder. "Soon, sir. Soon."

"Water? Got any?"

"We'll see you get a drink, sir."

He let go of her skirts, collapsing back to the ground with a groan. She pulled his blanket up to his chin.

"How long have they been out here?" She burned with fury at what she saw and what inefficiency it implied. How many men lay here? How many needed water, morphine, more?

"Must be two hundred here, at least." Flo grew red in the face. Gwen had never heard her so angry. "Jesus Christ, Gwen, and they diverted us from these men for that one Limey?"

"I know. I know."

More soldiers reached up, appealing to them as they flowed past. Some grabbed at their boots and skirts. Others tried and fell backward, unable to summon the strength.

Flo urged them along. "Come on. The sooner we're in there, the better off they are."

"Why are those men outside, Colonel Hightower?" Gwen asked him as the nurses assembled in the grand foyer.

"We don't have room for them in here. Come with me. I know how it looks out there, and we are operating as quickly as we can. But we have to clear those we have and send them down the line because we have word more wounded will come tonight."

"There's a battle going on?" someone asked.

"There is always a battle going on, Nurse. Someone is always fighting. And the ambulances come only at night. They run that way so the Huns won't bomb them from their planes."

Gwen recalled her discussion with Dalton about Germans hitting hospitals. At Camp May, she'd learned more. "That's supposed to be against international laws."

He stared at her, his brown eyes made ghoulish by heavy circles of fatigue. "Their job is to kill us. Win the war. I don't know what they've been ordered or even if they aim for our ambulances, but I do know that our vehicles have been hit. And we don't want to lose our men. Now. Any other questions before I open these doors?"

He surveyed them, and they told him to carry on. "Very well. Down on this main floor is our ward. All cases are together because we don't have rooms to separate them. We do whatever triage we need out there on the grounds."

Flo winced. "Then some of them are dead."

"Before we can get to them, yes, sadly so, Nurse. Upstairs in four former bedrooms, we have our Operating Rooms. The ORs are in need of nurses to assist in surgical. Any of you wish to volunteer or have experience with that, we need at least six of you. Okay.

You. Yes. You. Anyone else?"

Gwen raised her hand.

"And you."

Hightower turned, swinging wide the double doors to a huge room. Bigger than any house Gwen had ever seen, nearly as large as the bay they'd slept in on board the *Siren*, the white and gold filigreed hall was full to the brim with men. Men in beds. Men on the floors. Men packed so close it was a wonder any one could reach them to move them or feed them or dress their wounds.

All in the beds seemed to be peaceful, sedated. Some had fractures, their legs or arms propped on myriad splints. Others lay totally quiet. The wounds they had suffered were of every size, shape, and to any part of the body.

Some wore bandages on their arms, others their legs. Some were naked, clothed only in bandages that wrapped their ribs or their hips. A few had suffered amputation. Some had lost more than one limb.

On the floor lay countless more. Untreated without dressings, they lay quiet, staring at the ceiling. Some lay on hay. Others on old uniforms.

The room was lit by a hundred candles and the air stank of rubbing alcohol, wax, and blood, urine, and feces.

"My god." Gwen whispered, not alone in her expression of despair. "How can you work this way?"

"Come now," Hightower bid those who had volunteered for the operating room.

And up the grand circular staircase she went with him and the other five. The first person Gwen saw when he opened the doors to the first OR was Doctor

O'Bryan.

"Nurse Spencer," he called to her beneath his surgical mask, his gray eyes bright with relief. "Come here and help me close this patient."

Chapter Eight

Gwen stripped off her surgical mask and her cap. Only five operations last night. But one had been an intestinal resection, a delicate operation to save a Welshman from gas gangrene. She could almost hear her bones creak as she murmured goodbye to Doc O'Bryan. He remained, determined to set the fracture of a French *poilu*, a boy of fifteen or sixteen. His femur had broken cleanly and would be a fast fix. Or so Doc thought.

When she told him he ought to quit for the night and let another set the bone, he rebelled. "I need to do the easy ones, Spencer. Just for the tally."

Tally, my foot. Sure, Doc had put himself in the betting pool to see which physician performed the most ops each month. Winner got a magnum of champagne bought by the other doctors. If they could find such a large bottle in the war-torn department of the Champagne. But Doc worked like a man obsessed, quickly and neatly, striving each morning because he wanted to fix up one more wounded young man.

Gwen shook her head at his persistence. The way his hands trembled, the way he rubbed his eyes and squinted after a few hours, he drove himself to exhaustion. Last night, she had had to point to a sloppy suturing.

Testy now, he ordered the anesthetist to get the ether ready for the boy. "Pay a visit to the X-ray technicians for me, Spencer. Tell them to get their asses in the saddle down there. What are they doing? Playing cards or taking whores?"

His language didn't bother her. She was used to that. But she balked at doing his bidding and reprimanding the men. Like many other nurses, she got a lot of lip from many of the male soldiers who refused to follow her orders.

"Tell them I sent you. I won't cut open another man's guts until they learn how to focus and get the films up here fast."

"He's right, Spencer," Doctor Hubbard agreed. He had volunteered in Scranton along with O'Bryan and had taken the night shift along with his older friend. "The sooner they can show us those films, the faster we can dig out the shit."

"That sergeant we had last night?" O'Bryan motioned to another nurse to secure a new mask on his face. "He would have been off my table in a jiffy if I'd known he had two hunks of iron in his large intestine, not one. Christ knows if he'll ever be able to eat solid food again." His bloodshot eyes turned to glass. "They give you crap, you tell them to come see me, blood up to my armpits looking for the shrapnel *they* should be finding."

"Okay." She'd do it. Why not? He'd back her up. Besides, she had an advantage since the technicians hated to talk to the doctors. Especially vocal, colorfully denigrating ones like O'Bryan.

Part of her itched to tangle with the techs. They

fought her because they disliked the fact that a woman could be right. And win. She loved winning.

"You look like hell," he told her. "Go sleep."

"I will. After I yell at your techs and wash my uniforms."

"Helluva note. Colonel says when our boys arrive in force, we'll have men to do all that."

She arched a brow at him, then stripped off her gloves and threw them in the sanitary bin. "Yeah. And I'm whistling Dixie."

He laughed as he motioned for the two orderlies to put the young *poilu* onto his table. "Get out of here."

"Gladly."

She pushed open the double doors to the hall and rushed down the grand staircase. Grabbing her coat from the hall rack, she ran to the front door. Standing all night next to O'Bryan as he picked his way through pink flesh marred by shrapnel and bullets took a high toll on her concentration, her eyesight, and her feet. She'd worked by his side now every night since February. They had lost hundreds, saved more. Sent them south toward the big recovery hospitals, the French coast, and onward home.

With a clockwork-like regularity that astonished her, more casualties came to take their places on their surgical table. Every night, all night, she and O'Bryan and the other nine doctors cut and probed and cut and sewed, over and over again. To measure their success, she would walk through the wards each morning to count how many wounded had left from the previous day.

Today, she had no desire for it. She simply wanted to sleep. And the way to that mindlessness came each morning when she stepped through the front doors to the veranda, lifted her face to the sky, and inhaled the fresh spring air.

She sucked it in as if it were her last full breath. The odor of carbolic acid, phosphorus, and iodine drifted up from her uniform as the chill spring winds blew some of it away. When she washed her butcher's aprons and her gray crepes in the huge cast iron pots each Monday, she flushed away the smell.

She wanted her clothes fresh for herself, but soldiers noticed, too, as she passed in the wards. How could they not? They had fought in the trenches where thousands of men lived, ate, slept, defecated and died, day in and out. That kind of proximity, that kind of poor sanitation meant they never smelled how they reeked until they were well away from the stench and the rot.

"We stink verra badly," one Scotsman, a private, told her yesterday.

His friend in the next bed, a ribald French *poilu* who always tried to grab her fanny as she passed him, followed with his own exclamations about the *tranch merde*.

She grinned at their vulgarity. Whatever would get them through the day was a good thing. *Like the warmth of this rare April sun.*

"Dreaming again, *Mademoiselle* Spencer?"

The gruff voice tinged with a rolling French accent was one she had come to know well these past three months. With a grin, she welcomed Count Valentin Chatillon to his own chateau. "I will be soon, *monsieur le comte.*"

The tall reedy nobleman hobbled up the path to his

chateau each morning at seven, leaning on his cane with his only hand. He'd lost his left in the French Army after he hastily joined in nineteen fourteen. The Germans had swooped down to take this sector in the first weeks of the war. He and his household staff had escaped in the tunnels under the chateau which two years ago, he gave to the use of the French and now the American military's medical corps. Each morning, with the hawkish mien of an aristocrat of blue blood and land, the congenial *comte* brought with him his cheer, his gifts, and his vegetables from the garden he tended in his small house in the village. "Is my *mademoiselle* still in her ward?"

"Of course. You know she never leaves on the dot." *She waits for you.*

He bobbed his dark head, his dark chocolate eyes dancing. "She is devoted to her men, my *Perle*."

Gwen liked his French name for her friend. Her funny friend who denied with all her might that she was enchanted by a man for the first time in her life. "I even think she might dally."

"Dally, eh? Hm. This dally is to—?"

"Wait." Gwen laughed. The *comte*'s English was impeccable. He knew this word and he enjoyed hearing Gwen speak the truth of Pearl's attraction to him. "Yes. She has come to expect you each morning."

"Ah. And I will not fail her." He hoisted a bottle of wine. "*Rouge* today. The wine from the Champagne is difficult to acquire. Not enough grapes. Too many men gone to the trenches."

Soon there will be hundreds of thousands more.

He cocked his head. "I am told the Americans swarm Bordeaux and St. Nazaire. You will save us, *mademoiselle.* I am certain of it."

"I think you are right, *monsieur*." Gwen wanted to be positive. From the French and Brits in the wards, Gwen had heard that both of those armies suffered from despair of the past few years' losses. The French death toll, to date, was over a million men, and everywhere, thousands mutinied. Others deserted by the droves. The French could not fill their front lines sufficiently without any reliable reserves. In the British Army, three years of repeated uses of failed trench warfare strategies had demoralized the soldiers. The will to win dwindled and died. Meanwhile, the new machine guns killed men ruthlessly and efficiently. Disheartened and sick of going like lambs to a slaughter, many who remained rebelled and questioned authority. Among the British and French staff, officers attempted to shore up morale by promising better rations, more leave, and better commanding generals. The British had held against major assaults by the Germans to the northwest. But the cost in wounded had been high. The hope that the American forces would settle in to the western front in massive numbers could not come soon enough. Even French Marshal Pétain declared he would wait for the Americans to arrive and turn the tide.

The *comte* cocked his head. "Will you share this bottle with me and my *Perle*?"

"*Merci.* But I'd fall asleep with the glass in my hand."

He arched a long brow. "Are you certain? It is the very best. From Burgundy. No one fights there."

"You entice me, but I must do my laundry. Afterward? I will sleep like a child."

"Another time?"

"Absolutely."

She said goodbye and headed for her barracks. More than a month ago, later than predicted, the engineers had finished the nurses' quarters. Adjacent to the doctors' and officers' quarters, the women enjoyed more comfort than they had known since Camp May. They had little gas heaters in their dorm rooms that housed four in a fifteen by fifteen space. And if they still complained about the horrible food, appropriately dubbed slum, they enjoyed their beds with real metal coils, covered in sheets and wool blankets. All of these, like their uniforms, the nurses washed themselves.

And today was Gwen's washday.

****

An hour later, she squinted in the bright sun, hefted the hammer the orderly had lent her and banged a nail into the wooden frame of the mess hall. That ought to hold her laundry line.

Something better work right today. It wasn't her relationship with the X-ray technicians, that was for sure.

"Self-satisfied shirkers." They had the audacity to sneer at her, informing her that if she wanted to take her complaint to their CO, she could. She had replied that they wouldn't like it if Doc O'Bryan did lodge his grievance with the man, and they had brushed her off. "Imbeciles."

She wound her rope around the nail and tugged at it.

"Okay, ladies," she called to two friends on her surgical team who stood over huge black pots stirring their garments in soapy water. "Time to hang your curtains!"

Gwen bent to her laundry basket and draped one of the sheets over the line. It smelled of strong lye soap. Bliss. She shook out one of her drab ward uniforms. Minus all the OR stains, it looked nearly as good as new. Water droplets sprayed over her cheeks and she lifted her face to the sun to let them dry.

Shouts from her friends distracted her. They pointed toward the road. As her laundry flapped in the wind, she glimpsed a figure driving a car and slowly coming to a stop. The driver was a man. Blond and big. Hair the color of new wheat. Huge and handsome. She took a step toward him, curious and shocked at who instinct told her this man was. The broad-shouldered, fair-haired giant screeched the Army staff car to a stop, yanked on the brakes, and jumped out. He wore a uniform, but it was so different from any she'd seen. An umber leather jacket, fawn trousers that flared at the thighs. Boots to his knees. A long red scarf around his throat and goggles over his eyes. He stared in her direction. Then he pushed his glasses up to his forehead and grinned at her. "Gwen!"

Shielding the sun with a hand to her brow, she melted in joy. She couldn't be imagining this. *Lex.*

The sheet rippled in the wind, obstructing her view. She whipped it back.

He ran toward her. "Ha! I knew I'd find you. Gwen!"

She broke into a jog, arms out, tears dribbling down her cheeks. *What was he doing here? Where had he come from?*

He swung her up into his arms and whirled her around. His hold, like a bear's, was what she'd missed for oh, so long.

"Let me look at you!" She cupped his ruddy cheeks when he set her to her feet. "Oh, how wonderful you are. A sight for sore eyes!" She reached up to hug him to her again. "Lex, Lex. How did you find me?"

"Well, let me see. *Have* I found you? The Gwen I know has no circles under her eyes." He pulled her against him, his iron-hard chest and thighs those of a robust and virile creature. His health, his vigor drew her like a magnet, and she couldn't get enough of his laughing green-brown eyes and his smiling lips. His hands slid from her shoulders up her throat to her cheeks and fisted in her curls. "You cut your hair?"

"Yes. I couldn't stand it. We wash our hair in our helmets. Mine was so long, it overflowed the damn bowl. I had soap in half my hair and the other half was filthy!" She reached up on tiptoes and planted a quick kiss on his warm lips. "Oh, I'm babbling. It's just that I can hardly believe you're here."

"Me, either. Had a game of round robin coming up through the Aisne valley." He brushed her temples with his thumbs, the caresses soothing, mesmerizing. "You look so tired. What are they doing to you here?"

"Working hard." She lifted one shoulder. "The night surgeries. Someone must."

"And you volunteered," he said with certain knowledge.

"Of course." She circled her arms around his waist and hugged him closer, her cheek to the solid comfort of his rock hard chest. "Tell me you can stay for a few minutes. I'll—I'll take you to the mess hall. They'll get you coffee. The men here talk about the famous American aviator."

"Forget famous, honey."

She pulled back from his arms, electric with the excitement to have him near her again. He always made her feel safe, secure, whole. How had she forgotten that? By pushing the memory to the recesses of her brain where she wouldn't yearn for him or fear for him. "You're modest. Shame on you. I hear folks back home would drool to have you to a war bond rally." She put up one hand as if building a marquee. "'Lex Learner Downs Another.' 'American Ace from Scranton fights for Freedom.'"

"Yeah. If they saw what I do every time I go up there, they wouldn't think it's so pretty."

No, war wasn't. Not for him. Not for her. Her heart hurt. She'd done him a disservice. She'd portrayed him as one who shot at Germans and enjoyed himself. He did it out of duty. "I'm sorry. I make your work too simple, don't I? I should know better. And—you—"

"Hey, hey," he crooned and caught her close, one hand buried in her hair and crushing her against his supple leather jacket. "Are you crying? Jeezus. Don't cry."

"No," she mumbled, her nose dripping. She swiped at her cheeks, hiccupping. "I'm—I'm sorry. I don't cry. I never do."

Fishing out a handkerchief, he handed it over and she blew her nose like a foghorn. He held her by her upper arms and bent down to look her in the eye. "You stop apologizing. You have a right to cry. With what you do here? God, honey." He yanked her close again and tenderly stroked her hair.

She sniffed, angry for her breakdown, astonished at it, too. She did not cry. Not in public. That kind of display the matrons declared was bad form. It would encourage the same and worse from others, and a hospital was not the place where those in charge could freely lose their emotions. Especially not this one where hideously wounded men whimpered like babies, their hands filled with their own blood, their hopes withering as minutes passed waiting for help, relief, a cure.

Other nurses allowed themselves the luxury of release. Sometimes as they got off duty. Sometimes in their barracks. One of the French women who had manned the chateau before Gwen's contingent had arrived allowed herself a regular old waterworks at least one morning a week. She worked receiving, cutting away ravaged uniforms, washing wounds caked with the thick loam of the Champagne, attempting to remove grime and pus while maggots crawled over the men's flesh. She had a gruesome job, that one. But she never broke down in front of the wounded. Yet, often when she left receiving, she'd run down the lane, tears streaming down her cheeks. Some days, she made not one sound. Other days, she sobbed as if the earth would crack. Gwen had never.

Never.

To see Lex now, hale and hearty, to feel his human warmth had broken her into little pieces. And put her back together again. He was her friend, her home, her finest example of all that was right about serving in France, fighting, striving, saving others, until it was over and they went home, victory in hand.

She grinned at him, tipping her chin at the crowd. "We have an audience."

For this reunion this morning out here in the fields, Lex and she had accumulated quite a draw. Her two friends who were doing their laundry laughed and snickered. Flo, who held a basket of her own dirty uniforms, had just strolled up. And two of the X-ray boys she had argued with this morning stood nearby. *Swell.*

Collecting herself, she hooked her arm through Lex's. "This is my best friend from home, Captain Felix Learner. With our Aero Squadron."

Lex stuck out his hand and shook with everyone all around, save for the privates who saluted him. "Hi. Good to meet you."

Flo stepped forward, a smile wreathing her face for the first time in weeks. "Nice to meet you, Captain."

"You a flyer?" One of the men whistled. "Were you with Lafayette Escadrille?"

"Certainly was."

Ever friendly, he impressed the technicians with his openness. The women hung on his every word. Descriptions of his charm would wind up as gossip in the wards.

"Heard great things about all of you," said one technician. "Blasting those Huns. Sending 'em down in flames."

Lex gave him a polite nod. "Thanks."

"Where are you boys based now?" another man asked. "Close?"

"A little town called Toul, east of here. Thirty miles, maybe more. Excuse us, won't you?" He threw them an apologetic smile, patting Gwen's arm looped in his. "Got to go. Not much leave."

She squeezed his hand. "Let me hang my clothes. Then we'll get coffee and talk before you have to go."

"Okay," he said, watching her throw her gray crepes over the line. "But I'm not leaving right away.

I'm on a mission. Can't go until I do my duty."

"What are you talking about?" She slid the clothespins on one of her uniforms.

"Came to give the Old Man my CO's gift."

It took her a moment to realize that the "old man" Lex spoke of was Pershing. She dried her hands on her skirt and grabbed his hand. Leading him toward the far wooden building, she chuckled softly. "Well, I don't know who you've been talking to, but the general is not here."

"Yes, he is. Passed him in his staff car about two miles down the road. Got the word on our hooter this morning, early. He's here to inspect your hospital."

"Oh, boy." She glanced back up toward the chateau. "I doubt they know up there. What a surprise that'll be. For them and him. He'd spend his time better inspecting the supply lines."

"Why? Do you lack things?"

"Yes. Everything!" She waved her arms.

He scoffed. "No. Can't be."

"Okay. So I exaggerate, but we use everything so fast. It's unnerving. I see the stacks dwindle and hold my breath."

"What do you need?" His pale blond brows crinkled in abject concern.

"We run out of bandages, thermometers, morphine, for God's sake. Needles by the hundreds! Everyone's aflutter because our First Division is supposed to swing into action soon and when they do, we're to save their hides. Well, we can't if they don't get those trains moving out of St. Nazaire. We sat on one of them. Not fit for firewood, I tell you."

He scowled at her. "Really pissed about this, aren't

you?"

"Wouldn't you be, if you didn't have any…?" Frenetic, she waved her hand in the air, at a loss. "Wings!"

He hooted in laughter. "I would. I definitely would!"

"Well?" She drilled a finger into his rib cage, miffed. "That's a *tiny* problem."

"Tiny. Maybe you should tell him?"

"Him? Pershing? Oh, shoot. That's jumping rank. Not done, let me tell you. Plus I won't see him."

"You will."

"You need that coffee." She wrinkled her nose at him. "You're dizzy and I think I am, too. Up all night, you know. Not good for the head or the heart."

"Yeah." He chuckled lightly, allowing himself to be dragged along by her into the mess hall.

Taking him back into the kitchens, Gwen grinned as the kitchen staff fell over themselves to serve their illustrious visitor. As Lex greeted this group with the same *élan* as the first one, she saw that his ease was, as the French would say, in his skin. She'd always known this about him, but never had she so valued it or recognized how unique it truly was. One private was so impressed by Ace Learner that he was ready to give him not merely coffee, but cook up an entire meal for him.

Gwen led him to a bench in the hall so they could sit and drink. "I will have you visit more often. Maybe we'd get something more recognizable for dinner."

"Bad, huh?" he said as he swung a leg over a bench and faced her. "Drink up."

She wrapped her hands around her cup and

absorbed the warmth of the porcelain. "Terrible. Let's not talk about it. Tell me how you found me."

"Mom."

"Your mother?"

"And Susannah." His sweet gaze delved into hers. "Your sister told my mother where you're stationed."

Susannah was getting her letters? Gratitude to her aunt budded. The woman was not being a monster, but allowing the girl to have Gwen's letters.

Lex took another drink of his coffee. "I looked up the base hospital list, wheedled a car out of my captain and here I am. Have a gift from him to welcome Pershing to the area. Kind of a bribe, to be honest, to get the old man to give us more planes."

"You need more supplies, too?"

"Yeah. Who doesn't?"

"Planes. Morphine." She pondered the costs of each and sipped from her cup. "How does he decide?"

Lex lifted a shoulder. "I doubt he does. Congress has to pay the bills. Bet the War Department screams in their ears, though, for whatever they need."

She grasped his hand. "I'm afraid, Lex."

All light left his face. "You'd be a statue if you weren't."

"No, I mean I'm not afraid for me," she hastened to explain. "Somehow I feel—"

"Invincible?"

"No. That would be stupid." Glancing out the window to the north, she listened to the roar of guns punctuate the silence. Over and over these past months since Anna's death, she had accepted the possibility she could be injured or die. Each night when she looked at a man with his jaw gone or his intestines spilling from his stomach, she peered down into the void of death and reached for the delicate thread of life to haul him back.

Lex frowned into his coffee. "When you're green, you think the worst can't happen to you. That means trouble. Carelessness and—"

"Don't worry about me. I'm not green, Lex. And I'm very careful. I think when I'm in there with Doc that I was always meant to be there. To do the delicate incisions he can't seem to do well anymore in the dim light. To remove the specs of shrapnel he can't see. To resection when—"

Beneath his breath, he swore. "Stop."

What had he seen that he wanted to forget? She squeezed his hand. "It's bad. I won't tell you anything else. But what I fear is not for me, but that we won't have enough to do a good job. Doc and I and nine other teams operate every night, all night. We're busy. We get Tommies and French, so far only a few Americans. Ones who've gone up the line to observe how the guns work or to learn strategy. But when Pershing puts the First Division in, as he's supposed to soon, we'll need more of everything. And quickly. We won't be able to wait. If you could see what I see…How these men come to us." She swallowed back more tears. "We can't cope with only forty-two nurses and ten doctors. We'll need—double that! Maybe more!"

"Tell him that then."

"Isn't that my base commander's job? To be honest with him?"

Lex arched a skeptical brow. "Maybe he hasn't."

She inhaled, unsatisfied with that answer. "He better or we all go down."

Lex drained his cup and tugged her to her feet.

159

"Come with me to headquarters."

She rolled her eyes at him. Her act covered her sudden awareness that the man was at least six inches taller than she. When did he get so big? And so appealing? "You're trying to trap me into complaining. I tell you they won't like it if one of their nurses becomes a fishwife."

"How will they like it if they lose men they needn't because no one would tell them they were sorely lacking supplies?"

"Okay. Okay! I'll go, but I'm not guaranteeing I won't put my foot in my mouth."

"Fair enough." He took her by the shoulders, turned her around and headed her toward the far door. "In any case, they'll like that you dress up headquarters."

"Right you are." She imitated the phrases of some British patients in the wards. "Just what I need to enhance my power around here. Become the fluff instead of the starch!"

****

As they walked through camp, others saw them together and smiled, or raised their brows in surprise or stopped to point. An airman was an unusual sight in this sector. One of their nurses with a flyboy was even more noteworthy. Then as she and Lex walked into headquarters, men fell over themselves to stand, salute, and greet the renowned Captain Learner. Beside Lex, Gwen felt the heat of dozens of eyes on her, questioning who she was, how she knew the Captain, and why he had taken her from the hospital before he presented himself to them there.

Lex took it in stride, the looks, the discreet

160

questions about when he had arrived and what his purpose was. In fact, he probably enjoyed it. The rascal. She could tell he got a rip out of it when he told them he was here to see the general. The staff appeared immediately contrite and delighted. General Pershing, they told him, was in conference with the commander of the base hospital and the colonel of the Services of Supply.

Lex caught Gwen's eye at that statement. "Good for them. Nurse Spencer and I will wait for him."

They got Lex more coffee. Gwen declined.

Would the captain care for a cigarette? A brandy?

"How about you, Nurse? A sandwich?"

"No, thank you." But after two aides left to do Lex's bidding, she huffed. "I had half a mind to tell him I wanted a cigarette."

Lex shot her a horrified look. "You're joking."

She folded her arms. "And what if I'm not?"

He hooted. "You *smoke*? Since when?"

"Since I am insulted that I don't even get offered the same as you."

He considered that a second, his eyes widening. "I understand."

She uncrossed and recrossed her arms. "Why is it that we get half the pay of a private?"

He stared at her, open mouthed. "You do?"

She fumed, pressing her lips together. "Had to buy our own uniforms, too. Oh, forget that. I don't give a damn about the pay. Money is only—" She curled her lip. "Money. But did you have to buy your uniform?"

"No."

"There you are then!" She swept out a hand, disgusted. "And you have rank. Men respect your stars and bars. What you say is law. What we say is questioned! Questioned!"

The sound of footsteps brought her up short. She froze—knowing she'd been heard. *Oh, great, Gwen, you have now made a spectacle of yourself. Please let it not have been in front of General Pershing.*

But it was.

"Good day, General," she greeted the American commander. Tall and gruff looking with steel gray hair, a trim moustache, and a stiff lip, Pershing walked to her with a courteous smile on his face.

"Good day, Nurse. What is your name?"

"Spencer, sir."

"And where is your home?"

She told him, aware that in her peripheral vision she saw a tall dark-haired British officer stand to one side of the commander. *Was this Adam Fairleigh?* Her urge to melt into the floor had never been greater in her entire life.

Adam stepped toward her. "Sir, this is the nurse who restored me to good health weeks ago. Hello, Spencer."

A cursory meeting of her gaze with his told her he was restored to vigor and the full promise of his excellent good looks. "Hello, Captain."

"You are to be commended, Spencer," Pershing told her, "for your service to all of us. I am sorry to say it won't be by adding stars and bars to your uniform. Perhaps some day that will come."

The general, she happily noted, was not being facetious. "Yes, sir."

"Although the pay may increase sooner, I am happy to tell you."

She looked him squarely in the eye for the first time in their conversation. "That would be most appreciated, General."

"What will you spend it on?"

Shocked by his question, she shook her head. "Pardon me, sir?" And when he repeated it, she chastised herself for sounding like a dolt. "Chocolate bars."

He chuckled. "Good chocolate here. Glad you like it."

"Yes, but it wouldn't be for me, sir."

"No?" His bushy brows rose.

"The men love a bit of chocolate. After they wake from a long night of morphine, if they're blue, sir, they love a treat."

"Good to know." Then he raised a finger and one of his aides stepped to his side. "Colonel Wallace? See if we have requisitioned any chocolate for our patients, will you? Our boys deserve a bit of sweetness, don't you think? I do. So do the nurses. See to it, Wallace. I will send you word of that, Spencer."

"Thank you." She couldn't believe what had just happened here. "Thank you, sir."

"I shall also take up this matter of your orders not respected in the wards."

Surprised, she managed to thank him.

"See you tonight, Nurse Spencer," the general told her and motioned for Lex to join him for a chat.

Wherever Pershing expected her this evening, she wouldn't be there. She had her shift. She scanned the faces of his staff arrayed before her. They either grinned or frowned at her.

Yet Adam Fairleigh looked like he was about to

burst like a balloon. With a hearty laugh, he leaned toward her and said, "I'll see you tonight, too."

"No. I'm on duty."

"The General gives a dance. Do come."

Chapter Nine

Back in her barracks, her laundry basket in hand, Gwen sank to her bed. The excitement of the morning warred with her fatigue. She felt alive as a lightning bug. As lethargic as one who'd not had any sleep for nineteen hours. She dumped her laundry beside her and idly began to fold it into neat little piles. The joy of seeing Lex, so healthy and jovial, invigorated her. The shock of seeing Adam Fairleigh in such quick succession had thrilled her in a totally different way.

He was dark, assertive, and insistent. She hadn't met a man like that before. His attention to her was heady. But she had no time for him, no interest in a friendship with him. Not even a dance.

She shook out one of her crepes and hung it on the makeshift hangers she and her barracks mates had created out of stripped barbed wire. Taking in the shapeless, drab color of it, she bet that Captain Fairleigh knew scores of refined, manicured, coiffed women in England who would outshine her. *Especially in these.*

Flo opened their door and walked in, babbling on about meeting Lex. "He is definitely the most handsome man I have ever seen. Lucky you."

"He's an old friend. Nothing more."

"Could have fooled me." She folded her own clothes. "Wish I had a friend who looked like that."

"Lex is a remarkable man. Smart. Generous." *Kind to come all this way to check up on me.* "Some day he'll run the Learner beer factory."

"Did he go back to Toul?"

"I have no idea. He was talking with General Pershing."

"He'll come say goodbye though, won't he?"

"Maybe. Yes, I guess so." Gwen ran two hands through her hair, then unbuttoned her uniform. "I have to get some sleep. Last night was hell."

"I heard Doc O'Bryan is on the warpath for the X-ray technicians."

"Correction." Pearl walked in, her own laundry in her basket. "O'Bryan sicced Gwen on the technicians. It's all over the wards."

"Please." Gwen sighed and crawled into bed. "I'm trying to celebrate how agreeable they were."

Pearl snorted. "That'll be the day."

Flo grumbled. "Why the hell make life unbearable for you? Why not bitch at them himself?"

Neither Gwen nor Pearl reacted to her language. All three of them, just like the other nurses, were calling spades spades these days.

"You know why," Pearl said.

Flo didn't say anything.

Nonetheless, her back to the room, Gwen felt the condemnation in Flo's silence. She pushed up on one elbow, turned and surveyed her friends. "Why? Oh, come on. Why?"

Pearl pursed her lips. "He's drinking."

When? How? But alcohol was easy to get. Too

easy. He could buy anything—wine, gin, vodka—in the village estaminet. "I don't smell it on him."

Pearl shrugged. "In the mornings before he goes to sleep."

Anger at this man who had taken her under his wing sliced through her, sharp as the blade of a knife. "Since when?"

"The past few weeks. Doctor Hubbard put him to bed himself this morning. O'Bryan was singing outside the doctor's quarters dressed in nothing more than the skin God gave him."

He wanted to get drunk more than he wanted the technicians to do their jobs? So he sent me to do his dirty work?

Gwen swallowed back her distaste. Doc was a fine surgeon. Blustery. Salty in his language. But dedicated to mending the soldiers broken and bleeding on his table. She could dismiss his actions. Say they didn't matter. But they did. They did if it interfered with his ability to operate. If others wouldn't respect him and take his orders. What was he thinking? That was it. He wasn't. If he were, he would stop. He wasn't here to drink his pain away. He was here to take it away for others who had wounds, open and garish and life-threatening and...

"Shit." She grabbed the covers and hauled them up over her shoulder, facing away from her friends.

"Want us to wake you at six for supper?" Pearl asked.

"Don't bother."

****

In the end, she couldn't sleep. She lay there for too many hours, alternately counting her blessings or

167

brooding about the disasters of her day. Finally she gave up, got up, took a sponge bath and headed for the mess hall. Dinner was stew. Again. When the war was over, she would have eaten so much of this stuff they called slum, that she was going to look like potatoes and carrots with a whiff of mystery meat.

"There you are." Lex caught up to her as she finished and let the screen door to the hall slam shut. "Did you sleep?"

"No."

"Ouch. Hey, what did I do?"

"Nothing. Everything. Sorry. You were the best thing to happen to me all day. Why are you still here?"

"I saw your friend Flo. She and your other pal said you were sleeping, so I waited."

"Don't you have to go fly off somewhere?" She stopped at the door to her own barracks.

"No. I came to see you. See Pershing. And now I am dying to dance with you."

Fighting laughter and his lure, she shook her head. "You are crazy."

"Yep. And I love to dance. But I am darned if I'll do it with the old man." He took her by both elbows. "Come on, kiddo. I know quite a few Yanks who want to dance with the beautiful blonde nurse."

"Yeah. I bet they do. After I let everyone have a piece of my mind in headquarters, they probably want to ship me back to St. Nazaire."

"No. Won't happen. They need you. I bet most of these guys have two left feet."

"That I can't fix!"

He pulled her away and she walked with him, admitting to herself that she wanted to dance with him to chase off the blues. After all, Lex had been the one to teach her to waltz and polka. In his parents' big conservatory, the two of them had glided across the wooden floor while he played tunes on the wind-up Victrola. "We have to show them how it's done. I doubt some of these guys have ever seen a proper lady cut a rug."

Inside the mess hall to the officers quarters, Pershing and his staff formed a receiving line. The old man was chatting liberally with everyone in line, evidently determined to meet as many of his soldiers here as possible. Lex led her to wait their turn, and Gwen couldn't help but seek out tall, dark Captain Fairleigh next to his American counterpart who'd driven to fetch him months ago.

Heaven knew what she said to any of the officers as she passed. She relied on Lex to make most of the introductions and ease the way with banter. Facing Fairleigh however brought them both up short.

"Hello, Captain," she said to Adam as evenly as possible. His eyes, dark and probing, gave her the jitters.

"Glad you came, Spencer." He offered a polite nod. "I feared you had opted for sleep. Captain Learner tells me you work the night shift."

They had talked about her? She stiffened. Lex wouldn't do that willy nilly. That meant Fairleigh had asked him for information. "I do. I work again tonight. I came to please my friend here." She gazed up at Lex.

But his lips were thin with strain. His eyes hard as glass. "Nice to see you, Fairleigh."

"Learner."

Lex led her away from the line and she was thrilled

to go.

"Well, there you are." Lex sounded like he thought over a puzzle. "He's very interested in you."

"Don't be silly," she told him and herself, her butterflies fierce with delight.

"How do you know him?" Lex led her toward a table where privates were handing out small coffee cups of champagne.

Accepting one, she took a sip and decided she really liked the bubbles. Liked it better than the white wine she'd get in the village on her afternoons off. "Evidently, he is a valuable entity. He had walked No Man's Land."

"Baloney." Lex grimaced. "Who does that?"

"Exactly." Then she told him the story of how the commander had stopped their train and rerouted the entire group of nurses. Fairleigh's activities crossing to the enemy lines fired his imagination…and then he believed the story.

Lex stared straight across the room at Fairleigh as the fiddlers and the piano player launched into their first tune.

"Nothing like a potential spy to make everyone sit up and blink. So you cured the man?"

"He was still in poor shape when I left. But I did what I could without the proper supplies, I hasten to add."

"Well noted. All right. Enough of him. Let's dance this one." Lex took her cup and set his and hers aside. She started to dig in her heels, but he took her in his arms. "No excuses."

"Let Me Call You Sweetheart" was a song they had both danced to at home. But she wasn't fond of being on display, the first on the floor. Not after her confrontation with the X-ray boys this morning and her outburst here in headquarters. "All right. We'd better be flawless."

"Nurse's orders?"

"You bet."

"Nothing less than perfect then." He smiled down at her, but as he wrapped one hand around her waist and took her hand, tension lined his face.

Other couples took the floor.

"Good. We are not alone." She went easily, so effortlessly that it might have been the old Victor record playing instead of this pick-up band of doctors and orderlies. Soon she was enjoying herself, moving with him as he glided in time with the melody. When the song ended and the band began "By the Light of the Silvery Moon," Lex took her off again.

But when that was done and he led her to the edge of the floor, he told her he would stand back and allow all the other men to have their turn with her.

"I'd like another cup of champagne instead," she told him, fearing Captain Fairleigh would come and ask for her hand. She didn't want to touch him. Not healthy and imposing and alluringly handsome as he was now. "Besides no one is as agile as you."

Lex winked at her. But his gaiety was a fake. "You never know, honey, until you try."

At her elbow appeared one X-ray technician whom she had argued with this morning.

"Is this a wise idea, Private Murphy?" She glanced from him to Pershing. She wanted no scenes here.

"Yes, ma'am, it is. We are just dancing. I like to dance and you do, too. Besides, I wanted to apologize for this morning. The way some of my buddies talked to you was not right."

"Thank you."

"You'll dance then? You're quite good, you know."

"The praise should go to my instructor." She tipped her head in Lex's direction. Then she allowed the man to lead her round the floor. Stilted though he was, he got the rhythm right.

"I wanted to dance with you, Nurse, because I had to tell you that I...uh...understand why you did it. Came to us this morning, I mean. We do need to be faster. I promise we will."

Surprised, she blinked up at him. He was seriously contrite. "Well, that really is good news." If he knew that Doc O'Bryan was drinking each morning after his stint in surgery, then perhaps he also figured that Gwen chewed them out to pick up Doc's slack. If he respected her for that, she wasn't certain. But he was promising to do his job better and that, she would take as his new leaf.

"What was that all about?" Lex asked her when Murphy had returned her to his side.

Gwen told him everything about the technicians and when she got to the part about Doc, she lowered her voice.

"Let's have a round of applause for good ol' Murphy who has the sense to know what the hell he's here for."

"Agreed. I think I'd better pinch myself," she told him, her back to the crowd so no one else would ask her to dance. "Or I've had too much champagne."

"Good for you to get happy once in awhile. What

do you do for fun up here?"

"When I have a half day or I can't sleep, I go into town with a few other nurses and share a flagon of wine."

He looked at her as if he was seeing her anew. "Bravo."

"But I always preferred beer," she told him with a broad grin.

"Do not pull my leg," he warned, his hazel eyes twinkling.

"But now I like the *Vin* Sisters just as well. *Rouge* more than *blanc*."

"Pardon me." It was Fairleigh with a nod to Lex and a strained smile for her. "I wonder if I might have the honor of this dance?"

Her stomach fluttered. It wouldn't be polite to refuse him. Trapped, worried, she cocked an ear to the band. At least the song they played wasn't romantic. She didn't want to be in his arms for any music that summoned any sugary sentiments. But "In the Good Old Summertime" suited her need to remain impartial to him. Detached.

"You don't like me much," he told her after they'd taken a few steps in silence.

How could he think that? "I don't know you to like you or not."

"True, I suppose. But you're very reserved."

Was she insulted or relieved? "It's my responsibility to be."

"Not when you're with your Captain Learner, it isn't."

She missed a step and crushed his toe. "Sorry."

"No, I'm the one who is. That was rude. He is your

friend from home and I am—"

She locked gazes with him. "You're what?"

He fought a self-deprecating smile. "I was shocked to see you here this morning. I thought...that is, I remembered this woman who nursed me and she—"

When he sought a word, she thought it best to supply one that encouraged laughter. "A harpy."

He chuckled. "Hardly!"

Others on the dance floor stared at them.

"I had this vision of this golden haired blonde with the largest deep purple eyes. Wild and angry at me for being ill. Frantic to save me."

She arched a brow. Being imperial could keep distance between them. "Would you rather I had been indifferent to your condition?"

"No. I welcome your...adamant nature."

She snorted. "Don't be absurd. You were delirious. On the point of shock. How could you know who it was who was there with you?"

"But I did," he said like it was the most important fact he had ever known. "You looked angelic then, but here now, you are simply stunning."

She gaped at him, charmed, yet incredulous at his eloquence. "Thank you."

He scowled. "Men do not compliment you, do they?"

"Not usually, no."

"They must be blind."

Her whole body flooded with warmth. He was too engaging. She was just too gullible. "They are discreet."

"Even Captain Learner?"

"Yes, of course. Lex would never—I've known

174

him forever."

"I see. And me you know not at all."

"This is true. The most I know about you is your extraordinary heroism to crawl across the hell of No Man's Land and the abominable condition of your hands. How are your hands, Captain?"

"At the moment, they are in excellent health." His fingers at the small of her back pressed into her spine. "Happy to hold you."

She cleared her throat. Trained her eyes over his shoulder to the other couples on the floor.

"What is your given name?"

She shot him a quelling glance. "Why?"

"I don't want to call you Spencer all the time."

"It's a good name."

"I'd like to know you better. Give me your name."

"And if I don't want you to have it?" *Use it? Pretend we are friends? Make me want what I can't have?*

"I'll find out somehow. I do have means."

She took in a shaky breath. Insulted, complimented, she was also aware others watched them. Lex, included. "Are you always so forward, Captain?"

"When I need something, yes."

She tamped down her elation. This was ridiculous. To find a man—an English man—an officer— appealing. She had no time to become attached to a man. She had a job to do. An all-consuming task that required her whole mind. "I cannot permit you to continue in this manner, sir."

"Tell me why."

"The conditions are—impossible. I am not—"

"Available?"

"What?" That confused her.

"Are you his?" He inclined his dark head toward Lex.

"No. No."

"Then finish your sentence." He pulled her incrementally closer to him as they took a turn and from the corner of her eye she thought she saw Pershing nod at their coordination. "You were saying you are not…what?"

When she shook her head, lost, afraid where this conversation led, he asked, "Are you not interested in me?"

She frowned at him. "I don't know enough about you to be interested."

"Really. Is that why you quiver like a bird as we dance?"

Stunned, she stared at him.

"You weren't afraid when you danced with Learner. I saw. I noted. I want to come back here. Call on you."

A wave of excitement washed over her. Fresh and invigorating, his interest in her had her blushing—and rushing to deter him. She had no time to go courting. "You can't. I work. You do too."

"You object too much." He chuckled lightly as the song wound down.

She wanted to stomp her foot at him. But couldn't in this formal crowd. "You press too much."

They halted in the middle of the floor.

"Will you dance another with me?"

"No."

The disappointment in his sultry green eyes gutted

her. "I'll return," he whispered. "Next week. Next month. Whenever I can."

The promise of his words suffused her with delight. His determination, she warned herself, should appall her. Knowing she should turn and run, she held her ground and her dignity. "Take me back to Lex."

"Of course." He wrapped her arm in his and like a gentleman returned her to Lex's side. Before he left, he caught her hand, lifted it and kissed the back. "Good evening, Spencer. *Au revoir.*"

With a nod to Lex, he walked away.

"Arrogant bloke, isn't he?"

Stiff as a board, Gwen murmured in agreement. "I should leave. I have to get ready for duty." That was a lie. But she had to escape this room with the men who examined her and nodded and smiled. Fairleigh who made apologies to General Pershing and departed. Flo who stared at her, her eyes gleaming in merriment. And Pearl who knit her brows and looked concerned about her, but who was company to a group of men that included the *comte* Chatillon.

"Okay. I'll walk you back if you like."

"No, Lex. Stay. I—I have to go."

"Yeah. Me too."

"You're leaving?"

He chucked her chin. "Have work to do just like you, honey." His smile was curt, unlike him.

They did their duty and bid good night to Pershing, then headed outside. The air was warmer tonight, the smell of dew sweet on the grass. Were it not for the cannon buzzing like angry bees in the north, she would have thought she was home.

When they got to her barracks, she grabbed Lex's

hand. "You'll come see me again. Promise." She wanted him back. Wanted him to visit her again. His presence wouldn't confound her. Wouldn't destroy her sense of peace. Or consume her sense of duty.

He took his time looking at her. Whatever he sought, he didn't seem to find it. "Sure. Yeah. Of course. You will promise me you'll get your proper rest. You do look a bit bug-eyed."

"Oh, thank you very much. Go back to your airplanes."

He glanced up at the night sky, then down at her. He looked at her as if he didn't know her. "You want compliments?"

She shrugged. She never had sought them before...before she met Captain Fairleigh. "After the war is over, I might collect them, yes."

"You never needed them. Not from me."

She glanced away, shy suddenly and feeling silly at this venture into feminine wiles.

"Forget it." He crooked his finger at her. "Come here and say a proper goodbye."

She went easily into his open arms, hugged him tight and reached up to buss him on the cheek. "No funny stuff up there in the air."

He leaned back, considered her lips a second, then kissed her forehead. "None. See you soon."

He jogged down the path. When he turned once as if he were checking to see that she was still there, she waved to him. She curled her arms around herself and watched him drive away.

Lex's return would always bring her comfort. Captain Adam Fairleigh's would bring her excitement.

Chapter Ten

Two days later, Fairleigh sat outside her barracks door on a chair he must have brought from the mess hall for the very purpose of waiting for her. He had the long view of her as she strode down the path from the chateau. Her smile, her delight grew with each step toward him.

"It's so early." She admired how wonderful he looked with his cheeks ruddy and his black curls windblown. "Why are you here at this hour?"

He shot to his feet, his gaze direct and absorbing. "I came to buy you breakfast and lunch. A spot of wine. Anything you want for as long as I can have you near me."

"This is silly, you must realize." She was giving propriety lip service because he looked so damn handsome and she was enchanted that he had come to visit her. So soon, too. She ridiculed herself for being foolish, but then ever since the dance she had committed to memory every word he'd spoken to her that night.

He took her by the elbows and drew her nearer to him. She held back, not allowing her body to touch his. She couldn't get that close. Not here. Not when others might see and remark and think her…loose.

"Change your uniform. Come walk with me to the village. Or I can drive if you wish. I have a staff car." He smiled, eager as a boy, and she had to grin back at him. As a suitor, he...well, she chuckled. He blossomed. No longer the spy, the lunatic raving in a bed, filthy and delirious, now he was a dashing creature with his impeccable accent and spotless uniform and the most delicious look to him as if he were about to eat her up. "Shall we walk or ride?"

Dare she tell him she thought him bold and much too devastating for her? "I think you are rash to come here. I didn't say I would see you."

"You didn't dissuade me." He cocked a brow.

"Didn't I? I thought I had put you in your place."

"No, you never did. Told me to return you to Lex."

The mention of Lex's name sobered her. Her mind raced. Becoming friends with Adam, becoming enamored of him could only end in a separation. Worse. Heartbreak. She panicked. *How to discourage this man?* "I've never had a beau."

"I surmised as much. You are so young. What in bloody hell is your name?"

She laughed in surprise. "I thought you could find it out all by yourself."

"I want you to tell me."

"Gwen."

He repeated her name as if it were a treasure. No one had sounded so fond of her in decades. Being regarded like that was mesmerizing. Captured by him, she warned herself not to allow it. But warnings meant little compared to a new and burgeoning desire to risk her heart.

"And I am Adam."

"Adam." She swallowed hard. Not Captain. Not Fairleigh. Not her patient. Not anyone but this man. "Very well. Wait a minute, will you? A few minutes, really. I am—" She brushed her hands down her butcher apron, stained with the blood of men who had lain on Doc's table last night. She wanted to go out with Adam in a clean uniform and what she wouldn't give for a full bath. But water was so scarce that the idea to lounge in a tub was pure fantasy. She'd do what she could because he was here and very, very real.

He smiled at her, his luscious mouth curling into a temptation. "Keep grinning at me like that, Nurse Spencer. I like the look of you taken by me. You try my restraint."

She parted her lips, the need to kiss him a wildfire in her chest.

"Oh, Gwen, you are quite devastating. Go inside before I forget myself and get us both reprimanded."

"Yes, of course." She spun away from him. Foolish and giddy, she opened the door to the barracks and fled inside. Within minutes, she stood before him again, her clean gray crepe on, minus an apron, her sturdy boots on her feet. *Would that they help keep me on the straight and narrow.*

He took her arm and began to stroll toward the village. "You do realize you are grinning again. A penny for your thoughts."

"I tell myself I have to behave with you."

He inhaled and beside her, though he looked straight ahead, she could tell he ground his teeth. "Honesty can create problems."

"I know. Let's be polite instead."

He feigned distress. "Let's not. Have you ever

misbehaved before?"

"With a man?" She chuckled. "Sorry. No, never. As you say I am too young and…"

He stopped because she had, and then he faced her. "And what?"

"I never even thought about…that."

He peered up at the sky, as if asking for forbearance, then locked his dark green eyes on her. "The fact makes me damn proud."

"Why? Because you're the first? Why do men think that way?"

"Males are encouraged to claim a mate. Fight for her. Command her. As for me here with you? I simply consider myself lucky."

She focused on her fingers tracing the cut of his cuffs, complimented beyond her ability to do more than enjoy him. "Don't be absurd."

He raised her chin. "I'm not. Remember, I saw you with Learner."

She was confused. How could Adam think she cared for anyone else? "Lex? Lex is—"

"I know. Your friend. You said. You say over and over again, actually."

"Do I?" She considered that a moment. There was nothing more to her relationship with Lex than a deep regard. "Finding a friend, a good one, here, so far from home is unusual. Heart-warming."

"Yes, I would guess for you Americans over here in a foreign country, that is true. For us, well, we came with the men we'd known all our lives. In school. At Eton and Sandhurst. For me, this is—" He paused, biting his lower lip.

She waited until he found words.

"What was expected of me. What I was trained to do. To be. To fight." In silence, they walked a few more paces. "And you? What is this war for you, Gwen Spencer?"

"Work I can do. Work I want to do. I—I have always done nursing because it meant so many things to me. At first, it was a way out of my aunt's house. A terrible confinement. Nurses' training was a way to become something better than a char woman scouring floors and toilets."

"My lord. You scrubbed floors." Admiration washed over his features. He took her hand in his, sweet and consoling. And they continued along the dirt road, no one else in sight.

She liked this solitude with him. This intimacy. Bulbs of tiny white lilies bloomed along the roadside. Pink and white cherry trees blossomed, their limbs swaying against the pale blue sky. She had not noticed them before.

"I gather that your family is not a happy one?"

She told him then about the deaths of her parents, her sister's and her adoption by her Aunt Mary. Keeping the more hideous details to herself, she thought prudent. She wanted his regard, not his pity. "And your family? Are they happy together?"

"A good question. Some are. Others have no idea how to define happiness."

She found that confusing and said so.

"My parents married because they cared about each other. They still do, only more so. Unusual for their set. I have an older brother, married and dreadfully unhappy with his wife. He's the heir and until he went off to fight in early 'fifteen, he did a damn good job of

183

running the estate. But he joined up, came out to France and wound up in the trenches. Not a month here and he went over the top. He is very badly wounded." Adam indicated his own face. "He has a terrible time coming to terms with it. So does his wife. Sad, because once they could not bear to be parted. Now? They are at constant odds. My father hopes George will learn how to face the world, literally, as he will be earl one day and need to be out and about."

Gwen sat rigid. Adam's family were nobles? What was she doing here with him thinking…assuming they could have much in common besides this fascination with each other?

He rambled on. "I have a younger sister. She recently returned to our parents' home from her own in London. She is, God love her, a widow. Her husband fell in Loos nearly three years ago. He remains among the missing. And she is lost without him."

Gwen squeezed his hand. "And you? How long have you been here fighting?"

"Too long."

He didn't seem to want to add more, so she thought it best that they walk along in quiet for a while.

In the village, a little restaurant she often visited with friends was open. The owner, an elderly French farmer who ran the place to earn American dollars, had flung open his whitewashed double doors to a stone patio. On the tabletops, he'd put out small jars with a wild flower or an early rose, whatever he could find.

"The gentleman's name is Armand, and he's a very good cook," she told Adam as he pulled out a chair for her to take the seat. No other patrons graced the place.

"What do you suggest?"

"*Jambon et fromage. Vin rouge. Salade verte. Du pain*, glorious *et* crispy. *Du pain*."

"Ha! Remind me to feed you often. You look glorious in raptures."

She wiggled her brows. "On occasion, he has offered *cuisses*, but I have not gotten the courage to try them."

"Frogs' legs? You should. They are as tender as chicken."

"The idea that Armand might have recently caught them in his garden"—she made a face—"disturbs me. Though my aunt raises chickens, and I've had to kill and pluck and gut them. I shouldn't be so finicky."

Beneath the table, he reached for her hand and tucked it in his lap. His affection was addictive. "Be what you are, Gwen. If you don't want frogs' legs, you don't have to eat them."

"Have you done many things you didn't care to do?" she asked, thinking of his venture into No Man's Land. What kind of dedication did it take to do that? What kind of cunning? "I'm sorry. That was ridiculous to ask. We all do things we don't want to do."

"I like my position with Pershing's staff. Even that jaunt across the barbed wire," he offered with a faraway look, "was exciting. I have been known to test the limits. That excites me. Does that make me a daredevil? Do you prefer men who are more ordinary?"

"I've never thought about who I prefer. I only know who I like."

He seemed not to breathe for a long while as his gaze traveled her lips and her eyes. "Like me." His words sounded like a plea.

"Can you doubt it?"

185

"I never want to."

His words were balm to an open wound she had not bothered to tend. If she let him do that for her now, would she be foolish? Or couldn't she permit herself to be charmed? Just for one small moment in her life. "You are doing very well. Shall I tell you if you ever disenchant me?"

"Do I enchant you now?"

"I'm afraid you do," she whispered.

"Don't be afraid. I'd never hurt you."

She had the urge to fling her arms around him, kiss his lips, and tell him she trusted him. "I don't trust our circumstances. If we were home... But then, you live in England and I live thousands of miles away and...and this is not appropriate for me to even talk this way." She covered her hot cheek with one hand.

Armand appeared and bid them *Bonjour*.

"Forget I said all that," she told Adam when the proprietor had disappeared into his little shop with their wine order.

"I can't. Look at me. We both know what we face. The possibilities. But I don't care. If you'll have me, I want to come back. Take you to lunch and buy you *vin rouge* and *jambon et fromage*. Anything you want. As long as you smile at me as you do now and blush and tell me with those extraordinary violet eyes that I am the finest man you've ever met."

Choked with emotion, her throat burning with tears of delight, she could only nod at him.

"Shall I drive over and see you again?" he asked as minutes later, they stood before her barracks once more and their interlude was done.

"Yes. Soon."

He raised her hand, turned it palm up and placed a tender kiss in the center. "Keep that for me, will you?"

Dissolved into a puddle of girlish need, she summoned a reply. "Will you want it back?"

He pressed her closed fist to her heart. "Many times over."

****

She had no time to moon over him. New spring assaults of the Germans along the French and British lines saw an entire American division take the field in support of their allies. The sound of field guns was an around-the-clock tattoo. The ambulances came trundling down the dirt road from God knew where, pouring out men every morning, the drivers telling them they couldn't run at night for fear of shelling and airplane fire. Four new Army Nurse Corps recruits joined Dalton in receiving, and according to their former matron, these four knew their stuff. Gwen noted that the wounded who came to her surgical table each night had their uniforms well cut away, their tourniquets newly tied, their morphine dosages rendering them oblivious when Doc gave the order to their anesthetist to place the ether cone over their faces—and make the first incision.

Gwen's operating room was now part of a larger hospital, accommodating two thousand men. Built by American Army engineers, many of whom were Negroes, it was a completed bungalow of wood with a tin roof. On the slopes, a soldier had painted two of the biggest red crosses Gwen had ever seen.

"That does no good," she told Pearl one morning as they walked back to their quarters. "I saw one of our planes overhead last night. They should know not to

187

buzz us."

"Tell Lex next time you see him," Pearl said.

"I will. If I ever do." She wondered where he was, how he was. *Is he one of those above us every night? Being shot at? Shooting us.*

"It rattles our men something awful," Pearl said. "They're weak as puppies, cringing when the planes come. They think they're going to be hit again. Some of them scream and others curse. I wish to heaven someone would realize we have men in dire straits here. Those red crosses on the roof are useless."

Pearl, who was head nurse in the post-op surgical *salle* in the far wing, often groused about the slow evacuations of her patients to larger base hospitals south. "I need more room again. Our boys are lying on the floor. On hay. Hell, I hate that mess. Gets in the dressings if they're delirious. Makes my life and my orderlies' lives hell. Plus, my back is killing me."

"At least we have more nurses," Gwen said as she opened the door to their room.

"None for you though."

"I keep hoping."

"Surgical experience is hard to come by."

Gwen rolled a shoulder. "The prejudice of men not to let a woman try is silly. Especially here."

She often watched the other doctors who wouldn't let a nurse touch a scalpel. Too proud, too covetous of their expertise, those doctors processed fewer wounded than she and Doc O'Bryan. If any of the men said anything to Doc about it, Gwen didn't know. She did, however, see them in the OR at night gazing over at the two of them and wondering, frowning, considering the reasons they did well. Still, it was not her place to make suggestions. None of the other doctors, including Hubbard who was Doc's best friend, would take kindly to it.

Both she and Pearl entered their barracks and halted in front of Flo's bed.

Their friend faced the wall, the blanket pulled up to her chin.

Gwen leaned over to see if she slept. Eyes wide open, Flo stared straight ahead. Gwen shot a glance at Pearl and shook her head. This pose of Flo's was becoming a regular occurrence. Pearl and Gwen had discussed it, worried over it. Was Flo sick? They didn't think so. Was she unhappy? Very.

In charge of the amputee *salle*, Flo ran the ward with two orderlies and six new Red Cross nurses. The orderlies had accepted her authority, so Flo told them, after one of their patients had fallen out of bed one night and broken his leg. But the Red Cross nurses were as dumb as stones, here for the glory of saying they were. Flo hated them, all society girls from Pittsburgh who flinched at the mere idea of changing a dressing.

"Hey, Flo," Gwen asked nonchalantly, "you awake? You want to go with us to get breakfast?"

"No."

"You need to," Pearl insisted. "You didn't touch your dinner last night."

"Not interested in that crap."

Gwen and Pearl passed each other a look.

"You can't go on like this, Flo," Gwen told her. "Come eat with us."

Flo whipped around and glared at the two of them. "I won't. Don't want to. Okay? Leave me alone."

"What if you talked with Dalton?" Gwen asked.

"Why? Is she going to give me a magic pill?" Flo sank back to her bed, facing the wall.

"You need to talk to someone."

"No. I. Do. Not."

"If those Red Cross girls are giving you shit, you need to whip their asses into shape!"

Flo reared back to stare at Gwen. "Golly. Listen to you."

"I wish you would."

"Go to hell."

Pushing her glasses up her nose, Pearl cleared her throat. "All right, kiddo, whatever the hell eats at you, you better get it out and over with. We're only going to get more casualties here and you can't be brooding when you need to be working. Cut this out."

"I can't."

"If you don't, you'll be shipped home."

"Good."

"You don't mean that," Gwen said. Flo might not be talkative or one to give wise cracks, but she was a smart, efficient nurse. Gwen had seen her croon to many a man who had lost an arm or leg and encourage him to buck up. Just last week, she'd heard Flo work with one man who'd awakened one dawn to rage at her that she'd robbed him of his boots and taken both feet with them. Flo had sat with him, gripped him in her arms as he sobbed in the realization of his new reality. "You can't, Flo."

"I can! I do!" Flo whirled around, sat up and flailed her arms. "I can't *do* this. The men come and come and come. The trail never ends! I'm learning new names, new conditions, new attitudes all the time. And as soon as one can accept what's happened to him, another wakes up, really comes to, and in a flash realizes he's got no arm or lost both legs, he's screaming and I'm running for the morphine. Night before last, one man sobbed all night long. Like a baby. Asking for forgiveness from his mother, for Christ's sake, as if he's to blame for the fact that the Germans shot him all to pieces. Last night, one of those goddamned planes flew over and the roof shook like a hundred tin cans. You heard it. I know you did."

"They're vicious," Pearl whispered, kneading her hands.

"You know what happened? The private in the last bed woke up, groping for his rifle, ready to shoot the plane, rolled out of bed and ran the length of the ward. Jesus, he has no arms! No arms! He stood in the middle of the floor and wailed like a stuck cow. We had to wrestle him to the floor. Tie him to his bed. Pump him full of morphine. Other men cried or cursed at him. Poor bugger. What happens if he does that again tonight? How in hell am I supposed to deal with that? Huh? Tell me!"

She shot up and crossed her arms, pacing like a woman possessed. "I thought I could do this. Be this…this saving grace. Thought I knew enough. But this is a nightmare! I can't cure these men. I can't even explain to them why they're cripples. I should be able to."

Pearl went to embrace her. "No, you—"

Flo shook her off. "What do you know? You only have to sedate them for a few days after Gwen gets finished chopping them up."

"That's not—" Gwen's stomach turned. She wanted to vomit.

"The hell it isn't! You don't have them weeping like children in your arms, asking you why they have to live their lives like this. You don't have to help them see that they're alive and that's the only answer."

Flo stood there, weaving, her tears running silently down her red cheeks. Then she crumpled like an old tent, sank to her bed and rocked in her misery.

Pearl and Gwen sat on either side of her and waited.

That morning was one of the longest in Gwen's life as the three of them mourned the losses of the men whose bodies they could only attempt to repair—whose minds the men themselves would have to find their own courage to save.

****

The next morning, Gwen emerged from the OR, stood before her barracks, and met the dark endearing gaze of Adam. Once again, he waited once for her in a chair he'd taken from the mess hall.

He shot to his feet. "I'm here for only an hour. But I had to see you. Your First Division is on the move to back our men near Soissons. There may be no time again soon when I could see you."

She took his hands and held them tightly. "Let me change. I'll be only a few minutes."

"Hurry."

They spent the hour at Armand's, drinking coffee and eating the morning's *baguettes*.

As they stood again in front of her quarters, he leaned over and kissed her on the forehead. "Take care of yourself."

"And you."

"I'll be safe. No more encounters with barbed wire

for me. But you? Here? If the Germans break through, you're in danger."

"You mustn't worry about me. I'm sure they'll pull us back in time."

He thought that over a long minute. "After this push, if we get it right and we're not on the run, I'm putting in for leave. You can, too. Come to Paris with me."

Paris. The city she'd told herself she'd see and hadn't. She'd glimpsed only a small part of France, the tiniest part of it in that operating room, her eyes trained on an eight-by-four table with little light and sometimes little hope for the patient beneath her hands. She needed to see something bigger and stronger, more full of life and hope. Before her stood the embodiment of a most alluring adventure. Days with Adam. Nights with Adam.

"I'll ask for it. I have time coming to me." *Time I need to spend with you.*

"Gwen, dear girl. You can change your mind. I won't rush you to Paris if you question we aren't—"

She put two fingers over his lips. He was so warm. His mouth so inviting. His words so dear. "I'll think it over. If I go, it's because I want to with my whole heart."

He kissed her fingertips. "Nothing less."

****

The battle of Cantigny tried everyone's patience. The skies had opened up two days ago, making the hospital grounds a swamp. The duckboard passages that the engineers put down to provide walkways were submerged under a foot or more of water.

The roof in Gwen's barracks leaked and pans under

the drips were the only help. To get to the different wards, she like the other nurses wore her boots, her floppy rain hat and her raincoat. In her operating room, the wounded came by the hordes. What had been a twelve-hour shift became eighteen and then twenty.

"Get the hell out of here, Spencer," O'Bryan barked at her on their third day. His eyes were bloodshot, his hands shook. "You reel where you stand."

She was certain she felt no better than he did. But she wouldn't leave him. "I know you'll stay. Work one more and one more. I go when you do."

"Stubborn."

"Yes, sir."

At least, she didn't smell whiskey on his breath. Who had time to drink? Or need? Oblivion came the second her head hit the pillow.

She had a flashing memory of Lex asking her if she smoked cigarettes. Hell. Maybe she'd try it. A woman had to do something to calm her nerves, didn't she?

She lit the newest gas lamp so that Doc might better view what he was doing.

And she smiled to herself. Soon she was going to Paris—and she'd have a different case of nerves.

****

Four days later, when only one ambulance arrived and the four wounded Doughboys inside were quickly dispatched to the care of her replacement shift, Gwen hoped this indicated a lull in the fighting. The rumor, sent down the line with the ambulance corps the past few days, was that the First Division had taken the hilltop village of Cantigny and run the Germans north. *They said if we held the line, if we could take the nearby town of Montdidier, then we could call it a victory.*

If they could rest a little more easily was the big question. *If we can get a good night's sleep is another!*

She washed up, removed her mask, then pushed open the door to the hall.

Doc O'Bryan stood there. "Want to talk with you, Spencer. Walk with me."

Still in his white blood-stained apron from surgery, he had not yet gone for his round of whatever the hell he drowned himself in each morning. He looked tired from the night's work, but that was nothing to how dramatically he had changed in the past few months. He had aged terribly. His gray hair was now shot with wide white streaks, his eyes were red, ringed by huge black circles. And occasionally, his hands trembled badly. During procedures, he noticed and would halt. In the last few nights, she had put her hand to his and he had winced, but calmed.

"Medical Corps has sent down a directive that we're to form teams to move closer to the front. I volunteered. I want you with me."

She had always been his right hand. *Sometimes his left, too.* "What does that mean?"

"We'll be in trucks. Live in tents. Operate in them. One, two, three miles from the front lines. It's dangerous, Spencer. The work will be…grueling. You have to commit to this with all you've got."

You, too. Can you? Will you stop drinking? "We'll be running with the troops?"

"As fast as they go, forward, back…"

"We'll have to be quick."

"Efficient."

Was he telling her he could go without his daily drunk? Whatever his answer, she couldn't let him go without her. Who would cover his lapses?

"Well?"

She gazed at her hands. Visions came to her of Anna and all the men whom she'd check on each morning in the post-op ward, men who had lain on their table, men they'd lost despite their devotion and skill, men they had saved. How could she do the best work if she refused to go forward to the line, to the limit of her abilities? "I'll go. I'll do it."

He put a hand to her shoulder, his tired gray eyes alight with pride. "Good old Spencer. Strong of mind and heart. We'll work hard and you'll learn more. I have aspirations for you."

"To offer me positions like this for the rest of my life?" she scoffed with good nature.

"No. Better ones. Have you ever thought you'd like to take the lead in that OR?"

He'd been working all night, every night, drinking all morning, every morning, but in that crush, he had also been speculating if she might want to become a surgeon?

She was speechless. And wildly excited. Yes. She had thought of that the night she had finished an intestinal section for him. Her neat little stitches had been a tidy sight.

"Think about it. But come with me. Tell Dalton. She chooses the nurses. Tell her. I already have said I need you."

"I will." Flustered, complimented, she heard someone say her name.

"There she is. Just knocking off her shift now," one

of the nurses told the soldier and nodding in Gwen's direction.

"Hello," she said to the private. "I'm Spencer. You needed me?"

"Yes, ma'am, I have this message for you. Captain Fairleigh said to deliver it to no one but you."

She took it from him with a decorum that belied the flutter in her belly. "Thank you, private."

"Captain says he needs an answer, ma'am. Today."

She read his handwriting, fat bold strokes done in haste. "Meet me. Tomorrow or within the next four days. Tell the runner, yes or no." He gave an address of a hotel in Paris, and signed it simply *Adam*.

"Can you wait for a few minutes, Private?"

He agreed and she told him she'd meet him in front of the base pharmacy near the main road.

She would have to get Dalton to agree to this. But as she went through the receiving area and found no one, then the surgical ward and into the amputee ward, she asked one of the men in the beds where the nurses had gone.

"Your matron came in and called them out to talk."

Gwen turned on her heel and headed for the nurses' mess hall where Dalton usually held her powwows.

But as she sloshed her way down the path to the meeting, Doughboys ran out of their tents. Laughing and slapping each other on the back, they looked like they had just won a thousand bucks.

"What's the commotion?" she asked one.

"You haven't heard?"

"No, what's going on?"

"We got Cantigny and now the plain! They're calling it for us! And those Huns said we couldn't fight.

Hell with them."

We won. It put a lift in her step and soon she was hurrying through the muck.

When she opened the door to the mess hall, she heard the strains of *Yankee Doodle Dandy* reverberate all around the camp. Even the nurses were singing.

Minutes later when she was able to have a private minute with Dalton and ask her for leave, the woman regarded her with a dire gaze. "Paris. Do you know how to get there?"

She nodded. "Yes, of course. I've heard from a few of the other nurses who've gone. I'll ask the Supply boys to take me to the train when they go down in the morning. Paula Dunbar told me which one to take and where to get off."

"Dunbar went with her cousin on their leave. You, I presume, travel alone?"

The woman's jaundiced eye was one that could have unnerved Gwen in days gone by. Not today. If she could stand all night operating on men with only a thread of hope to help them survive the hideous deformities this war had foisted on them, then she could face up to the moral question her matron posed. *This is my decision. To meet a man does not make me into a less worthy creature. It makes me human. Taking what joy I have found.* "Yes, ma'am. I go alone."

"But you meet someone, don't you?"

Dalton had no right to ask her who she met or why. Nor could she deter her. She wanted this…freedom. She wanted this man. "I do. I'll be safe."

"You must wear your uniform on the street at all times."

"Yes, ma'am."

"The uniform entitles you to travel for a third of the cost, but it also sets you apart as someone who is to be respected."

"I know. I'll wear it." Gwen heard the note of concern in Dalton's tone. The woman did not want her to be hurt by falling in love with a man who would break her heart. Gwen had to know, had to learn what she felt for him. And her uniform was hardly satisfactory attire for a rendezvous. *But what else do I have to wear anyway? Nothing I brought with me would be even halfway interesting to an accomplished, complicated man who must have had a dozen sweethearts.*

"You are entitled to twelve days. But I cannot give it to you."

Gwen opened her mouth to object.

Dalton put up her hand. "We're gearing up for a run, changing the way we work and I will need your stability. And Doctor O'Bryan...is not well. He does better with you...and he needs your expertise."

"He told me about the mobile units. Ma'am, I'll return, but I must go."

"This British captain means that much to you?"

"Yes." Dalton had seen them dancing. Had she learned that Adam visited her here? She should not be surprised. Everyone on base talked like a bunch of magpies. O'Bryan drank. Flo had acquired an *ennui*, hating her ward duties and sinking further into a silent fury. Pearl was infatuated by *comte* Valentin Chatillon, who courted her despite her every blasé objection to his suit. Now Adam Fairleigh wanted to take her to Paris— and she wanted to go, to kiss him, to learn if this marvelous thrill she felt for him were foolish and fleeting. She was entitled to do that, old enough, if perhaps not terribly wise enough to deal with the consequences. "He does."

With compassion in her eyes, Dalton warned her of the danger here. "Be careful, Spencer. I cannot afford to lose you."

"You won't. This," she said with a look around, "is where I've always been meant to be."

The older woman shut her eyes a second. "Very well. I'll write you a pass for three days. I want you back here by your shift on Thursday night."

Chapter Eleven

The train she boarded at Meaux resembled the one she'd ridden from St. Nazaire like night from day. No nurses on this one. No available seats. But crammed to the windows and doors with French peasants carrying small carpetbags and French *poilus* in their muddy blue uniforms, smelling still of the trenches, clumps of earth stuck to their boots. A few American Doughboys rode, standing up, whether on leave or running messages, she did not ask but kept to herself.

The ride was slow, but uninterrupted by the delays and changes of track and trains she had encountered when she arrived in France. She stood the whole way, blessing her hours of practice in the surgery. She didn't care about the discomfort or the eternity it seemed to take to arrive at *Gare de l'Est*.

She walked out onto the *quai*, drifting at first with the crowds toward the center hall, the huge glass dome above her letting in gray light. Inside, people milled about. Many looked as lost as she. They were dispossessed. Refugees from the fighting in the north, they carried all their worldly goods. Small satchels of clothes hurriedly collected and shoved inside, fabric bursting at the seams. One little girl carried her doll. A boy held a chicken, the poor animal as dazed with fatigue as his little owner. Old men and women, weary, in rags, on the verge of silent despair and begging for a coin to keep them going.

This side of war was as heartless as the one she saw on her table. She rushed outside, eager for fresh air, different air. There on the sidewalk, the rain poured down in sheets. She hailed a taxi and showed the driver Adam's note with the address.

Minutes too soon to collect her thoughts or rev her courage, he pulled up to a hotel. A doorman opened the taxi door for her while she paid the driver. Scurrying in under the portico, she walked inside. Her skin prickled at the grandeur. She was so very out of place.

Cut glass windows and chandeliers dotted the foyer. Thick vermilion carpet lay beneath her feet. The walls gleamed of polished white marble and this was no place for her. She expected a small establishment, discreet, where no one would know she had come and gone. But as she stood in the middle of the lobby and surveyed the patrons who sat here and there in settees or in the circular velvet couches, she breathed more easily. No one knew her here. They would see only the uniform and know an American nurse had met a British officer. They'd never know her. Soon forget her. *After all, out there not fifty miles away, men went to a slaughter they never predicted so that others might be free to walk in their chosen paths. Surely then, I can come here with all my good intentions and never be beholden to any one.*

She debated if she should ask the reception clerk for the room of Captain Fairleigh when at the far corner she saw Adam stand. He wore his uniform, crisp and beribboned. Debonair. His hat, he hooked under his arm. He threw a newspaper aside, put glasses in his inside pocket and beamed at her as he walked toward her.

He took her hands in his, the forest green depths of his gaze flashing with eagerness and apology. "You look wonderful. I hope the trip was not dreadful."

"Not that, no. But sad. All those people dispossessed, lost to themselves."

He looked at her hands, thumbed the edges of her nails. "Let's not speak of them. I don't want to spoil this with words, things we already know."

"Yes, you're right, of course."

"I'm so glad you're here. I worried that you'd change your mind."

"No. I told you if I came, I would be committed."

One of his brows dipped. "The sound of that makes this sound like a mission."

She sniffed and straightened her spine. "Maybe I'm so new at this, I can't describe it well. You can understand my discomfort. Can we leave the lobby, please?"

"Are you hungry? Thirsty? There is a wonderful bistro around the corner and I already know the *maitre d'* very well."

"Did you tell him you had invited a woman to share your hotel room with you?"

"No. I didn't want to jinx it and disappoint him— or myself."

"Do you have wine in your room?"

"Is that what you'd like? Wine? In our room?"

She noticed the difference in his words, his hesitation, his longing, his endearing chivalry. Without debating, she told him yes. "That's what I'd like."

He looped her hand through his arm and led her toward the gilded elevator. The lift was tiny and they stood, their hips and thighs touching, her heart flooding with romantic expectations meant for some other woman. Surely not her. Could she be so lucky?

When the conveyance jostled to a stop, Adam pushed back the caged door and led her down the hall. At the last room, he paused, extracted a key from his pocket and turned the lock.

Inside—*oh, my*—the appointments were much grander than she'd expected. Expensive red velvet draperies, frilly white lace curtains behind. A red damask coverlet on a huge bed. Pale white walls. A chaise longue covered in a chintz with a riot of red roses. The lobby should have provided a hint, of course, but who was thinking?

"This is very elaborate," she said to him, rooted to her spot near a table where he had laid the key and his hat.

"I'm glad you like it." His gaze drifted over her as if he thought her a mirage. "We have a bathroom, too."

"Really?" He recalled how she had complained of the lack on base. Overcome with his thoughtfulness, she set down her suitcase.

"Through there." He indicated the far door. "All the things you need. A huge sink. Commode. A tub."

A tub. Heaven. "May I see?"

He strode forward and took her hand to lead her into a large black and white tiled room where on one side stood a huge claw-footed affair.

"My lord." Her hand went to her throat. "I don't think I've seen anything quite so lovely."

His eyes gleamed. "I haven't either. You, your joy,

I mean."

She left him in the center of the bath then. Wandering into the bedroom, she surveyed the bed. Fit for a king, a queen and maybe more. She smiled and told herself to smarten up. When she turned, he stood in the middle of the Turkish carpet and he looked as lost as the little boy she'd seen on the train.

She wasn't lost, but found, right to be here. Down in her bones, she understood it to be so. "When you left me the first time you told me to keep something for you."

He blinked, hope and desire flaring in his eyes.

"I have it."

"Do you?"

She took the few steps to stand right before him. "Quite a few, as a matter of fact."

Gwen, he breathed her name.

She sent her hands over the lapels of his uniform, up around his shoulders and sifting into his silken hair. How exquisite he felt. So much more enthralling than she had predicted. Against his lips, she tried to express how she had yearned for him. "You must tell me if they're good enough. I've never kissed a man before."

He wrapped his arms around her, his thighs braced against hers, his strength the most vivid red aura in her world.

She reached up and brushed her lips on his. His mouth fell open. Met hers. And melded and crushed and took and returned all the fervor, all the desire she had locked inside her imagination. "You taste better than I dreamed."

He made some ungodly sound, then bent to pick her up in his arms and lay her crossways on the bed.

"You must have more of me then."

He took her mouth, over and over, a ravenous exploration of tongue and teeth and all her inhibitions. "We should have dined," he said against her ear. "We should have seen the city."

She took his hand. "But why?"

"Because now that we're on this bed, I may ravish you and never let you up."

She squeezed him tighter. "Oh, wonderful." She wrinkled her nose at him. "Except we have one tiny problem."

Still off balance, he searched her eyes for answers. "What's that? Tell me. I'll get it. Fix it."

"You still have on your uniform."

He laughed at the ceiling. Relief flooded his features and suddenly he became her beau again. Her man. "Darling, if I take this off, there's no putting it back on for ages and ages."

"That's what I hoped."

"Did you?" He thumbed her lower lip. "And then you'll have to remove yours."

"I hoped that, too."

He trailed kisses down her throat. "Gwen, there is so much of you to enjoy, sweetheart. And I don't want to shock you."

"You can't."

He seized her hand and pressed it to the placket of his fly. Beneath the wool, he was long and hot and iron hard. "I can."

"Oh, Adam. What you have, sweetie, I've already seen. A thousand times. A thousand men. None of them was you...wanting me." She skimmed her fingertips over his brows, his nose, his cheeks, his full enticing lips. "I want to see you needing me. Charming you, wanting Gwen Spencer."

Tears dotted his lashes. "I can do that. I was made, I think by God, to do just that."

Pulling her to her feet, he carefully undid his jacket and shirt. His trousers and small clothes. His shoes and socks.

Naked as God made him, he was perfection. Her hands drifted up of their own free will to caress the breadth of his shoulders, the corded columns of his throat and his biceps. She counted his ribs, a rack of virile bones, so straight. His waist, tapered. His hips, lean with a line of muscle that led straight down to his groin and his body's declaration that he wanted her. Wanted her.

She closed her eyes.

He took it as his cue to unclothe her. The jacket, the blouse, her skirt, her shoes and socks, her slip, her bra and her step-ins. As she had done with him, he treasured what he discovered. He did it with his hands and his lips, with his small inarticulate declarations of how he enjoyed what he found.

And so did she. She loved his gentle touch of her clavicle, his caress of her arms. His warm hands that cupped her heavy breasts and his mouth that blessed the tips and melted her into liquid desire as he sank to his knees. He murmured about her beauty and she reveled in his praise. He shocked her and she wanted more. She went willing, aware that she inched to a precipice of mindlessness. Aware this must be bliss, she welcomed his caresses as he nuzzled her belly, kissed her hips and parted her thighs to kiss her there, *there* where she'd never imagined a man's mouth would ever be.

He scooped her up then, walked with her into the bath, sat on the bench and turned on the spigots to the tub. And as she lay in his arms, he kissed her lips and her eyes, her cheeks and the tips of her aching nipples.

He helped her to stand, dazed as she was from his kisses, and then led her to dip her toe in the water. "Tell me if it's too warm."

"It's perfect," she said, tugging on his hand, "but only if you come in here with me. Please."

He stepped in, sinking down with her into the luxurious warmth and wrapping his arms and legs around her. There he held her back against his chest and kissed her nape and shoulder, fondled her and petted her until she was afire to have him.

"Will you never make love to me?" she beseeched him.

"Now." He cupped her chin, kissed her frantically, then helped her to stand. "Now I will and hope to God to never let you go."

****

They left their bed for dinner and afterward, immediately returned to it. They emerged for breakfast and a walk in the park across the street during a break in a rainstorm. They strolled, arm in arm, no need for words, replete. When he kissed her beneath the pink buds of a tulip tree, she let tears declare her ecstasy of what they were together. He brushed them away and led her down the boulevard where he bought a small bouquet of purple pansies from a crippled vendor. Back upstairs in their room, he undressed her, laid her down and kissed her until she gasped with pleasure.

He took her into the bath again, ran the water, and this time, he did not climb in but washed her tenderly, slowly. Helping her to stand, he wrapped her in one of the towels, dried her down as if she were his charge and scooped her up. In their bedroom, he sat in the chaise and pulled her into his arms.

"Tell me about your aunt and your sister. Your parents. I want to know more about you."

"Some of it is not pretty."

He toyed with locks of her hair, his lips pressed against her crown. "I could have guessed. You are so young, darling. Yet older than your years. Tell me."

She began, praying it did not sound like some litany of woes. The years of injustices, the slights, the illogic of how her aunt had treated them all and driven her away were perverse to her. Ordinarily, she didn't share such facts, lest she sound like a child. But what had happened had provided her motivation to leave the house, her family, her sister, and then, in many ways, to find the courage to come abroad. Then she told him about Doc's need to have her with him on the front lines. Though Adam visibly balked, he did not object but held her more tightly. She wanted him to understand she was an average woman, so she thought, doing the next most beneficial thing for herself and her future. "I don't like pity and I don't want—"

He waited for her to find the right words, his sweet eyes drifting over her own.

"Help. I want to earn what I get. Go where I am needed, wanted, appreciated."

He hugged her so close she could hardly breathe.

"And you?" She gazed up at him, her cheek to his solid chest. "Who is Adam?"

He brushed a finger over her lip. "He is Gwen Spencer's lover."

"He is," she breathed. "And good at it, too."

A corner of his mouth lifted, but he glanced away to consider middle space.

Gwen panicked, his dispassion and reluctance to reveal facts about himself creating a hole in her perception of him.

"I am an invention of my class, my family. My father is an earl. Fourteenth of his line."

A frisson of dismay ran up her back and she tried not to freeze.

He noticed and caught her gaze. "He is a fine man, really."

Yes, but sons of earls do not mix with daughters of coal miners. Not in England.

"He's a good manager of the estates, a stout-hearted fellow with many friends. My mother is an arbiter of taste in London and in the country. She dresses, she dines, she deigns to recognize which ladies will enter her coveted circle of select friends. Don't mistake me. She was a loving mother, saving all her sweetness for the family, to our benefit, thank God." He lifted Gwen's chin and kissed the tip of her nose. "You would love her."

Gwen wanted to believe that.

"I have a younger sister, twenty-four, wearing widow's weeds. Poor Natalie, married in bliss for only a few months before her Trevor went to the trenches. Now? I'm afraid she parties too often with a fast crowd and my parents despair of her future. Nat'll come round, though. She does have a head on her shoulders.

"As for me, I am the second son without a hold on the estate. When my father passes on, my older brother, George, takes the title and all the work of the farms and renters. Good luck to him, I wouldn't want it. Such a bore."

He inhaled, as if he sorted his own thoughts about how to continue. "I went into the Army because that is what the spare son does. I never questioned it. Never thought about it. When I went to university in Germany, that was my own deviation from the norm. I returned after I got this in a thoughtless duel. A bet. Glad I didn't lose my sight." He touched his scarred eyebrow.

"I went to Sandhurst. Got my commission two years before we declared war. Because I speak fluent German, I was posted to Berlin. Military attaché, a ceremonial post but useful for gathering snippets of intelligence. Whetted my appetite for it, I must say. Later, I went to B.E.F. headquarters in London and since America declared war, I have been Pershing's man in his G2."

Somehow, his speech seemed too cursory, as if he rehearsed it. And if he did, why? The very idea such a speech might be necessary frightened her. Yet she couldn't fathom why.

Tucking it away for a later exploration, she curled into his embrace. "And do you like this work?"

"As you say of yourself, it's what I'm good at. Where I am needed and appreciated."

He had sidestepped her question and she thought it best to let it pass. After all, he performed a delicate function, and she was not entitled to know the details of what his job was. Only this outline was hers to hear. So be it.

"And why are you not married?"

He arched a wicked brow at her. "Do I detect you

wish to know my romantic past?"

"I do."

"There was never anyone I loved. No one until you."

She adored his confession, let it fill all the hollows of her heart with tenderness she had so sorely missed in her life. "How is that possible? A man like you? From a good family. How old are you?"

"Twenty-eight."

"My God, you *are* old."

He tickled her mercilessly and she squealed. Her towel dislodged and fell away. "Old enough to make love to you."

"*Again?*" She chuckled, feigning outrage.

He whirled her under him. "Do you object?"

She flung her arms around his neck, at once contrite and eager for him inside her. "No. I want all you wish to give me."

"Gwen," he said, his hand cupping her jaw, "when this is over—"

"No, don't, please talk of that." She had meant all he had to give her here, now. Today she could control. But forever? That loomed too large, too dangerous an expanse.

"I can't bear to think I might not have you after all these years searching for you."

His endearment squeezed her heart with joy. "Have you been? Searching for me, I mean."

"Yes, I never knew it until I saw you in that hospital. It was as if you were all my yearnings put into this beautiful body, this gorgeous and talented and dedicated woman." He ran his hand through her curls and brushed his lips on hers. "Each time I see you, I want to savor you and applaud you and—"

His compliments could overwhelm her common sense. She mustn't allow that. She'd be absorbed, consumed by him. She'd learned the importance of standing on her own two feet, not beholden to anyone. "Don't ascribe qualities to me that may not be so."

"I could say the same to you."

"You could." That he could think her more noble or wise or smart than she was scared her. "What do you think I am?"

"Mine. Are you mine?"

That made her smile. She was a fool to agree. She had always felt wholly, solely her own. But she adored him for his largesse, his unerring gallantry. She owed him a few words he could treasure. Not a declaration of love but as close to it as she dare. "I am."

His eyes narrowed to slits. He examined her for so long that he tipped his head in question.

The time dragged out—and she understood he wanted more. He wanted words to cement what they could become for each other when, in fact, she knew it wise to have ones only for the present.

"You can't say it, can you?" His nostrils flared. He was hurt, angry.

Yet she had promised him nothing but honesty. "I'm not that brave."

"What is it you fear?" He sounded almost incredulous.

Cornered, she turned her head away from him. "That the war won't ever end. That we'll all be here stuck in this mire until we're old and gray. That you'll stop loving me or I'll lose you to—to No Man's Land or a shell or—" She remembered Flo and the man who'd gone berserk in her ward. "Or some man who goes crazy with despair!"

"You won't lose me."

That appalled her. Roiled her. "You can't promise me that. You have no right to try."

He stared at her. The despair she had seen in his face the first moment they met reappeared. He had seen worse than she. Had walked it, crawled through it, subsisted in the dregs of hell. And she had brought the visions back for him. "I see. May I hope for anything for us after the war is over?"

For moments, her mind spun. She had not thought beyond this moment. This excitement. This rendezvous.

Tears cascaded down her temples. She had lost her mother and father, that was one thing to lose them as a child. But she had lost patients. Here in this strange place where cannon roared and men came to her so broken and torn that she'd kept her mind averted even if she could not avert her eyes. She had helped to save hundreds. But lost scores of them. Men she had labored over, prayed over, cheered for to no avail. She had pumped into her veins a resolution to never care so much for each one…and she had failed. Now to love one man was a rapture and a crime. "I hope so. But I don't know how that can be."

He threaded his hands through her curls and rocked her in his arms. "Don't think of it. I'll find a way."

She heard him, but did not believe him. How could she? The noble Englishman and the nurse from a small town thousands of miles away. Then she cried. Liberally, never stopping until she had drained her head of whatever the argument had been. She wanted sleep, to forget, to rest and he led her to the bed where she did.

The lights of Paris glimmered through the lace curtains when she awakened. Adam stood by the window, in silhouette, looking out. From his stance, she saw he brooded.

"Come to bed," she asked of him. "I'm lonely here and cold without you."

He slid in beside her, his naked body long and strong against her own. Gathering her close, he kissed her and stroked her hair. "Go to sleep. You need rest for the push that's coming."

Her heart ached that he seemed to accept her injunction not to press her for a commitment to him. But she would not promise fantasies.

****

The next morning, they went out to dine on coffee and croissants. The sun dazzled, refracting off the raindrops clinging to the tree leaves. A few solitary tulips bloomed, crimson and purple among the lime green tufts of grass. He held her hand. They sat in silence. He smiled politely and briefly at her now and then.

But their rendezvous had progressed too far from a madly romantic one to a realistic love affair. She had no idea what to say to him, uncertain how to explain to him her motivations. She could not even explain to herself these new, uncanny fears. His life was suddenly too precious to her—and she loathed her knowledge that she could lose him to any number of outrageous misfortunes.

They returned to their room and she undressed frantically. Naked, needing him once more, she saw he would not remove his clothes so she did it for him.

Then she led him to their bed. He allowed her to welcome him into her arms and then he made love to her with an intensity that blinded her. This time, they did not speak, but used their lips and hands to offer up the eloquent despair they could not say aloud.

She rose to fill the tub. He did not follow and she was quick about it. When she emerged, he sat on the edge of the mattress to watch her as she picked up her clothes.

Buttoning up her jacket, she bit her lips. Ready for the argument he would give her, she picked up her hat and twirled it round and round. "Don't come with me to the station. I need to leave alone." *I'll cling to you like a grieving child if you accompany me.*

He nodded once.

"Will you kiss me goodbye?"

"Do you want me to?"

"Yes. Please." *One more memory I can treasure.*

He stood, a strong man in build, elegant and honed as a marble statue, his face a wreck of despair. But as he strode toward her, naked and beautiful, his expression turned fierce. This man who stalked her was all steel, forged in a cauldron of circumstance and determination. He pulled her against him to take her lips once more and brand her as his own. "I will see you again."

"I don't know where I'll be—" She tore herself away from him, cursing her cowardice to commit to him.

"I'll find you, Gwen. I'll always find you."

Chapter Twelve

June 20,1918

Dear Gwen,

Big news! Helen has accepted Mr. McIntosh's proposal. They'll be married next Saturday in church. Helen is so happy. And Mr. McIntosh seems like a swell fellow.

Win is to be his best man. And Helen has asked me to stand up for her and carry her bouquet. She told Mr. McIntosh she wants lilies and he told her he would buy her an arm full of them. Isn't that wonderful?

I am off to visit the Learners. My piano lesson is today and Herr Schuler says I have a gift for playing. Imagine that. I am happiest on the keys.

Did you know that Will has joined up? I can't remember if I told you when I wrote my last letter to you. But he has. Mr. and Mrs. Learner are not happy with him because he could have gone to Yale just like Lex did. But Will told me he had to go and do his duty, just like Lex and you. I am afraid for him. He leaves next week for camp. I wish the war would end and all of you would not have to be

217

so far away.
Love to you. Be safe.

Susannah

Gwen crushed the letter. Helen was marrying the owner of the store where she worked? He had to be twice her age. An even-tempered man, a good businessman, yes, but a widower and not terribly attractive. Whereas Helen was a beauty, delicately wrought, fair as a daffodil. She could have had any young man. *Why Edward McIntosh? Why now?*

Gwen let the letter flutter to her mattress, the most recent of the six she'd received from her sister at this morning's mail call. From the postmarks, they'd been lost somewhere in France for months while Gwen had fretted that her aunt had prohibited the girl from corresponding with her. Her delight at receiving them washed away on her wave of dismay at Helen's marriage. Had Mary incited Helen to this drastic measure? Or had Helen, in some stroke of outrage, seen the possibilities to escape her mother's domination, and wrongfully accepted the man's proposal as her only road to freedom?

Oh, Helen.

Gwen nibbled her lower lip. Helen had it in her to do this. She could be led, influenced. Had Mr. McIntosh seduced her? Gwen winced, not having anticipated that in his character. But who couldn't love Helen? She was a kind girl, sweet, silently suffering under the demands of her mother. Would a man appear to be her saving grace?

And now that I am not there to—
Stop that.
For two years when I was in training, I was not

218

there day in and out to stop Mary from her tirades, her injunctions.

Why pride myself now that I was the strongest block in any bulwark against Mary's demands?

Helen has done as she thought best. And I am thousands of miles away.

Gwen glanced at the postmark on Susannah's last letter. Helen was already Mrs. McIntosh. Had been for more than two weeks. There was nothing Gwen could do about her cousin's decision.

Sighing, sad and sorry for herself and for Helen, Gwen stepped outside her barracks. For once, the skies were clear. The moon hung low and shockingly opaque in the black velvet expanse. To the north, the horizon glowed in a thin red line and the pounding guns punctuated the night with their thunder.

Tomorrow she would leave with Doc O'Bryan, the anesthetist Therese Reynard and a special surgical team of four others for that ridge of red. How close they would go to it was a determination of their chief medical officer and his cohort, a quartermaster of the front line. Gwen yearned to go, she loathed to stay.

What had she signed up for?

Shivering, she clutched her elbows and abhorred the chattering of her teeth. She'd never been afraid before. Oh, hell, of course she had. After Anna died, she'd come to a few hard terms with the possibility. Since her arrival in France, she'd become accustomed to her routine and now she had volunteered for this front line duty and so increased her odds of never going home. Ironic, really, when she had reasons to live a long and happy life. A profession she loved. A man she loved...

What was she thinking?

She winced and shook her head at her decision to join this mobile unit. A *groupe complémentaire*, after the French model of transported hospital units, this unit moved quickly to war-torn battlefronts. With one surgeon, his assistant, an anesthetist, two nurses and two orderlies, it offered speedy surgery to those men most grievously wounded. Orders were that patients with head, chest or abdominal wounds were to be operated on within three to eight hours of their front line injuries. Gwen had seen hideously wounded men in her time here. Now she would see them sooner. In worse shape. Some without morphine. Some with only a scrap of dressings. And she had volunteered for this because she thought herself able to meet the challenge. But now, she was afraid. Afraid she would fail, afraid she would crack, afraid she would die.

She clamped a hand to her mouth to stop her sob.

Hearing from Susannah today had brought home her responsibility to her sister. After all, she could stay here in her base hospital, work in the OR at nights without O'Bryan and still be useful. She could tell the team she had second thoughts. As she had gone through the specialized training these past few weeks, the CO had emphasized that any of the volunteers could back out if they wished. This was hazardous duty.

"No cake walk," he'd said. "Step down now. You won't be able to once you're up the line."

If she went to his billet tonight and told him, she could stay here in her own hospital, and still learn from the other surgeons. Assist them. Let O'Bryan go to the front with another surgical nurse as his assistant. Why not?

Why?

Because I want to know what happens up there. Because I hate what I see, wonder how men destroy others, how men witness it and do not lose their minds.

She ran her hands over her face and stared at the moon. She had to go. Call it mad. Call it morbid. Call it need. Raw, itching need.

Because I am drawn to what can be remedied. What can be repaired. What can be mended. By my own hand.

Silliness to be so proud! But she had raised her hand, committed herself to this and now she was honor-bound to fulfill her promise to the men she might aid.

Resolved, satisfied with her decision, she marched down toward the village. She checked her watch. Ten o'clock. All who had leave tonight or were off-duty had gone earlier to the village *estaminet* to drink wine and sing. She should have gone with Pearl and the *comte* when they invited her earlier. A little carousing would have taken her mind off her troubles.

"*Bon soir, Mademoiselle Spencer!*" *comte* Chatillon greeted her from across the smoke-filled room. He flung out his arm wide to beckon her to him, then took tight hold of his *Perle*. "Sit here. *Rouge* or *blanc?*"

"*Rouge.*" She'd welcome the rich red tonight. Who knew when she would have any of it again?

The Count poured her a small glass and motioned for Pearl to slide over the board of *chèvre* and pieces of a baguette.

"Didn't think you would come," Pearl said, sipping her own wine. "Thought you wanted to pore over those letters."

"Changed my mind. Good news mixed with bad makes me want to drink."

The Count pulled out a package of cigarettes from his coat pocket and extracted one. "You must have more than one glass then and perhaps a smoke?"

She nodded and took one from his crumpled blue package. "Tonight is my night to try it. *Merci.*"

Pearl groaned. "Don't Gwen. Really. That is the most horrible stuff."

"Enough!" He admonished her gaily. "She must know what it is to go up in flames."

Memories of Adam had her grinning at her two friends. "I already know a few ways. This should be child's play." Gwen bent to him as he struck a match for her.

Pearl scoffed. "Don't listen to her. She volunteers for front line duty and she gets light in the head. A crazy woman. She curses, she drinks, and now she smokes! It will be the end of her."

Gwen drew on the lit cigarette and rolled her eyes at her friend.

"A crazy woman is one who lives to the fullest!" The *comte* leaned over and nuzzled Pearl on her neck. "I expect she has learned much from you in that regard."

The thick smoke burned a fiery path down Gwen's throat—and she coughed.

Pearl giggled and pushed him a discreet distance away. "I have taught her nothing."

Gwen hacked, a hand to her chest. She'd never imagined smoking could kill her!

The Count dismissed Pearl's idea with a wink. "Thank God. She would have disappeared on us!"

Gwen gasped for air. "Hell! The cigarette—What *is* that?"

The man grinned like a fool. "Good French *tabac*, my Spencer."

Gwen could not catch her breath, and held out the cigarette for him to take from her.

He was chuckling, lifting his handkerchief to her mouth. "Cough, *ma petite*. You will feel better."

"You should not have given her that, Val."

"Nonsense. You see, she is fine. Are you not?" He rubbed Gwen's shoulders.

"*Oui*, wonderful. Although I may never eat or drink again."

"Nonsense. The *poilus* in the trenches demand the black *tabac*. It keeps them sane. Ready for battle."

"If smoking these doesn't kill them, then I'd say they're primed to fight the Bosch," Gwen told him, reaching for another draught of the red wine to line her throat.

"What time do you leave in the morning?" Pearl asked.

"Ten."

"Enough time to have a decent night's sleep. I am pea green with envy."

Pearl still worked the night shift in the post-op ward and she was becoming good at sleeping through any ruckus during the day. After suppertime, though, she was up and ready for the night, usually here with Val, drinking wine with him, or in his tiny house, making love to him.

"When the war is *fini*," Val said as he chewed a bit of bread, "I am not certain you will be able to sleep at night."

"Oh?" Pearl lifted both brows high, so uncharacteristically *femme fatale* for one bright second. "Do you want me to?"

Cursing, he hauled her close and kissed her. "She toys with me, this one," he said to Gwen. "Is she this way with you?"

Gwen twirled her wine glass. "You mean, does she tell me one thing one day and another the next?"

"*Exactement.*"

"No. To me she says what she means." Gwen switched her gaze from Val to Pearl. Her friend scowled, drawing patterns in the red checked tablecloth with her nail. "You will have to give her an ultimatum."

"I see." He scowled, unhappy with that order. "I want her to be bold, strong. Change her life."

Is that so? Gwen tried to catch Pearl's gaze. She would not do it. "How so?"

"She tells me she hates Scranton, Pennsylvania."

Ah. Did that mean that Val didn't want Pearl to return there? "It doesn't match Paris."

"This can be a lovely place, too, when there is no war," Val said with pride and a touch of sorrow. He had explored a future with Pearl? Here?

"Stop, Val. Please." Pearl sniffed, pretending insult, yet not a little undone by his persistence.

So. Pearl is conflicted about love. That, I understand. "I should go. Let you two talk."

"No. Stay." Pearl said, sliding off her chair. "I'm leaving."

"You're going back already?" Gwen glanced at her watch, wishing she herself had not entered this conversation. "It's early. Oh, please, Pearl."

"I can't stay."

Val put a hand atop Gwen's. "She does not mean she cannot stay here with you tonight. She means she cannot stay here with me after the war."

What?

Pearl's eyes filled to the brim with tears. "You don't know what you're asking." And then she grabbed her cape and hurried out the door.

Gwen and Val stared after her.

"Tonight, I asked her to marry me, Gwen. She refuses me." He sounded hollow, as if he faded from the little café like a ghost into the still night.

At last Gwen found words. "She may have reasons."

"Not one. She has no husband at home. No child. No attachment. Or does she?"

"No." Pearl had never spoken of a beau. "She has her mother and father, both well. But no brother or sister."

No Susannah waiting at home.

"She must marry me then. She has no reason to return. I live to see her each day. She gives me laughter. And I had lost that, lost it in this deluge. I must have her after the war is over."

May I hope for anything for us after the war is over? In the past few weeks, she replayed Adam's question to her as if it were a record on the Victrola.

My circumstances are not Pearl's.

Gwen shoved back her chair, scraping the wooden floor with an ear-splitting shriek. "Forgive me, Val. I cannot listen." She squeezed his hand. "Ask her again. She loves you. Ask her again."

****

At ten the next morning, half the base hospital staff

225

showed up to send them off. Gwen shifted from foot to foot, uneasy at the hullaballoo. This was no occasion for revelry or congratulations. She didn't want the recognition, either, and that was what was about to happen.

The hospital CO had requested a receiving line. All mobile unit personnel lined up in front of their vehicles. The CO, who was an administrative sort who never walked the wards, worked the formal line like he was at one of Pershing's dances. Chatting with this one, smiling at that one, he took forever to reach her.

"Spencer," he read her name tag. "Good of you to volunteer for this. Not a picnic, you know. Means you will be required to show our wounded boys how to carry on."

"Yes, sir." *I know more than you. When were you last in the OR, sir? When have you ever walked the amputee ward? Or talked with any of our boys with facial ticks and violent dreams?*

Thankfully, he soon passed on to the next nurse. Therese Reynard, who had joined up with them in Scranton and become a new fast friend of Gwen's, appeared to curl her lip, not thrilled with the CO's pap, either.

At last, he dismissed them and it was time to say goodbye to Pearl and Flo. Both, as usual, had worked the night shift in their wards. Both, as ever after twelve hours on their feet running a staff of twenty, looked like hell. They were losing weight, hollows in their cheeks, a more somber maturity to their demeanor. Pearl was dealing better with her duty among her post op patients. She had finally whipped her subordinates into an efficient team of whom she was proud. Flo, too, had managed to improve her unit by requesting a transfer of two of her nursing staff to the contagion ward. To four others, she had given private instruction in the art of administering the hypodermic. Her amputees still woke up, horrified at their altered physiques, wailing at the injustices of how they were to live the rest of their lives. But Flo coped with their shock, offering as much sympathy as perspective. She did not take to her bed each day with despair. Recently, she had purchased a bike in the village and rode each evening before dinner. Her eyes were brighter. Her skin glowed. Last week, after a rainstorm, she returned to get them for supper and told them she'd seen the most beautiful rainbow.

"I will miss you both something awful," Gwen told them as the three of them huddled together. Tears burned her eyes. "Promise me you will be kind to *monsieur le comte, ma Perle*."

The woman laughed through her tears. "He is nothing but a problem. It is you who must be kind to yourself."

Pearl had argued with Gwen when she told them she would volunteer for the mobile surgical team. *Too dangerous. Too far up the line, Gwen.* But Gwen had reassured her this was what she needed to do, even if she could not quite describe why except in vague and glowing terms that made her sound more noble than she intended. Her need to go and see and do this was a compulsion she had to feed. A desire she had to serve. How could she explain to her dearest friends that her need to go forward was ingrained in her personality? Just as she had had to stop picking coal and scrubbing floors, just as she had to go into training and come to France, she had to go forward. Somehow *forward* was not a destination, not a frightening place, but instead a goal she had to reach. A mission she had to experience to understand. Who would understand that? Even eloquence would fail her. She would keep her own counsel.

She cupped Flo's cheeks. "Keep riding that bicycle and finding rainbows."

Flo broke into a sob and threw her arms around Gwen. "You must look for them. *You*! Wherever you are."

"I will. And each time I'll think of you."

"You will come back to us," Pearl said, tears dribbling down her cheeks.

Gwen nodded like a fool. "For leave, yes, if we get any. We'll go find the *Vin* Sisters together, I promise."

Pearl wiped her eyes. "Flo and I will have to train a new tent mate. They'll send us some brat who'll whine that she can't wash her hair in her helmet. And then she'll get cooties. We'll have to cut her hair and burn her clothes."

"Heaven help her."

"Let's mount up!" A colonel sitting high on a large butternut quarter horse grinned down at the two hundred men and nurses who had signed up to move closer to the front lines.

Gwen hugged her friends once more, lifted her suitcase and marched to their convoy.

This cadre was the new face of Army medical care and as Gwen looked at her cohorts, she warmed with pride for them. Her unit, the mobile surgical team, would receive the most severe cases first. Right behind her unit, the mobile hospital would take her team's post-op patients and perform secondary care, then later hand off those recovering quickly to a larger group, dubbed an evacuation hospital. All of them would charge into action immediately after the carpet barrage of a new battle. But those closest would be Gwen's team a mile or two behind the Doughboys. Immediately behind cannon fire and machine guns, bayonets and grenades that ripped and tore and destroyed beautiful young men's bodies.

That knowledge this morning had made the very thought of breakfast turn her stomach. In fact, she had huddled near the latrine for over an hour. Out of breath. Pulse racing. Dry heaving. Never vomiting. Truly, she went forward with nothing inside her but her resolve.

How many Doughboys went to their first battle in precisely the same condition?

More than we'll ever know.

Gwen piled into the transport truck assigned to the nurses. There were only thirty-one of them. Twenty-two for the evacuation hospital and two each for the three mobile units. Each of the three nurse anesthetists rode with the surgical nurses. Meanwhile, all physicians boarded another truck. Ahead of all personnel stood the x-ray and sterilization trucks, the field kitchen, laundry, and supply wagons. One for each of the four units going forward. They started their engines, the racket drifting backward to the personnel, a huge grumbling animal on the move.

Therese plunked down next to her. "Ouch. Plywood. Should have brought my pillow to sit on."

Gwen broke into a smile. "Got your hot water bottle?"

"Yep. Without it, I can't brew a decent cup of tea."

The two of them snickered.

229

"Glad you came, Spencer." Therese looked to be about Gwen's age, but had the dark refined looks of the French women Gwen had seen in Paris.

"And I'm tickled you're here. For tea time, I brought chocolate." She patted her suitcase.

"The little joys."

"Golden moments." Gwen grabbed for the overhead bar to steady them over the bumpy road. "When I get home, I will sit in a tub for a week."

"And I will eat bonbons and guzzle champagne." Therese crossed her arms. "I joined up to see the world. My grandfather came from the Lorraine and left because he hated how his little farm was always trampled by French and German soldiers. He went to America to be free from that. And now here I am, fighting for his little farm. A fine kettle of fish, don't you think?"

"Maybe this time, we'll get it right."

Therese's dispassionate eyes zeroed in on Gwen's. "I want to believe that."

"It's for the best we both do." Gwen reached out to take her hand and hold it.

They rode like that for two hours until the crump-crump-crump of the guns made them cringe and the ground shook so badly, they had to break off and grip their plywood seats with both hands. Murmurs grew louder. Shouts of men and orders by commanding officers swelled to a crescendo. Soon, the transport swung into a rutted road—and they rode beside long lines of Doughboys who threw them jumpy smiles and waved too gaily. They were for the front, too, and Gwen could read in their eyes the valiant hope that they never saw nurses any closer than this.

I don't want to see you, either.

Within another hour, the trucks halted. The engines stopped. The evac hospital team dropped off, taking up a permanent position on the shoulder near a burned out village. The rest traveled onward. Minutes later, the mobile hospital team detached in the hollow of a valley marred by abandoned trenches. They were ugly crevices filled with the detritus of a hasty advance, tin cups, old boots and rifles, one with the bayonet still fixed. To one side, a hundred or more small wooden crosses dotted the ravaged land beneath one lonely tree. Hung on each cross was a metal tag like the ones Gwen wore. *Our boys, then. Here beneath that tree.* Lush with green leaves in this burnt and bitter desolation, it blossomed with soft pink flowers as if it were springtime and all was right with the world.

Gwen tapped her toes on the floorboard. Therese nibbled on her lower lip. The other nurse on their team, Janet Fulmore from Chicago, sat with a stone face. With a head of wild auburn curls, she appeared to be fiery. But she tended to be quiet, introspective, and at the moment, she clenched her knuckles white.

A mighty din vibrated though the valley. No one spoke of it. No one spoke now at all. A few fluttered their lashes, the only sign they gave of acknowledging the noise. Some crossed their arms and comforted themselves by rocking to and fro. Others sat without a muscle moving. Finally, their truck stopped. The drivers killed their engines. The few horses in the line neighed, grew silent.

"Dismount!"

The teams climbed down from their vehicles and near the edge of what had once been a copse of trees but was now a series of stumps, a few trucks formed a circle with the sterilization wagon and the x-ray unit.

"Let's go!" The colonel on horseback shouted, gesturing for them to move toward the circled trucks. "Our ambulances come down the road now. Now!"

Gwen stood with Therese, the two of them blinking at the ghastly terrain. Trees, once a forest, now were charred stalks piercing a steel sky. Their feet sank in the sopping wet soil, a mucky mess. No birds sang. None dotted the silver sky. A stream flowed to one side of the clearing. Gwen's nostrils flared, assaulted by the putrid smell. Chock full of debris, the water was black. No wash or drinking water there.

She choked back bile. "Time to go to work."

****

Gwen's team lined up beside one of the tables inside the tent. Three other tables dotted the interior.

Doc O'Bryan held out his arms, letting one of their orderlies suit him up. Of the seven on his team, Doc, Therese, and she had worked together before. Doc's assistant surgeon—a man named Baldwin, the two orderlies, and Janet were their new members. O'Bryan had called them together before the first wounded entered from the admitting officer. Tonight, he had bloodshot eyes but no other signs of inebriation.

Gwen focused more closely on him. He inhaled, puffing himself up for this first meeting of the seven of them. Was his strength a pretense? Or false courage? She told herself not to fear for him. What price he paid must be his own. Still, she held her breath.

He began, urging on them a well-oiled efficiency. "I want to see you analyze the patient's needs before he reaches your hands. I want to see you," he spoke to the orderlies, "read the x-rays and describe to me the diagram of the wound that the receiving officer drew. I want to hear it as you put the boy on our table."

Doc's organization had always been precise. That was one reason, given his drinking—maybe the only reason, he'd been approved to head this team. But these new mobile procedures were meant to streamline an OR op. To emphasize that, the Army now imposed quotas. Brass wanted one man per hour processed. If anyone could meet that quota, that would be Doc. *If he were totally sober. If he would stop drinking every day. Every morning, for Christ's sake.*

"Reynard, you do nothing except replace those cones, calibrate the ether. Fulmore," he spoke to the nurse whom none of them knew well because she had worked in the contagion ward. "You make certain I have the correct number of sterilized instruments at the start of each operation. Wosnicki," he addressed one of their orderlies. "You keep her line of supply flowing from the sterilization unit, you hear me?"

The orderly agreed.

"Fulmore." He frowned at Janet. "You look nervous. Bury it. It's disruptive. For us all. Spencer, here, can tell you I bark only when one of you is slow—or scared. I assume Dalton approved of you moving up the line with us because you think on your feet. So tell us now before we start, what's your nemesis?"

"Sir?"

From the look on Janet's face, she had no idea what Doc asked of her.

"What's your weak point?" He sniffed, averse to repeating anything.

"I need to eat regularly or I faint."

Gwen wondered why she didn't collapse from hunger herself.

Doc narrowed his gray eyes on Janet. "Epilepsy?"

"No, sir. Of course n—"

"High blood pressure?"

"Definitely not, sir."

"How much food do you require?"

She stiffened her back, appearing insulted. "I—I need an egg now and then, but—"

"Good. Hartman?" He crooked a finger at one of their orderlies. "It is now your job to fetch Nurse Fulmore a boiled egg every morning. Better yet, get one for each of us."

"Seven eggs?" The orderly gaped, incredulous. "But, sir, we're—"

"In France, Hartman. Farms abound. I'll give you money. Buy them. Boil them. Seven of them."

Gwen bit back a smile. So did the others. Even Janet. But not Hartman. Poor man. She'd take him aside later and explain that if he could keep Janet on her feet with her rations, Doc would be happy.

"Ready?" he asked them all, checking their expressions. "Come now, Fulmore. If you faint at the sight of blood in my OR, I will make you walk back to base."

"I won't, sir. Promise."

He waved her to silence. "Let's get the first poor bastard in here and set him right."

Wosnicki marched toward the receiving area and called to the officer to have the receiving team carry in the first man.

Four men, two at each point of the canvas stretcher,

jogged in, double time.

One glance at him and Gwen resisted the urge to rock on her feet. *My God.* The man's face was half gone. His left cheek was pulp and she could see his tongue working, gulping back saliva and blood. The four orderlies set him down, not even removing the stretcher.

Like so many whom she'd seen before, this one was caked in the rich black loam of northern France. The receiving orderlies had efficiently cut down the neck of his uniform. His paper medical tag that described his wound, attached to his front shirt button by the first aid station, was black with blood, unreadable.

Gwen looked up and away, steeling herself for this procedure.

The man grabbed her hand, burbling some phrase. His eyes burned bright with pain and fear.

One glance at his remaining sleeve and she saw he wore the insignia of a chaplain. She bent to him and patted his arm. He stilled. *How many morphine pills had they given him? How many had he really been able to swallow? Not enough. Not enough.*

Therese leaned into Doc. "I don't know if I can fit the cone to give a good vacuum."

"*Do it,*" Doc growled.

Hartman recited the description of the wound.

As if we need it. We can see it. All too clearly.

Gwen bit her lower lip, glad—*glad*—she hadn't eaten much that day.

Therese dropped ether to the gauze. An eternity passed as she measured and to Gwen's calculation, over-saturated it. But when she cupped the mask over

235

the chaplain's nostrils, she held it to his ravaged flesh to form the best vacuum she could make of it. The man drifted, woozy. His hand dropped from Gwen's. She rushed to aid Doc as he probed the edges of the damaged tissue.

"We can do this, folks," he assured them. "Let's irrigate him. Trim the edges. See if we can save enough skin for a temporary flap. He isn't lost. By damn, if I'll let God steal him!"

Chapter Thirteen

Gwen reeled at the ripe odor of the man the two receiving orderlies put on the surgical table. No different than the man before him except this one had half his brains hanging from his field dressing and the previous one had— *What did it matter?*

She closed her eyes, looking for strength in her weary bones, but finding none. The past ten weeks of eighteen-hour shifts had drained her energy to a trickle. The never-ending work was a marathon, patching up one boy and then another and another, each one desperately near death's door, each one needing every bit of their expertise and devotion to outwit the hideous fortune that had ravaged his body.

"I can't go on, Doc." She locked eyes with him, pleading for relief.

He glared at her, scalpel in one hand, the other up to stop Hartman from reciting the man's condition. "I continue, you do too."

"Really, I—I'm not well."

He snickered, a new habit he'd adopted. *A new personality he'd revealed.* Until now, he had used that tactic only on Therese and Janet. But not on her, he wouldn't.

Gwen stared at him, hating this creature who

arrived for duty reeking of gin or whiskey or whatever he had managed to buy in the village that day. Each night, this man turned more nasty.

"Cut open his dressing, Spencer. Be quick." He snapped his fingers, trying to intimidate her. Control her.

She wouldn't allow it. With a yank, she pulled off her mask.

He leaned over their patient and ever so quietly said, "So then you *are* pregnant."

She jerked ramrod straight. *What gall.* "Sir?"

"I know you went to Paris with that Limey!"

"That was months ago and I'm tired—" *What was she doing?* She had learned years ago that arguing with logic never worked with those bent on controlling her.

"And he's been here since. I saw him taking you behind the tent the other day!"

Her mouth fell open in outrage. "He most definitely did not. I saw him for five minutes, no more. He's—"

"A horny bastard can work in one minute." Doc chuckled. "Get his end in and—"

Gwen couldn't find proper words to tell Doc to go fuck himself. "I'm leaving." She turned to her colleagues. "I'll be back after a nap."

"That's right. Get the hell out! Don't come back until you can do what we do!"

She grabbed her raincoat from the rack and marched down the path to her tent, her mind on fire with hatred for what he'd said. How he'd tried to humiliate her. How he'd tried to tarnish Adam and destroy her delight in his visit.

Adam who had taken a few minutes to see her on

his way to deal with German prisoners. Adam who had not even touched her hand yesterday. "Propriety," he had said smiling with his heart in his eyes, "tries me sorely."

How dare Doc do that to her. What kind of man stole something lovely and made it sordid and small?

One who is sick.

One who is unraveling.

She ducked into the tent she shared with Janet and Therese, stripped off her raincoat and sank like a stone to the only chair. On her feet since noon yesterday, she needed just a few blessed hours to sleep before she started again. Yanking at her boots, she let them drop to the mud floor, careful to leave them standing.

"The only thing that is," she murmured to herself as she fell backward onto her cot. Eyes closed, half asleep already, she felt for the front buttons of her uniform and realized she still had her butcher apron on. *Hell.* She reached around, tugged it off her shoulders and lost interest. Too tired to move. *Too tired to breathe.* She closed her eyes and listened for the next round of air raids. The Germans were coming. They always did. Three, four times a night. Tonight, she dared them to come before she got twenty winks. Just twenty…

Her eyes drifted open. Ear-piercing sirens rent the night.

"Damn Germans," she muttered and refused to move.

From the front lines a mile away, the screeching warnings screamed at her. She put one ear to her cot, no sheets, no pillows. No use, she couldn't block the wails or the whomp-whomp-whomp of the bombs striking earth.

"Lights out! Lights out!" someone outside hollered amid the tumult.

Who could hear him? Who needed to?
We know what it is.

"Take cover!" someone else yelled.

Gwen rolled over, her hands over the back of her neck, her body curled in a ball like a child playing hide-and-seek. She was damned if she was crawling *under* her cot. What protection could it give if a piece of shrapnel was meant for her?

None.

She cringed, the roar of the planes, the bombs coming closer and closer, exploding tents, trucks, machinery. The howls went up, human cries of soldiers struck. *Who? Who this time?*

A gush of wind rushed over her. The rat-tat-tat of machine guns plowed into metal. A sharp sting grazed her wrist. Thwapp! She gasped as the tent groaned and collapsed around her, a suffocating shroud. Shocked, she froze. The German Junkers flew away, whoosh whoosh, whoosh. Silence, too weird, too welcome stretched to a void. She waited, testing her own sanity, counting interminable seconds as she asked herself, *Am I hit? Where? Where? Can I move? Hand? Yes. Fingers? Yes. Toes? Yes. Is this real or am I imagining that I am whole and capable?*

Over and over, she flexed muscles in her abdomen, her chest, her arms. Breathing became hot under the weight of the tent. *Move. How?*

Beyond where she lay, she heard men running, scurrying, demanding. calling, asking who was hurt, who was hurt, who needed help, over here, over here, can you talk? "Can you talk to me, Gwen?"

Mist covering her face, she gazed up at Private Hartman. "Spencer! Speak to me!"

A sliver of dawn sat on the horizon. *Must have slept then. Or I passed out in the raid.*

Hartman ran his hands over her limbs. Other men worked around her, rolling up the tent. "Spencer, are you okay?"

She found her gratitude before she found any words. "Yes, I think so."

"Your arm." He lifted her wrist.

"What?" she asked him, knowing her speech was slurred with fright.

"Wosnicki!" he called to his buddy. "Get over here. Bring that lamp closer! Spencer's hit."

"I am?" *No, can't be.*

"Over here! Hold it here. Let me see this." Hartman gingerly held her elbow as he examined her hand and forearm. "Well, hey. Aren't you a lucky lady?"

"Am I?" *Please God, let me be. I can't feel a thing. Except—* "My wrist."

"Yeah. A cut. Not serious. Sliced off your watch! Clean! Not bad!" He was chuckling like a silly kid, unnerved, relieved. "Come on. Stand up. Lemme make sure you're fine. Got others to help if you've got nothing broken or needs mending."

He hauled her up to stand with him. Trembling, she leaned on him with the aftershocks of trauma.

"You're fine. Just shook. Need to sit, don't you?"

She nodded, incapable of many words now that terror ripped through her like a chill wind.

As much walking as dragging her, Hartman led her

to the officers' tent, announced he had a nurse with him, said the women's tent was zapped and lifted the tent flap. The admitting officer stared at her, too weary to do more than raise a finger in greeting and sink down to his cot to return to sleep. Her team's assistant surgeon, Tom Baldwin, glared at her and she returned the favor. The man had the personality of a doorstop and she expected nothing from him except his dedication to the surgical team.

"Sit here. Do not move," Hartman ordered her and left her reeling in the chair.

Absently, she gazed at her wrist. Minus her watch, her new one she had purchased more than a year ago, her wrist looked naked. *Naked. Adam, my wrist is naked.*

She grinned at Baldwin, acting foolish, in a bit of shock, but she was too tired to care. Baldwin wouldn't know a foolish thing if he fell in it. "Why are you here?"

"Same as you, Spencer. Working till I drop."

"No." She waggled a finger toward the OR tent. "Aren't you operating?"

"I persuaded O'Bryan to take a break. You left. It was a good excuse. Now? In the raid? Worked out, didn't it?"

Outside, a man was singing.

What idiot would sing after an air raid?

She grinned more widely. *You are silly with fatigue to imagine a man would sing after—*

The tent flapped backward. A hulking gray figure stomped in. Singing. Singing and growling his displeasure that a woman sat in his tent.

"Schpenser?" Doc O'Bryan put his ragged old face

in front of hers. "What the hell you doing here, girl?"

She hated to be called a girl. Never had he done it. But then never had he insulted her like he had this evening, either.

In careful answer, she raised her wrist. "Got hit. Our nurses' tent is gone. Collapsed. All around me, Doc."

"Shiiiit. When will these fuckers ever leave us alone?"

His crudeness put metal in her spine. He would never speak like that around her or any of his nurses if he were sober. But he was so far gone, he had become another being. A caricature of himself. A cartoon. A mean one.

He grabbed her around the throat. "Speak to me. You hurt?"

Rank with whiskey, his breath appalled her.

She grimaced. "A cut. That's all." *I think it is.* "Please, Doc, you're hurting me."

"You defy me? Here? In there!" he roared, his fingers tightening.

Baldwin yelled at him to take his hands off her.

Gwen found her own breath even as his fingers bit into her skin. "Let me go!"

Blinking, coming to for a second, Doc dropped his hand and yanked on her arm. "Stand up!"

So tired, so apprehensive, she rose but her knees went to water. She fell against him, unbalancing him. Her head spun. "Doc, I'm…dizzy. I need to sit."

He stumbled, bellowing now. "Stand the hell up, I said!"

Finding her footing and her dignity, she scowled at him. *Where in hell did he get his supplies of liquor?*

Whoever did that for him was aiding a sick man and she had promised herself one day, if that person ever came to light, she would kill him.

"Doctor O'Bryan."

Gwen blinked at the man taking Doc's other arm. *This was Baldwin to her rescue?* She suppressed the urge to snort.

"Doctor, our Spencer needs to sit and rest. She's had a shock. She's hurt. And you, sir, need to give me that flask of yours and go to bed."

"Hell I will." Doc pushed at Baldwin's chest.

"You must." Baldwin lifted his chin in the direction of the chair. "And you, Spencer, will sit down. For your own good." He leveled an imperious look at her. "Wait for Hartman."

She dared not defy him. But then she didn't want to, either. She wanted only to sleep, preferably now, preferably anywhere.

Hartman appeared in the entrance and at the sight before him, he cursed a blue streak beneath his breath.

"Yes, well," said Baldwin as he led Doc away to his cot, "this is a fine mess, Hartman. Take care of Spencer, will you? And for the love of God, do ask yourself why you buy the good doctor here his daily ration in the village. You are driving us all crazy, man."

Gwen wanted to cry, to scream, to mourn. *Hartman supplied Doc.* She shot to her feet. "You buy his liquor for him?"

"He gave me an order," the private managed. His eyes begged forgiveness.

Gwen had little to dispense. "Buying him alcohol is not Army business."

"Either way, he can send me down the line. Make

up anything he wants. I wind up digging ditches in St. Nazaire. You can't stop him."

Oh, Christ. How true. How powerless she was. She would change that. She would find a way to make brass understand the disservice the Army had done to the thousands of courageous women who gave their lives and yes, their sacred honor, just like any man over here, to win this goddamned war.

She stood right in front of the private, a man she had liked, appreciated, and now one she would watch carefully, diligently. "Listen to me, Hartman. You might be obeying orders, but you are aiding and abetting a very good physician to speed the day of his own death. Trust me, none of us thanks you. Except of course, O'Bryan here. Continue to supply him with wine or beer or local hootch and you not only kill him, you kill any number of Doughboys on his table. Do not let me see that you supply Doc with anything more. Do not. Or I will go to the CO and have you both sent to the Services of Supply to dig ditches. And maybe your own graves. Do you understand me, Private Hartman?"

"Yes, ma'am."

"Dismissed," she told him. For a moment, the man didn't move, looking as though he couldn't believe he'd just been dressed down by her, but when it dawned on him, he pivoted and ran.

When she turned, she faced the two doctors.

Baldwin stared at her, his mouth slowly curving upward at the corners.

Doc glared at her. "Fuck you."

"I already have been, sir. I work for you."

****

The next morning, Gwen rose from sleep in a tent

245

Hartman had set up for her, Therese, and Janet. Both of her friends snored, sleeping like the dead, flat on their backs like she had last night and still in their uniforms. *No surprise.* Wandering out to the latrine, she was stronger for the rest she'd had—and for the comeuppance she'd given Hartman. But she was grubby, grumpy, pining for a bathtub and clean clothes. At least Hartman had done one good deed by finding her boots and sticking them on her feet or she'd be trotting around in this muck in her socks. She needed food and some plan to retrieve her clothes from her collapsed tent. She wrinkled her nose, leery of meeting Doc again.

Hell with him. I need to take care of me.

She headed for the mess tent and breakfast. The ground was pock-marked from last night's attack. Her tent was the least of the destruction. One ambulance stood in the road, a charred shell. A sterilization truck had been sheared in half. One corporal in the admitting team stood by the truck talking with a friend of his. Gwen overheard him tell his pal that they had lost one of their officers when the man had stood near a boiler tank that had been hit and exploded.

At the death, another little piece of her heart broke off and landed in the dense mud. This loss was her small sign of a larger grief she bore for those whom she knew and had passed on. Losing one man in this small band was like losing ten. This one Gwen had liked and appreciated. He was an admit man, extensively trained not only to do secondary triage here, but also to analyze which men got immediate surgery and which went to the less critical teams farther back. Gwen had met him months ago in base camp, liked his humor and his expertise. She would miss him and she mourned him. Right there and then. A moment for a silenced comrade. A second to honor his life. She prayed his family gave him more than she could. Her job was not to mourn too much. Not to succumb to grief and fail to see what she could do for the next man.

She wiped away tears and hurried to the mess tent.

Inside, she got a bowl of oatmeal, a piece of French bread and coffee, then sat on a bench in the back corner. Usually she would sit and talk with others. Today, awash in the aftermath of her confrontation with Doc, she preferred her own company. Like so many others who sat alone occasionally, her buddies understood her signal and left her to herself.

As she got up to take her dishes to the line, a corporal came in and stood at the front. "We have the Commanding Officer of Evacuation Hospital Twenty-Three coming in. We're all to report to the Admin tent at ten hundred hours."

Swell. Enough time to see if I can salvage any of my clothes in that chaos that used to be our sleeping quarters.

Luckily, the Supply boys had come up from the evac unit and removed her ruined tent. There for all the world to see out in the open was her stained butcher apron lying on her crushed cot. Beside it, standing up, whole, was her own suitcase. Terrific. In there, she had four step-ins, three bras and three clean gray crepes and aprons. How in God's green earth she would be able to replace her cape, wool coat, and hat was anyone's guess. She'd have to notify the Supply guys and hope she'd get replacements sometime before hell froze over.

She headed for the briefing. The CO who rode up

from the evac hospital ordered them to leave, head farther east through the Champagne. Furthermore, they were to prepare for this and leave by noon. The team was desperately needed as Doughboys moved to take another salient south of Verdun, called St. Mihiel. While many base hospitals had their quarters in that sector, few as yet had mobile surgical units ready to travel and equipped to quickly operate. Plus, Gwen's team was considered the finest, most experienced. Out here in the field for more than three months now, her team would be observed by others who were training to form new units.

"Just what the hell we need. Observers. Shit." Doc O'Bryan groused as he left the briefing tent. Never glancing her way, she doubted he remembered what happened last night. *No matter. I do.* This morning, he looked like hell and smelled—*still*—like a distillery.

Gwen's stomach rolled.

Baldwin passed her by as he walked behind Doc. "Did you get any sleep?"

"I did. Thank you for last night." She owed him that, at the very least.

"My thanks to you. I'm tired of picking up his slack."

"Yes, well. We'll have to make certain we don't pay prices for his illness." Dear God, she sounded like Bernice Dalton.

"Let's see what happens with Hartman."

She snorted. "Doc, I am not a betting woman."

"In this case? Very smart."

She could hope Doc O'Bryan was.

****

Picking through the ruins of the nurses' tent

minutes later, she helped Janet and Therese find their clothing. They had a tougher time than she. Both came up with scorched bits and pieces, asking each other how they could replace their uniforms out here in the back of beyond.

"Spencer, what God do you pray to?" Therese asked with good nature. "I need to go to your church. You could have at least scrambled to save a few of our gray crepes."

"I wish I had thought of that," she told them sincerely. She was tired again, sad about the loss of her friend the admitting officer—and sad at the loss of her friend and mentor, Doc O'Bryan. "I might have saved my watch."

"Oh, hell." Janet shrugged. "Sorry, sweet. I'll buy you a new one whenever we get leave again."

"We're getting leave?" Memories of her days with Adam glowed like a good fire, luring her from the chill of the autumn morning.

"Heard the CO say he'll grant it for the whole unit once he gets another up and running to replace us."

"I will not hold my breath," Gwen told her.

"Me, neither," said Therese. "COs promise but rarely deliver."

"Isn't that the role of men the world over?" asked Janet.

"Wow," said Therese, "do I detect a problem with the males of the species?"

Janet harrumphed, throwing clothing in her suitcase helter-skelter. "You might say."

Therese widened her eyes. "Do tell."

Janet glanced from Therese to Gwen and back again. "Baldwin is an ass."

Gwen was ready to add her two cents, but detected that might not be appreciated by Janet. Besides, she was curious that Janet felt compelled to discuss the man. Why would she? Unless Janet knew Baldwin might have emotional depths to him Gwen hadn't anticipated. "Why? What's he done?"

Janet rolled a shoulder. "He could have stood up for you last night, Gwen, when you asked O'Bryan for a nap. Instead, Tom acted like a statue. He is too closed, and other times, too rash..."

"*Tom?*" Therese asked, use of the physician's first name and sign of a closer relationship than permitted between doctor and nurse.

"*Tom is rash?*" Gwen nearly choked on the idea.

"He is," Janet defended him. "He could have been more...himself."

"Himself? Please go on," Therese urged her. "I'm loving your train of thought."

Gwen sidled near her. "What is more characteristic of him than his...silence last night?"

"He can be supportive. Kind. Sweet."

Are we talking about the same Tom Baldwin here?

Janet shook her head. "You don't know him. And this morning, I told him he has to be more—"

"What?" Therese spit out, exasperated.

"Commanding. Charming."

"Well, I'll be damned," Therese said under her breath. "Count Dracula has a heart. Since when?"

Gwen chuckled at Therese who had hit the nail on the head.

Janet bit her lower lip, unready to talk. "Since about a week ago..."

Therese looked impressed. "A week ago, eh? When

he did what?"

"Kissed me in back of the sterilizer."

Gwen and Therese burst out laughing.

"Didn't know the man knew how to kiss," Therese offered.

"Didn't know he could even think of sex," Gwen added.

To which the two other women turned toward her with astonished eyes.

"Sex?" Therese savored the word.

"I said kiss," Janet added with mirth.

"Now we know how our friend Spencer's mind works when she isn't handing O'Bryan a scalpel," added Therese. "Want to tell us about sex, Gwen?"

"No." Her cheeks burned as she blushed like a sixteen-year-old.

"Why not?"

"Because it is none of your business."

Therese gazed at her just like a spinster schoolmarm. "We'll ask again. We need to know."

"Like hell, you do. Pack your bags, ladies."

The three of them finished, giggling like girls.

****

More than an hour later, Gwen carried her suitcase toward the baggage truck when the sound of an automobile engine had everyone along the road turning to identify the car. Without a top, the Ford car was the new brown of the latest Army vehicles and the driver was alone.

He wore a dark brown leather jacket, a leather skull cap and goggles over his eyes. The red scarf trailing in the wind behind him was the item that made Gwen catch her breath. In another second, she dropped her suitcase and ran toward the driver.

In a flash, he halted his car, jumped out and opened his arms to catch her.

"Oh, Lex! Lex!"

He swung her around like he always did, his embrace warm and fierce. His lips were buried in her hair and he muttered things about being crazy to find her.

"Let me look at you." She pulled back in his arms to examine him and pushed up his goggles. Oh, lord, he was tired. His hazel eyes dull with fatigue. His blond curls peeking out beneath the ugly leather cap. His cheeks tanned and red, too. Sunburned? And gaunt.

"How are you, honey?"

"I'm fine, fine. Thought I might have the flu, but I don't. Just tired. Bone tired. But you look…" She put a hand to his brow. "Ill. Are you?"

"Nah." Jerking away, he rejected her idea soundly. "I scared the medical boys in Chaumont, said it was life and death to find you. Been looking for you for two days now. Christ, you people move like the wind."

Proud of that, she hugged him close. "We have to."

"You can take up bank robbing when you get home."

She pretended to turn a steering wheel. "I'll drive the get-away car."

He looked horror-stricken. "They teach you how to drive up here?"

"Yeah. In my spare time." She elbowed him. "You kidding? Maybe I'll take up flying when we go home. Become a fly girl."

"God help us all." He settled his arms around her and tipped his head toward the activity around the trucks. "Where are you going, babe?"

"East. Always east. They don't tell us battle plans, you know that."

"Word is this team is the crackerjack."

"We are. Best there is." *If our head surgeon doesn't get plastered and our assistant surgeon doesn't fight with him and reprimand our orderly. Or me.*

He stilled, his green-brown eyes refracting in curiosity in the morning sunlight. "What's wrong?"

"Perceptive Lex." She glanced away, irritated with herself for breaking her own code of never snitching. Even though she had only looked askance when he complimented her unit, she had been disloyal. Unprofessional. "Nothing we can't fix. If I only knew how."

"That bad?"

"It could be. If we…" *Lose a patient because of it.* "Never mind. Ours to do." She looped her arm in his and pointed toward a fallen tree. "Sit with me for a few minutes before we leave. How is everyone at home at your house?"

"Well. Mother is on the warpath that Will enlisted. Dad says beer consumption is rising. Good for us. Bad for customers who like our product too much."

"Amen to that."

The wind picked up and the two of them huddled close on the log.

"I hear from Susannah that she really loves her piano lessons. Of course, she's angry that Will signed up. Why did he do it? Why not go to college, let you fight the war?" She noticed that Lex concentrated on her lips as she spoke. "Was he afraid of not doing as well as his big brother at Yale?"

"Will isn't afraid of a man or woman on this earth."

She turned away from him, suspicious of the way he had listened to her. "But he hasn't done as well in school as you. Why was that?"

"School? Will hated school."

That was okay, but not exactly a fitting response. She stared at him. His complexion looked splotchy. He wasn't sunburned so much as wind burned. He hadn't removed his cap, either. He usually disliked hats. What was wrong with him? "Take your cap off."

Quick as could be, he put his palm to his head. "No. Why? I like it."

"Do you? Suddenly?" Now he was hiding something. "Have you been in a dog fight lately?"

She had never seen him look sheepish. The sight roiled her. "Take it off."

He complied.

She caught her breath. A long red scar ran across his forehead in the hairline. "What happened?"

"A little scrape. Doing a little fly-by over German lines lately."

"Un-huh. And that?" She pointed to the scar.

"A memento from a Fokker that came a little too close to my Nieuport."

She scoured his eyes. "How close?"

He smacked his lips. "Forty, fifty yards."

Jesus. "Were you shot down?"

He winced. "Not really. I came gliding in." He simulated with one hand a gentle swoop to earth. "Engine shot, though."

Now she was gloriously pissed. "And the scar, Felix? How did you get it?"

"Hit my head on the way in."

"Were you knocked out?"

"No."

"Good." She narrowed her eyes on him, frantic for facts he did not volunteer. "Where did you go after you landed? For medical treatment, I mean."

"I didn't."

She cursed. She wouldn't ask why. Men could be such cretins when it came to their own health. "That's what I thought. Stay here."

"Where are you going?" He was on his feet, grabbing her by the arm.

"To get a stethoscope. Sit down there."

"Damn! You are bossy."

She pointed.

He sat.

Furious that he would be so blasé about his condition, she marched toward the equipment trucks and found Hartman who was just closing one of their satchels. "Hate to do this, but a friend of mine from Aero Squadron just came over to visit and he's sick." She told Hartman she needed to listen to Lex's heart and lungs. "And give me a otoscope, too, while you're at it."

"Sure. Better be quick." He fished inside a box for her equipment, then handed them over.

"I'll do my worst."

"Go, get 'em!" he urged her.

Lex paced. As she approached, his pinched look told her he was going to give her hell. "I came to visit, not for you to play doctor."

She stuck her tongue out at him. "Open your coat and shirt."

He sat on the log, complaining about how cold her stethoscope was.

"We pack them in ice so patients will know when we touch them."

He scoffed. "I know when you touch me."

"Yeah? Well, tilt your head and let me see your ear."

"Hell."

"As I thought." She sat beside him, took his hand and frowned at him. "You have pneumonia."

"Bullshit."

"Not serious, but it will be. You march yourself down to the evac hospital and admit yourself."

"Like hell I will. I need to be back down the road to Toul by midnight. I have a sortie to lead."

"If you don't check yourself in to that evac, you won't be leading anyone ever again in the air or on the ground. Not only do you have pneumonia, you have an ear infection. You couldn't hear me when I turned away from you. Do you realize that if you—"

"Okay!" Both hands in the air, he was shouting. "Okay! I'll go."

She coiled up her stethoscope. "If you don't, I'll never speak to you again."

"Well, that would work, because I wouldn't be able to hear you."

"Not funny." She pulled him up. "Ear infections are not simple things. You could lose function in your facial nerves. Your face would go lax, frozen."

"I'm convinced. Honest!"

"Good. Go. Stay there until the docs say you are well. They can send a telegram to your CO that you're sick. Didn't you know? Aren't you in pain? Your ear, I mean?"

"It felt odd. Flying so much, I got used to not hearing as clearly. Guess I didn't notice."

Relieved at his compliance, she sagged. "I'm glad you came so I could notice."

He slid his arm around her waist and squeezed her to his side. "Me, too."

"Tell them you have a fever, too."

"All right! Anything else?"

She admired his good looks, even ill as he was, he was a very handsome man. "Find a way to let me know when you are better."

He took his time examining her then, his gaze traveling her eyes and lips and back again. "Promise. On one condition."

"Name it."

"You find a way to tell me where you are once, twice a month. I'm out of Toul. You are—" He waved a hand at the crowd of folks in the surgical unit bustling like bees around the trucks. "Ghosts in the night."

"Yeah. Good ghosts."

"Angels."

"Hey, let's not mix medicine with religion." Many nights she questioned if any god came near this hellhole. How could he see this and turn away?

"I would bet many a Doughboy thinks you're better than God."

"He'd be wrong. We're just people trying to do the best we know how."

Chapter Fourteen

Gwen struggled up from her cot and drove her hands into her unruly hair. Her head pounded with a splitting pain. She winced, the drilling in her head in syncopation with the bombardment on the front a mile or two away. *It might even be more than that by now.*

And she had better get up. The team could move at a few minutes' notice to pack.

Ever since the end of September after the victory in the valley of St. Mihiel, American forces had pierced every German bulwark along the Meuse River up into the dense Argonne forest. At many spots along the route, the Germans ran. Literally ran. They abandoned anything they could not carry, not bothering to even take food or water before they jumped into trucks or on top of tanks. Those who could not hitch a ride, followed the vehicles at a jog. Their retreat was so fast, so dire, they left behind their own dead and severely wounded.

She had treated them, only after their own Americans were patched up. But as her unit piled into their own trucks and rushed to keep up with the Doughboys' advance, she had seen more Germans. She'd glimpsed hundreds of them, perhaps thousands, in the pitiful grotesque postures in which they had died, their black and bloated bodies lining the makeshift roads up through the dark and deadly woods north to the German border. These dead, too, awaited the services of American boys in the burial teams. Their duty was to inter the remains of their enemy, but only after all American casualties had been buried. Each— American or German—merited a small cross, their identification tags plus a plywood coffin, lowered into hastily dug holes, suitably covered to cut the risk of contagion and wild animals destroying them. *As if any living creature can survive in this desolate landscape now.*

Gwen inhaled, rubbing her temples. She was turning sour, negative in her exhaustion and her worries. Each evening when she awoke from her allotted four-hour nap, she took up her litany of worries. Counting them like sheep, she allowed herself this one short venture into personal reflection.

She worried about Lex, but he had sent a note up the line through medical services two weeks ago that he had recuperated from his bout with pneumonia and ear infection and returned to his aerodrome and flight duty. For what comfort it was that he was well, Gwen took it and pushed aside her fear for his life. Up here on the lines, she had heard tales of pilots shot down, dying in the flames of their own planes. One had survived the crash of his Nieuport and an ambulance driver had rushed him to their team. The man had been so badly burned, his flesh a pulpy mass, that the best they could do for him was to inject massive doses of morphine and let him die in peace.

Adam, she had seen three times in as many weeks. Until he strode toward her tent one night, she hadn't worried for his safety. That realization came as a shock.

Yet, for some reason she had no time to examine, he seemed impervious to war or death or accident. She'd led him to a quiet nook between the mess and nurses' tent where she had hugged him and told him she never feared for him. He, on the other hand, had been sick with concern for her. Knowing she and her team were up in the north, he had volunteered for the job of interrogating captured German officers. That he could find her comforted her, but finding her, she knew in her soul, was the major reason he had this job. He spoke German fluently, so well he had masqueraded across No Man's Land and back. As he left her, he'd spoke of peace negotiations.

"Soon, very soon," he'd said wistfully, "this will be over." He'd promised to see her often in future, and true to his word, he had come once each week since then, finding her wherever her team had been sent.

The worst of her fears was for those at home. Susannah's last letter to her had arrived more than a month ago. None had come since then, but mail delivery was often weeks or months late. Gwen was not alarmed until days later when she heard from Helen who announced that her mother had taken to her bed with influenza. A second note from Helen came days later in mid-October. Aunt Mary had suffered badly and the new young doctor in Peckville did not expect her to survive. Helen had assured Gwen that if that happened, she would take Susannah to live with her, just as she would take her brother Winslow. Gwen had replied, a hasty note given to the postmaster as he passed through camp collecting mail. She'd thanked Helen and prayed for everyone's health. Susannah's, Win's, Helen's and her husband. Gwen even wished for Mary's recovery.

After all, I never wished her ill. I only wished her civil. Loving.

But the flu had felled thousands of Doughboys. Even now Doc Baldwin was down with it, ordered backward to the evac hospital and on to the contagion ward at the nearest base hospital. Janet looked a little green herself these past few days. And if anyone on the team thought Doc O'Bryan might have improved his disposition by being deprived of alcohol, they were terribly wrong. He had become an ogre, erratic, yelling at Janet and her. Cursing at Hartman and Wosnicki. Missing a few stitches, here, there, nothing yet life threatening. *But eating away at everyone's composure. Mine, too.*

Biting her lower lip, she winced at the headache that seemed never to leave her alone these past few weeks. She was hungry. That malady she could fix by eating supper. Stew again, most likely. It was food. Once Janet and Therese woke up, Therese would brew tea from the water in her hot water bottle. They'd huddle, the three of them, their fingers clutching the hot tiny *ventouse* cups, heated to reasonable temperature only because Therese took her hot water bottle to bed with her.

"At least I have something warm under my sheets," Therese would rib Janet now that Baldwin was no longer around and word came from the SOS boys that he was recuperating quickly.

"I never had him." Janet retorted, cheeks flushing pink.

"You should have," Therese stuck out her tongue. "Do it when he returns."

Enjoy whatever you can, was Gwen's new

261

philosophy. No clock measured tomorrow.

Meanwhile, their orderly Private Hartman had ceased his daily search for eggs. Up here in the forest, village farms were few and far between. He hadn't found eggs—and he hadn't found booze for O'Bryan, either. Gwen had sung a mute halleluiah to that, but then rued it when a sober and somber O'Bryan began to have the shakes so badly, he dropped instruments, ignored the wound analysis, making his own and yelling his way through surgeries. Brow-beating them all as if they were his slaves, his idiot servants. The night duty was becoming a battle, of Doc with himself, and Doc against the others. No matter what they did, he found fault, found it fast and damned them to hell for it all.

Gwen reached for her wool coat and pushed her arms through. *Can't think of O'Bryan. Shouldn't until I must. Not when I have to wrestle with this ridiculously long coat.* She turned up the cuffs of the coat that Services of Supply had requisitioned for her. Fit for a woman a foot taller—and maybe a foot wider, the coat hung on her like a tent. *What the hell. It's wool.*

And the snow today, she saw as she stepped out of her tent, was fresh—and the coat deliciously warm. But the gray dusk was thick, acrid with smoke and fumes. All of it blowback from the fighting at the front. Gwen ducked inside her tent again to get her gasmask. *Better take it now than to have one of the officers bark at her in the mess for failure to carry the ugly thing.*

Good thing, too, because as she ate she could feel the earth shake with the force of a new carpet barrage. Going toward the Germans or headed toward the Americans, she wasn't sure yet. If the Germans were charging their way, which she doubted, the sirens would warn them soon enough.

Half way through her stew and coffee, Therese walked in.

"Eat up," she urged her as she sat beside Gwen and began to down her own meal. "Ambulances coming. Another all night stand. God, do I wish we had a replacement for Baldwin."

"That'll be Baldwin," Gwen figured. She hadn't told Therese or anyone at all that she'd spoken with the evac hospital CO the last time he'd made his rounds up here. Breaking protocol of a nurse's reverence for a physician's status—and Army rank of a contract worker complaining about a captain, she explained in the most diplomatic terms she could summon that Doctor O'Bryan, in her humble opinion, needed a leave of absence. Her CO's reply was short. He had no replacement for O'Bryan. Not now nor in the foreseeable future. She had to "make do."

Therese sighed. "Think Baldwin'll recover by Christmas?"

Gwen lifted her coffee cup in a toast. "Merry, Merry."

The commotion outside had them and the ten officers inside gobbling their food.

An orderly ran in to announce the arrival of two ambulance convoys.

"Two?" one of the admitting officers asked him. "Jesus. This war is killing me."

"One from Verdun. Shell-shocked boys."

"No." Gwen checked Therese's eyes. "Why here? They go to neuro-psych in La Faure."

"We can't handle them." The admitting officer

threw down his fork and stalked toward the door cursing. "Not our job."

"Hello, my baby," Therese said with an evil grin. "That one has a temper on him."

"Nerves."

"But he's right. Those boys need a soothing hand, not—"

"A crit team that slices and dices?"

"Boo."

"Let's go." Gwen scooped up the last of her stew, then headed for the chow line where they deposited their dirty dishes.

Therese strode right behind her.

Outside, the two lines of ambulances converged to a point in the far clearing. Janet stood stomping in the snow, reaching up to help the shell-shocked men from their vehicles. The ambulances they came in were the usual eight to a wagon, four bottom, four top, all reclining on cots. But the commotion inside those wagons was nothing like the wounded ones that the women were used to receiving. Casualty wagons came with moaning, writhing men inside, some half bandaged, others half dead. The shell-shocked patients came silent, scared, with nervous twitches or paralyzed arms or legs, and all with eyes like glass.

Neither woman was surprised to see Janet assisting the psychiatric team. She had a way with them. In the past, the team had had a few surgical patients fight them on the table, their field station sedation not up to snuff, and she had calmed them with a few kind words and gestures.

Sirens turned the air to chaos.

"Raid! Raid!"

"Lights out!"

"Cover!"

"Aw, hell," Therese complained. "These Heinies interfere with my digestion."

"Where would you like to cower, my pretty maid?" Gwen asked her as she hooked her arm through hers. "Our tent?"

"That didn't work too well for us last time we were hit."

"No, but— Oh, *hell*!"

Over the treetops rose a roar, a fleet of black planes, five in V formation, flying low, too low. *Too low.*

Gwen flung back her head, staring at them, frozen. Therese tugged at her hand.

The machine guns chunk-chunk-chunked as bullets hit, splitting trees and punching metal, collapsing the mess tent and exploding the ambulance…the ambulance from where Janet helped those men …

Metal flew in the air, landing, piercing the earth with thunks. Men cried. Bloodied. Limping. And where the ambulance had stood, only a black, smoking hole remained. Around it lay chunks of pulsing masses. An arm. A leg. Vermillion swatches on a carpet of pure white.

Gwen gulped, dying for breath.

Therese sank to her knees.

Others ran, shrieking, shouting orders.

Gwen commanded herself to stand. Stare.

In a treetop, yards away, bits of gray crepe hung from a limb.

****

Arm in arm, the two of them walked to the OR tent

265

twenty minutes later. Men who might be saved had arrived on that ambulance train and the admitting crew had most likely processed them through registration and x-ray. Janet would be best honored by saving the men whom she could not tend this night.

But the attempt to proceed with work as usual was bitter. Hollowed out by the unrighteousness of Janet's death, neither Gwen nor Therese found words, nor wanted any. They'd mourned Janet in an uncanny silence, rising from their cots in unison to report for their duty.

As senior on the team under O'Bryan, it was time for Gwen to figure out what how the hell they were going to deal with patients minus yet another of their unit.

"I hope to God O'Bryan has his head on straight tonight," Therese murmured as they neared the tent.

My exact thoughts.

"Anything you want tonight, you ask me. I'll do my damnedest to do Janet's job as well as my own."

Gwen patted her hand. Hope was always a good recourse. "Maybe we get a reprieve tonight."

Hartman and Wosnicki had performed their own tasks well, scrubbing down completely from the last patient they'd processed hours earlier. The mud and blood was gone. Their tables—gray, spidery metal—sparkled. Soon they'd be covered once more in the miseries of the Argonne.

"How are we doing here?" Gwen asked them, noting their faces were haggard, their eyes red from crying for Janet and the injustices of this war. "You've done a fine job. Thank you."

The two men accepted her gratitude with their

usual *aw, shucks* attitude. She liked them. Especially Hartman who had distinguished himself in her eyes by ending his service to Doc outside of the OR. He was that extraordinary man who could learn from the error of his ways. He could stand tall, denying those in power the ability to do whatever they wished and call it necessary.

"Ready?" One of the admitting officers stuck his head in the tent.

Gwen finished lining up the instruments. "We need Doc. Have you seen him?"

The man shook his head. "Shall I go hunt him down?"

This officer had done that twice this week. She hated to send him again. Doc cursed a blue streak when he had to be "fetched like a child."

Gwen bit her lower lip. "How many do we have?"

"Twenty-two."

"What's the first one's condition?"

"Chest wound. Sucking."

Lungs, then. Surprised the man made it here alive.

Therese and she locked gazes.

Gwen nodded. "Find O'Bryan. Bring in the chest wound. We'll prep. Hartman, get the analysis and read it."

The corporal with the chest wound lay on their table, bare to the waist, boots hanging over the edge, Therese's gauze cone to his face, resting, resting, waiting. Gwen set her jaw. *Where was he? How dare he come late. This man needs—*

"Well, well, look here." O'Bryan strolled in. "Starting without me? That'll give this poor man a ticket to hell. You four can't do it. Can you, Spencer?"

267

He had it in for her. Had ever since that night back in September in the air raid. Maybe he knew or suspected she had snitched to the CO, but she didn't really care. He could taunt her all he wanted. *Just do your job.*

"Answer me!" He circled around her.

"Sir, the man is ready for you." That statement was a sin, too, because O'Bryan didn't even have his whites on yet. "Wosnicki, get Doctor O'Bryan his—"

"Shut up, Spencer."

Gwen went still.

He leaned over the man on the table, giving him a once over. "What do we have, Hartman?"

"Shall I read the—?"

"Yes, God damn it! Do it!"

Hartman glared at Doc. Who knows what indignities the orderly had suffered at the doctor's orders since he no longer supplied the man with daily doses of alcohol.

Doc sidled right up to Hartman. A few inches taller than the orderly, O'Bryan sneered down at the private—and Hartman did not back away.

The older man's nostrils flared. "Do it, I said."

Hartman raised the analysis and began to read, his voice sure and even.

At the end of the recitation, O'Bryan simply stood there as if he were memorizing the report—or dreaming.

Gwen stepped forward. "Doctor, our patient has been under sedation for more than five minutes. He is ready for you. Allow Wosnicki to proceed. Have you washed your hands?"

"Yes, Little Miss Muffet. I have washed my hands.

Have you? Huh?"

If she ever left this godforsaken forest, she vowed she would never work for an alcoholic again as long as she lived. She'd find men who were whole, able to accept life's losses, addicted to nothing. "I am ready, sir, as we all are."

He moved around the room.

Therese cleared her throat. "Sir, I will have to give this man more ether if you don't start soon. It's not prescribed. He could be overdosed. Sir."

"Reynard, you are a pain in the ass. I'm getting to him." He turned for the sterile water and the sink, rolling up his uniform sleeves as he went.

If this man dies, I will hop a ride down to see the CO tomorrow, complain from the roof tops until someone drums you out of the United States Army.

Refusing to let Wosnicki dress him, O'Bryan stepped beside Gwen. "Smells like shit, doesn't he?"

She stared straight ahead.

"Let's see." He wrinkled his nose and bent over the Doughboy. "Need a rib spreader. Get it."

Gwen turned and opened the sterile metal.

"Get it in him." He took up a scalpel. "Let's go."

She did as she was told, putting all her muscle into the act of opening the boy's chest. Although she knew this was not the first procedure O'Bryan should be using on him, she went along hoping O'Bryan knew a technique she didn't.

But his hands shook, and he swayed on his feet. She didn't smell liquor on him, so what the hell was wrong with him?

He laughed.

Laughed!

"Poor sunuvabitch got shrapnel in his left lung. See that. Stepped the wrong way in that trench, eh, buddy boy?"

"Stop this." She confronted him, relaxing her hold on the spreader. "Do your job!"

"Says you."

"Says me. This man is dying and you are wasting all our time."

He inched closer to her and now she knew he had not been drinking. But this, whatever it was, was just as dangerous to them all, as him in his cups.

He waved the scalpel near her lips. "What if I shut that pretty mouth of yours in a permanent way?"

Every cell in her body turned to stone. "Wosnicki? Hartman? Please remove Doctor O'Bryan from the OR."

Hartman stepped right behind O'Bryan in a heartbeat, one arm restraining the hand that held the knife.

The doctor grappled with him, shaking off Wosnicki.

O'Bryan broke free and in one flick of his wrist, he sent the scalpel flying toward Gwen.

His aim was off.

She sidestepped it, tracking the instrument as it clattered against the metal table and dropped to the mud floor. The attempt to hurt her, wound her, kill her was not a surprise. But it did appall her. Once more, she had met a person who wished to control her, compel her to actions not of her own choosing or of her own moral sense. Once again, she would not permit this one to prevail.

"Take him away."

"*You bitch*!" he bellowed at her, as the two orderlies hauled him toward the exit. "This is my operating room."

"Now it's mine."

She considered the patient on her table. *Hers.*

She flexed her fingers, testing her own dexterity, physical and mental. She knew what to do to help this man. Now she could.

Chapter Fifteen

Stepping outside the tent, Gwen squinted at the skyline to the east. The sun burned her itchy eyes and she raised a hand to her forehead to shield the glare. The wind whipped up, chilling her, refreshing her after more than thirty-two hours of straight surgeries. She and her team had operated on one Doughboy after another until minutes ago. Yesterday after noon, the never-ending flow of dreadfully wounded men had slowed, then trickled to a full stop.

One of the admitting officers gazed at her from across the clearing.

"Any word?" she asked him for confirmation of the rumor of a cease-fire.

"Nothing definite. Ambulance drivers said the front has been told to stand down. We got a telegram from evac said to stand by." He gave her a watery smile.

Yes, let's not celebrate too quickly. Let's not believe this could end so abruptly. Or hope too desperately that we're done. "I'm going in to sleep. Wake us if we get more."

Turning away from him, she headed toward her own quarters. She'd already sent the rest of her unit to sleep, needing time in the OR alone. But she had sat on one of the metal stools, staring at her empty table, unable to process more than her pride that she had dealt with O'Bryan—and that she—without assistance save for Therese—had mended more than thirty-five severely injured men.

Rain pelted her cheeks as she walked toward her tent. Here, there, clusters of the support team stood, conversing in hushed tones. *The war might be over. How can that be? What will you do? When will we go home?*

Gwen heard them, but she was too tired to think of answers. Flipping open the tent, she ducked inside and found Therese sitting on her cot, her legs crossed under her, staring straight ahead.

"I can't sleep," she murmured as her gaze met Gwen's. "I don't think I know how to act if the war ends."

I don't know how to act if it doesn't. What happened last night invigorated her, astonished her. Working on those men had filled her with a sense of achievement that surpassed all she had ever felt before. Being Doc's assistant, his fall-back, was nothing compared to being the one who decided the best way to open, the most efficient method to proceed, the way to close. The way to save each man from the most harm. Each man's survival, the goal. Each man's wound so drastically different from the one preceding him. Fascinated by the depth of her own accomplishments, she needed to treasure her memories. Make more of them than mere self-congratulations. Discover why she had lost herself in those hours. Why she craved them yet again. How could she explain that to Therese? She couldn't yet explain them to herself.

She shrugged out of her raincoat and pulled off her

hat, then sat on the edge of her own cot.

"I haven't allowed myself to think of going home. Have you?" Therese asked, uncharacteristically solemn.

"Not much. All of this was so demanding."

"I don't want to go." Therese shook her head with a reverence that shocked Gwen.

"Would you stay here?"

Therese glanced around the tent as if this were the very place she might hang her hat. "Not France. I loathe the place. Every hideous event. Every hellish shock. The mud. The flu. The air raids."

"Anna and Janet, gone."

"The men beneath my masks torn all to bloody hell."

"Their mothers would tear their own hearts out if they ever learned how this war destroyed their beautiful boys."

Gwen had visions of the first man who'd been placed on their table. The chaplain with his jaw torn away. He lived, a miracle. Forever scarred, he had gone on to one of their base hospitals that specialized in facial reconstruction. She recalled another man, a boy, whose arms they had removed. This one, the young man who had made such a commotion, screaming his dismay in Flo's ward, had been transferred to the neuro unit, a victim of his despair at his crippling condition. There had been so many, too many, most of whom she'd had no time or opportunity to ask about their recoveries.

"I want to use what we've learned here," she told Therese. "But I don't know yet what that is."

"Too tired."

"Too crazy. We should be talking about drinking

274

champagne and going on leave to Paris."

"You should. You can. I'd go if I had a man like your British captain."

Gwen wiggled her brows. "I just might."

"He is more than a fling, isn't he?"

"Truly? He is my biggest concern." *Until the past two days.* "I've committed that thoroughly modern act and had an affair with a dashing man."

"You aren't the only nurse who has. Look at Pearl."

"And she should. She loves him. God." Gwen ran a hand through her hair. "Things will be different for women soon, very soon. They have to be." *Even here we've seen that a woman must have equal status with a man. If she is denied that, everyone loses. And people can die from the failures to ensure it.* "It won't be a crime to be a complete woman and think and feel and do and even make love."

Therese waved a hand. "Let's applaud the day when girls from our class can keep company with any man without bearing a heavy price."

"Wearing a scarlet letter?"

"Life is hard enough without that." Therese widened her eyes. "What will you do about Adam?"

"I care for him. But he has a family who are…well to do. And I have my sister to consider. My aunt and my cousins—" She was about to say they relied on her. But her aunt didn't. And after Helen got married, Susannah and Win counted on Helen. "I may have done the most outlandish thing here and fallen in love with a man I can't have."

"What does he say about that?"

Gwen shook her head. "I'll have to find him and

ask."

Therese winked. "I should say so. If I had a man who looked like that, I'd settle our differences."

"At any price?"

"Oh, I don't know. What would you lose? If you love him and want to marry him, why couldn't Susannah go to England to live? I hear they speak English there."

She smiled. "He hasn't asked." *And I question if I want him to. Now that I might want to be more than a nurse. More than a wife.*

"Give the man a chance, woman. He's been at Pershing's beck and call. Running off to British headquarters. He's had no bloody time!" She arched her brows and slapped her hands on her knees. "Okay. I see you no longer want to discuss this. Very well. Shall we go to breakfast?"

"Frankly, I can wait for more of cook's oatmeal. I'm too overwrought to eat. Peace is so new. I don't dare think beyond war."

Therese grinned. "I do. Soon? No more eating slop. Working my ass off. Fighting with doctors. *Jeezus!* I think I like this crap!"

"You're punchy." Gwen laughed, purposely steering the conversation to a lighter note.

"You bet I am. I mean, have you thought about this peacetime business? How can Scranton be as...demanding as all this?"

As rewarding. "What you want is a new challenge."

"Not in this man's Army." Therese groused about lack of respect for the nurses. "Women got the butt end of it."

Gwen nodded. "That's the truth. I'm fed up with playing second fiddle to privates and officers. What we did here these past months must count for something to someone."

"It will if we make a stink about it. And I tell you, especially what *you* did these past few hours, better count to a few big *someones*."

"Don't bet on it. But I'll make a point to tell them what we need. Rank and pay and equal responsibility." She rubbed her hands over her face. She shouldn't allow herself to fear consequences from an act that at the time had been so necessary. So right. "They could send me home tomorrow."

"They'd be damn fools if they did. After how you saved those men?"

Gwen looked at her friend with all the gratitude in her heart for her support. "You did, too."

"Oh, big stuff! I gave them drops of ether. *You*, my darling woman, stitched them up!"

I did. I did. I was useful, absorbed, possessed by the challenge. But being a surgeon is not my duty. And I could pay prices for usurping the role. "I expect anything from O'Bryan. After last night when he threw the scalpel, I don't know who he is."

"Hey, honey. *He* doesn't know who he is."

"He's sick."

"You've got that right. But he also had a responsibility and he reneged on it. His career? *C'est fini*." She drew a finger across her neck.

"We'll see. He could press charges against me." *Ruin me. Say anything. Anything.* Had she been naïve to think she'd never have to fight this kind of perversion ever again?

"For what? Throwing him out?"

What could Doc do? Would he lie? Why not?
"Wosnicki and Hartman can testify he was crazy. That he threw the knife at me." She trusted that both men would tell the truth.

"Exactly. O'Bryan wasn't drinking. He didn't have the DTs. But he was on a dry drunk." Therese rolled her eyes. "Call it whatever, the man had to go! He can't do anything to you now. Besides, you are contract labor. Remember that. He might be an officer, but by God, he was no gentleman, and no leader. Let him rot. Besides, it's you who should charge him with attempted murder."

"Oh." She was repulsed by the idea. "I wouldn't."

"He threw that knife at you and we three were witnesses. If brass comes to ask questions, we'll give them an earful."

Gwen bit her lip, her mind running a mile a minute. Hartman had handed Doc over to the admitting officers right after the incident. He'd told Gwen and Therese that when he'd returned to the OR. "I wonder what admitting did with him. Did you talk to Hartman this morning? Did you ask?"

Therese shook her head. "I don't care where he is as long as he is not in the same OR with me."

Gwen reached for her raincoat and hat. "I have to find out."

"Aw, hell. Me, too." Therese slapped her hands on her knees and struggled to her feet. "I can't sleep anyway."

****

"Where is Private Hartman?" Gwen asked Wosnicki when they found him outside the enlisted men's mess tent drinking a cup of coffee.

"Got one of the ambulance boys to drive him and Doc O'Bryan down to the evac hospital," he said, eyeing her, wary at her question. "Why?"

"I wanted to know what happened to O'Bryan."

"He told you that he turned him over to the admitting staff after you threw him out of the OR."

"You told them what happened?"

"Yes. Why? Didn't you want us to?"

"Of course. How was he this morning? Doc, I mean."

"Quiet. I got a glimpse of him as they put him in the car. Hartman said they told him that Doc just sat in admitting, quiet as a mouse. Didn't sleep. Not for all those hours. I'd say he's got his own shell shock. Catatonic maybe officially."

She grimaced that O'Bryan suffered so. "Any idea when they'll be back?"

"Nah. They're probably waiting for word from Chaumont. I'd want to be where the party is, if there's peace."

"Right. Thanks." she gave him a small smile as she listened to the uncanny silence of the morning. "Shall we take a walk, Therese? Up there?"

Therese followed her line of vision toward the road the ambulances took from the front lines to their tent. "Let's."

The road was a rut of mud and snow and rocks churned by tanks and trucks and the feet of thousands of Americans on their way to the war to end war. The two of them trudged along, catching each other as they slipped and slid in the melting snow. Atop a hill lay the remains of a village, the stones gray, scattered on the ground and covered in slime. The roofs had collapsed. The walls stood, lonely sentinels to the white winter sky. Here and there were a trestle table, a chair, a bed, now rotting remnants of lives once passed here. The church, bare of all adornments, sat on the pinnacle. The altar window was blown out. The pews blasted to smithereens.

Gwen and Therese nodded at each other, mutely agreeing to continue on the path down the northern side of the mountain. But at the ridge, they paused and clutched each others' hands harder at the sight. Before them lay the American Army, thousands strong, in miles' long front formations of silver tanks and dark gray cannons, a sea of muted browns and brass, soldiers moving slowly, waiting to hear the word that would take them home or send them forward again onto a plain of destruction.

"If there is no cease-fire, we're back in our surgery tonight," Gwen said to her.

"We'll do it."

"We will."

"You loved it, didn't you?"

Gwen nodded, not daring to look at Therese lest her friend think pride the reason she valued the experience. "I would do it again. All of it. Send O'Bryan out."

"Because you are capable."

"Thank you. I'm grateful that you think so."

"I watched you. I know so."

"Let's go back then. I've seen enough here."

"And I'm tired now," Therese said with a consoling smile. "You?"

"Like never before."

****

By the time they entered the clearing, men were laughing, slapping each other on the back. One danced a jig in the snow.

Peace had come.

Gwen and Therese walked to their tent, flopped down on their cots and agreed that this time when they slept, they could for as long as they needed. They did not have to rise to mend another wounded man.

"Get up! Get up!" Hartman called to them outside their tent.

"What's wrong?" Gwen was the first to sit up and inquire. "Is the cease-fire over? If we're at war —?"

"We're pulling out. Pack. The convoy moves in ten minutes."

"Christ!" Therese moaned, scratching her head like she had cooties.

"Enough time to pee and put your drawers on," Gwen groused.

"If I had any! I lost mine in the air raid!"

Gwen stared at her and the two of them burst out laughing. "That doesn't sound right."

"Yeah, well. It doesn't feel right either." She was up and scurrying around her cot. "Hell, why can't I just burn it? Or leave it all here for the crows?"

Gwen pointed a finger at her. "Not a bad idea. We could buy new lingerie in Paris."

"Paris. I could get so lucky. You, I predict, are going with a gorgeous man. Me? I'm probably going with Wosnicki!"

Minutes later, they were piled into the transport truck, the last few on, Gwen sitting next to Hartman and Therese next to Wosnicki.

Gwen turned to Hartman. "So this cease-fire is real?"

"We're going down the line, aren't we?"

His tone had a note of comeuppance to it.

Therese arched a brow at her.

Gwen had to ask. "What bothers you, Hartman?"

He flexed his shoulders and tore his gaze from hers to the passing landscape. The convoy had joined a contingent of ambulances carrying first aid station personnel, and their laughter felt like balm for an old wound. "Doc O'Bryan refused to be examined. You need to know."

"He recovered his ability to speak, then." Did he recover his ability to act like a man?

"Yes, ma'am. He dismissed himself from the chief surgeon and the idiot let him go."

That didn't sound safe to her. "Where did he go?"

"The village of Le Couret."

"Do they have a café there?"

"They all do, don't they?" He crossed his arms and focused on the roof of the truck.

Therese sighed. "Shit. So he bided his time, got himself out of Dodge and headed down to the local watering hole."

"Did you file a report with the chief?"

Hartman snorted. "Only what I told him. I couldn't write it down. The man was up to his armpits in secondary surgeries from us and the other mobile units." He shifted, tears glistening on his lashes, the first time Gwen had seen the orderly break down. "Fucking war should have ended years ago. Years ago."

Wosnicki caught Gwen's eye and shook his head briefly.

"Did you get bad news recently, Hartman?" she asked him.

He swallowed. Hard. "One of those boys in the yard is my best friend. Was my best friend."

"I'm so sorry, Hartman."

Therese met her gaze.

"Don't worry about Doctor O'Bryan," Gwen told him. "I'll talk to the chief when we pull in. Tell him what happened up there with us."

"Yes, ma'am." He wiped his nose with the back of his hand. "And I'll back you up, ma'am. Doc had no business acting like that with you. I know he was ape shit and he coulda killed us all. Coulda but didn't. Don't you worry none."

"Thank you, Hartman. I appreciate that."

****

More than two hours later, their convoy came to a halt outside Varennes, a small town where once the king of France had fled from revolutionaries with his wife and children. The church where he had taken sanctuary still stood in the square, so said the captain who checked in their team.

"You folks had it tough up there near the line. We're in pretty good shape at the moment. Rested and fed. Any of you want to fall out and go to chow, do it. Nurse Spencer?" The captain looked up from his roster and motioned her forward. "Come with me."

They strode in silence as the captain headed toward the old red brick building where Gwen saw the regimental flags flying.

"Wait here," he told her after they climbed a narrow staircase and entered a small hall with a few chairs. "Colonel Hendricks wants to talk to you."

She cooled her heels for long anxious minutes until a private opened the far door and ushered her inside a large room with a portly white-haired officer behind a large desk.

"Spencer!" He barked. "Sit there."

She took a chair in front of his desk. "Yes, sir."

"I have a report here from your Private Hartman, your orderly in the mobile surgical team up in sector five. Very disturbing. Very."

She waited for an indication that the colonel had read the report.

"Tell me what happened, Spencer." He looked upon her with a calm expression.

She took his polite tone to mean her statement might really be heard and that he would weigh her description and search it for truth. She spoke softly, her recollections facts, her description spare and hopefully, useful. She told of the incident of a few nights ago, but also indicated O'Bryan's behavior before it. The months of drinking. The nights when his performance was less than perfect, but adequate. And then the deterioration of that to the chaos of a few nights ago.

Hendricks pursed his lips, taking his time to speak again. "Doctor O'Bryan seemed rational when he was here, Spencer."

"He changes. Under the influence of continuously drinking alcohol, he has become a different man." *Barely civil now.*

He tapped his fingers on a sheaf of papers. "These are serious charges."

"I realize they are and for months, I've debated discussing them with any staff. I did tell the CO of the evac hospital about this weeks ago. But what occurred the other night was so distressing, I know it is my duty to tell you. Just as it was my duty to relieve the doctor of his responsibilities. Had he continued, we would have lost men, sir, not saved them."

"There may be an official inquiry."

He wished to see if she would flinch from the challenge? "I am aware."

"You would endure that?" His tone rose, a threat inherent.

"Sir, what I told you is the truth. I would endure the anxiety of such an inquiry, but I do not shrink from it, if that is what you seek to know."

"I do." He did not move.

Neither did she as she stared back at him. He could not intimidate her.

"Thank you. You are dismissed."

She rose and turned her back on him.

Outside, she stood on the top step, inhaling the bracing air. Across the street, a tall gray haired man stepped from the tavern into the lane.

She caught her breath.

Doc.

He saw her immediately, his lips drawing tight across his teeth. His haggard eyes bloodshot. "Bitch," she saw him form the word more than she heard them.

She shivered in her raincoat. *Go back to the unit. Ignore him.*

But he started to run. Lope. He slipped, slid. He was ungainly…and drunk.

He yelled at her, waving like a madman, bellowing that he wouldn't let her ruin him, after all he had done for her, all he tried to teach her and—

He stepped into a ditch just as an Army truck came

285

careening around the corner. Behind the wheel, the Army driver fumbled with the steering wheel and brake, but the vehicle ran so quickly, it skidded in the mud and sleet, veering into the ditch at breakneck speed. O'Bryan scrambled to find purchase. The muck was too thick, sucking him backward. The truck slammed into his back, bending him over the hood and throwing him high and wide.

No! No, no, no.

Gwen ran, crossing the square, screaming at the driver, dodging the truck herself as she squatted, went to her knees and bent to his battered body.

She called to him, pleaded with him, cried over him.

But people came to urge her away.

The chief.

Hartman.

Therese. "Come along, Gwen. He's gone, honey. Let Hartman and Wosnicki take him. He's gone."

Chapter Sixteen

Inside the Chateau du Jardin, the quiet voice of the priest reciting the marriage vows brought a new tranquility to the building that had so recently been hospital to hundreds of recuperating Doughboys. Now, a month since the Armistice, the house had once more become a home to its former owner, *comte* Chatillon. And within minutes, it would be home to his new wife as well.

Her eye on the front door, Gwen had hoped that Adam would arrive in time for the ceremony. He'd sent a telegram promising to be here, but she had learned his time was far from his own. He had sent word three times since the Armistice that he would visit her here, but arrived only once last week. Then he had stayed for a total of four or five minutes. Running between Pershing's staff and British headquarters, he could not predict what new crisis would consume him day to day.

"Gwen," Pearl whispered, "did you bring the ring?"

"Oh, yes. Sorry." She dug in her jacket pocket for the simple gold band that Pearl had made in Paris to bind her to the Frenchman she had come to adore.

Beside Gwen stood Flo and Therese. All of them wore their dress uniforms. But for the bride, who had recently resigned her contract with the Army Nurse Corps, a new ankle-length gown of ivory satin graced her tall figure. Pearl wore the luxurious gown with dignity and a hint of revelry.

Gwen smiled at the memory of the trip the four nurses had taken to Paris for Pearl to buy wedding attire and Val's ring. The women had to seek permission from Bernice Dalton who was once more the matron for all of them now that Gwen and Therese had returned to base hospital. Dalton had shooed them off with a two-day pass.

"Do not return later than that eight o'clock train from Gare de L'est," Dalton had warned. "If you do, I will have you on report. You, Markham, are not free of me until next Saturday at midnight. Reynard and Spencer, you two are still on surgical shifts. And all of you,"—she had run a jaundiced eye over them—"are my only reliable nurses until headquarters finds me four who have volunteered to stay on."

"What else is new?" Gwen asked with a light heart. The base hospital was emptying quickly, becoming a ghost town of cavernous wooden buildings on the Chateau du Jardin's grounds. Each morning, the ambulance crew took ten or twelve Doughboys whose conditions had stabilized enough for them to travel long distances, down the line to the hospital complexes in Mars or on to the French coast at Brest or St. Nazaire. She and Therese had been assigned to a new surgical unit that performed secondary surgeries. Flo still headed the amputee ward. All three of them had volunteered to extend their service with the Army in France until all American wounded cleared all medical facilities abroad. "With us, you don't need anyone else."

"Yep. I've lost so much sleep here in sunny fun-filled France," said Flo with a newly developed sense of satire, "I'm already ten years older."

"Get out!" Dalton handed over their leave orders. "When you return, come to my quarters immediately."

Pearl had frowned at her. "Oh, you won't make them work the midnight shift. Will you?"

"I might. Unless—"

Gwen had caught a note of mischief in Dalton's mood. "Unless what?"

"You show me the lingerie you buy."

Gwen had hooted. She could laugh so easily these days. The stress of combat duty had dissolved like a bad dream. "Really?"

"Of course. You ladies have been to Paris before. I have not had that pleasure."

That was true. Even Flo had gone for two days just before the Argonne push. With two of her Red Cross staff, Flo had gone to Montmartre and even the Rue Pigalle. She had seen can-can dancers, women gymnasts, female impersonators, and even women of the night. She had smoked, drunk wine—and danced with strangers. Best of all, Flo had learned how to belly laugh.

Dalton surveyed them all. "I await my Parisian holiday. Till then you will bring me all your purchases to view."

When they had returned and revealed their stash, the woman had blushed at the sheer silk panties and lace cupped brassieres Pearl had purchased. But she approved them all. "Love is to be celebrated. What better way than to dress for the experience?"

"Or undress," Gwen added and got a royal ribbing from all the women.

Now, here stood Pearl before the local Catholic priest wearing her luscious unmentionables beneath the rich fall of pale satin. And from the looks of her groom, he could not wait to take it all off her.

Gwen blushed at the thought. She envied Pearl. Envied her adventurous spirit to accept the Count's proposal. Applauded her willingness to live for the rest of her life in a country that was not hers, among people who were virtual strangers to her.

Could she do the same herself?

Last week, Adam had arrived in base hospital one afternoon in a staff car on his way to Paris. He'd stayed for only a few minutes and vowed to return later for a long talk with her. In his eyes, she had seen and heard the compelling desire he bore her. Her blood rushed in her ears, excited to have him so devoted to her. His enchantment with her never seemed to diminish.

Hers for him, meanwhile, grew more precious, more uncontrollable—and more inscrutable. What could she bring him that he could love? What was it he saw that inspired him to want her in his arms?

Truly, she could be so bold as to say she thought herself lovable. She was a woman with drive, some education, and perhaps more courage than the average female. But to be desired by this extraordinary man who was neither her countryman, nor any type of man she had ever known, shocked and pleased her.

"Now I will kiss you," Chatillon told his new wife as he pulled her flush to him and bent her backwards against a tall chair in a smacker worthy of lovers in the picture shows.

"Gee," said Flo, fanning herself theatrically. "Do they let you do that in the Catholic ceremony?"

"That," the Count said, wiggling his brows like a lothario, "is why we have been wed in my home."

Pearl put a hand to his chest, restraining him, even as she laughed like a girl. "I told him we will have this wedding supper like civilized beings. Oh, ohh, *mon cher*, do catch the priest and have him stay for the meal."

Her husband hurried off after the pudgy little man whom he had had brought up from the village church to perform the ceremony.

"Let's go into the kitchen." Pearl hooked one arm through Gwen's and another through Flo's who then took hold of Bernice Dalton. "Val has a surprise for us, he says. Won't tell me what it is."

Just as the four women were seated at the kitchen table, Val returned with the cleric. With flourishes, he pulled out the chair for the priest and told everyone to wait. Off he trotted out the back door into the snowy afternoon.

Minutes ticked by.

Pearl folded her arms. "Do you think he has deserted me on my wedding day?"

"Abandoned you to his chateau," Gwen said, her arms opening wide to the beauty of the centuries-old abode that only in the past week took on the color and form of a residence of a nobleman. Valentin had resurrected his family's Rococo furniture from the cellars. As he sorted and patched and repaired the woodwork and upholstery, he had hired a few discharged *poilus* to whitewash the rooms, wiping away all traces of Flo's amputee ward and Pearl's post-op room. Even upstairs—especially upstairs—where the operating room had once taken over his master suite, Val had somewhere found and then reinstalled the most enormous bed any of them had ever seen.

Pearl had gasped at the glorious size of it.

Flo had chuckled and bet "if anyone can make use of each inch, it is Val...and you."

Gwen had laughed and yearned for as wide and lovely a marital bed as this one.

Now she bit her lip, pushing aside her envy of Pearl and Val, and vowing to find the same happiness for herself. *If she dared.*

"Here he comes," Bernie Dalton said as she took another sip of her champagne, now a favorite of hers on off duty hours.

Through the back door, Val entered with a large wooden box. Engraved and gilded, the box was decorated in a delicate decoupage with golden grommets at each bottom corner. He lifted the lid and his guests peered inside, then blinked and stared at him, peering down again into the painted box. There in the faded red satin sat countless glistening, gleaming glorious jewels. The first item he removed was a string of perfect white pearls, as long as his arm. These he took in hand, moved behind his wife and told her to sit down, please.

She sat, with a thud.

Around her throat, Val hung the length of translucent pearls. His fingertips lingered on the nape of his bride's neck, then slid to the hollow of her throat, pressed her head back so that he could kiss her with all the passion he could now display for her in public.

"For my wife, the *comtesse* Chatillon, the pearls

whose beauty she outshines. You are the jewel of my life." He claimed her lips yet again.

Gwen raised her glass to the others assembled and silently toasted the embracing couple.

Pearl flushed beet red when Val took his mouth from hers. "They're stunning."

"They are all yours." He inclined his head toward the box.

She took another glimpse of the array of gems. "But—there are so very many of them. Where did you get them?"

"Well, let me see." He removed a ruby brooch big as his palm. "This was my grandmother's. For court dress. My grandfather bought it for her when she was presented to Napoleon the Second Emperor. This—" He held up a sapphire-studded hair bob. "Hmm. This belonged to my Aunt Delphine, who wore wigs because, poor soul, she was bald. Father declared that her love of natural hair pompadours nearly bankrupted us."

"And these?" Pearl stroked the chain of pearls.

He shrugged. "I have no knowledge of their past."

"You went outside to get them. Where were they?" Gwen asked.

"Perceptive of you, Gwen. I hid them before I left to join the Army in 'fourteen. I did not know when I would return, and as it happened, when I was wounded in Meaux and lost my arm, I did not come back for almost a year. But I had buried them in the root cellar near the hen house. When I returned here from Paris, I thought it wise to leave the box in the ground. I did not need them. They were safe where they were. But now. *Viola!* They aspire to adorn your throat and hair and breast, my pretty *Perle*." He chucked his wife under her chin.

"Oh, Val. Be reasonable." She looked flustered and totally embarrassed. "I cannot wear all these. I would not know how. When would I even have the chance?"

"Every day, *ma cherie*. You will choose one and wear it in the house."

"Absurd. I am not royalty, not really a…a countess."

"My wife," he intoned as he raised her chin. "You are the fifteenth Countess Chatillon, cousins to the Valois, descendants of the Capetians and you are to be the mother of the next *comte*. You are my countess. You will wear them."

Not one person in the kitchen moved a muscle.

Then Pearl blinked. And then she cried, tears cascading down her cheeks. "You are so good to me. What can I do but love you?"

He shrugged. "Well, there you are. A perfect duo. Soon to be a trio."

Oh, my god. Gwen locked eyes with Pearl. "Then you are pregnant?"

She winced, glancing at Dalton. "Yes, I am. Due in July, I estimate. I'm sorry, Bernie."

"Oh, dear Pearl, please do not be. I knew you two were not simply holding hands. I might be a spinster, but I am not blind or dumb. It is a wondrous thing that from this hell you have found each other and we all may have a baby to cuddle and coo." She raised her glass. "I am empty, Valentin, and I wish to propose a toast, man. Hop to it, will you?"

The sound of a car engine outside made all eyes turn toward the front door.

Gwen beamed when it opened and there stood Captain Adam Fairleigh in all his spiffy glory. He had two men with him, too. One was the American who had come to collect him that first time Gwen had met Adam. The other man was new to her.

"I've come for the wedding and brought a few chaps to help all of you celebrate," Adam announced, his grin big and joyous.

"And we brought other soldiers," the man whom Gwen had met announced as he hoisted a bottle of wine in each hand. So did the third gentleman.

Val rose to welcome Adam, his arms going around him like a long lost friend. "*Bon soir*, Captain. Welcome, welcome. We need more to celebrate our happiness. Who do we have here?"

Adam introduced his American colleague and the other man. Then he took Pearl in his arms to offer his congratulations. "May you have many happy years together, Pearl."

"Thank you, Captain."

"Adam, please. You are out of the Army and I was never one for ceremony with civilians."

Gwen stood back, allowing him to make his way to Therese and Flo, both of whom he had met briefly the last time he came through. But Dalton he had never met.

Amid those who knew of Adam's and her romance so well, Gwen debated how to greet him. She was still in the Army. He was still an officer, albeit British. His colleagues stood close by. And Dalton was present, the warden of propriety. Protocol demanded a polite approach.

Then he turned to her, his green eyes bright with

delight. "Hello."

Gwen smiled, feeling awkward about walking into his arms to greet him. "Captain, I want you to meet our matron, Bernice Dalton.

He arched a brow at her in surprise, but with a finesse that soothed her, he put out his hand to introduce himself to the matron. "Bernice Dalton. How do you do, *madame*. I am honored at last to make your acquaintance."

"And I yours, Captain. I am delighted you have come today. I have often wished to see the cut of you, sir. Our Spencer is a brilliant young woman, bold and dedicated. No flibbertigibbet, sir. And I want for her a substantial man who values her, heart and soul."

"Thank you, ma'am." He gave a little bow to show his deference to her words, then threw Gwen a crooked smile. "I shall endeavor to prove my mettle. I, too, know our Spencer is worthy of the finest of men. I attempt to be the one man she chooses."

Gwen flushed with delight. He could charm the paint off walls. Dalton certainly thought so as she allowed him to lead her back to her seat.

"Oh, for God's sakes, Captain," Dalton scolded him, "take Spencer outside for a few minutes will you, please?"

Gwen didn't wait for him to act, but with a grin and a toss of her head, turned on her heel for the door.

Adam followed her out to the porch in the frigid air. He wrapped his arms around her and held her in his solid embrace. "Gwen," he said as he kissed her with the reverence that never ceased to astonish her.

She cupped his cheeks, then ran her fingers through his hair, knocking his cap askew. "You feel wonderful.

But you're cold. Can I warm you up?"

Laughing, he whirled her to the corner of the porch where the wind was blocked by the house and by his body. "Kiss me again and I'll tell you when I've gone to ashes."

"I'm cinders myself," she whispered, grabbing his lapels and giving herself up to the abandon he inspired.

In between lingering kisses, he told her he could stay only an hour or so. "It's not enough. Never enough. How long will you be here? Does Dalton know when the hospital closes?"

She stood on her toes to bring him closer, sampling his lips and sighing. "No idea. She thinks we're to be posted in St. Nazaire or Brest. Those will be our big embarkation points."

His fingers traced the outline of her lower lip. "Ask for Brest. When you go, send me a message through the mail pack."

"I will, but won't I see you again?" She sounded as if she were pleading, and God knew, she was. She hated to think her time with him was at an end, brief and glorious as it had been. Selfishly, she had even volunteered to stay on so that she might see him more often. "When do you go home?"

"I've been a few times. As courier, mostly." He shook his head, binding her closer to him. "But permanently? I don't go for months. But you mustn't fret. We'll be together. I'll see to it."

"How?"

"I'll come here as often as I can. Brest, too. Perhaps I would see you more frequently if you were stationed there. It's closer to England. Certainly closer than St. Nazaire. But I did ask the medical brass in headquarters the other day about expected dates to close all your American hospitals. They're thinking six to eight months."

"That long?" She hadn't expected that. Guilt over leaving Susannah with Helen leapt through her. "I signed up until all our hospitals are closed. All our men returned home."

"I'll have an idea when your medical corps are packing up for good. I'll send you word. Before then, you'll be entitled to a few days' leave. Take it with me."

"Paris?" She grew wistful, wanting to relive the days and nights with him that had melted her heart.

"No, better. Gwen, darling, come to England with me. Meet my family."

There it was. The invitation she had fantasized about—and dreaded.

"I assure you they are polite and charming people. Father can be stuffy. Mother is...unhappy since my older brother George was wounded in 'fifteen. He...he has a facial deformity. Rather frightening to look at him. But he will soon enter a facility where the doctors treat such wounds. We hope for him, if not for his failing marriage. My sister, too, suffers from the death of her husband. But we carry on. They all want to meet you."

"You've told them about the American nurse?"

"They have only the finest reports of that accomplished woman. Except, of course, that her German is frightful."

"Oh, what a claim to fame." She frowned, glancing down at the gold burnish of the buttons on his uniform. "I want them to think me acceptable."

He lifted her chin. "I know you are. Their opinions, their challenges are their own. Tolerate their foibles. Dismiss their transgressions. You know what I want for us."

She shivered at the giddy hope that the two of them could have more than this relationship fraught with torrid longing and all-too-brief rendezvous. "I do."

"Come home with me then. See who I am. See what I am when I am not this. Not here."

And what would you do if you saw what I am when I am not this, not here?

He took her by her shoulders. "Look at me. I want you as you are, beautiful and wise and smart. I want you. You owe it to yourself to come to England with me for a few days. You owe it to me."

"You're right." She couldn't deny him or herself. She wanted this love affair. She needed him in so many ways. To laugh with him. To fill the lonely spaces in her heart where a lover should dwell. To complement her existence, be her friend and supporter. Her mother and father had had that. She deserved that, too. Especially now, after all she been through. How she had worked, and slaved to save herself, her integrity. Didn't she deserve the glory, the reward of a man to love and one who loved her? "I'll go home with you, Adam."

He sealed their agreement with a kiss. "I will prove to you I am worth every bit of your devotion."

"I never doubted that."

****

Three days before Christmas, Dalton invited her into her quarters. "We have to talk."

"Shall we go have coffee in the mess?"

"No. We need the privacy."

"Okay." Were they going to rehash the story about Doc? A twinge of panic hit her and she fought it back. She had thought that Hendrick's inquiry had been settled weeks ago when all of them who had been in the OR that night had given the same testimony about O'Bryan's wild behavior. Gwen removed her apron and sank to the wooden chair Dalton indicated. "What's this about?"

"I received my weekly orders from headquarters of the Occupation this morning." The Army had renamed itself after the Armistice, taking over parts of the German border even as it processed home most American troops to the continental United States. "Inside, I have a message from the medical chief in Mars hospital center. About you."

"Oh?" *Why Mars?* They wouldn't want her to transfer there, would they? That was east, not west, not Brest, not closer to England. "What does it say?"

"They are processing the death records of Americans and one of them is Doctor O'Bryan's."

Gwen swallowed, fighting the rush of emotions that could envelop her. Love, hate, respect, despair jumbled together. She still mourned him, hearing his voice as he gave her directions in surgery, seeing him nod in approval when she aided him with a Doughboy's sutures. He had been her teacher, her friend, her model physician. Then as his health deteriorated, he no longer represented anything to her. His death was a void, a vacuum, a dull and ever-present echo of his loss.

Dalton took from her pocket a letter. Gwen could see from her vantage that it was an official document, typed, formally addressed, bearing many signatures.

"They sent a copy of the letter to me, as your matron. I will let you read it for yourself."

She took it from her Dalton's hands, reading it once, then again. This was from the adjutant's office? She had no idea what that was. A notice of death beneficiary from the estate of Captain Joseph O'Bryan, physician, late of Scranton, Pennsylvania. "What does this mean?"

"Read on."

The paper declared, in its own grand legal terms, that Captain O'Bryan purchased a life insurance policy in the amount of ten thousand dollars when he joined the Army Officer Corps in nineteen seventeen. The beneficiary of that amount is Gwendolyn Spencer, contract nurse, Army Nurse Corps, last home address Prospect Street, Peckville, Pennsylvania.

Ten thousand dollars? From Doc? His life insurance. Dear God.

Gwen put a hand to her brow, her heart racing. "Why would he do this?"

"He cared for you, saw potential in you. Here is proof. Here is a gift of his admiration."

"Oh, ma'am, how can I take this?" She shook with grief. "He was so ill."

Dalton took both her hands and urged her be calm. "Doctor O'Bryan was an excellent physician, a talented surgeon. He saw the same skill in you."

"Oh, I only assisted him."

"But you did it so well that he wanted you to be rewarded, praised, and encouraged. In Scranton, he saw it. He told me after you volunteered for the Corps that he would take you under his wing here, train you, give you openings to try your hand, literally, at surgery. He knew that here we would all be tried and tested to the last degree. Of course, he did not foresee the one who would be most tested and break was he, himself." Dalton pressed her lips together, suppressing the grief that welled in her voice.

"He has no family? No wife or children? They should have this."

"He lost his wife many years ago, my dear. She died in childbirth and he could not save her. I do not know the circumstances, but it was after that he began to find solace in whiskey and wine. Over the years, he would stop, then start again. Each time, his behaviors became more erratic, more incurable. There is no one at home who loves him, Gwen. But you did, when he deserved it. And he knew it. He did. You were his prize, his surrogate daughter, his golden student. You are to have this, Gwen."

Tears slid from her eyes. "But I was the one to turn him out of his own surgery."

"And rightly so, my dear woman. Rightly so."

She raised the letter. "What will I do with this?"

"Make your life better. Happier. He wanted that for you. What your heart desires is what he thought you most worthy to have. Take it in the spirit he gave it. With love and hope that whatever you choose, it fulfills you. "

She sat there for the rest of the afternoon, mourning with Dalton a man they had both admired and lost to his own hopelessness. They discussed at length what this gift could do for her. The money could be spent to accomplish so many goals for her. A house for herself and Susannah. A financial base that would mean neither she nor her sister would ever want for a home or a loving hearth. Never need to submit to another's control or irrationality.

But it could mean more.

Gwen rose and left Dalton to ponder what else Doc's gift could grant her.

She wandered down the lane to the stone wall where first she and her friends had come upon the wounded that night they arrived on the transport trucks. There on the ground so many hundreds of them had lain writhing in an agony she could not then contemplate. Here she had vowed to aid them. Here she had dedicated herself to using every ounce of her energy and health to heal them, if she could.

That night, when she had ordered Doc from his operating room and it had become her own, she had become empowered with the ability to finally fully do that. She had taken Doc's responsibility. She had taken his role, his job. She had taken his instruction and turned it to her own hand, her own talent.

And that night she had grown into the fullness of what she could become. A physician.

A surgeon.

She stood with her hand on the gray stones and wept for what she might never have known, save for Doc. Might never have learned, save for him. Might never have been able to afford, except for his gift.

Now, now she had to find a way to do that.

In England?

She had no idea how.

But then, she had no idea of how to enter medical school in the States either.

And what would Adam think of that?

What would she gain, what would she lose to use

Doc's gift to gain the goal that totally fulfilled her?
****

The first week in January, Pearl drove Gwen down the frosty lane in a shiny new Renault to the village train station. Beside her sat Val. Gwen rode in the seat behind, but she smiled at the sight of Pearl who occasionally let one hand rest protectively over her little belly.

"I wish you had left for Paris yesterday." Pearl had been complaining about Gwen wearing her uniform the whole time she would be in England. "Then you could have easily stayed overnight so that you could go to that lingerie shop in the Rue Haussmann and buy a few things for this visit."

Gwen fidgeted at the idea of appearing before Adam in frilly laces and trims. She was bold enough, brazen enough to want to be naked with him again. "I am not there to seduce Adam." *Though the lure of it dances through my imagination.*

"Nonsense. He wants you there for more than one reason," Pearl went on. "Yes, of course, he wants you to meet his parents, but at night—"

"At night, I will be sleeping, and in his parents' home, I will be sleeping alone."

"Oh, darling, why waste the chance?"

Val reached over to grab his wife's hand. "Hush, *madame*. She is nervous as it is. You must not pester her."

"Okay. Okay." Pearl gave up with a shrug. "But you can accept him. If he proposes, you can accept him, Gwen, you do realize that?" She turned quickly to try to capture Gwen's gaze. "Say you do."

To Pearl over the last few days, Gwen had

disclosed all her concerns about this trip and what it implied. She would tell Adam about Doc's money and reveal her desire to go to medical school. She hadn't had but a few minutes at Val's and Pearl's wedding to tell him what had happened to her that fateful night north of Varennes when she had ordered Doc O'Bryan from the operating room. She had summarized what occurred, Doc's outlandish behavior, how she had banished him from the team and then his accidental death. Now she would tell him what it meant to her future. She had no idea how he would react and that alone had her asking herself if she truly knew him. If he knew her. If they loved each other enough to commit to a life together. "I do."

"It is simple," Pearl rattled on, her eyes on the road. "You love him. He adores you. What better way to live your life?"

Indeed. What better way?

"You can have children. A home of your own. You could bring your sister to live with you."

Gwen noted how vast the countryside seemed these weeks since the Armistice. Solemn and still and empty of everything. Cannons, horses, soldiers. Where were the farmers, their wives? Where were all the children?

"Are you listening to me, Gwen?"

"I am. You sound like Therese now."

"We all want this for you."

That was so true. Therese, Pearl, and Flo, all urged her to marry Adam Fairleigh. *If he asks. And he will.*

She welcomed the proposal.

And debated what her answer might be.

Chapter Seventeen

January 1919

An old hand now at traveling to Paris, Gwen climbed aboard the spartan train headed for *Gare de l'Est*. The car was half empty. No frantic refugees with all their worldly goods under their arms, no French *poilus* with fretful faces going home for a rare, sad visit. Instead, a few businessmen took seats. A priest. American Army officers, too.

She found a seat at the end of a car and took from her suitcase one of the novels she had bought in Paris weeks ago. Soon though, she shoved it back inside. She couldn't read, too excited to have five days with Adam—and too terrified of meeting his family.

She scolded herself for her sensitivity to her social standing. Was this a remnant of her subjugation to the will of her aunt? She had worked to be free of that. She was no miner. And what if her father had been? She had still done much to extricate herself from menial work and accomplished it by herself. She wasn't a nobleman's daughter, but she claimed some nobility in her own right for her own actions. *That should count.*

With that infusion of iron in her backbone, she disembarked and headed outside for the *Gare du Nord* only a few blocks away. Today, the sun shone down creating a brilliant glaze upon the melting snow. She took it as an omen of bright events to come.

Inside the station's central dome, she sought out the listing for the London *quai* and hurried to the track. Beside a news kiosk stood Adam. In his greatcoat, the brown a rich complement to his swarthy complexion, he projected a perfect picture of authority. She might even have said he appeared imperial, except for the way he glanced at his watch and beat his rolled up newspaper against his palm.

He spotted her and his frown became a beam of welcome. Here, where no one knew them, he opened his arms to her and she walked right in. Sighing against him, she relaxed for the first time in hours.

"No troubles on the trip?" he asked, his hand raising her chin, his lush green eyes admiring her.

"None. Only a thousand butterflies in my stomach."

"May I assume I caused them?" he whispered, squeezing her tightly.

"You may."

"I bought our tickets. Let's get inside, then I can greet you properly." He steered her toward the first class compartments, slid open the door, and helped her step up. When he had secured the door, he swept off his hat, took hers, too, and dropped them to the seat. Then he kissed her with thoroughness they had not enjoyed since their first meeting in Paris last spring.

Breathless, she smiled at him. "I feel decadent. I've never traveled first class."

"It's best done," he said as he pulled down all the window shades on the corridor and the outside, "with someone you cannot live without."

She laughed at his gallantry to provide privacy. "I've met that requirement."

He led her to sit down and took her against him to kiss her once again. "So have I."

She cocked a brow at him. "I hope you are not expecting some kind of scandalous behavior in here?"

"I expect innumerable kisses and a chance to hold you for hours uninterrupted by any woman or man, British, American, or German. For that, I asked the ticket clerk to put me in a compartment without any other passengers."

"You bought all the seats?" She was astonished.

"I smiled like a scoundrel and begged her to allow a soldier of the Great War to *rendezvous* with his *amour* in a bit of peace." He winked. "She was terribly understanding."

"I bet she was. The French love a hint of romance."

He grew serious, his knuckles stroking her cheek. "This is no hint."

"No," she agreed and nestled against him. "Nothing small or insignificant, but very grand."

"No snuggling. Too tempting, you see." He pushed her to the corner of the seat. "Get comfortable. Here." He lifted her legs and placed them across his thighs. "Let me remove your boots. Take off your coat and jacket."

"Yes. It's so deliciously warm in here." She waggled a finger at him. "You need to do the same."

"Yes, ma'am." He removed his greatcoat, but as he watched her undo the buttons of her jacket, he stopped her and pointed to her array of ribbons. "When did they give you that?"

"Last week, one French general from our sector sailed into the hospital with an entourage. I think he had a truck load of these to dispense." Still awed by the pretty medal on her chest, Gwen had been embarrassed when the fussy little officer pinned the *Croix de Guerre* on her breast pocket. "Therese got one, too. The mobile unit was such a unique idea."

"You weren't going to tell me?" His eyes danced with pride.

"Oh, phooey. I'm not certain I deserve such a thing. I never fought."

"Of course you did."

"Oh, Adam. I never held a gun, went over the trenches." She reached out to grasp his hand and hold tightly to him. "I never crawled through No Man's Land."

"You went through a no man's land of your own, stitching up men's faces and arms and guts…"

She put her fingertips to his lips. Said that way, it sounded obscene. War was. "It's what I know."

He blessed her fingers with a kiss. "You braved as much as any man. A man in the trenches, can see one, two, ten of his pals blown to pieces. But you saw how many? Hundreds, broken in a thousand different ways. I marvel that you understood what was best done for each and did not lose your mind."

"I thought about only what was possible." She went quiet. She had told him briefly at Pearl's and Val's wedding about Doc's outburst that last night when she had forced him out of the OR. To tell Adam about her desire to go to medical school and how she hoped Doc's life insurance made that possible did not seem appropriate right now. That discussion would cast a pall over their reunion. It could come later. Besides, she was becoming a glutton for happiness and seeing Adam again was the most she'd had in a long time. "Let's not talk about the war. I want you to tell me more about your family. I know so little and I want to look intelligent."

He sat back, massaging her feet as he took his time to begin. "I cannot recall what I told you before. Forgive me, if I bore you."

"You won't."

"Let's see. My family are—rather, *were* lovely people before the war. Very sociable. Lots of friends. Many of my parents' set are much changed now, selling off their London townhomes, retired to the country, lost in grief over sons and daughters killed in the action. Others have lost their fortunes, their lands, their household staffs. Taxes are high. The farms lie fallow. Many men are gone, sacrificed to the misery of the trenches. My parents are only slightly different from their friends. My mother and father count themselves fortunate to still have their three children, but two of them are...shattered. George cannot bear to look at himself in the mirror. Natalie, I'm afraid, doesn't look at her reflection often enough, but prefers to dance at all night parties and gamble away her husband's fortune at cards."

Gwen took Adam's hand, as the misery in his family dimmed his light-hearted mood. "And your parents? What do they think of George and Natalie's behaviors?"

"Ah, what can they do? Tolerate them? Hope for change? Neither my father nor mother had to boost any of us. We each seemed so...so set along a pre-ordained path. George to be heir. Natalie to marry well, give her husband a brood of happy children. Me, to the Army. We never asked for anything else, never thought beyond our noses, never predicted any of our lives would change." He held Gwen's gaze. "So different than you, my darling. Working all your life to rise above your circumstances. And we three?" He laughed ruefully. "We needed no reason to rise. No reason to change. And here we are."

He toyed with her fingers, tracing the edges of her nails. "That said, I will tell you that my parents do attempt to keep some semblance of normality amid the shambles. Both are idiotically devoted to the three of us. After that? My father likes horses, the hunt, his home, his club and his banker. Not in that order. My mother loves her social prominence, her home, her horses and the hunt. Definitely in that order."

She heard reverence and a hint of tolerance in his voice. "And you love them."

"They have their quirks. But yes, I like them better than others I've met."

She waited as he knit his brows and debated how to elaborate.

"My parents began their courtship with money and position as their motivations. That was the norm. Nothing argued against it, except of course, a wretched eternity bound to one you hated. But love hit them quite unawares as they courted. They have grown in that affection, for which we three offspring have been grateful. My sister Natalie took their example and married for love. Her marriage, sad to say, ended too quickly when her husband died in 'fifteen in France. George, too, married the woman he loved. However, his wound—his anguish—has brought them new challenges. I haven't been home but for a few days here and there since he returned from hospital, and I'm not privy to all their conflicts, but he and his wife Clarice have immense problems. She takes great pleasure in being a royal pain in the ass." He stared out the window for a long moment, then looked at Gwen with trepidation clouding his eyes.

"I'll tell you true. Prepare you in case Clarice is at home. She has created quite a stir with us since George was wounded. The problem stems from an incident two years ago." Adam cleared his throat. "She went to the townhouse in London, so she said, to do volunteer hospital work. Who knows how or when precisely she decided to end her work, or if it was an excuse, but she began an affair with a colonel well-known to all of us in the family. George's best friend in university, in fact. Soon, she became pregnant, but aborted the child. We knew only because she had gone to some hack whose butchery nearly killed her. George shook loose of his doldrums and journeyed to bring her home, but she refused. When she recovered, she went away supposedly to Cornwall to her mother's, but in truth, she had gone to live in Wales with a reclusive aunt. George this time hired a detective to find her, but to no result. Finally, out of the blue, last fall, she returned to Fairleigh Haven and claimed she was there to stay. Except she isn't. She leaves at the drop of a hat, returns days or weeks later. When she is at home, she either rides all day or shuts herself up in her suite. My father has talked to her, cut her funds. But she makes herself a right harpy, arguing with George and my mother. And there you have the Fairleighs. What the war has done to us all may never be measured."

She remained silent, any consolation she might offer too insipid, too tasteless for the severity of his family's woes.

"Tell me about your own family," he said, combing her curls over her ears. "I know you have one or two who must challenge your wits. You've intimated as much."

She wove her fingers together. "I want to tell you about her and yet, I don't. I dislike talking about her, and rarely do. I don't want you to conclude I hate her. I don't. But I can't understand her, either. And I can't live with her or allow my sister to live with her. She—" Gwen met his mellow eyes. "She could have destroyed me and I wouldn't allow it. Couldn't."

He drew her closer into his comforting embrace. She told him about the death of her father, her years with her aunt and that woman's attempt to manipulate her and thwart her ambitions. She recounted for him her need to work, to earn, and to give to the family. She described her desire to become more than her aunt had decreed, to discover a finer calling than picking coal or scrubbing floors. She recounted her excitement to enter nurse's training, to join the Army and work beside O'Bryan.

And now she once more came to a juncture in their conversation when she could tell Adam about her total absorption in her surgeries the night she'd thrown Doc out. This time, she went on.

"I never felt fear. When he left, I simply knew what I had to do. I knew how to do it well. With each new patient, I examined his wounds, heard Hartman's description, and I saw the means to cut away or patch or redirect or irrigate as if I envisioned the diagrams on a chalkboard. I never stopped or questioned or debated this or that. I simply did." She saw herself that night, unharried, consumed, driven to another realm where she understood only the rightness of her next move and the next and next. "I must do that again. I want to be a surgeon."

The range of emotions that drifted over his face was the most loving array she'd ever witnessed. Used to others who had objected or argued or counseled or debated, she saw Adam do differently. His expression told her with silent praise of his surprise, his pride, and his support. The gift of his acceptance flowed over her like a benediction, and the shock of a man who could love her and see what pleasure this gave her overwhelmed her.

She threw her arms around him and held on to him with all her might.

"It's okay. Are you crying?" He pulled back. "My God, you are. Why? You didn't think I could accept what you want for yourself?"

"I had no idea what you would think." She took his handkerchief that he shoved into her hand.

"I think it wonderful, darling, that you want to become a doctor. You'll be damn good at it, too."

She sniffled, wiping her cheeks and grinning. "You don't know what it means to me that you won't try to stop me."

"Stop you? Dear Lord. You must think me a real bounder. Why would I try to stop you from having your heart's desire, hmm?"

"I know, I know. Terrible. I need to learn to open my mind where you are concerned. Of course, you would see the value of me being a doctor. You do what you love."

"Ha! Let us please not ascribe your accomplishments to me, my darling."

She could scarcely believe his words. "You don't value what you've done? You're not proud of the Army? Your interrogation of prisoners? The way you crossed the lines? Risked your life?"

"Pride is one reward. But what you found in that tent that night?" He cupped her cheeks. "That is bliss."

The word froze her. Gratified her. "But what of your dedication? How you were trained and—"

"How I was trained, my love, was not what I wanted. It's what I was ordained to become. Second sons take a commission. It's that or the bar or a bank. I daresay, compared to the law and money, I find the army more intriguing." He settled her against him, but she kept her eyes on his matter-of-fact expression. "It's what I do well. It's where I'll stay."

"But you don't stay because you—?"

"Love it?" He shook his head, derision in his grimace. "No. I love only you, Nurse Spencer."

****

Adam's reassurances about how she would fit in to his family evaporated like mist as they drew closer to his home. One indication after another told her she was out of her depth. The black touring car that arrived at Houghton's tiny station with the family chauffeur to greet them was one thing. The iron gates at the entrance to the family estate were the second. But as the car took the road round a natural pond and a fountain filled with stone nymphs, the sight of Fairleigh Haven came into view and Gwen fought a bad case of the shakes.

At the front door, a white-haired liveried butler appeared just as Adam stepped out from the car.

"Hello, Roswell. How are you?"

"Wonderful, sir. Thank you."

She gave the man a curt smile, having no idea if she should speak to him or not. Then thought, *what the hell.* "How do you do."

He blinked. Was he shocked? Had she committed some social sin? *Oh, how to survive this?*

The servant murmured something innocuous sounding, as Adam put his hand to her waist and let her toward the open door. "The staff, what's left of them, will be lined up to greet us. All you need do is smile."

A footman took her overcoat and Adam's. Another had her suitcase in hand. The attention seemed too terribly efficient. And so unnecessary.

All along the servant's line, she nodded and looked congenial. At the end, Adam spun and grinned toward the stairs. "My mother," he told her.

Following his lead, Gwen looked up, stunned by the riot of colors in the life-size portraits adorning the walls and the refracted light from crystal chandeliers. In the center of this dazzling glory stood a grand staircase of polished black marble. The regal steps, Gwen was certain, must lead to heaven. Down them, descended an older steel-haired woman in a mint green diaphanous tea-length gown like those Gwen had seen weeks ago in the boutique windows in Paris. Compared to this fashionably dressed and rigidly coiffed creature, Gwen felt dowdy. Out of place. Worse, the lady examined her with leisurely indifference.

Was this the one whom Adam thought was his loving mother? If so, she was not welcoming his friend to the house with any largesse.

Did he notice? He seemed oblivious as he introduced Gwen, hugging his mother and dropping a kiss to her rosy cheek.

"I am delighted to meet you, ma'am." Gwen put out her hand.

The lady considered it a moment. Then gave in and shook. "And I you. Welcome, Miss Spencer. We have heard much about you from Adam and we need to know more. Ah." She glanced down the hall. "Here is Herbert. Darling, do greet Miss Spencer."

"Gwen, please," she said as Adam's father came upon them and took her hand.

A smile wreathing his face, Herbert Fairleigh raised her hand and kissed the back of it. "Charming. Adam told us you were lovely, Gwen. He did not say you would hypnotize us. My god, boy, you did do well here." He chuckled.

"You are very kind." Gwen blushed, the heat burning her cheeks as she glanced at Adam and pleaded silently to him for intervention.

"My father," he said while embracing the man, "is an old rogue. He will compliment you at every turn."

"But you deserve the praise, Gwen. Is it Gwyneth or Gwendolyn?" The older man whose dark good looks he'd given Adam, took her by the arm and led her toward a room off the foyer, leaving Adam to accompany his mother.

"Gwendolyn, sir. But I have always been known simply as Gwen."

"So shall you be. Let us all go in to the salon and warm you up. George is resting and will join us later. Clarice is not with us these past few days." He looked pained to impart the fact. "Nat went out for lunch but should return soon. I apologize she is late, but what can I say, eh? Tea? Coffee? What would you prefer, Gwen?"

"Tea, thank you." She took the chair Adam's father indicated. Her fanny sank into the upholstered cushion and she mellowed. This kind of comfort she hadn't ever experienced. As she listened to the three Fairleighs discuss the finite details of the train ride and the weather in France, she absorbed the magnificence of the rest of the room. She would bet the room was as large as the entire first floor of Aunt Mary's house on Prospect Street. The walls were a peach-tinged cream, the upholstery shades of vanilla, spring green, and orange. The furniture was ivory wood, curved and elegant, with gold etching the edges. One large tapestry, faded in centuries of sunlight, hung on the widest wall and told tales of knights in armor assaulting a castle.

"Gwen?" Adam stood before her.

"Yes?" She'd been caught, gawking like a child whose face was pressed to the glass of a candy store.

"Your tea, darling."

At his endearment, his mother stilled. "You have four nights with us, is that correct, Gwen?"

"I do, yes." She took a sip of her tea, scalding hot and sweet with honey, the best she'd had in ages. She nodded at Adam in thanks for him dressing it for her exactly as she liked.

"I will return with her," Adam told them as he took his own cup from his mother.

"But I thought you wrote that you had a full week." His mother pouted. "We have much to discuss, dearest. I am..." She pressed her lips together and drank from her cup to hide her distress. "We are quite in need of good company."

"Liv," the elder man prompted, "do not harry the boy."

"I understand, Mother." Adam sat in the sofa nearest Gwen, crossing his legs one over the other and placing his cup and saucer on the nearby table. "But you know my time is not my own."

"But do you have seven days or not?" His mother trained a hard eye on him and then Gwen.

"I do. However, I will not allow Gwen to travel all the way to Paris alone."

"Pardon me, Gwen." The woman seemed to abhor the way her name felt on her tongue. "But you can do without his escort, can you not?"

"Mother!"

"Olivia!"

"We have bread riots in London, Mother." Adam bit off his words.

Gwen had never seen him angry. But incensed was what he really was. It frightened her.

"Honestly, Mother, be sensible. I would not want Nat to travel alone so far. Nor would you. In addition, I have work to do in Paris at the peace conference. The fighting may be over, but the dust and clean up is a frightful mess. The paperwork could fill this house. The scrap heap of cannons, tanks, and planes fill acres of northern France. Land dotted with unexploded bombs and grenades. All our war graves must be organized, our men laid to rest properly. My god. Gwen has men in her hospital still, waiting to recuperate so they can take the damn train down to the coast to sail home and—"

His mother put up her hand. "I do apologize. I am not privy to such scenes. I merely wished to discuss family matters with you and thought an extended stay might provide that opportunity."

"Don't bother him with Nat's and George's woes, Liv. For Christ sake. But these two have fought a grisly war for years and now they have a few days to enjoy themselves. We are very fortunate they want to do it here with us. Don't badger them."

"Yes, of course, Herbert." She set her jaw, her reluctance bitter. "I am sorry, Gwen, Adam. My concerns are parochial, compared to yours. I see that. Please, do go on," she urged them, sat back and suffered. Oh, yes, Gwen had seen that look before. Olivia suffered in silence.

Shall we see the results in some shocking new way?

Gwen drank her tea to warm her against the chilling premonition.

****

That evening, fresh from her bath before she dressed for dinner, Gwen heard a knock on her door. Fearing it might be the maid who'd been assigned to unpack her meager belongings, Gwen secured the sash on the robe borrowed from Natalie earlier and asked who it might be.

"Your personal footman, darling," Adam joked. "Do let me in."

Laughing, she slid it open a crack and warned, "I'm not decent."

"All the better to kiss you," Adam proclaimed, pretending to twirl a wicked moustache. He hoisted a bottle of champagne and two glasses. "We need this after that rigorous lesson in bad manners you got this afternoon."

She agreed, the only balm for a somber teatime with his parents, George, and Natalie would be cheerful hours with Adam. "Do come in."

As he popped the cork and poured, he apologized profusely. He sounded gay, but she could see the tiny lines of anger etched from the corners of his eyes.

"It's not your fault." She threaded her fingers through his hair.

He straightened and took her against him, his lips to her forehead. "That was horrid. I've never seen Natalie so drunk. Nor George so self-righteous."

She nestled close to him. "Natalie I cannot explain. But George has an enormous burden to carry." The poor man's face was a ghoul's. His left cheekbone was gone, crushed. She assumed fragments had been removed. His left ear was gone as well. Whoever the surgeon was who had initially received him had failed to bolster his eye socket and the left side of his face drooped. Though his skin was not marred by excessive burns, his face seemed pulled to one side, the effect eerie. "You say he will go to a reconstructive hospital?"

"Yes, next month. A military hospital near London. Sidcup, it's called. As soon as they have space." He handed her a glass and led her to a sofa where he sat, patted the cushion beside him, and she settled next to him, he with his arm around her. "Here," he said with a clink of his crystal against hers, "is to better times."

"I had patients with similar wounds. One chaplain who lost his jaw. Another who had been terribly burned, poor creature. He would have been in enormous pain. I wonder whatever happened to him. If he survived." She forced her mind back to George. "What do you know of the successes at Sidcup?"

"Not much. Father heard of this from one of his friends, looked into the services and insisted George give it a go. But I do believe George would rather hide here in the house forever and a day."

"You mustn't let him. None of you."

"No, of course not. He does have motivation though." Adam drained his glass and went to bring the bottle over.

"His wife, you mean."

"I do. They once were enchanting to watch. Now?" Adam sighed, pouring more champagne for them both. "She needles him. I wonder that she doesn't throw her affair..." He raked a hand through his hair. "I'm sorry. I was about to say, throw it in his face. Poor choice of words."

His shoulders slumped in gloom. "Mother took me to her sitting room after you left to dress for dinner."

Gwen tucked her feet under her and faced him, her hands stroking his hair. Naked beneath the silk robe, she tingled to be this close to him. "And did she reveal what bothers her?"

Gazing into her eyes, he inhaled and glanced away. "She did. It seems Clarice was here last week, down for one of her horrid little visits from London, only to bring her usual bad news. She has announced to one and all that she has been to her physician in Harley Street, had tests and whatnot, and learned she cannot bear any children."

Gwen felt a sting of sadness for the woman. "That's very difficult to accept."

"For her, yes, I would guess it might be. For George? It crushed him. Mother said he did not move from his rooms until yesterday. I suppose it took a mighty force from Mother for him to appear this afternoon to meet you."

"It's his responsibility to sire a successor," she said with a small understanding of the English inheritance system. "And now he won't be able to."

"Unless he divorces Clarice and marries another."

Gwen foresaw the larger problems. For George. And for Adam. She shivered. "But he won't."

Adam pursed his lips. "No."

"Because he loves her."

"Yes."

Gwen narrowed her gaze on Adam. There was something more. "And so that means what?"

"It means, my darling, that if Clarice can't produce an heir, and George can't or won't summon the courage to find a woman he loves, then the next male issue of the family is the heir to the Earldom of Arun, with all rights, duties, and rewards." Adam ran his gaze over her face. "And any firstborn son of mine succeeds me."

She went to stone.

"I can tell you see the problem."

"Do I?" She stared at him. "I don't dare imagine the...Tell me."

He cupped her cheek. "I planned to say this to you in the garden outside at midnight with the sound of the fountain splashing in the background. But I love you, Gwen. I love you. I want you to marry me. I want you to be my wife, my friend, my succor. And if we are fortunate, I want children with you."

He was so right. She never thought he would propose to her this way. But what did it matter how he had? She loved him and he wanted her to be his wife.

She kissed him quickly, but he was tormented by other thoughts that made his eyes wide and his heart pound.

She hated to ask. But her mind raced. The joy to marry him drowned in the prospect of what obstacles this appeal by his mother would mean to the nature of her own existence.

"Oh, Gwen," he said, his voice full of sorrow, "I never wanted to be saddled with this...this relic." He waved a hand to denote the appointments of the house. "It's a dying estate. Father knows not how to manage the place. He has never collected proper rents. He allows the tenants to farm and never pay their due. He cannot afford to keep up the repairs on the cottages. What do I know of tractors and cows and ducks? My life has been a regimen of men, diplomacy, and deception. I know little of Arun's affairs and do not want to learn more. The land, the estate, the title were George's forte. He should keep them. But he won't."

"What are you saying? That—that you'll give up your commission?" *Would he learn to accept such a sacrifice? She doubted it.*

"My mother would have it so. Yes."

"And live here?"

"To learn the running of the estate. Of course."

"And you?" Gwen asked very quietly. "Have you no say in the matter?"

He studied her. "I do. I want you to think what it would mean."

Bewildered, she shook her head. "I have little idea."

"We would live here. Father and George could coach me. I could learn. And you would learn from Mother how to run the household of Arun."

She was aghast at the outrageous possibility. "I am no countess, darling. You know this."

"You have been many things, my love. Could you not become this, too?"

"But I have never aspired to this. Never." She uncurled herself from the sofa and paced the carpet. "I have no idea how to live here. In the country. Among butlers and maids. I barely knew how to behave with them this afternoon. And your mother balked at something I did. I know she did. It was wrong and I—"

"Stop." He was up, taking her into his embrace. "Stop."

"I can't." She was breathless, witnessing how her hope to cherish him for the rest of her life was collapsing before her eyes. "I love you, Adam. I do. But I cannot be a countess. I cannot be just a wife, an ornament. I was born to work and do."

"I'll give you a job then."

She froze. "You're actually thinking of doing this? Resigning the Army?"

"What choices do I have, Gwen? My life was never like yours. Free of all restraints. Free to be as I wished."

His words riveted her. "Is that what you think of yourself?"

"I was bound to a system. Trained to follow and obey. Not you."

"Me? You thought me free? I was bound. Bound by poverty. Bound by illness and mine cave-ins. Bound by lack of love. And education. And money." She took two steps back from him.

"Don't put words in my mouth. I didn't imply that you—"

"I can't do this, Adam." Tears coursed down her

cheeks.

"How do you know?" He pursued her.

She put her back to the wall. "I can see it. Feel it. If I try to live it, I will be mired in it. I'll die here just as George does, just as Natalie. Just as you will if you give up your profession that you worked so diligently to make your own bright future."

"You're being irrational."

"Am I?"

"You are." He was angry. Incensed. "You love me. Say it again."

"I do love you."

He caught her arms. "And you belong to me."

"I belong to myself."

Chapter Eighteen

June 1919
Brest, France

Gwen paced the dock, the American sailors urging stragglers aboard the naval transport home to New York. Therese, Flo, and Bernie Dalton had taken the gangway nearly an hour ago. She couldn't wait much longer for Adam to arrive.

If he can get away.

He'd been assigned to the military staff at the Paris Peace conferences and since that began a week after their disastrous trip to his parents' home, they had met briefly only twice. She'd met him in Paris on a one day leave in March. He'd come to Brest once after her transfer here in early May.

On neither occasion had they solved any of their problems. He still considered resigning his commission, perhaps after the conference in Paris officially ended the war and he could return home, free to choose his next assignment or leave the Army forever. She had researched how she might attend medical school, largely by discussing the possibility with Dalton and with Tom Baldwin who had returned to duty in the base hospital near Chatillon. Knowing that to enter medical school, she would have to take an entrance exam to show her competency to read and write accurately, Gwen felt confident. If Doc's insurance funds would carry her, she had no idea.

Tormented that she would lose Adam in the process, she nonetheless owed it to herself and to Susannah to return home. Once there, she could learn more about entering medical school. She had told Adam this and, noble creature that he was, he did not argue with her but agreed that she must go.

"I want you to return to me because you want me as I am," he had told her.

She did not do more than agree with that statement. Because he had not yet decided what he wanted for himself, or indeed, offered her any ideas how they might live together if he decided to remain in the Army, she could not do more than nod and smile.

Up ahead, a black Renault displaying British flags pulled alongside the huge black anchor. The driver stepped out and opened the back door. Adam emerged.

In the past few months, he seemed to have become more striking, more worn. His black hair streaked at the temples with gray. His large eyes, always so expressive and warm, were lined with worry. Yet he stood taller, more regal. If the role as military adviser to his delegation at the conference or his view of the Army or even of the war had done this to him, she could understand. What caused her remorse was that she might have added to his transformation.

Spotting her, he broke into a jog, then hugged her close. "Thank God you are here. I was late getting away. Had I missed you, I would have gone back and shot the little man who chewed on my ear."

She caught his face between her hands. "I don't care. You came." Then she pressed her lips to his once and then again.

Around them, sailors and longshoremen on the docks hooted and whistled.

Adam chuckled, but his eyes were grim. "Last chance to stay, darling."

"I can't." Her eyes clouded with tears.

"I know," he whispered against her ear. "That slipped out. Wrong of me."

"I must decide what to do."

"I will, too."

She clutched him close, a part of her he possessed breaking into pieces. "You won't forget me?"

"How could I?" he said with words too bright. "I am not whole without you."

She wanted to sob then. "Write to me. Tell me all you decide."

"And you will do the same."

She nodded, tears dribbling down her cheeks. "I will. Whatever I do, wherever I go, I will write you reams and reams of news."

The same sailor who had urged her aboard minutes ago appeared at her side.

"Ma'am? You must board. The captain is insistent."

Adam lifted her hand and as he had done when first they met, he kissed her palm and closed her fingers over it. "We'll be together again and then you'll return this to me."

She turned away from him then and ran. If she didn't, she knew she would never be able to leave him.

****

Her cousin Helen's home was only a few blocks away from Aunt Mary's former house on Prospect Street. Gwen had come from the train station in Scranton by herself, giving strict instructions that no one was to meet her. She needed to feel the earth beneath her feet, see her hometown with new eyes and understand with her heart how far she had traveled— and how much of what she had learned here made her what she was now.

Nothing had changed, of course. She recognized this building and that. The coal dumps. The collieries. The Methodist church. The park. The school house.

The only one who had changed was she.

She paid the taxi driver, tipped him well, and earned a smile from him. He thanked her and, because she wore her uniform and he eyed her service stripes and medals, he thanked her for her service, too.

She walked up the slate sidewalk to Helen's house, her suitcase in hand. The front screen door banged open and out rushed a flurry of people.

Susannah—taller and more curvaceous than when Gwen had left—led the pack. Her arms out, she squealed in delight and hugged and kissed her sister. "Oh, you are so swell! Look at you!"

"And you, my dear." She was whole again to have her in her embrace. So long, too long, she had been without the presence of this sweet child.

Helen cried as they hugged. Winslow, too. Both of them so much older, so much more mature.

"Come inside," Helen beckoned and the four of them walked together up to the porch. "Edward will close the store and be home in a little while. I have a roast pork in the oven. Susannah made a chocolate cake."

"Did you?" Gwen ruffled her sister's hair. "You are a baker now?"

The girl stuck out her tongue. "Only when I have to be. I am a great pianist."

"A pianist, is it?" Gwen rolled her eyes, well aware from Lex's letters sent to her in Brest, that Susannah's lessons with Herr Schuler had transformed the girl into a startling talent. "Oo, la, la!"

Inside, Win took her suitcase from her. "I'll put this upstairs. You'll sleep in Susannah's room."

Gwen nodded. Where was her aunt?

"Come." Helen took Gwen's hand and led her to the parlor.

Only one in the family remained. One who no longer posed a threat to her peace of mind. One whose motivations Gwen no longer needed to understand. One who was only owed one thing from Gwen—respect for having taken her and her sister into her care when all else seemed lost.

On the threshold, Gwen paused at the sight. In the center of the room was Aunt Mary. Diminished in every way by the Spanish flu that felled her months before, the woman sat in a wheelchair. Her hair had gone stark white. Her body frail. Her fingers thin reeds that tapped in palsy upon the armrests. Her blue eyes sought Gwen's, but they strained to focus, rheumy and pale.

"Hello, Aunt." She went to kneel in front of her.

"You have come home." The woman patted her hand in a tender touch, new and extraordinary, the first gentleness that had ever passed from the lady. "I knew you would. Knew you would. They would not hurt you."

331

Gwen's eyes filled with tears at the sentiment. For all the years and pain, for what she had learned as a result of this woman's indifference, this statement of Mary's measure of affection for her was suddenly enough salve to heal all her wounds. "No, Aunt. No one hurt me."

The next afternoon, she walked up the hill toward the Learners' home. She had called ahead to ask if she might visit. Lex had answered, warning her she had better come within the hour or he would never let her in the door.

"Why's that?"

"You dawdle in France. I'm home six months before you are. Hell, even Will got home last month. Mustered out. Poor kid, he complains he never saw combat."

"For that, I will wash his mouth out with soap when I get there."

"Hurry or I will come charging around with the Ford to abduct you!"

"I am putting on my jacket. Hold your horses."

Like the day before, she was only half way up the walk when she was greeted. Lex bounded out the front door, caught her in a whirl and squeezed the stuffing out of her.

Breathless, she pushed him away. "God in heaven, you look wonderful. You've put on weight and your eyes are brighter. How are your ears?"

"Tip-top. How are yours?" He chuckled and hugged her again.

"Fine," she managed, her face smothered in his chest.

"Let's go inside. Take all these official looking

items from you." He walked her in the front door and took her hat, then he halted. And whistled at her French medal to which she'd recently received a companion from the British. "Look at all your icing."

"Stop that. I bet you've got a closet-full yourself. Where is your mother? Will?"

"In the garden, waiting for you with tea and cakes."

"Wonderful. Let's—"

"No, let's not." He clasped her wrist and she stared up at him. "I want to know before you go out there how you are. Really."

She flexed her shoulders, unsure what to say, how much to give him, what he wanted to hear. Her thoughts about her aunt? Her sister? Her future?

"That's a long conversation. You must tell me as well about you and what you plan to do."

"I'm home for now. Putting a business together. Airplanes. Mail service."

She grinned. "That's utterly exciting. Although I do not want to see you delivering mail and getting ear infections. I won't be around all the time to diagnose them for you."

"Why not?"

"What?"

"Why won't you be around to diagnose them?" His hazel eyes turned dark with worry.

"I just meant that—" She swallowed hard. "What the hell. I'm thinking of going to medical school."

It was Lex's turn to look shocked. "Medical school? You want to become a doctor?"

"Not so crazy, is it?" she asked, reacting to his incredulity with a giggle.

"Definitely not." He draped his arms around her

waist. "And where will you go?"

"You mean where and when and how can I afford this little venture?"

"Okay. Tell me all that."

"I will when I know all the particulars."

"Ah." He nodded, smiling, pleased with her answer. "Sounds reasonable."

"Good. Now can I have some tea?" She pointed toward the garden doors. "I've developed a maddening craving for boiling hot tea."

"One thing more."

Exasperated, she narrowed her gaze on him. "Fine. What?"

"Why did you extend your contract? Why wait to come home?"

"I wanted time to think in peace. I needed the distance. Who could think about anything in the midst of bombs and air raids and—" She met his level gaze, but the sad curve of his lips told her there was an emotion in his question she had not seen before. A hint of remorse that she'd never recognized. "I wanted—"

He tipped his head, his move encouraging her to be frank.

"I had a relationship with the British captain whom you met that first time you came to see me. I needed to see it through before I left."

Lex seemed not to breathe. "Is it through? Over?"

"I'm not sure."

"Why not?"

"That's...a long story." *Not one I am able to discuss with any rhyme or reason just now.*

"Will you tell me?"

She frowned at him. "I could, but why?" The

words barely left her lips when she saw the answer written on his face. As if a thousand suns dawned, she blinked. Blinded by the revelation that Lex cared for her with a romantic intensity, she stepped back from his embrace.

"I'd like to know," he said simply. "I'm thinking about my own future. I need to know about yours."

"I see." He thought of her as more than a friend? This revelation alarmed her. When had this happened and she hadn't seen it, felt it? Had she been so wrapped up in Adam or her work or—? When or how Lex began to feel this way wasn't what was as important to explore at the moment as telling him what was in her heart and mind about Adam. Still she had no desire to hurt Lex. Yet she had to be careful telling him and she'd need time to think that through. "I'll do my best to explain it to you. Only not today. Not for a few days, if you don't mind."

"Okay. I'll wait." He grinned, once more the man who had been her friend for many years. Then he put a hand to the small of her back. "Come see Mother and Will before they scalp me for keeping you too long."

****

Gwen ran out to meet the mailman each morning. Most often in her robe, she no longer startled the man but greeted him, waving and eager to see what he might hand over.

On a humid morning in August, he gave her a letter that looked very official. Typed and postmarked Washington, D.C., the letter was brief. Pointed.

She ran inside, waving the paper at Helen and Susannah who sat at the table over their eggs. "I'm in! Accepted!" She danced around the room. Kissed

Susannah, then Helen, and went to the telephone on the wall.

"I've been accepted," she told Lex the second he answered. "No questions. I'm going."

He volunteered to accompany her, if she wished. But she refused, feeling oddly about him escorting her to find an apartment, even if it was in a strange city.

He insisted. "I will not have you and Susannah lost in the capital. I've been there, know it well. You have to take Susannah to register for school, and you want her to have music lessons. There is no impropriety between us, Gwen. We've been friends too long."

Friends. His affirmation of that smoothed the way for Gwen to accept him and gratefully thank him once she and Susannah were secured of home and hearth in the city. She rented a walk-up west of DuPont Circle not far from the White House. For Gwen, now a freshman at George Washington University, the apartment was a twenty-minute walk to classes. Admitted without high school diploma to the undergraduate college because of her Army Nurse Corps service and Bernie Dalton's letter of recommendation, Gwen was required by their Medical School to take two years of courses before she could be admitted to the four-year doctoral program. Six years seemed forever to wait for her degree, but at least she had the money. Tuition each year for her undergraduate work amounted to a pittance. Her yearly rent cost twice as much. But as of that September, the annual fee for doctoral classes and the final examinations were fixed at seventy-five dollars. At that rate, she would become a doctor with money to spare.

September became October, then November

approached and memories of those few nights on the front lines last year consumed her. The men she had treated, she wondered where they were. How they were. Had she done well by them? How many had she not been able to save? She had to be content never to know those answers.

She doubted she would enjoy the month of November ever again.

She tore her thoughts from gloom. She had much that was so right with her world. Save for her lack of Adam. Adam, whom she had not had any letters from in more than a month.

His last few had been short. Full of detail, minus any emotion. After the Treaty of Versailles was announced and the parades in Paris ended, he had gone home to Fairleigh Haven for an extended leave. George had gone into hospital at Sidcup. His first surgery had been a success, though George did not acknowledge that. He was due for another the first of the year. No news of Clarice graced Adam's letters. Whether George's wife had come or gone or simply was of no import any longer, he did not mention her. Natalie had not changed. The family was quite beside themselves about her.

About himself, he told her he was talking with his Commanding Officer. "Discussing what the future might hold. A post to Palestine or Hong Kong. A new position as British military attaché to the new Weimar Republic. None of it appeals to me. We are at an impasse."

After a few letters more, all missives from him stopped.

She feared the worst. He'd resigned his

commission and gone home to learn the business of being a country gentleman.

He will die there.

And I will miss him.

And all that love will have gone to waste.

Stifling her tears, she huddled into her new red wool coat and walked through the falling snow south toward Lafayette Park where Susannah studied piano each Wednesday afternoon after school. Her sister was taking to the demanding tutor with excitement. Would that she took to her regular lessons as well.

Gwen glanced at her watch. Four forty. Twenty minutes until Susannah darted out the teacher's door and joined Gwen for their weekly dinner out. Gwen liked the restaurant in the famous old Willard Hotel. The fish was fresh and grilled. The chardonnay crisp and French.

She sat on one of the emerald green benches, raising her face to let the snowflakes fall on her skin. The crunch of footsteps made her glance up.

Before her stood a tall dark man in a military uniform, a rich brown greatcoat, his hands in his pockets. His gaze was dark and deeply green, expectant, hesitant.

"Miss Spencer," he said in that mellow bass voice she heard in her dreams, "I wonder if I might interest you in a rousing round of a German drinking song."

It took her a long minute to find her own voice, her throat clogged as it was with surprise and desire for him. "I would love it, but only if we sing that one that repeats how you live in my heart."

He stepped closer and so near now, she could see his face more clearly. Lined with worry, his face was haggard. "You live in mine."

His sorrow was palpable. Her hope was too. "Might I expect we can sing together for many years to come?"

"You may. That is, if you will marry me."

"You want a student for a wife?"

His lips spread into a devilish grin. "Can she cook?"

Gwen shook her head, swallowing any tears. They were so unnecessary now. "She makes a damn good pot of tea."

"Ah, well then." He shrugged. "I want her still."

She waited, daring to believe he was no mirage. "Can she live with you? Here?"

"She can. You see, I am fully employed. Worthy husband material. The military attaché at the British Embassy."

Gwen caught her breath. "You didn't resign."

"They promoted me. Colonel Fairleigh at your service, Miss Spencer."

She stood and walked into his firm embrace and simply held him for interminable minutes. "Do you have an apartment?" she asked him when finally she had stifled her sniffles.

"I have lodgings."

So he was here to stay. "Would you like to come have dinner with Susannah and me?"

"My fondest desire. Aside from this." And then he kissed her.

Kissed her. Kissed her.

She clung to him then, crying freely. Once stoic, sedate Gwen Spencer, now an emotional geyser. She laughed, then pulled him to sit with her on the bench.

"You'll come home with me and Susannah."

"No scandalous behavior for the new medical student. We will live together only after you marry me."

"Oh, I will. How soon can we do that, I wonder?"

"What would you say to the day after tomorrow?"

"Do not tease me. You have to have a license for that," she offered in her ridiculous glee.

He patted his breast pocket. "Miss Spencer, I helped to win the Great War. I have powerful friends in many places and I am prepared for anything, most especially to be your loving husband."

"A man after my heart."

"Say I have it."

"You do. You always will."

Reading Group Questions

As I wrote this book I hoped that it not only would portray the first group of courageous women who volunteered to go to war zones but also become an educational and thought-provoking novel. I hope you and your group will share your impressions and the effects this book has had on you. Here are a few questions to guide you.

~~

1. Heroism in all its forms is the central theme of *Heroic Measures*.
Define heroism. What does it mean to you? How many kinds of heroism do you think there are? Name one person you admire for a heroic act he/she performed.

~~

2. What is the highest form of heroism for you? Is one type of heroism more difficult to accomplish than others? How extreme does an act have to be to call it heroic? What actually makes a hero? How do you measure heroism?

~~

3. Do you think men and women experience different degrees of heroism or different kinds of heroic actions? Why?

~~

4. Many characters in the novel display varieties of heroism. Looking at Gwen, Pearl, Flo, Lex, and Adam, would you praise one more than another? If so, why?

~~

5. American women, as a whole, had experienced a few social and political advances by 1917-1919. In the novel, you read of many instances in which lack of

equality with men created a challenge to the nurses. Describe what changes you know have occurred for women's equality in the United States since these years. What others remain?

~~

6. The United States did not declare war on Germany-Austria-Hungary until April 1917. Still, it took the United States nearly a year to build a million-man combat army, supply it, and ship it overseas. In *Heroic Measures*, you see a few of those challenges of cooperating with and fighting in a foreign country.

Do you think many of those same challenges exist today? Do more challenges exist to international cooperation now than then? Why?

~~

7. One of the great challenges to writing a historical novel is to ensure that readers enjoy an enriching experience that is true to the period. Here in *Heroic Measures*, you get a picture of life in the early years of the twentieth century. From child labor, to lax childhood education rules, to types of transportation and food, you can paint a picture of everyday life for many of that era.

What other facts about transportation, music, education, social mores, medical care, and Army life can you pick out from the text that depict the quality of life in that period?

Which advances in each of those areas are the ones you value most, and why?

~~

8. In the United States, the events and aftermath of World War One are often considered merely a prelude to the events of World War Two. Defined by President

Woodrow Wilson as "the war to end all wars," World War One is considered the conflict that the British-French-American military coalition won and the politicians lost.

List the negative outcomes of World War One.

Name any outcomes of World War One that you consider beneficial to individuals or societies.

~~

9. When a disgruntled peasant shot Archduke Ferdinand in 1914, the powerful nations of the world declared war against each other within one month. Over the next four years, more than 10 million soldiers would die in combat, while more than 9 million civilians died, too. More than 3 million more were maimed, disfigured, or disabled. Others lost their families, their homes, their jobs and farms. An entire generation of young men between the ages of 16 and 40 was demolished, cut by more than one third.

Some criticize that this war was too blithely declared. Under what circumstances is declaring war justifiable to you?

Under what circumstances would you join your country's army and fight a war?

A word about the author...

Whether the story calls for immersion in history, the always-volatile corporate world, or the demanding environment of journalism, Jo-Ann Power brings her expert writing talent to draw readers into exciting worlds portrayed with an accuracy that is unique.

Her versatility with genres has brought her success as well as thousands of readers in genres such as mainstream, mystery, and romance, and drawn praise from multiple reviewers and readers.

Romantic Times said of her work, "She draws readers into a carefully constructed novel that is brimming with…passion, brilliant colors and fascinating history…" Others compare her "powerful" style to that of Daphne DuMaurier and Phyllis Whitney. *Publisher's Weekly* said, "Her ability to 'cleverly weave politics, murder and romance, creating intense, breath-catching suspense' is a hallmark of her works." Her mysteries have been Featured Alternates of The Mystery Guild, and her historical romances were selections of both Rhapsody Book Club and Doubleday Book Club.

In her latest historical novel, *HEROIC MEASURES*, Jo-Ann takes us from the coal mines of Pennsylvania to the battlefields of France in World War One. Recreating the decision of one young nurse to join the Army Nurse Corps, sail to France, and serve on the American front lines, the novel follows her courageous journey under brutal conditions. The story of the hardships and triumphs of these women has been woefully neglected. Fascinated by the valor of these nurses and their grace under pressure, Jo-Ann researched the topic for decades, including trips to the actual battlefields where much of the book takes place. Now, as we approach the Centennial of the outbreak of World War One, she brings the bravery of these women to life in the person of Gwen Spencer, a young girl from Peckville, Pennsylvania, whose heart led her to serve others in their time of need.

Read more about *HEROIC MEASURES* at Jo-Ann's website,

http://jo-annpower.com

For more information, pictures, and details about the Army Nurse Corps, American experience in World War One, and Jo-Ann's research trips in the States and to France, read Jo-Ann's blog,

http://theyalsofought.blogspot.com

Thank you for purchasing
this publication of The Wild Rose Press, Inc.
For other wonderful stories of romance,
please visit our on-line bookstore at
www.thewildrosepress.com.

For questions or more information
contact us at
info@thewildrosepress.com.

The Wild Rose Press, Inc.
www.thewildrosepress.com

To visit with authors of
The Wild Rose Press, Inc.
join our yahoo loop at
http://groups.yahoo.com/group/thewildrosepress/

CPSIA information can be obtained at www.ICGtesting.com
Printed in the USA
LVOW06s1453131113

361171LV00017B/702/P